PENGUI

THE
PALACE
GIRLS
AT CHRISTMAS

Emma Royal is the pen name for established romance writer Katie
Ginger who also writes as Annabel French. She has always loved
historical fiction and has a Master's degree in history. When not
writing, she can be found running around after her two children
and two dogs along with her husband.

Also by Emma Royal

The Palace Girls
The Palace Girl's Secret

THE
PALACE
GIRLS
AT CHRISTMAS

EMMA ROYAL

PENGUIN BOOKS

PENGUIN BOOKS

UK | USA | Canada | Ireland | Australia
India | New Zealand | South Africa

Penguin Books is part of the Penguin Random House group of companies
whose addresses can be found at global.penguinrandomhouse.com

Penguin Random House UK,
One Embassy Gardens, 8 Viaduct Gardens, London SW11 7BW

penguin.co.uk

Penguin
Random House
UK

First published 2025
001

Copyright © Emma Royal, 2025

The moral right of the author has been asserted

Set in 10.4/15pt Palatino LT Pro
Typeset by Six Red Marbles UK, Thetford, Norfolk

Printed and bound in Great Britain by Clays Ltd, Elcograf S.p.A.

The authorised representative in the EEA is Penguin Random House Ireland,
Morrison Chambers, 32 Nassau Street, Dublin D02 YH68

A CIP catalogue record for this book is available from the British Library

ISBN: 978–1–804–94550–6

Thank you to every single person who has read one of the Palace Girls stories. I cannot tell you how grateful I am.

Inside Buckingham Palace, Queen Elizabeth II is left reeling from the announcement by her sister, Princess Margaret, that she is in love with a member of staff: her father's former equerry, Peter Townsend.

Queen Elizabeth The Queen Mother still mourns the loss of her husband, King George VI, while coronation plans are causing unease and ill feeling between parliament, the monarchy and within the royal family itself. The charismatic Duke of Edinburgh leads the Coronation Commission while his traditionalist wife seeks to appease the Prime Minister, Winston Churchill.

Christmas 1952 is fraught with tensions.

November 1952

Chapter One

'Margaret,' Queen Elizabeth said, her voice steady and calm, though with an edge that indicated rising tension. 'You must think clearly.'

'There's nothing to think about, Lilibet. I love him and he loves me. I simply don't understand what the problem is. Just because he's not nobility—'

'The problem is not that he is not nobility.' The Queen's hands were clasped in front of her. The sensible dark navy suit tailored beautifully to her figure was adorned with a pearl and gold brooch. A matching string of pearls sat at the base of her throat. She touched one gently as she spoke. 'The problem is that he is currently in the courts divorcing his wife.'

Silence.

'He also has two children that you would become step-mother to, and let us not forget that he is significantly older than you.'

'She cheated on him,' Margaret replied sullenly. 'I don't see why he should get all the blame.'

Through the crack in the door, Caroline Stratton, cleaner and member of staff in the Royal Household, watched the young Princess cross her arms over her chest. Caroline bent her head and polished the ornate gold detailing on the door that separated the 1844 Room from the Bow Room as though her life depended on it. It wouldn't do to be caught prying and Mrs Edie Barnes, her unofficial supervisor and something of a palace mother, was always watching.

As the gold reflected the light from the chandeliers above, she realised it wouldn't be long until lights glittered throughout as the palace was decorated for Christmas. The smell of spiced biscuits would emanate from the staff and royal kitchens and their strange city within a city would become enchanted and magical. She just hoped the tensions that ran through the walls of the palace now would have gone by then.

They were similar ages, Caroline thought, eyeing the glamorous Princess. Caroline was only a year younger, though her life couldn't be more different: one of hard physical grind and long hours while the Princess's was one of late nights, lie-ins and fashionable frocks. She was incredibly beautiful with unblemished porcelain skin, striking, violet-blue eyes, a small nose and full mouth. Caroline meanwhile was pale with freckles and a tangled mess of red hair secured in place with all the pins she could find, many of which would be lost throughout the day as her mane came loose with scrubbing and cleaning.

The Queen and her younger sister looked small in the immensity of the Bow Room, one of the largest reception rooms in Buckingham Palace. Although all the rooms were excessively large: larger than the house Caroline had grown up in and the small staff apartment she lived in now, which was nothing more than a bed and a sink. A plush crimson carpet dominated the eye, a shocking shade compared with the pale walls, white marble columns and white ceiling with gold decoration. It was one of the barest rooms in Buckingham Palace, with its lack of chandeliers and large empty spaces. Of course, the walls were still adorned with priceless paintings, the mantelshelves covered in antique clocks and candlesticks, and the alcoves full of precious porcelain. Her ma and pa's home in the East End had very little in it, and all they had, they'd worked hard for. Nothing had been inherited. Not that she begrudged the royal family anything. She'd seen first-hand how hard they worked, how they felt grief and loss just as anyone did. It was just a strange world, very different to the one she'd grown up in.

'It isn't Peter's fault their marriage didn't work out,' the Princess continued. 'War weddings don't always, you know.'

'I know, darling.' The Queen's tone was softer. Her own wedding had taken place in 1947, not long after the war had ended. Was the softness of her tone sympathy with Peter Townsend or an attempt to defuse the argument? Caroline couldn't tell.

Princess Margaret turned away from her sister, facing the door through which Caroline had been watching. She jerked back from the gap, holding her breath, eager not to be seen. With her hair pinned up, Princess Margaret's neck was as long and graceful as a swan. However, beneath her angelic exterior lay a temper that had become increasingly apparent as her love for Peter Townsend, now Comptroller of Queen Elizabeth The Queen Mother's household, had been revealed. Sadness at her father's death was fading as she grew used to the grief, but more than one member of staff had been on the receiving end of her mercurial temper.

Gossip over the matter was rife in the palace. Only a month or so before, Peter Townsend had visited Tommy Lascelles, the Queen's private secretary, and declared his love for Princess Margaret, asking the more senior officer what he should do about it. According to whispered stories below stairs, the reply hadn't been very positive. Mr Lascelles was a stickler for rules and decorum and this nobody's supposed love for the Queen's younger sister couldn't be countenanced. The royal family had, so far, managed to keep everything from the press, but arguments like this one had been raging behind closed doors ever since.

'If you only tried to like him, Lilibet, you'd see that—'

'I do like him. Immensely.' The Queen turned back to the window that overlooked the gardens of Buckingham Palace, her eyes drifting towards the vast lake and the belt of leafless trees, their naked limbs twisting in the heavy winter wind. Her calm exterior remained intact, but Caroline wondered what was going on inside. If it had been Caroline and her sister Nancy, they would have been shouting at one another, Ma and Pa intervening to try and calm the situation down. But the Queen had always hidden her emotions and it was often difficult to know how she truly felt about anything. 'He was wonderful with Papa, always putting up with his gnashes and never caring a jot about them, but you must see this is different, Margaret.'

'I'm twenty-two years old, for heaven's sake.' She cast her hands into the air despairingly. 'I don't see why I can't make my own decisions. Every other twenty-two-year-old woman in the country can. Why do I need your permission to marry before I'm twenty-five? It's utterly preposterous.'

'You are a princess, Margaret,' Queen Elizabeth replied matter-of-factly, her voice detached and lacking emotion. 'The rules are different for us, as well you know.'

Behind Caroline, Mrs Barnes cleared her throat and Milly, Mrs Barnes's niece, a fellow cleaner and one of Caroline's best friends, appeared at her side.

'Aunt Edie's watching you. You better be careful.'

'I am,' she whispered. 'I'm just doing my jobs. It's not my fault they're talking. We're supposed to be moving in there next. What are we going to do if they don't move?'

'I don't know,' Milly replied with a shrug, tendrils of her blonde hair escaping and falling in front of her ears. She tucked them behind with a swift move of her hand. 'Aunt Edie will tell us. We'll either go into the Belgian Suite or come out and go around the other way into the 1855 Room. Just don't look like you're earwigging, or she'll have your guts for garters.'

Conversations like this were normally kept within the royal family's private quarters or Queen Elizabeth's study. Buckingham Palace might be their home, but the royal family valued their privacy as much as the next person and exchanges of a personal nature remained within closed walls, with footmen and butlers dismissed before they began. As cleaners, she and Milly had occasionally heard something more intimate if they were called to clean a spillage, but even then, voices would quieten or talking might stop altogether until they'd left. Yet, that winter, as tensions rose within the palace for a thousand and one reasons, including the Queen Mother's unending grief, the upcoming coronation the following summer and Princess Margaret's need for a more suitable husband, conversations spilled into more public areas. Especially where Princess Margaret was concerned. If she had something to say, she was going to say it no matter who was around.

Milly edged away, polishing the marble columns, tilting her head to see where the pale winter light reflected on any smudges or fingerprints left behind. Caroline knelt, working on the lower panels of the door, polishing the gold elements until they shone.

Princess Margaret took a step nearer her sister. 'The rules need to be changed.'

'That is not within my power to do.'

'You're the Queen, damn it!' She threw her hands in the air, anger dripping from every pore. 'Everything is within your power to do.' When the Queen didn't respond, Princess Margaret fled towards the door, her trim figure rapidly growing closer as she made short work of the space. Caroline jumped back just as the door swung open, catching it when the edge was only millimetres from her face. Margaret glanced at her and for a moment seemed to consider apologising or asking if she was all right, but then she quickly turned away and hurried off in the opposite direction. The tapping of her heels was softened by the carpeted floor as she marched through the 1844 Room and out the other side, no doubt heading towards the family's private apartments.

As Caroline closed the door, she caught sight of Queen Elizabeth walking down the stone steps from the Bow Room out into the gardens of Buckingham Palace, two fat little corgis hot on her heels. The weather was frigidly cold, the biting wind finding its way under coats and clothing until skin puckered with goosebumps, yet the Queen strode out as if the freezing air didn't touch her.

'Are you done over there, Caroline?' Mrs Barnes asked. 'You ain't half taken an age on one little doorknob.'

'I haven't just done the doorknob,' Caroline replied, her cheeks colouring. 'I've done all the shiny bits. Like you told me.'

'Hmm.'

'I think the Queen's gone. Shall we move into the Bow Room now?'

'Let me see.' Mrs Barnes joined her at the door and knocked. When there was no reply, she opened it tentatively and stepped through. The Queen was just climbing back up the steps; her cheeks were rosy from the wind but she showed no trace of being uncomfortable. 'Oh, I'm sorry, Your Majesty.' Mrs Barnes bowed her head.

'Not at all, Mrs Barnes. Would you like me to go somewhere else?'

'You're very welcome to stay where you are, ma'am. We can do the Belgian Suite if that's more convenient.'

'No, no, I can—'

Before she could finish, the Duke of Edinburgh cast open the door that led into the Bow Room from the Marble Hall and marched through. His handsome face was a little red with frustration and his normal smile missing. 'Ah, there are you, Lilibet. Those bloody old duffers – there's no reasoning with some of them. You'll have to do something.'

'Excuse me, Mrs Barnes,' she replied serenely, turning to her husband. Mrs Barnes curtseyed and began to close the door. All Caroline could hear were the fading words, 'What is it now?' followed by the Duke's reply:

'The blasted coronation, of course.'

Caroline tried to get a final look at Philip, her heart rate increasing at his presence. She'd always had rather a thing for him. Not that she told anyone. But he was devilishly handsome and lively too. Unlike most of the people who came to the palace, and even most who worked there, she thought with a smile. She edged away and, through the heavy door, the Queen and Philip's voices merged into a single sound as they spoke about the challenges of the coronation: balancing the pressure to televise the ceremony to appease the public and the broadcasting services with the government's wish to protect tradition and respect the solemnity of the occasion.

'Right then,' Mrs Barnes said, her hands on her hips as though she were guarding the door. At forty-nine she had a soft, womanly figure, and she had recently begun to take better care of herself; the rosacea that for years had marked her cheeks was fading and the skin growing less pink. She seemed younger than she had when Caroline had first started at the palace; but, she supposed, happiness could do that to you, and Mrs Barnes did seem happy with Mr Newington, a senior clerk. 'Looks like we're doing the Belgian Suite. Come on.'

They trudged through the opulence of the 1844 Room, with its blue-silk-upholstered furniture, pale, dusky-pink-hued wallpaper, gold columns and mirrors, and on towards the Belgian Suite.

'I hate the Belgian Suite,' Caroline muttered to Milly.

'Why?' she asked with a laugh.

'I don't know. It just seems a bit tired to me. Like it needs a good spruce-up and some new wallpaper. And it smells of mothballs even though we air it every day.'

'I know what you mean. It isn't the only part of the palace fading a little, but there's no money to do any sprucing up right now. Every penny's going into the coronation. I heard the Duke of Edinburgh say that it had to be held next year because there just wasn't enough money in the economy to do it this year. I'm not sure what that means exactly, but it must be costing a fortune, and . . .' She leaned in closer, not wanting her aunt to hear her. '. . . apparently, the Duke said Churchill didn't want people taking too many bank holidays off.'

Caroline scoffed. 'Chance would be a fine thing. I'd love an extra day off.'

'I know,' Milly replied sagely. 'Anyway, come on, it'll be lunchtime after we've done the Belgian Suite and Helen's meeting us in the dining room so that'll be nice.'

Caroline followed though she couldn't help glancing over her shoulder at the closed door behind which the Queen and Duke of Edinburgh were still talking, wishing she could hear just a snippet more of their conversation.

Chapter Two

Settled in the Household Dining Room, Milly and Caroline were joined at a table by their friend Helen who worked on the telephone exchange at the palace. Grateful to be out of the small, stuffy room full of enormous switchboards, Helen relaxed in the dining chair, careful not to lean her elbows on the plush white tablecloth or nudge the shining white crockery. For those who lived on site, lunch and dinner were served in this room, a bank of silver warming trays at the side. Breakfast was served in the Household Breakfast Room which was set up the same way. Though Helen lived off site, she was always welcome to join them, especially for lunch or dinner, and Mrs Chadwick, the cook, and a great friend of Mrs Barnes, welcomed her with open arms.

Helen stretched her back, placing a hand there. She was pregnant with the prospect of being a single mother stretching out before her, yet her spirits were high even though her father had died only a couple of months before and the man who had betrayed her had returned to his wife. Jake Walker, reporter for the *Daily News*, hadn't mentioned his wife when he'd been wooing Helen, even taking her to Brighton, but as soon as she'd told him about the baby, the words had come tumbling out, stealing the life Helen had imagined out from under her. Some men simply weren't ever to be trusted. Caroline knew that from her own bitter experience.

Helen had been able to keep her job thanks to an intervention from Princess Margaret and Queen Elizabeth, who were ushering in a new age for women. Perhaps it was because they worked, visiting here, there and everywhere no matter how ill or tired they felt, or perhaps it was because the Queen never really stopped working at all. Whatever it was, the three friends were grateful. If the royal family hadn't made an exception, Helen would have been unemployed and without a chance of getting another job. They would have rallied round and done what they could, but the very real possibility of ending up destitute had been significant. Today, now the morning sickness had abated, Helen looked happy and healthy. Her appetite had returned, and she ate her sandwich, brought from home, with glee.

'Was it busy on the telephone exchange this morning, Helen?' Milly asked.

'Rather. I don't think I stopped from the moment I sat down.' She ran a hand over the back of her neck, squeezing the muscles. More than once she had complained that the headset all the telephonists wore weighed more than some of the palace's furniture.

Caroline repressed the urge to ask if she'd heard anything interesting that day. She knew Helen wouldn't be allowed to talk about it, but that didn't stop Caroline wanting to know, and it wasn't just idle curiosity or gossip driving her interest, it was something more. She was tired of being on the periphery of palace events: a tiny cog in a huge wheel. A wheel that would continue to turn even if her cog fell out.

She was a nothing. A nobody. But since the Queen had come to the throne, Caroline had wanted more for herself. Seeing what a young, albeit privileged, woman could achieve, she'd wanted to stretch her wings and try for something more than her parents and even her sister had.

Caroline's family and friends back in Whitechapel had been so happy when she'd got the job at Buckingham Palace. Her ma and pa couldn't believe that someone from their family had ended up somewhere like that. Being in service was a fine profession, but after a while, a new desire had grown inside her. A need for something more. Now she'd completed a Pitman's secretarial course and learned skills such as shorthand and touch typing (not to mention elocution and poise so her cockney roots wouldn't be quite so obvious), she wanted to put them to good use. It had been hard going over the last few months, working all day and attending evening school afterwards, and then completing homework tasks, and she hoped one day it would be worth it. She aspired to be more than a part of the palace machine, yet she didn't want to leave for a job elsewhere. The palace provided everything she could hope for, including meals and somewhere to live, but there was a well of untapped potential inside her. She could feel it in her belly and desperately wanted to be more than just a cleaner.

Helen sighed, once more twisting the tension from her neck. 'And things are only going to get busier as the coronation plans progress. At least there'll be a lull at Christmas when the family go to Windsor. Or is it Sandringham?'

'I think it's Sandringham this year,' Milly replied.

Caroline glanced at Helen's stomach. At almost four

months pregnant, she didn't really look any different. When it was noticed that her stomach did seem rounder, it was as if she'd eaten a particularly heavy meal, not that there was a child growing inside her. Caroline wondered how their friendship would change once the baby arrived, and she couldn't decide if she was excited or scared for what was to come. Perhaps both. Babies were common in her street back home, and she always loved a cuddle with them when she could, but she didn't want the special friendship that had developed between them all over the past year to change. 'Can you feel the baby move yet?' she asked quietly.

Helen pushed a crumb into her mouth and spoke as soon as she'd finished her mouthful. 'No, not yet. I don't think that happens till later. I really should get a book from Whitechapel library or go and see another doctor. That nice one who treated me before, perhaps. There's still so much I don't know about it all.' She brushed her black hair from her face. She was wearing it down, with curls pinned back at the front, and it looked lustrous and thick, her body finally responding well to the pregnancy after months of sickness. Her hands rested underneath her stomach, cupping the growing belly.

Mrs Morton, one of the particularly gossipy older women who also worked as a cleaner but in a separate team, passed them, curling her lip in disgust as her gaze roved over Helen.

Though the Queen and Princess had set a new precedent by allowing Helen to remain in post, it didn't mean attitudes were changing everywhere. Helen had still been subject to lots of sneers and sly glances, whispers and muttered slurs. She'd been the subject of gossip at the exchange and those rumours had spread throughout the palace, as gossip always did. Caroline and Milly defended her, as did Mrs Barnes. With everyone who didn't know the truth, and hadn't known Helen before, they stuck to the story that her non-existent husband had died in a traffic accident. Some were happy to let it lie while others passed their own judgements. Caroline often wondered how blameless their lives were and if they had any moral ground on which to stand and judge others.

'You need to be prepared,' Milly replied to Helen.

'I am getting there.' She dropped her eyes, an unspoken gratitude for their love and support radiating from her. 'You must tell Johnny that I'm ever so grateful for the fruit he brought round the other day. It was very kind of him.'

'What fruit?' Caroline pressed a hand to her mouth, aware she'd just spoken with a mouthful of food – something she'd been told off about more than once at secretarial college and by Mrs Barnes.

Her brother had taken fruit to Helen's house? When had he done that? And why hadn't he brought any home? More than that, where had he got it from in the first place? Caroline loved her brother dearly, but he didn't always play by the rules and Helen couldn't afford to get caught up in his nonsense.

'Oh, didn't he say?' Helen blushed, the pinkness of her cheeks emphasised by her dark hair. 'I think he just wanted to make sure I was eating properly.'

This time, Caroline made sure to finish her mouthful before she spoke. 'Seen him much lately, have you?'

'No, not really.' Helen brushed her hair behind her ear. 'Just once or twice.'

Johnny and Helen had met the month before when he'd 'borrowed' a van from his work to help Helen move into her new flat. Caroline hadn't known they'd even spoken since. Just as Caroline was about to press for more details, Robert, Milly's fella who had been promoted from pot wash to trainee cook, arrived full of excitement.

'M-Milly, have you heard?'

'Heard what?' she asked with a laugh, seeing his eyes shining and his inability to keep still. They were utterly smitten and observing them together always warmed Caroline's heart, giving her hope of a love that might one day come her way.

'There's going to be a Ch-Christmas dance.'

'Why's that a good thing?' Caroline asked. 'It'll mean more work for everyone.'

Robert rocked on to his toes. 'It's for the staff. For all of us.'

'How do you know this?' asked Helen.

'A poster's been put up in the Household L-Lounge and I overheard the head of the Royal Household Social Club t-talking about it.'

'A dance!' Milly exclaimed as the news sank in. This was exciting news indeed. 'I can just imagine dancing in the Household Lounge with the Christmas tree up. But how will we all fit?'

'It's not here. It's in the ballroom.'

Milly gasped. 'How wonderful! I can't wait. What will I wear?'

'What will *I* wear?' Helen asked, her eyes shooting downwards.

'Surely you won't have grown that much by then?'

'Another month? I think I will.'

'We'll sort something,' Milly said. 'Aren't you excited, Caroline?'

Though a kernel of excitement sprang inside her, trepidation took over. Dancing would mean someone's arms around her, and she didn't want to think about the last man who'd held her tightly. Yet her mind ran immediately to him: Timothy, the charming footman who'd befriended her and tried to take advantage of her. She shuddered at the memory and the lucky escape she'd had, grateful that he no longer worked at the palace and she'd never have to see him again. 'Yes, yes, of course,' she lied. 'Just wondering if I've got anything suitable, that's all.'

Others overheard their conversation, and soon the room was filled with lively chatter.

Jane, a new coffee maid with rosy cheeks and a supremely positive nature, joined them. 'I can't believe there'll be a dance! Do you think the Queen will be there?'

'I shouldn't think so,' Robert said; then, seeing her face fall, he added, 'But you n-never know.'

Mrs Barnes appeared and hurried over to them, Mr Newington following. The handsome gentleman who worked as a senior clerk at the palace was now officially courting Mrs Barnes and the three younger women couldn't be happier. Jane moved back to her friends.

'Have you heard about the dance?' Milly asked, interpreting her aunt's fluster as excitement.

'The what? Oh, yes. Yes, that'll be lovely for everyone, won't it? It's been a tough year. Nice of the Queen to show her love for us all.' She waved a hand in the air, catching her breath. 'But that's not why I'm here.'

'Is everything all right?'

Mrs Barnes turned towards Caroline. 'It's you I'm after.'

'Oh? 'Ave I done summat wrong?' In fear, her accent had reverted to the dense cockney she'd had before months of elocution lessons. Milly's aunt was very rarely in such a flap and concern began to weigh heavy in her stomach. She knew she shouldn't have listened in for so long that morning.

Now fully recovered, Mrs Barnes placed her hands on her hips. 'You're needed.'

'Needed why? What's happened?' She pushed herself out of her seat. 'Is it Ma or Pa? Nancy? Has something happened to one of them?'

'No, no, no, nothing of that sort. Everything's fine with them as far as I know.' She clasped her hands together in front of her. 'It's your lucky day, my girl. Mr Newington's got a job for you.'

'A job?'

Mrs Barnes's faintly pink cheeks lifted as she smiled. 'In the offices!'

Chapter Three

Caroline sat, her mouth hanging open, her eyes wide as she attempted to take in Mrs Barnes's words.

'A job?' she said at last. 'You mean . . . has someone spilled something? Do I need to—'

'No, you daft thing.' Her tone more reassuring than cross, Mrs Barnes smiled as fondly at Caroline as she did Milly. 'As a typist. Mr Newington said someone else has gone off sick with the flu and they're droppin' like flies over his side of the palace.'

'We're incredibly short-staffed,' he added. His lined but still handsome face was animated. He wore his salt and pepper hair slicked back and his brown eyes shone with intelligence. 'I was telling Edie about another young lady who's been sent home, so when she reminded me that you'd just finished secretarial college, it seemed like the perfect solution. It wouldn't be permanent, I'm afraid, but you never know. Put on a good show and there's every chance something more might come of it.'

'There now,' Mrs Barnes added. 'What do you say to that?'

Caroline had watched each of them intently as they'd spoken to her, her eyes darting from one to the other. Now they fell on Helen and Milly, who were both eagerly awaiting her reply, as pleased for her as Mrs Barnes and Mr Newington were.

'But—' Fear forced a million and one reasons to refuse into her mind. 'I've not done anything like this before. I—'

'Well, now's your chance,' Helen said, reaching out and taking her hand.

'But I'm too inexperienced. And what about the Bow Room?' She turned to Milly. 'We were supposed to clean that this afternoon.'

Milly took her other hand. 'We'll just have to manage without you.'

'And we'll manage just fine,' Mrs Barnes said.

Caroline dropped her eyes, wishing she didn't feel terrified at this unexpected opportunity. She'd worked hard for this: toiling all day and night. There'd been days when her fingers had ached from practising touch-typing on the noisy typewriters and her brain had felt like soup. Yet she'd got up and worked the next day, her hands still sore as they'd clutched a duster or polished the wooden floor. Was all that work to be wasted simply because she was scared? She'd been scared when she'd first come to the palace, but it hadn't stopped her. As her brain whirled with the familiar voice that always sought to tear her down, she could hear her ma and pa egging her on. 'Go on,' they were saying. 'You can do it. You can do anything you put your mind to'.

'What will I have to do?' she asked Mr Newington.

'Oh, the usual sort of thing. Typing reports, taking letters. I'm in the Private Secretary's Office, so we look after the needs of the Private Secretary to the Queen, the secretaries to the ladies-in-waiting, the press secretaries – lots of people.

It's rather exciting work, really. Never a dull moment, as they say.'

Mrs Barnes beamed up at Mr Newington like a love-struck schoolgirl and he gazed down at her in return. Caroline smothered a smile, a moment of light relief in this wonderful but odd moment.

For the first time, she felt as if her life was at a crossroads. Before now, it had run smoothly, down a single-track road, moving ever forward just how she'd expected it to. Her Ma's life had run in a similar way, and now that of Nancy, her older sister, was doing the same. She'd found a chap and was hoping to get married and start a family. When she did, she planned to give up work. That's what women did. They went to school, got a job and worked until they were married. Ever since she was little, Nancy had wanted a husband, a house of her own and children to run around after. Caroline suddenly realised that her life might take a different turn. She'd gone to college to improve her chances of getting an office job, but now she had the prospect of not just an office job, but one here at the palace. Somewhere she loved. Mr Newington had said it wasn't permanent, but it would be good experience, nonetheless. She was only hesitating because, despite all the deportment and elocution training, she still felt like the stupid, good-for-nothing cockney her schoolteachers had told her she was. With everyone's eyes still on her, waiting for her reply, Caroline cleared her throat. She wasn't a child any more; she was a woman and one who was determined to do whatever she could to make a worthy life for herself.

She lifted her head to look directly at Mr Newington. 'All right then. When do I start?'

'Today,' he replied, opening his hands. 'Now, if you've finished your lunch. Don't worry, Mrs Barnes and I agreed it all already.'

But as Caroline stood Mr Newington's face dropped.

'Ah—'

'What is it?' Caroline glanced down at herself.

'I'm afraid you'll need to change first. Do you have a suit or a nice skirt and blouse?'

She'd forgotten she was still in her white cleaner's uniform. 'I've only got my formal dress for Household events.' This was normally only worn to line up in the Quadrangle and see the royal family off to one of the other estates or to welcome them home after an absence. The short-sleeved navy dress was old but in good condition as it wasn't used that often. With a cardigan over the top, it would do perfectly well and a cardy was most definitely needed, given how cold and draughty the palace was.

'Why don't you change into that, and I'll meet you back here in ten minutes or so? Then I'll take you round to the offices and get you settled.'

'All right then.'

Milly and Helen stood too, Helen adjusting the waistband of her skirt where it was getting tighter. They each embraced her as she moved around the table.

'I'm so proud of you,' Helen replied, giving her a squeeze.

'You'll show them all how it's done,' Milly added when it was her turn.

Mrs Barnes didn't say anything; instead, she pressed her hand to Caroline's back, guiding her towards the door.

'Hurry up now, you don't want to keep Mr Newington waitin'. Are you sure you've had enough lunch? You can't be losin' concentration because you're hungry.'

Mrs Barnes and her motherly ways filled Caroline with love for her friends at the palace. Friends she was leaving behind. 'I'll be fine.'

If she was honest, she felt a little sick at the prospect but wasn't going to let it get the better of her. She swallowed down her nerves and hurried to her room to change.

Ten minutes later, she arrived back in the Household Dining Room to find that Helen, Milly and Mrs Barnes had all returned to work. Mr Newington stood in the near empty room looking out of the window, turning as she entered.

'Ah, Caroline, wonderful. You look splendid. Shall we get going?' He checked his watch and led the way through the palace corridors to the clerks' offices.

He walked quickly, slightly stooped and leaning forwards as though it might help him get there faster. She trotted along behind, pulling down her skirt and brushing it with the flat of her hand. Back in her room, she'd added a touch of powder to her nose. When cleaning, she didn't normally bother as the tough nature of the work meant it washed off with sweat within minutes of starting. She couldn't believe her afternoon now looked so different.

'Ready?' he asked as they paused at one of the heavy wooden doors that lined this side of the Quadrangle. She nodded and he cast the door open.

Caroline felt as if she was about to enter a magical new world, so it was somewhat odd but also reassuring to see at her feet the familiar crimson-coloured carpet that ran through Buckingham Palace, one that she had swept many times before. The room smelled the same, though less of the beeswax polish she was used to and more of cigarette smoke and typewriter ink. No one was currently smoking but the remnants of it hung in the air. The quiet of the State Rooms was replaced by the clicking of keys and rustling of papers and despite there being so few people – or perhaps because of it – the atmosphere was more harried than her cleaning team experienced. Tension and expectation were rife in the air.

Dark wooden desks were arranged in two orderly rows, each with a typewriter in the centre and a notepad to the side. Most were empty where the staff were off ill. One woman turned and caught sight of Caroline but immediately looked back at her notepad, covered in the swirls and swipes of shorthand, and resumed her work. A young, handsome man in a dark grey suit bustled past her, clutching papers to his chest. He approached the door and Caroline stood to the side to let him through.

'Ah, Mr O'Keefe,' Mr Newington said. 'Do you have a moment?'

Mr O'Keefe paused, frowning in what Caroline hoped was confusion, but suspected was annoyance.

'May I introduce Caroline Stratton. Miss Stratton will be joining us for a few days until we're back to full strength. I trust you'll make her feel welcome.'

The young man, no more than a few years older than her, cast his eyes over her face, and she could feel them as if they were fingers touching her skin. Her stomach tightened under the gaze of his almond-shaped, pale blue eyes. His chocolate-brown hair had been combed back with Brylcreem, the separated strands where his comb had run through it still visible. He was attractive in a stuffy, bookish kind of way. She waited for him to smile, but his gaze ran from the top of her head to the scuffed toe of her shoe, and he all but sneered. She had the awkward feeling she'd been assessed and found decidedly wanting. Her fears threatened to over-rule her, but she lifted her chin, and met his gaze defiantly.

His tone was full of impatience. 'How do you do?' He thrust out his hand hurriedly. She caught the melody of an Irish accent: the soft rolling of the letters as if every word were a lyric in a song. If only he'd said it as if he meant it. Instead, it was clear he'd rather be anywhere else than way-laid by her.

Her backbone, while not as strong as people like Helen, stiffened, and she refused to be cowed. Caroline took his hand strongly and shook. 'Nice to meet you.' Her voice was as firm as she could make it, though it wavered slightly as she began to speak.

'Caroline will be a real asset to the team,' Mr Newington said. 'Are you—'

Mr O'Keefe signalled to the papers held firmly at his chest. 'Sorry, but I really must dash. The Press Office is waiting for these to be sent out today. In this afternoon's post. And they want a final read of everything.' He rolled his eyes. 'You know what they're like.'

'I won't keep you then, but do try and make Miss Stratton feel welcome, won't you?' He didn't answer and Mr Newington turned back to her. 'Right, let's get you settled next to Miss Finnigan and I'll find you some work to do. There's more than enough – I just don't really know where to start.' He led the way into the room, signalling to a desk next to the woman who'd glanced at her. 'Perhaps with the assistant private secretary's backlog.' Mr Newington scratched his head and moved to the furthest side of the room where wooden filing cabinets were pressed against the wall. On top of them stood several trays, all overflowing with papers. He tapped his chin as he assessed each one.

'Who's he assistant private secretary too?' she asked as they crossed the office floor.

'The assistant private secretary? He assists the deputy private secretary, who's second in command to the Queen's private secretary.'

'Right.' Caroline tried to make a note of the hierarchy, though it seemed overly complicated. She'd worked at Buckingham Palace for eighteen months and knew some of the job titles, but this area of palace life was new to her, along with most of the people and what exactly they did.

'Here we are then.' Mr Newington slapped a pile of papers down on the desk beside her typewriter. 'These are all minutes of meetings that need typing up, copying and circulating. Can I leave you with those to get started on?'

'Of course.'

'You've used a duplicating machine before?' He signalled to the back of the room where a large machine with a crank handle stood.

Caroline nodded. 'Yes, we had one at secretarial college.'

'Good. Right then, I'll leave you with Miss Finnigan here. I must just go to the Press Secretary's office.'

He closed the door behind him as Caroline sat and took

up the first piece of paper, scanning the shorthand. She began to search for a sheet to load into her typewriter.

'Paper's in the bottom drawer,' Miss Finnigan said. 'That one there.' Caroline followed her finger to the bank of drawers under her desk. 'We all have a stash that we have to replenish every evening from the pile in the corner there. They don't want us getting up and wandering around all the time, getting in each other's way.'

Caroline took some out, loading it into the typewriter. 'Thank you. I'm Caroline. Stratton,' she added, seeing as how everyone was much more formal in this part of the palace. 'Have you worked here long?'

'Oh yes, couple of years now. I'm Barbara – when we're not "on duty", so to speak.' Her deep red lips parted to reveal wide, white teeth as she grinned. Her yellow-blonde hair, which Caroline suspected, from the dark line of roots at her forehead, came from a bottle, was short and curly. Caroline's own red hair curled so tightly that she'd learned long ago to keep it long so she could at least pin it up out of the way. She was slightly jealous of Barbara's neat, chic hairstyle. She had the sort of voice that indicated she wasn't quite middle class but most likely came from more money than she did. She probably lived in one of the nicer suburbs of London and could afford new suits every few months. Hers weren't frayed and darned, and her shoes were high-heeled in shining burgundy leather.

'It's lovely to meet you.' Caroline began typing, eager to work through as much as she could and impress Mr Newington. He was giving her this chance and she was determined not to let him, or Mrs Barnes, down.

'I'm so pleased you've joined us. Mary normally sits there and she's a right laugh when they're not cracking the whip, but she's left now to get married and the woman they replaced her with was awful. I was quite relieved when she went off with the flu, but then I thought, hang on, it's only going to be me, Connor and old Newington.'

'Connor?' Caroline asked, the name unfamiliar.

'Mr O'Keefe, or matinee idol as me and Mary used to call him.' Her eyebrows had raised knowingly. 'Not to his face of course, but he is a dish, isn't he? Lots of people don't like the Irish. I don't know why. He's got a lovely voice.'

He was handsome, but he was also rude. Having grown used to the feeling of family that abounded in the Household staff, Caroline had assumed the offices would be similar, especially as Mr Newington was so nice. However, she knew from Helen's experience that some areas of the palace weren't anywhere near as friendly. The telephone exchange being one of them.

'He lets you call him Connor, does he?'

Timothy had suggested they be on first-name terms because she'd been away from home and in need of a friend – a friend he wanted to be. Too friendly as it had turned out. Those two near escapes still haunted her in the dead of night, when the spectre of his face appeared out of the shadows.

'Not likely. But I heard him say his name to Mr Newington once. Mr Newington said that in other parts of the palace, people who work together call each other by their first names but it hadn't taken here. Mr Lascelles – you know, the Queen's private secretary – got wind of it and put the tin lid on it PDQ.'

29

'PDQ?'

'Pretty damn quick. I think poor Mr Newington was quite embarrassed about it, but he was only trying to make life a bit nicer for us all. Anyway, Connor's such a lovely name, don't you think?' Before she could answer, Barbara continued, thankfully changing topic, 'This flu's getting everyone at the moment, isn't it? No doubt it'll be me next. It's a wonder I'm still here.' She had been typing all the while and suddenly ripped the paper from the typewriter and began on a new sheet. 'You're new to the palace then, are you?'

'Sort of.' Caroline's speed wasn't as fast, but she took a breath, knowing that as soon as she relaxed and grew used to the weight of the keys, she'd quicken. Every typewriter was different, she'd learned, and though the keys were all in the same places, the weight and stiffness of them varied. 'I've been working in the Royal Household as a cleaner, but I've been going to secretarial college one evening a week too.'

The door opened, and Mr O'Keefe re-entered the room.

'It was hard work but worth it, I think. I hope anyway. This'll be my first—'

A derisive snort sounded from behind her. With a disdainful glance at her as she continued speaking, he took his seat. Caroline's face began to flame but at least he hadn't heard Barbara describe him as a dish.

'—my first proper secretarial job.'

'Must make a change from scrubbing toilets,' Barbara said cheerfully.

The skin on the back of her neck prickled but there was

no trace of malice in Barbara's words and Caroline decided it was more likely she had spoken without thinking, as she herself was wont to do.

'We do have to do that, but we also clean the State Rooms and the royal family's private apartments. Queen Elizabeth The Queen Mother's room was always my favourite. She has so many lovely little trinkets.'

'Oh, I'd love to see more of the palace than just this place,' Barbara replied, gazing around. 'I'm quite jealous. You must know so much about them.'

'No more than anyone else. It is hard work though. Not all tea and crumpets.'

This time, Mr O'Keefe sighed and when she turned, she saw him smirking.

Not so long ago, after her experience with Timothy, she would have hidden away, kept her mouth shut, been frightened, but something about Mr O'Keefe's attitude lit a fire within her. She'd show him, just as she'd show everyone else, and she'd begin by proving she wasn't to be pushed around. She might not speak like they did, and she might clean toilets for a living most of the time, but that didn't mean she was stupid.

'Summat funny?' she asked, relapsing into her fierce cockney accent, startling him so he looked up, a flash of shame passing over his eyes.

His jaw tensed. 'Not really. I just wondered if you two were ever going to stop talking and get some work done.'

'Sorry, Mr O'Keefe,' Barbara trilled in a flirty way, turning to face him. Caroline was sure she'd stuck her chest out, the buttons on her thin white blouse straining as she pulled her shoulders back. 'It won't happen again. I was just trying to make Miss Staunton—'

'Stratton,' Caroline corrected. Even Barbara couldn't get her name right.

'Sorry – Miss Stratton – feel at home. We need all the help we can get, don't we? We don't want to scare her off.'

Though she wasn't scared, Caroline did have the feeling she'd made a terrible mistake in attempting a new role she didn't feel at all ready for, despite the hours of training she'd undertaken.

'I suppose we do,' Mr O'Keefe conceded. 'But there's no need to pretend this is a mothers' meeting. You can natter during breaks or after work.'

Caroline turned back, annoyance burning the skin on her neck, and began to type. As she'd expected, her fingers soon grew used to the different typewriter keys and began to fly.

Mistake or not she was here now, and she'd show him. She'd show them all.

Chapter Four

On Sunday lunchtime, Caroline approached her parents' house on Cannon Street Road, Whitechapel, with a racing heart. News of the temporary office job had been kept secret. She'd wanted to tell them in person, to see the looks on their faces rather than send them a letter. She'd spent all of Friday afternoon in the office with Barbara, who she'd discovered was quite nice but a bit blunt, and dismissive Mr O'Keefe. Mr Newington had come and gone, hurrying from one place to another taking papers and reports with him as he'd tried to catch up on the vast number of tasks he was in charge of. He'd been pleased with her progress, and especially complimentary of her typing speed, which had forced another sigh of annoyance from Mr O'Keefe. A part of her had revelled in it. It would teach him to judge her for her appearance. When the time had come to leave, she'd rushed back to the staff quarters and found Milly and Mrs Barnes eager to hear the details.

All afternoon, as Caroline had watched Mr Newington flitting about like a harvesting bee, she'd felt the familiar burn of ambition that had forced her to undertake the secretarial course in the first place. Despite his frowning, tie-pulling and stress, she wanted what Mr Newington had. Not just to be important and in command of others, but to be responsible. To be respected. Perhaps one day she would run an office. Even one in Buckingham Palace, if they ever let women climb that high. She was getting ahead of herself, she knew. She was getting ahead of the world and tried to quell her ambitions. If she were lucky, she might one day oversee a typing pool. Thinking of anything more was to invite disappointment.

The temperature was just above freezing, and the heavy white clouds overhead were laden with unshed snow, the weather unusually cold for November. The forecaster on the radio had advised it was only going to get worse, and Caroline pulled the neck of her coat and tucked in the ends of the scarf her ma had knitted the year before. If the temperature continued to fall, as it surely would overnight, there would be a dusting of snow, perhaps more, by morning. She'd have to make sure she left her family home in good time to make it back to Buckingham Palace before the roads became icy and treacherous.

She secretly hoped for a white Christmas, imagining waking up on Christmas Day to find the world covered in white, the fires blazing in the palace, decorations adorning each and every room, sharing presents with her friends. She'd miss home of course, but she'd manage and her parents would understand.

Her parents' small house was sandwiched between a grocer and a newsagent, and she marvelled at how it had contained them all for so many years. When she and her siblings had been little, they'd all shared a room. As they'd grown, the room had been split in two by a blanket and Johnny had been forced to dress only when they left the room.

Compared to Buckingham Palace, it was the size of one of the garages in the Royal Mews. In fact, it was more akin to a horse stall in the stable block, but it was home, and returning always gave her a sense of calm and peace. The small house had been her sanctuary, thanks to her loving parents. She'd only had to look down the street to see children who didn't have it so easy. Some fathers were free with their belts and mothers scolded on the slightest provocation. Hers had always been kind and caring and for that she was grateful. Yet, despite the love that existed between them, she had never told them about Timothy and the way he'd tried to take advantage of her. Once she'd been saved by her own ingenuity and a second time by Milly, though they never spoke of it, Milly too having been manipulated by him. A mutual silence had developed around the subject, and it was one Caroline was happy to maintain. She didn't like to think back on such events and had decided those unhappy moments wouldn't colour the rest of her life. Timothy had been sacked and she hadn't seen him since.

She pressed her key into the lock and pushed the door open. 'Only me,' she called as she stepped inside. Despite the freezing weather of the city, the house was reasonably warm where her ma was cooking dinner. Her parents were saving their coal for when the snow came and once the cooking was over the house would be filled with cold, damp air. The deep, savoury scent of steak and kidney pudding filled every room, making her mouth water. There was nothing quite like her ma's cooking. Alongside it, she could almost taste the carrots from the garden, the vegetable patch still regularly tended to even though the war was long over. Her ma was shelling peas in the kitchen at the back of the house. Caroline could just see her through the open doorway, humming to herself.

'Tea's in the pot,' she called as Caroline closed the door behind her and took off her coat, hanging it on the nails her father had knocked into the wall.

No fancy coat stands for them. As with so many people, their life had been one of make do and mend even before the war had started. Her memories of it were hazy: nothing more than a jumbled collection of half-remembered feelings. There'd been fear, of course, but also comfort and safety as her parents had held her tight, protecting her from the bombs and fires that surrounded them.

When she got her first permanent office job, she'd save up and buy a coat stand for them, Caroline decided. Something elegant and made of good quality wood. Although she'd have to leave the palace to secure a position like that and that would mean finding somewhere of her own to live. She wasn't sure how she felt about the prospect. Perhaps she could find somewhere with Helen and the baby, and they could split the rent.

''Ello, treacle,' her pa said, appearing in the doorway that led to the living room. He was wearing a thick jumper her ma had knitted for him and old trousers that were faded and patched at the knee. 'Get 'ere all right, did you?'

'Yeah, no bother, Pa.'

'That wind's bitin' though, innit?'

'Not half.' She rocked on to her tiptoes and gave him a kiss on the cheek.

'Reckon there'll be snow tonight.'

'I wouldn't be surprised.' She glanced back through the

36

small glass panel in the door. 'The light's gone all funny like it does when snow's on the way.'

''Ere.' He handed her his empty, chipped mug. 'Fill that up, will you? If you're goin' to the kitchen.' She took it, returning his grin.

Her ma embraced her as she entered, leaving the pea-shelling for a moment. A bowl of fresh bright green peas sat on the countertop and beside it sat the discarded pods that would be chopped up and used in a soup or stew. Nothing was wasted. Not when rationing was still in place and money was tight for everyone. Austerity, they called it. The country still had to rebuild itself after the war. But for most, it was just more worry on top of everything they'd been through. Surely with the new Queen on the throne and a grand coronation planned for the following year, rationing would stop soon?

'All right, my darlin'? 'Ow's it been at the palace this week?'

Her ma loved saying that, the word 'palace' filling her face with pride.

'Good,' Caroline replied, keeping the excitement from her voice. 'Actually, I've got some news. Pa? Pa, come here.'

She heard him push himself up from his chair with a heave and joined them. His tall frame filled the doorway, his red hair as vibrant as Caroline's own. His beard, she could see, had been recently trimmed by her ma, probably while he sat in one of the old wooden chairs around the small kitchen table, the tablecloth tied around his neck.

'What's all this then?' he asked, removing the pipe from the corner of his mouth. The sweet smell of tobacco mingled with the cooking smells and Caroline wished she could bottle it and take it with her back to the palace.

'Caroline's got some news for us,' Ma said, her eyes brightening.

'Oh yeah? Good news, I 'ope.'

'I think so,' Caroline began. 'Mr Newington, you remember him? He's the one stepping out with Mrs Barnes. He's asked me to work in the offices for a few days.'

Her ma gasped and pressed a worn red hand to her mouth. 'Oh my goodness! Pa, did you 'ear that?'

'I did.' His chest puffed with pride. 'What a piece of news that is. Come 'ere, treacle.' She stepped into his embrace and her ma joined in from the other side. 'Well done, flower. We're ever so proud of you, ain't we, Lils?'

'Thanks, Pa,' Caroline replied while her ma patted her cheek affectionately.

Just as they were moving away from each other, Johnny, her brother, rattled down the rickety stairs and into the kitchen. He was taller than their father and Caroline noticed for the first time her pa's slight stoop, as though the weight of the world were pulling him down. His wrinkles had deepened since the last time she'd seen him, and he seemed older and more careworn. Her ma, now she took her in, had more grey hairs dotted through her once lustrous brown hair and creases gathered at the corners of her tired eyes.

'What's going on here? Has someone died?' Johnny winkled his way past them and, grabbing the pot of dark, deeply stewed tea, he poured himself a cup.

'Cheeky beggar,' Lillian replied, waving the tea towel she'd kept over her shoulder at him. 'Our Caroline's workin' in the offices at the palace. For a Mr Newington. Ain't that wonderful news? She's goin' up in the world.'

'He's a senior clerk,' Caroline added. 'It's just some typing work but it's a start, isn't it?'

'That's brilliant! Well done, sis. Not bad at all.' His genuine smile hid the teasing in his words.

High praise indeed from the brother who'd spent his entire life pulling her pigtails and calling her carrot top.

Suddenly remembering what Helen had told her, Caroline said, ''Ere! I want a word with you.' The more refined accent vanished as it always did when she was home, partly because she didn't want her parents to think she was getting above herself and partly because it made her feel closer to them to speak without having to think first. 'Helen told me you brought 'er some fruit the other day.'

Though his skin was darker than Caroline's paler, opalescent complexion, a ruddy pink rose into his cheeks. He stirred his tea, keeping his eyes on the mug and the dark, swirling liquid.

'Where did you get it from?' she finished, enjoying his embarrassment. Ma and Pa had turned to face him too.

He still wouldn't look at her but spoke over his shoulder. 'Fell off the back of a van, didn't it?'

'Oh, Johnny!'

Ma crossed her arms over her chest. 'You can't go mixin' Helen – a pregnant woman – up in that sort of thing, Johnny.'

'What sort of thing?' At this, he turned and faced them, truculent, adamant he'd done nothing wrong. 'It was just some fruit. And it was given me. I didn't ask where it came from, but I weren't the one who took it from wherever they

39

got it. I just thought she might like it, that's all. The rozzers ain't going to care about fruit, are they?'

'Still,' Ma continued. 'She don't need that sort of trouble. She's got enough on her plate with that baby and no husband.'

'Couldn't you buy any?' Caroline asked, moving from the crowded end of the kitchen down to the worn table and chairs just big enough to sit the four of them. They were virtually in each other's laps when Nancy joined them, which wasn't very often now she had a fella and was gaining a reputation as a decent dressmaker. Caroline sometimes wondered if she was forgetting her roots, but never saw her enough to ask. 'You're still working at Whitelock's, ain't you?'

'Course. Wish I weren't though. I'd much prefer a job with better prospects. And that man's a crook. Make no mistake.'

''E's no such thing,' Pa remarked, coming to join Caroline. The chair creaked and moaned under his weight and Caroline worried that it needed replacing. 'Arthur Whitelock's 'ad that warehouse for donkey's years. Respectable, 'e is. And you'd do well to remember it. You could do much worse than work for 'im and the docks is good employment. It'll serve you well if you keep your nose clean. Job for life.'

It had been like that for her pa. He'd worked on the docks since he was a young boy, but he was suffering for it now. In a way, Caroline was proud her brother wanted to make something more of himself. There had been a time she'd worried he never would, but then he'd pulled himself together and knuckled down.

'What were you visiting her for anyway?' she asked.

There was silence for a moment and Caroline's ma and pa looked at each other knowingly. Caroline had the horrible feeling Johnny was taking more of an interest in Helen than she was happy with. She hadn't thought they'd said more than a few words to each other the day he'd helped her move.

Johnny shrugged and placed his hands in his pockets, leaning back against the kitchen worktop only to be shooed along by their ma. 'I dunno. Just thought she might want some, that's all. She needs to eat proper, don't she? In her condition.'

'Well, she don't need no trouble,' Caroline replied. 'So you just leave 'er be. Don't go dragging 'er into any of your messes.'

'I won't,' he replied, annoyed by her accusation. 'And I ain't in no messes. I ain't been in no messes for years. I'm not like that any more.'

'You're always in messes,' Ma said, placing a hand on the side of his head and tilting it towards her so she could plant a kiss on his temple. 'Now, all of you, get to work so we can eat this dinner. I don't know about you, but I'm starvin'.'

Through dinner they discussed the fact that it had been Remembrance Day: a poignant reminder of the struggles the nation had gone through and the losses everyone had suffered. The Queen had attended a service and laid a wreath at the Cenotaph for the first time as monarch. There was also excitement at the palace as Prince Charles would celebrate his fourth birthday at the end of the week.

Lillian had asked questions about what Caroline had to wear for work now that her role had changed, what sort of minutes she'd have to take and whether she'd get to see Milly and Mrs Barnes as much. A week could seem a long

41

time when there was no telephone. Buckingham Palace had a staff one, but as her parents didn't own one it was of no use to Caroline. No one they knew had one either. Letters took too long to write, and something was always lost when she committed the words to paper. With the cost of telegrams, any news would have to wait till next Sunday when she returned to see them. Caroline reassured her ma it would, in all likelihood, be a boring and quiet week.

'There was one funny thing that happened this week,' Caroline said. 'We heard there's going to be a Christmas dance.'

Ma couldn't have been more excited if she was attending herself. She leapt from her chair, fairly dancing around the kitchen. 'What will you wear?'

'I don't know,' Caroline replied. 'I need to buy something for work before I think about a party dress.'

'I might have just the thing.' With as much speed as she could muster, she made her way upstairs. Caroline didn't follow and instead shared confused glances with her brother and Pa. A moment later, Ma returned with a dress that was as good as new, though too big for Caroline. It was a little old-fashioned with short, puffed sleeves and she worried the V-neck would reveal too much flesh, but the dark, navy-blue satin was beautiful.

'I ain't worn this in decades,' Lillian said wistfully. 'But a bit of tinkerin' and it'll be lovely on you.'

'Are you sure, Ma?'

'Course I am. Better you wear it than it sits in my wardrobe. See?' She turned her attention to her husband. 'I told you it was right not to throw it out.'

Once dinner was eaten and a fruit flan with custard consumed, they settled in the cramped living room to listen to the wireless.

'Are you here next Sunday, Caroline? I was thinkin' of makin' the Christmas puddin's, givin' them time to stew before Christmas proper. I need you all here so you can have your stir.' It was tradition that everyone had a stir of the pudding. Her ma swore it tasted better that way. Caroline said she would be and her ma continued chatting. 'Betty Hardy told me that those posh people she cleans for over in Belgravia are buyin' a television.'

'A television?' Pa echoed. 'Cor blimey.'

She nodded. 'To watch the coronation on next summer.'

'It's all right for some, innit?'

Johnny turned to Caroline. 'What will you lot at the palace do?'

She was about to answer that she didn't know when a knock at the door forced their ma from her seat. 'Now who could that be?'

Low muffled voices sounded from the hallway before she returned, white as a sheet, two tall policemen behind her, their helmets tucked under their arms.

Everyone leapt up, Caroline's eyes flicking from the concerned faces of her parents to Johnny, whose normal bluff and bluster when faced with authority had disappeared. He looked scared. His eyes were wide, and she could see from the rise and fall of his chest he was breathing heavily. Her own stomach contracted, tightening on the dinner she'd just eaten.

'Mr Jonathan Stratton?' the policeman on the right said.

He edged around Ma, and she shuffled to stand beside her husband.

'What's all this about, officer?' Pa asked, his posture stiffening as he removed his pipe from his mouth.

'Are you Mr Jonathan Stratton?' the officer asked Johnny again, ignoring the question.

'Yeah. What of it?' Johnny puffed his chest out, but Caroline could tell it was all bravado. He was pale and sweating, and there was a wildness to his gaze like an animal about to flee.

The copper stepped forward, reaching out for Johnny's arm. 'You're under arrest for burglary and theft.'

'What?' he exclaimed as his arms were manhandled behind his back and cuffs placed on his wrists.

Ma shrieked. Pa said, 'Now 'ang on a minute. You can't just come in 'ere and—'

'We can and we must,' the other officer, who was still standing in the doorway, replied coldly.

'What have you done, Johnny?' Caroline asked, her chest tight.

'Nothing. I swear! I ain't done nothing! I've never robbed anyone. What're you talking about?'

The officers dragged Johnny away as Ma sobbed into her apron, her raw, red hands dabbing at her eyes. Pa stepped between them and the open doorway.

'If you're arrestin' my son, you 'ave to at least tell me what for.'

'A van from Whitelock's Warehouse was stolen last night and used to rob Oclee's jewellers down on Fieldgate Street.

Whoever did it beat the living daylights out of old Mr Oclee and stole most of his stock.'

'I had nothing to do with that,' Johnny shouted, wriggling in their grasp.

That? Caroline thought the choice of word strange. Did it imply there was some other meaning to it?

'Was your son here last night?'

Pa clenched his teeth around his pipe. 'I can't say for sure. We went to bed early, but I'd 'ave 'eard if he went out. I'm sure of it.'

'Your son's known to us. Got a criminal record a mile long—'

'That was years ago! 'E was only a kid then. A stupid one at that, who got caught up with the wrong crowd, but he ain't like that no more.'

'Someone saw him out the same night. Late. He works at Whitelock's and it was a Whitelock's van that was stolen. Then Oclee's jewellers is robbed. That all just a coincidence, is it?'

'My son would never do anythin' like this.'

Sadness passed over the copper's face as he looked at Pa as if he'd heard it all before. Then his gaze shifted to his colleague. The colleague signalled for Johnny to be taken away. They followed them outside, the cold nipping at their skin as they stood there coatless. All Caroline could do was slip her hand into her pa's as they watched Johnny be hauled into the back of a police van. She squeezed his hand tightly and he wrapped his other arm around his wife.

'It'll be all right,' he said firmly, trying to convince himself.

'What are we going to do, Pa?' Caroline asked, her voice shaking. She should have said something, defended him. Guilt swamped her that she'd stood back and watched her brother be dragged away.

'I don't know yet. But I'll think of somethin'. If Johnny says he 'asn't done anythin', he 'asn't done anythin'.' There was a waver in his voice: a hint of uncertainty, just as there had been in her own thoughts.

'Did he go out last night?' she asked quietly.

'I don't know.'

''E did,' Ma said between sobs. 'I 'eard him. I was just about to go to the outhouse when I 'eard the front door.'

'What time was that?' Caroline asked.

'I don't know.' She collapsed again, weeping against her husband's chest.

As a boy, Johnny had been easily led; he'd also had a talent for trouble. He'd been in difficulty with the law as a teenager, getting himself into scrapes and stealing the odd apple, but he'd worked hard for years now, trying to turn his life around and make something more of himself. He might be a bit cheeky, but he wasn't a bad person and would never do anything like burglary or theft, she was sure of it. Yet, for all Caroline's hopes that those days were behind them, she knew her brother too well, and she worried that if he had fallen in with the wrong crowd again, he could have been forced to do something, too afraid to say no.

Something that might ruin them all.

They went back into the house, none of them speaking, all in shock. She made her ma a cup of tea, adding a tot of whisky to her pa's.

'I have to get back,' she said. The weather was turning and if she didn't hurry, she'd end up in a snowstorm.

'Course you do,' her ma said. She followed her into the hallway and watched as Caroline took her coat from the nail. 'I'll write as soon as I know more.'

Pa joined them in the hall. 'Do us proud,' he added, engulfing her in another hug that spread warmth through her body, fighting the cold that permeated the house now the oven was out.

'I'll come home on my next half-day, and you can always write to me. I'll try and come by after work if I can.'

'We'll let you know as soon as he's 'ome. Most likely it's just a mistake.'

She wished she could believe him. The first snowflakes began to fall as the old front door closed behind her and she hurried towards the tube and the comfort and warmth of Buckingham Palace. However, nothing could remove the hard stone of dread that had settled in her stomach. Only Johnny's innocence would do that and right now she wasn't convinced that he was.

Chapter Five

When Caroline had returned to the palace, she'd gone straight to her room. She hadn't been able to bear seeing Milly or Mrs Barnes. It was all too shameful. A brother arrested and for such serious crimes. Instead, she'd closed herself in her bedroom, and shut the world out. What would happen to them all now? Her family would be shunned. Nancy's beau might finish up with her. Everything was at risk because of Johnny. Rage at her brother had filled her, but then she'd remembered his terrified face, his quick breathing, and collapsed into sobs.

This morning, she wished more than anything to stay in bed until the last moment and then go straight to the offices. Mrs Barnes and Milly would knock for her soon. They always did and she wasn't sure she was a good enough liar to convince them everything was fine when it most certainly was not. She climbed out of bed and dressed and as she'd expected, the knock came right on time.

'Morning, Caroline,' Milly said, cheerful and smiling. 'How were your ma and pa? We didn't see you last night to ask. Is everything all right?'

'Yes, yes,' she lied, closing the door to her staff room, and walking with Milly down the corridor. 'I was just cold from the snow, so I went straight into bed.'

'That was a good idea. You don't want to get the flu as well, do you?'

Milly began to talk of the dance. Her excitement was endearing but not enough to distract Caroline from her thoughts. What happened when you were arrested for something? Would Johnny be kept at a police station? Interviewed? Interrogated? Would he be sent to prison? She had no idea how it all worked and hated that they were about to find out. The neighbours would be talking and soon, if she wasn't careful, the palace would be as well.

'Are you sure you're all right?' Milly asked as they walked into the Household Breakfast Room. 'You're ever so quiet.'

'Just nervous,' she replied. It wasn't a complete lie, but her guilt grew.

'Don't worry, you'll be marvellous. Have some breakfast. That'll make you feel better.'

They joined Mrs Barnes at a table and Caroline ate as much as she could manage, claiming it was nerves at her first full day in the office stealing her appetite. Mrs Barnes's eyes roved to her on several occasions and, unable to risk the older woman intuiting something as she so often did, Caroline left to get to work early. Mrs Barnes caught her in the corridor.

'Caroline,' she called and, slowing her steps, Caroline cursed under her breath before turning around. 'Are you sure there isn't somethin' wrong?'

'Honestly, Mrs Barnes, I'm fine. Really.'

'If you say so. Go on then.'

The whole charade would have to be repeated in front of Barbara and Mr Newington and tonight when she met her friends for dinner. Could she claim a headache and eat in her room? Not without people visiting her to help. As grateful as she was for her friends, all she wanted was to disappear. To be alone. To be so insignificant no one would care or notice her. She'd felt like that her whole life and it had only changed recently, since her friendships with Helen and Milly had grown. How strange it was to be wishing them away now.

In the office, she knuckled down to work, ignoring the looks and huffs of Mr O'Keefe, who clearly wished she wasn't there. Little did he know she too wished she were somewhere else. She wanted to be at the local nick to find out what was happening with her brother, but all she could do was concentrate on her work, on the next word she needed to type, the next paper she had to copy.

At the end of the day, having not eaten anything since breakfast as she couldn't stomach it, she needed something to fill the hole in her belly. She couldn't go a whole evening and night without eating, even though it would mean seeing her friends and pretending again everything was all right. She'd eat and claim a headache or stomach ache and go straight to bed after, asking them politely to leave her be and let her sleep. It wasn't a lie that could last forever, but she wasn't ready to admit her family's shame, even to those at the palace she loved.

That night, her sleep was fitful and uneasy, as she'd suspected it would be. Her thoughts strayed constantly to Johnny. She didn't know which station they'd taken him to or if he'd been locked in cells with murderers who would eat him alive. For all his faults, he was at heart a kind and generous soul like their pa. She could only imagine how scared he'd been, how his bravado would have faded.

The next morning, a resounding knock on her door signalled Mrs Barnes was there to fetch her for breakfast. She'd dressed in a skirt and blouse, adding the best-fitting cardigan she had over the top. She'd worn a little more make-up than usual, though nothing as daring as Barbara's bright red lipstick. Her nerves were biting more than they had yesterday or on Friday afternoon, but then, she'd been swept up in the doing of things: making the decision to try, following Mr Newington to the office, and finding her feet with the tasks given to her.

When she opened the door, she saw Milly by Mrs Barnes's side and they marched into her room, demanding to know what was going on.

'I'm no fool, missy, and you should know that by now.'

'I – umm—' With no way out, Caroline crumpled, burying her head in her hands. As she slumped on to her bed, she told them the whole sorry tale.

'Why didn't you tell us?' Milly asked. 'We've been through enough to trust each other, haven't we?'

'It's not about trust,' Mrs Barnes said sagely, sitting beside Caroline and rubbing her back. 'It's about shame. But you needn't be ashamed around us, lovey. Come on, you need some food.'

Supported on both sides by her friends, they led her to the Household Breakfast Room and sat her down, Milly insisting she'd fetch some breakfast for her. Caroline felt the need to cry all over again. She could have had this warmth and support immediately if she hadn't been so foolish.

When they were all settled, Mrs Barnes thought for a moment, then said, 'Arrested. I can't believe it.'

'Do you think he did it? Whatever it is they're accusing him of?' Milly asked, leaning forwards, her arms resting on the table.

Caroline twisted the teacup in its saucer and, below the table, she crossed and uncrossed her feet at the ankles. She couldn't keep still. The snow that had fallen all night piled on the windowsills in uneven white lines.

'I wish I could say no, but I know my brother too well. He trusts people and then they let him down, or they turn out to be different than he expected. It's happened before.' That was how he'd ended up the wrong side of the law in his youth, egged on by people he thought were his friends. She hated admitting it out loud and wished she could cover her face with her hand, hiding her shame. She looked around, grateful that everyone else in the room was discussing the Christmas dance. 'I don't think he would have done anything that could've hurt anyone, but . . . sometimes he just doesn't think things through. Like when he "borrowed" the works van to help Helen move. But he's harmless. What worries me is that Ma said he went out that night.'

'Right,' Mrs Barnes said, brushing a stray grey-brown hair from her forehead. 'We need to think about this rationally. What exactly has he been accused of?'

'Theft of a works van and burglary of Oclee's jewellers.'

'And they didn't say anything about why? They didn't mention the evidence against him?'

She shook her head. 'Just that he was seen out—'

'By who?'

'I don't know. I need to talk to him. I need to know where he went that night. And what did he do if it wasn't that?' Her voice cracked and she looked again to the window. Snow continued to swirl down, obscuring more of the view, and fat white flakes dropped like confetti from the sky. She'd always loved snow as a child. Had played out in it with Johnny and Nancy.

'Maybe he was just in the wrong place at the wrong time?' Milly offered. 'Johnny seems like a decent sort to me. We've all done silly things in our youth but that doesn't mean he's silly now. Maybe there's a logical explanation.'

'I hope so. I really, really do.' Yet Caroline still wasn't convinced and that brought with it a flurry of guilt that threatened to overwhelm her. 'Where are you two working today?' she asked, feeling tired beyond measure. Her eyes were heavy, and her brain felt used and empty. She wished she were joining them, that she would have the comfort of her friends around her and the routine she'd always known.

Milly answered, 'We're cleaning the Queen's private quarters and office. Peter Townsend's gone with her to High Wycombe or somewhere like that.'

'Has he now,' Mrs Barnes said, loading her bread with a spoonful of jam.

'It makes a nice change from scrubbing everything ready for Christmas. I'm not looking forward to the Christmas tress getting here. You know how the pine needles get everywhere and those floral displays always drop leaves.'

Caroline scooped kedgeree on to her fork, wondering

if the offices would be decorated for Christmas. She had to admit that if she were still there, she'd miss working in the State Rooms that always looked enchanting at Christmas, filled to the brim with wide, lush Christmas trees decorated with ribbons and baubles. 'Do you think that's because they want him away from Princess Margaret? They certainly seem to be keeping him busy and on separate outings as much as possible.'

'I think that's the plan,' Milly replied. 'Maybe they hope the infatuation will end if she doesn't spend much time with him.'

'In my experience,' Caroline replied, 'it can do the opposite.'

They shared a secret look, both knowing to whom she was referring. Timothy had been in her thoughts often over the last few days and she wasn't entirely sure why these things would only occur to her now. Perhaps it was because it was only nine months since everything had come to a head. Back then, when she'd thought him a good man, the time they'd been apart had been painful, only heightening her need to see him. An icy shiver rippled down her spine and she shuddered. Milly placed a hand over hers: a gentle gesture that was both reassuring and brought her back to the present. She wouldn't think about him any more today. That part of her life was over and there were other, more pressing concerns right now.

'Well,' Mrs Barnes said. 'Better get this eaten. You don't want to be late. Mr Newington said he was very impressed with you when I had lunch with him yesterday.'

'He's a very nice man.'

The older woman's cheeks coloured. 'And all this business

with the Princess and Peter Townsend will blow over soon enough. You mark my words.'

'When we were cleaning the other day, I heard her say that Margaret must have the Queen's permission to marry before she's twenty-five. Why is that?' Mrs Barnes scowled. 'I wasn't earwigging!'

'You were!' Milly added with a teasing grin. 'I've never seen anyone take so long to polish a door.'

'I told you: I was doing all the gold bits.'

The lighter tone to the conversation brought an unexpected smile to Caroline's face, and she forked some kedgeree into her mouth.

'Well . . .' Mrs Barnes took a piece of bread and began to butter it liberally. 'My understandin' from Leonard is that it's somethin' to do with a Royal Marriages law or some such Act like that. Basically, any member of the royal family under twenty-five needs the monarch's consent and I can't help feelin' that's a good thing in this instance.'

Robert sat down at the table, his cheeks red and sweat prickling his brow from the staff kitchens. 'Morning, M-Milly.' He leant forward and gave her a peck on the cheek. They'd been courting for eight months now and Caroline, Helen and, no doubt, Mrs Barnes were all eagerly awaiting news of an engagement. 'Morning, Mrs Barnes. How are you f-feeling, Caroline? Nervous?'

'A bit,' she confirmed, wishing he hadn't reminded her of it. She'd been quite happy talking of the royal family and not thinking too much about herself or Johnny and the mess he'd got himself into.

'You don't n-need to be. You know what you're doing.'

She sighed. 'I hope so. Actually . . .' She pushed her plate away. 'I think I'll head off now. I'd prefer to be early.' She hoped they'd meet for lunch, but it depended on when she was allowed hers and when they finished tidying the rooms. Cleaning the Queen's apartments could only be done when she was out, so they'd have to make the most of the time.

The maze of corridors had become so familiar to her now, and that familiarity brought comfort, an anchoring to something solid so she wouldn't be swept up in the fear that threatened to engulf her. As Caroline passed friends and colleagues, they smiled affectionately at her; they'd heard about her temporary new role and were glad to see her hard work had paid off, the palace looking after its own. If only they knew what else she was dealing with.

The unrhythmic noise of inexpertly pressed typewriter keys sounded behind the office door. She took a breath, banishing her worries over Johnny and ignoring the sleepiness that burned her eyes. She opened the door gently to find Mr O'Keefe leaning over his keyboard, trying to type while at the same time reading his notes. She made no comment and moved to the desk that had become hers.

'You're back again, are you?'

'As you can see,' she replied without turning around. She placed her handbag by the side of her desk and sat down, reading the topmost page on the pile of papers beside her typewriter. She'd worked through almost half of it since Friday and wanted to get it finished off today, helping Mr Newington to ease the backlog.

'You're quite full of yourself, aren't you?' Mr O'Keefe had sat back in his chair, one arm resting on the desk.

'Me?' She turned around, pointing at herself. 'I'm not the one who's full of myself.' If anyone could be accused of that it was him. Especially with that smug look on his face, but she was too tired, too stressed to argue. 'I'm just trying to work.'

She turned and he huffed out a breath. Caroline loaded a sheet of paper into the typewriter only to hear Mr O'Keefe mumble over his papers. She didn't catch it the first time, but when he repeated himself a second later, his frustration apparently growing, she heard him say, 'What's that supposed to be?'

The smugness had fallen away as he bent over a sheet of paper, one hand on his forehead, pushing his dark chocolate-brown hair back from his face. She was struck again by how handsome he was, but she reminded herself she was done with handsome men who thought too highly of themselves.

'Is that accession or accessing?' he whispered, lifting the paper and studying it closely.

'Can I help at all?'

'Not unless you can read my writing.'

'I might be able to. Do you want me to have a look?'

He studied her for a second, paused, and then shrugged. 'You might as well. I can't figure it out.'

She stepped towards his desk and took the sheet he held out. 'Oh, you write longhand.'

'So?' His face hardened, and his tone was defensive.

'I just thought everyone used shorthand, that's all.'

'Not all of us have had the time for secretarial college.'

'I've made the time,' she replied fiercely, the anger he'd sparked in her earlier returning. She was already tired and on edge. Connor O'Keefe was going to have to watch himself unless he wanted to end up on the wrong side of her temper. 'I worked all day doing a hard job – one that leaves your bones aching – and then went to college and did homework. It wasn't easy. But I did it. If you really want to learn shorthand, you could do the same.'

He scoffed, his lyrical Irish accent unable to soften the harshness of his reply. 'I'd look rather daft in a class of young women, wouldn't I?'

'Then teach yourself. You can get books on it, you know. And it would be quicker than writing longhand.'

'Look, do you know what that says or not? I don't really need a lecture on the benefits of learning shorthand.' She studied the words and from the context decided it most likely said 'accessing'. 'Right. Thank you.'

The office door swung wider and Mr Newington entered. 'Ah, Caroline, wonderful to see you here so promptly. And you've already got started, I see.' He motioned to her typewriter, the page halfway out, filled with type. 'Marvellous. I'll have some more for you later. We're expecting the minutes of the Coronation Commission, and they must take priority. There's a lot of hoo-ha over televising the coronation and complaints have come in from the BBC and other international broadcasters who all need answering. Mr Lascelles has written the responses and said we'll have them today, ready to type up and pass to the Press Office.'

'Is that Tommy Lascelles?' she asked.

'That's right. Lovely man but a stickler for deadlines. He won't be happy if I don't have his minutes ready for him either. Now, where did I put them?' Mr Newington began to look around, tapping his finger to his lips.

'Can I have that back, please?' Mr O'Keefe said, holding out his hand for the paper.

'Of course.' She returned it, meeting his gaze squarely. As he looked at her, she was sure some thought or feeling passed behind his eyes, though she didn't know what it was. Loathing, most likely. Whatever it was, something in his features had taken hold for a second, and then left as fleetingly as it had arrived. She cleared her throat and returned to her desk, brushing her hands down the sides of her skirt.

Shortly after, Barbara arrived along with two other women who had returned from illness. The first was of a similar age to Caroline, who peered around nervously. She reminded Caroline of a mouse. The second, an older lady, walked in at exactly nine o'clock with a stern expression, a small, pursed mouth and glasses that perched on the end of her nose.

'You're new,' she said, standing next to Caroline's desk and towering over her.

'Umm, yes, I am. I'm—'

'Ah—' said Mr Newington. 'Mrs Coniston, this is Miss Stratton, who has joined us temporarily from the Household Staff.'

'The Household Staff?'

Caroline knew her pale skin was beginning to flame. She could feel the heat building, prickling her hairline.

'Yes. She's been training at secretarial college too. Quite a feat I'd say, wouldn't you? We all know how hard the Royal Army of Cleaners work.'

It wasn't an official term but there were so many of them that they'd named themselves that and it had spread around the rest of the palace. Though Caroline was grateful for Mr Newington's support, it did nothing to sway Mrs Coniston.

'If you say so,' she replied, and then moved to her desk. Caroline could feel the look the woman was giving her from the corner of her eye.

Her face now alight, Caroline turned her attention back to the keys, placing her fingers over them and typing speedily.

'Don't worry about old battleaxe,' Barbara whispered. 'She thinks a lot of herself. Knows everything and can't be told otherwise. I hate her. She's always miserable.'

Mr O'Keefe cleared his throat loudly and Barbara shifted, training her eyes forward on her desk. Caroline had thought it was another veiled caution, but then Mrs Coniston walked past to the duplicating machine at the back of the room. Had it been a warning to stop talking, or a signal that the old crow was about to move from her desk? She glanced behind her to see his head down, his attention firmly on the task in front of him. Most likely, given his attitude towards her, it was the former.

The morning progressed far quicker than Caroline had thought it would and soon it was time for the Changing of the Guard. The familiar sounds greeted her and she took comfort in them. The stirring notes of the military band – the trumpets, horns and drums – soothed her fraught nerves. The rhythmic marching of heavy, booted feet across the gravel of the forecourt was a sound she'd heard a hundred times before, yet it heartened her. They gave a sense of normality. Of something that would never change no matter what else altered around her. She needed that while this new world and Johnny's predicament untethered her.

Before long, lunchtime was approaching. She had cleared the pile of work Mr Newington had given her on Friday, and he was just about to hand her another when Tommy Lascelles, the Queen's private secretary, walked in.

'Ah, Newington, there you are.'

'Mr Lascelles, I've been expecting you.' The two gentlemen shook hands. 'I understand the work is urgent?'

'Isn't everything?' Mr Lascelles had a dour expression and a well-kept but bushy moustache. His face was rather angular with prominent cheekbones, as though he needed to eat more. Had her ma been there, she'd have offered him a pie: something to fill him up. 'There are the complaint responses I warned you about but also some highly sensitive papers regarding a personal matter between . . .' He lowered his voice, but Caroline was still able to hear. '. . . the Queen and the Duke of Edinburgh. I'd prefer your most trusted person to deal with those.'

'Of course.'

Mr Lascelles left and as Caroline assumed Mr O'Keefe was Mr Newington's most trusted person, she returned to her work.

'Caroline,' Mr Newington said. 'Can I speak with you a moment please?'

She stood and followed him to the end of the room where his small office was located. Inside, it was as she'd expected: incredibly neat and tidy, with everything in its place. He closed the door behind them, clutching Mr Lascelles's papers to his chest.

'Mr Lascelles has asked for my most trusted member of staff to deal with these. I'd like you to take them and work on them this afternoon, please. Ideally, you'll finish everything, but if you can't, anything left must be given to me so I can lock them in here overnight.' He held out the file towards her.

'Me?' She squeaked, taking them in shaking hands. 'But what about Mrs Coniston or – or Barbara?'

'I know this is all new to you but let me tell you something. When it comes to personal matters between the Queen and the Duke, I would normally deal with them myself. As you know, I don't have the time to do that presently, and in fact' – he checked his watch – 'I really must be off to a meeting any moment now. You've worked in and around the royal family since you started here. You've seen and heard their conversations, no doubt their secrets, but you have never broken their confidence, have you?'

'No, sir. Mrs Barnes always said that was the first rule of our job. We might see and hear stuff, but we have to pretend like we haven't.'

'That's why I want you to deal with those.' He pointed once more to the papers now in her hands. 'Mrs Barnes trusts you and so do I.'

'Thank you. That's ... I won't let you down, Mr Newington.'

'No need to thank me, but you better get started. Give them to me when you go for lunch and fetch them when you're back. They mustn't be left out.'

'I understand.'

She exited his office to see Mrs Coniston glaring at her as though she'd just done something unimaginably rude. Mr O'Keefe's jaw was set tight, his features hard, and any trace of that slight softening from before had gone. From the coldness in his gaze and the way his eyes fell to the papers in her grasp, he must have heard Tommy Lascelles's words too, and it was clear he hated her. In that moment she longed for the comfort of her friends, the camaraderie she'd grown used to. The only person who seemed pleased for her was Barbara.

'Looks like you're going up in the world,' she whispered.

But at what cost?

As proud as she was, no amount of success in her professional life was going to make up for losing her brother, which she would if he was guilty. Capital punishment was only kept for the worst crimes like murder but losing him to a life in prison would be just as hard.

Chapter Six

'Johnny's been charged,' Caroline told her friends later that evening as they sat in the Household Lounge. The news she'd heard earlier that night from her parents was still ringing in her head.

As soon as she'd finished work, she'd caught the bus home to find out if they'd heard any more and had been surprised to find them sitting in silence, the shock and worry evident on their faces. Her ma had been dazed and confused. Pa had visited the police station earlier that day, but it still hadn't sunk in. She'd hated leaving them but nothing she'd said had brought them out of their shock and after making them dinner – her ma unable to cook – she'd reluctantly returned to Buckingham Palace.

In the warmth of the lounge, Caroline dropped back into a comfortable armchair, her shoulders aching where they'd been tight with tension. There was snow again and the journey had been exhausting, her thin coat no match for the freezing temperatures.

Groups of people gathered, relaxing after a hard day's work. Someone had put a record on the gramophone and its tinny, scratchy notes could just be heard under the chattering voices. It was a Christmas song, but her mind couldn't focus on Christmas. Would her brother still be in prison then? The thought made her feel sick. Her friend's sympathetic faces warmed her heart but did little to remove the mounting worries and doubts that filled her mind.

'They're talking about assault as well now. Someone beat up Mr Oclee while they were robbing him and as they haven't arrested anyone else yet, they're blaming Johnny for that too, but he wouldn't ever do anything like that. He wouldn't hurt a fly. He's not got a violent bone in his body.'

'What I don't understand', Helen said, 'is why they think he was involved in the first place, just because he was out that night.'

'Pa went to the police station. Apparently, there's a witness who saw him out walking near the docks, but they won't say who it is. They said they were going ahead and charging him and now they're moving him to Pentonville Prison.' She looked around to ensure no one had heard her say the words. A chill ran down her spine. 'Pa said trying to see him there would break Ma's heart, but she's determined to go. I wish she wouldn't.'

A raucous burst of merriment rang out from the other side of the room where a group of footmen were playing cards, using matchsticks for currency. One of them had their hands in the air in celebration while the rest laughed. A group of maids sat opposite them on the other side of the room, and they were frowning. Seeing Caroline, the new coffee maid, Jane, waved. Caroline and the others waved back, pretending they'd been talking about something frivolous.

Excitement about the Christmas dance was still buzzing in the air. It had invigorated them all and everyone, from the groomsmen in the Royal Mews to the paper-pushers in the offices, were talking about it. Another jeer came from the footmen and Mrs Barnes spun to face them.

'Oh, do be quiet, you lot,' she shouted. 'Some of us are tryin' to talk here.' Turning her attention back to Caroline, she said, 'You don't think he did any of this though, do you?'

Caroline thought for a moment. Though at first she had worried he might have, she'd come to the conclusion that he had enough sense not to be involved in anything like this. 'Course not. Nothing like this. He was a bit of tearaway but that was years ago. He's not got into trouble since. I should like to know where he was that night though. He hasn't said and that makes me worry that he was up to no good. But he wouldn't go stealing jewellery or beating up defenceless old men. Ma knows Mr Oclee. She knows everyone. And he's a lovely old chap.'

'Will he be all right?' Milly asked, placing her teacup on the table. 'Surely he can identify who did it?'

'He's still unconscious,' Caroline replied. 'I just wish there was something I could do to help. I've got half a mind to go and visit Johnny and demand he tell me what he was up to. If he did go out, I need to know where he went so I can tell Ma and Pa. I don't know why he hasn't just told the police, and he can't have done, can he? Not if they're still charging him.'

'Perhaps he was seeing a lady-friend,' Helen offered. Caroline detected the note of sadness in her voice. Given the way Johnny had spoken of Helen and how Helen was now speaking of Johnny, Caroline wondered whether to warn her friend off, just as she had her brother. But this didn't seem the time or the place and she didn't want to embarrass her in front of everyone.

'He hasn't got a lady-friend,' Caroline replied. 'I'm sure of that. No, he must've been up to something else. But I don't know what. He's been doing so well for such a long time now.'

'Maybe you should talk to a solicitor? The one I spoke to after my father died was very nice indeed. I don't know if he works in criminal law, but I can find out. Would that help?'

Caroline brightened. 'Are you sure you don't mind? That'd be so helpful if you could, Helen.'

'And in the meantime, I'll come with you to see Johnny.'

At this remark, everyone stared at her.

'Really?' Caroline asked, her voice carrying the uncertainty she and everyone else felt. 'Are you sure? I mean . . . in your condition?'

Helen tilted her head, frowning. 'I'm not giving birth anytime soon, Caroline, and I'm not about to keel over either. Yes, I'm absolutely sure. If I'm to speak to the solicitor, I'll need to tell him all I know, so I think I should come with you.'

Though Caroline was still hesitant, Helen wasn't to be swayed. Caroline said, 'I can't say I wouldn't like the company. I've never been to a prison before.'

'I can't say I have either, but we'll get through it together.' She reached out her hand and Caroline took it.

After a second, both let go and took a sip of their tea. Caroline's was cold now, the dark liquid stewed and unpleasant. Still, she drank it.

'How are you getting on in the office with all this going on?' Milly asked Caroline.

'I'm just not sure I'm cut out for it.' She nipped her lip between her teeth. She'd been trying not to face that as well, but her doubts had been overwhelming her. She'd had another day of disdainful looks from Mr O'Keefe and every time she spoke she felt self-conscious. Too self-conscious.

'What do you mean not cut out for it?' asked Mrs Barnes. 'The work can't be any harder than what we do here.'

'It's not physically as hard but it's hard being there with people who'd like to see me fail. Who can't wait for me to mess up or make a mistake.'

'And who's that?' Mrs Barnes's voice rose in outrage.

Caroline leaned in closer, not wanting to be overheard. Mr O'Keefe and Mrs Coniston weren't in the room. She was sure they lived off site, as Helen did. But you didn't know who knew whom in the palace and she couldn't risk someone telling them she'd been talking behind their backs. She lowered her voice, so it was hidden by the raucous group playing cards and the music.

'There's a chap who works there called Mr O'Keefe. He's nicer to everyone else than he is to me. He's got a real problem and I don't know why. He always speaks all cheerful like to Barbara and that evil old crone Mrs Coniston, but when it comes to me, he just sort of mumbles as if he can't bear to talk to me. And Mrs Coniston thinks she's Lady Muck. She's always explaining things to me like I'm stupid and she can't help but check my work as she walks past, trying to find fault. I made one mistake this morning and she was there over my shoulder, pointing it out to me. She couldn't have been happier.'

'Perhaps you should stand up to her?' Milly said. 'Put her in her place a bit.'

'Maybe. It's just not as nice as working here with you and Mrs Barnes. To be honest, I was thinking I might ask Mr Newington if I could move back. Especially with everything else that's going on.'

'You can't do that,' Helen cried. Milly echoed her sentiments.

'This is what you've been workin' for,' Mrs Barnes added.

'I know but—'

'And Leonard told me he'd given you some important work to do. He wouldn't do that if you weren't up to it.'

The lads playing cards gave another guffaw. Someone turned off the gramophone and switched on the wireless.

'I know for a fact that he's happy with what you've been doing, so you don't need to worry there.'

Caroline had worked on the important papers that afternoon and, despite the looks from Mr O'Keefe and Mrs Coniston, she had found them utterly intriguing. The sensitive situation Mr Newington and Tommy Lascelles had referred to was between the Queen and the Duke of Edinburgh regarding which name she would take as reigning monarch. Though Elizabeth had confirmed the name of Windsor when she'd acceded to the throne back in February, the Duke of Edinburgh was still petitioning her to take the name Mountbatten before the coronation next year and so were his relatives, some even writing to the Queen. Though

Caroline had been close to the royal family as a cleaner, she'd never heard these sorts of discussions and was seeing a different side to palace life. But was that enough to make up for everything else?

'I appreciate everything Mr Newington's done for me . . . honestly. But everyone in that office hates me and I just don't fit in. I don't sound like they do, and I don't look like they do neither.' She signalled to her dowdy blouse and skirt, the best things she owned and had worn in the office that day. Mrs Coniston was always looking her up and down, judging her appearance, as had Mr O'Keefe, his face set in his usual sneer.

'You can get something new when you next get paid, can't you?' asked Milly. 'What's this really about?' she added gently. 'I've a feeling this is more about how *you* feel than anyone else. You know you're up to the job. Is it this business with Johnny?'

'Partly,' she confided with a sigh. 'I know I should keep hold of this job to help Ma and Pa out, especially as they've now lost Johnny's money too. But it's just hard and I'm sick and tired of life being hard. Everything I do's a struggle, with people looking down on me because I'm from the East End and ain't never had much. And now with Johnny and the rozzers—'

'Police,' Mrs Barnes clarified gently.

Caroline could feel the heat that had sprung into her cheeks and the tears threatening the back of her eyes. 'Police,' she repeated, feeling again like the stupid, ignorant girl everyone thought she was. 'My family could be ruined. Johnny could end up in prison for the rest of his life and—'

'Right,' said Mrs Barnes, slapping her hand down on the arm of the chair so Caroline jumped. 'Are you finished now?' Caroline nodded. 'Good, because this self-pityin' nonsense is not what I've come to expect from you, Miss Caroline Stratton. You're a strong, clever girl. Time to sort yourself out. I once heard someone say that what you do today can improve all your tomorrows. Are you really going to let some miserable old witch – and I know she's a miserable old witch, I've heard talk of Mrs Coniston before – and some sniffy young man stop you doing what you want with your life? Hmm?'

Caroline lapsed into silence, mulling over Mrs Barnes's words. She particularly liked the saying she'd recited. The situation at work wouldn't last. They'd get used to her and even if they didn't, she was only there temporarily, and she'd never been one to give in to bullies. Not those of Mrs Coniston's ilk anyway.

'All right, Mrs Barnes,' she conceded with a slight straightening of her posture. 'You're right.'

'I'm always right.'

The three younger ladies laughed.

Milly agreed, gazing up at her aunt fondly. Helen nodded alongside her.

'A good night's sleep's what you need, and to go and see your brother. The sooner you get his mess sorted out the better. Once you know where he was you can decide what to do next. It's time for action, my girl. Not sittin' around mopin'.'

Action. Caroline mulled the word over in her mind, silently mouthing it behind her closed lips. Yes, she would take action. She wouldn't leave her ma and pa to deal with this situation with Johnny, and she didn't trust the police to do a good job either, seeing as they were judging her brother based on the silly things he'd done in his youth.

Oh yes, she thought, feeling relief flood her body. She'd take action all right.

Chapter Seven

Caroline's working week continued in the same vein she had described to her friends the previous Tuesday. Mr O'Keefe sneered and mumbled begrudgingly whenever she was around while Mrs Coniston continued with snide remarks about Caroline's previous role as a cleaner. She constantly remarked on the state of her hands which, although they were less red and dry than they had been, were clearly those of someone who had spent their life undertaking manual work. Caroline had ignored her and worked hard to finish the papers Mr Newington had asked her to complete. She had heard from him that Tommy Lascelles had been pleased with the work she'd produced, commenting on the clarity and speed with which she'd done it. Mr O'Keefe had sighed as this piece of praise was delivered but it hadn't dented the glow of pride within her, or her determination to remain strong in the face of their disparagement. There had been moments of happiness, too, as they'd all enjoyed the news of Prince Charles's birthday. Caroline had missed her old job more than ever, thinking about her friends cleaning his sticky finger marks off the palace walls and brushing cake crumbs from the carpet.

On what should have been a quiet and peaceful Sunday afternoon spent with her family, eating her ma's delicious cooking and chatting with her pa about his week, she was on her way to Pentonville Prison with Helen. There'd been heavy snow through the previous night that hadn't abated this morning and the bus had made a valiant effort to get them there through the slushy drifts of snow that lined the roads. They had left the palace just as the Changing of the Guard was ending and Caroline was sure that, though they couldn't say anything, even the hardy soldiers were happy to be nearing the end of their time outside.

The journey had taken almost an hour as the bus trundled north. Shops were beginning to display Christmas gifts and paper chains hung in swathes. Helen was by her side as they stood opposite the imposing gates, shivering in the plummeting temperatures. From the glance Helen gave, Caroline knew the dark, medieval-looking door was just as intimidating to her. They had already entered through a gate in a high brick wall. The wide, dark building was bleak and menacing. Even the bare, leafless trees outside looked as if they didn't want to be there. How could Johnny have ended up here with people who must have done far worse things than he ever had? Or so she hoped. If she'd come all this way and gone through all of this to find he had had something to do with it, she'd never speak to him again.

'What do we do now?' asked Helen.

'I don't really know,' Caroline replied, looking at her watch. 'We're a little early.' She spotted other men and women, some with children in tow, heading their way. Perhaps they too had worried there'd be problems and delays due to the inclement weather.

They filed in through the same gate but instead of heading

to the medieval door, the visitors carried on around the side of the wall. She and Helen followed, joining the end of an informal queue. They paused behind a woman with two children aged seven or eight, one holding each hand, who wore ragged clothes, their knees visible through the badly darned holes in their trousers. Caroline saw the door they were waiting to open. Although it was smaller, it was no less bleak. Above it was a sign that read 'Visitors' Entrance'.

Flurries of snow surrounded them as they waited to step inside, knowing it wouldn't be warm and welcoming, but hoping it wasn't as freezing as standing in the gusty wind. The queue moved quickly and before long they were inside the door, faced with an intimidating man in prison officer uniform.

'Name?' he asked brusquely, staring at a clipboard that was splitting apart at the edges. He had a doughy, angry red face and long, old-fashioned sideburns. His bulbous nose was thread-veined and pitted, pink from the cold.

'Caroline Stratton and Helen Hill here to see Johnny – sorry – Jonathan Stratton.'

His eyes skimmed over the two pretty young ladies in front of him. 'Open your bags, please.' They both obeyed, sliding them down their arms and into their hands, then unclasping them. Holding them open, they showed them to the guard. He tilted his head left and right, stuck a hand into each and rummaged about, not that there was anything in there to find, then straightened up and pointed to another door. 'Through there, if you please. Next.'

They moved along, and he spoke the same way to the man behind them, sending him through a different door.

Caroline had the sudden feeling they had been sent that way because they'd done something wrong, and she worried she wouldn't be allowed to see her brother. With a firm breath she calmed herself. Most likely they were seeing people in different parts of the prison. The horrible situation was destroying her nerves.

'This reminds me of a hospital,' Helen said, leaning in. 'Though it's a lot noisier. It just has that disinfectant smell to it.'

'It's not hiding the boiled cabbage though, is it?' She'd hoped to lighten the mood. Her courage was failing, fear gnawing at her stomach, tying it into a tight ball.

'Why do places like this, or hospitals, always smell of boiled cabbage?'

'Makes you realise how lucky you are at the palace, doesn't it?'

As she said the words, she was even more aware of the contrast in her surroundings, as though someone might hear and begin to shout at her, calling her names or making fun of her. Aggression and violence lingered on the air, and one false move would be like a spark to a flame and a riot would erupt. The last time she'd felt tension like this had been when Timothy . . . No, she wouldn't finish that thought and rubbed the goosebumps from her arms. Below the atmosphere of barely contained anger was an undercurrent of fear. She could almost smell it beneath the cabbage and carbolic soap as if it seeped from everyone there: the visitors and inmates alike.

Through a second doorway they were met by another officer. He was tall and slim, and looked as though he'd get picked up and thrown around in a fight. Then she noticed a scar on his chin and another by his ear. His front tooth was missing, causing him to whistle slightly as he spoke.

'Who are you here to see?'

'Jonathan Stratton,' Caroline replied, her heart beating so fast her words were fearful, unsettled.

'Names?' She repeated them again and he checked the papers on his clipboard. 'Over there.' He pointed to a table. Other people were already seated, waiting at theirs.

The small room had been laid out with tables barely big enough for a person to sit at. On the further side of each one was a single wooden chair for the prisoner and on the other side, one or two seats. The woman with two children was sitting in one corner. Her hair had been tied in a headscarf, the knot under her chin, and one of her boys sat on her lap, playing with it, irritating her. The other boy glumly leaned on the table with his head on one hand.

Helen and Caroline made their way to the table assigned to them. Both held their bags tightly on their laps, hands clasped around the small handles. Helen nudged her, nodding towards a large sign on the wall that read: 'No Touching, No Gifts, Remain Seated At All Times'.

Caroline read it with a shudder. It all seemed so cold, so hard, and whilst it might be necessary for most inmates, it wasn't for Johnny. All she could think was that no matter where he'd gone that night, he shouldn't be here. As if reading her thoughts, Helen took her hand.

'It'll be all right. Try not to worry.'

'This is worse than when old King George used to be in one of his gnashes. And them guards are scarier than any

77

we have at Buckingham Palace. They have guns and swords there, but they don't frighten me like these chaps do. They look like right bruisers.'

A heavy lock clicked, and a door opened. The inmates began to file out of a door at the end of the room. Caroline craned her neck and spotted Johnny, his head down, his dark hair uncombed and messy. He wasn't making eye contact with anyone. She could tell he was scared and now, Caroline was too. Her stomach contracted, as did her throat, tightening and squeezing shut. She was just glad it was she and Helen there to see him. It had taken both her and her pa to convince Ma not to come. She would have died watching her son like this. Johnny sat down opposite them, finally looking up. His cheeks were sallow, his skin pale and grey, and his eyes lacked their usual mischievous glint.

'All right, Caz,' he said, clasping his hands in front of him on the table. She automatically reached out, but he pulled back. 'Sorry.' He nodded towards the sign. 'No touching.'

'Oh, Johnny.' Tears pricked her eyes, but she clenched her jaw to control her emotions. She loved her brother deeply and seeing him laid so low was heartbreaking.

'Hello, Helen. It's nice to see you, but I do wish you hadn't come.'

Helen shrank at this remark, folding in as if the air had been knocked out of her. She pushed a few stray strands of her black hair away from her face. 'I don't. I'm glad I'm here . . . for Caroline.'

'You're too good to be in a place like this, I mean. But it's nice of you to come with her. You keeping well? The baby doing all right?'

Helen twisted her mother's wedding band that she used as her own to stop the looks and judgements. 'We're both doing well, I think. Everything seems to be going OK.'

Knowing their time was limited, Caroline gathered herself. They didn't have time for idle chit-chat or pleasantries. Not that you could describe anything said here as pleasantries. 'You have to tell me what's been going on, Johnny.'

He met her eye, but then dropped his gaze. 'Ain't nothin' going on, Caroline. Just like I told the coppers. I had nothin' to do with that burglary business. I never went near Oclee's.'

'But Ma said you went out that night.'

'Did she tell the police that?' There was a note of panic in his voice, forcing the same emotion into her.

'I don't know. But you can't expect her to lie to them. Apparently, there's an eyewitness too. Do you know who that is?'

He shook his head.

Now all the inmates were seated, one of the guards began patrolling the room, wandering between the tables, watching everyone.

'You have to tell us where you were that night.' Johnny lifted his head. She could see he was hiding something, and a surge of bile rose, stinging her throat. 'It's the only way, Johnny. Just tell us the truth.'

He glanced at Helen and then back to her. 'You won't like it.'

'I didn't think I would, but you've got no choice now.'

Johnny took a deep breath, moving his clasped hands across the table. She was tempted again to reach out and touch him but knew she couldn't. Instead, she gripped the handle of her bag tighter, readying herself for whatever he was going to say.

'I did go out that night. I borrowed a works van. But I didn't steal it. I returned it, undamaged, and I didn't go anywhere near Oclee's jewellers. I swear it.'

'Where did you go then?'

After checking that the guard patrolling the room had moved past, he lowered his voice. 'I went to help Don Green shift some boxes, that's all.'

She should have felt relieved but the fact he'd said boxes, not specifying what was in them, made her stomach roil. 'Boxes? Of what? Please don't tell me it was stolen jewellery?'

'Course not! I've already told you I had nothing to do with that. It was . . .' He leaned in even closer. 'It was boxes of meat.'

'Meat!' With some effort Caroline controlled the pitch of her voice though she wanted to scream. 'You were shifting black-market goods? Meat's still rationed. Where did Donald Green even get it from?'

'I dunno, and in my experience it's better not to ask.'

'So you *were* doing something illegal? And you nicked a works van to do it in? Oh Johnny!'

Johnny's face filled with shame but instead of looking at Caroline, he looked at Helen before dropping his eyes to his hands, the fingers pressed so hard together they were turning white. 'I was trying to help Don. He's already been nicked once; he needed help. He's got a wife and kids to look after.'

'Then maybe he should get a proper job and stop doing things he shouldn't.'

'He's got a job,' Johnny said through gritted teeth. 'But it pays next to nothing, and his kids were starving. He didn't have a choice. He was doing what any dad would do for his family. And who are you to be so high and mighty? You might work at Buckingham Palace now but once you were at home with us and you knew this sort of thing went on all the time. You know how hard people have it round our way.'

A prickling warmth crept up Caroline's spine. She thought she hadn't changed. Faced with the condescension of people like Mrs Coniston, she'd felt belittled, judged. But perhaps she had altered. More than she knew. She felt ashamed of herself for judging so harshly even though she wasn't exactly wrong.

'What we need to do', Helen said, her voice calm, filling the tense silence between the two siblings, 'is decide what we do now.'

'We have to tell the police the truth,' Caroline said, dropping her voice further as the patrolling officer circled their table then moved on.

'If you do that I'll still be stuck in here, won't I? And I can't bring Don into this. His family would never forgive me.'

'But at least you'll only be charged with fencing stolen goods—'

'And stealing a works van.'

'That too. I know you don't want Don to get into trouble but what else can we do? You're in here because of him.'

Johnny's tone changed and he looked at his sister fondly. 'I did this off my own back, Caz. Don didn't make me. He didn't hold a gun to my head and force me into the van. He needed my help and that's what we do round our way, ain't it? We help each other. He's got a lovely shin of beef I was going to give to Helen.'

A small smile lifted the corners of Helen's mouth, a faint blush coming to her cheeks; Johnny's too. Caroline sat back, too angry to cry.

'I've seen the duty solicitor, not that he was much use – I couldn't tell him the truth, could I? But he kept saying I should tell them where I was. I didn't give him the details, stuck to the story I just went for a walk, but he knows I'm lying, and it ain't helping. I know it's making me look guilty, but I can't land Don in it, Caz. I just can't.'

'Then we have to prove you didn't do it and keep the rest of it quiet. What *did* you tell the solicitor and the police?'

'That I couldn't sleep and went for a walk. They asked me if anyone can verify it, but I told them I didn't see or speak to anyone.'

'That could have been when the eyewitness saw you,' Helen added.

'Possibly,' Caroline said. 'Do you have any idea who might have done it? Some of the people Don knows aren't exactly upstanding citizens. Could they have information that might help clear your name?'

'I can't let you near them, Caz, they'd eat you alive. What I can tell you is old Arthur Whitelock ain't all he seems to be. I know Pa said he was a good, respectable man, but there's something not right about him. Something shifty. Oh, and there's more than one van. Whitelock has two and they're identical.'

'Did the police say what the van looked like when they were questioning you?' Helen asked.

'Just that it was dark and opened at the back.'

'No shop name on it?'

'No. Nothing.'

Caroline said, 'And Whitelock's Warehouse doesn't have a sign on the side of their vans, does it?'

'Nope. I asked Whitelock about it once. I said, "Why don't you get the name painted on the side, let everyone know who you are when you're driving around London. People'll remember a name like Whitelock's Warehouse."'

'And what did he say?'

'Said he didn't like people to know. They might try and break into the warehouse at night. Steal the vans. Or worse, the goods.'

A loud, hard voice rang around the room, startling everyone. 'Time's up!'

Around them, visitors began to stand, gathering coats and bags. The woman with two children dashed forwards, hugging a large, bearded man before the guard could stop her. The children followed suit and two guards leapt to separate them all. The children were crying, and the mother was close to tears. All Caroline wanted was to get out of there as quickly as possible and to take Johnny with her.

'Thanks for coming. It's nice to see you,' Johnny said, his eyes lingering on Helen's face. She nodded, her expression unreadable. 'You do believe me, don't you? I didn't hurt anyone. I wouldn't.'

'I know,' Helen replied and a speaking glance passed

between them. Caroline watched the fondness they had for each other tear at their features.

'Just stay out of trouble, all right?' Caroline added. 'I'll find a way to get you out of 'ere.'

'Out you go, please,' a voice commanded again, and Caroline and Helen shuffled out.

The air outside was freezing and within seconds Caroline's nose and lips were stinging, growing numb. Snowflakes swirled and danced around them as they made their way to the bus stop, but she was grateful for the freshness of the wind, as if it were blowing all traces of that horrible place away. She could smell lingering touches of the disinfectant and boiled cabbage on her coat or in her hair, and hoped that another few minutes would rid her of every last drop.

'Are you all right?' Helen asked as they waited at the bus stop with all the other visiting families.

Caroline pushed her hands deeper into her pockets, her fingertips like ice. 'I don't rightly know. Not really, I suppose. But I will be.'

'What will you do now?'

'Get Johnny out of there. I just don't know how yet.'

Chapter Eight

The typewriter keys clicked with their usual intensity as Caroline wearily eyed the clock.

When she'd returned to the palace, after her visit to the prison the day before, she'd been exhausted and couldn't face socialising with Mrs Barnes or Milly. Instead, she'd gone to her room, curled up on her bed and read. All she'd wanted was to escape the fearful thoughts circling in her mind but no matter how hard she focused on her novel, the words simply wouldn't sink in. Unable to lose herself in another world, she was forced to place her book on the small bedside cabinet and lie back to stare at the ceiling. Eventually, she'd fallen into an uneasy sleep, her dreams nothing more than veiled versions of the worries that plagued her while awake.

Today, as the clock neared six, her eyes heavy and tired, she couldn't wait to leave the small, noisy room. The sounds of the duplicating machine, the typewriters and voices discussing the latest palace gossip sounded even louder than usual. Barbara had been especially talkative about the man who had come to the gates of the palace a few days before, demanding to see the Queen so he could convert her to Catholicism. Clearly unsound, he'd been taken to Cannon Row Police Station, but he'd created quite a scene and the guards who'd dealt with him had told their stories freely.

The details were no doubt embellished with each new telling so that by the time the story had reached Caroline, via Mrs Barnes, a knife was involved along with cursing and threatening behaviour. How much of it was true, she couldn't say.

'Mr Newington?' Tommy Lascelles called, striding into the room, causing them all to look up.

'Mr Lascelles,' he replied congenially. 'Is everything all right?'

'I'm afraid it isn't. There are far too many mistakes in this piece returned to me earlier today. I'm sorry to say this isn't of the standard I'd expect from this department.' Below his bushy moustache his mouth was pursed.

Caroline's skin grew cold. She'd been the one working on Mr Lascelles's correspondence today. Mr Newington had made another great show of handing her the most confidential work, citing how pleased the Queen's private secretary and, by extension, the Queen had been with what she'd produced. She swallowed, feeling Mrs Coniston's smug stare fall on her. She could only imagine what Mr O'Keefe was doing behind her. Probably dancing with joy or making streamers from the used paper on his desk. Barbara shot her a sympathetic glance, but it did little to stop her embarrassment. Caroline lowered her head and continued to type.

'Oh, I am sorry,' Mr Newington replied, his brow creasing in concern as he stepped forwards and received the papers. 'That's clearly not acceptable. I'm very surprised though. I gave this to one of my most prudent members of staff. I assure you I shall deal with it immediately.'

'See that you do. I couldn't hand these to the Queen, and she was expecting them this afternoon. We're all most

86

disappointed.' He turned to speak to the room, and everyone responded by giving him their full attention. 'There is no room for error at Buckingham Palace. We all rely on each other to ensure the wheels of monarchy continue to turn uninterrupted. Who worked on these?'

How she wished she could sink into the carpet and disappear. Since last night her thoughts had been far too preoccupied with Johnny and how she was going to get him out of that awful prison. She'd thought she'd done well to silence them during the day, but clearly she hadn't. As silence rang around, she knew she had to respond before Mrs Coniston did. The old bag was always waiting for a moment like this – a moment when she could show her superiority – and would love to be the one to land Caroline in trouble. The best thing she could do was own up and apologise.

'I did,' Caroline replied as humiliation climbed up her body scorching her skin. 'I'm terribly sorry. I—'

'I'm very surprised it was you, Miss—'

'Stratton,' Mr Newington supplied.

'Hmm. A shame. The work you submitted the other day was very good indeed. Quality of work is just as important as quantity.'

'It might have been the typewriter,' came a voice from behind her and Caroline spun to see Mr O'Keefe replying to Mr Lascelles. He held a pencil in his right hand and was flicking it backward and forward so fast that it blurred in her vision. 'Some of the keys were sticking and getting in an awful mess. Miss Stratton informed me, and I thought I'd fixed it, but perhaps it was still sticking. Could that have had something to do with it?'

'Yes, perhaps,' Mr Newington added his agreement. 'Some of these machines are very old and could really do with replacing. It can make life very difficult for our typists, you know.'

Tommy Lascelles twitched his moustache. 'I'll speak to the Queen about replacements. Until then, can this be retyped? Please.' He pointed to the paper in Mr Newington's hands and his 'please' was somewhat disingenuous.

'I'll do it straight away,' Caroline said, bringing her attention back to the issue and away from Mr O'Keefe's surprising comments. 'If you're happy to give me another chance. And you'll have it before the end of the day.' She'd have to stay late but it would be worth it to prove she could do this job well.

Tommy Lascelles glared at her. 'Mr Newington may assign the work to whomever he chooses. Perhaps someone else should take this on if you cannot maintain the standard we expect.' With that, he marched out of the room, his short steps beating a fast rhythm on the floor.

Despite her shame, her mind lingered on Mr O'Keefe's words and she turned to him. He looked down as she caught his eye, the pencil still moving rapidly between his fingers. Why had he helped her? If anything, she'd expected him to revel in her distress. Mrs Coniston scowled at her as usual.

Mr Newington handed her the pages. 'Well, that's rather put a downer on the day, hasn't it? Very embarrassing.'

'I'm terribly sorry, Mr Newington. I don't know what happened, but I'll put it right and I won't leave until it's done. If you're willing to give me another chance, that is.'

'Thank you, Caroline. This sort of thing doesn't normally

happen, and I don't want the powers that be to think we're not up to the job.'

'Some of us are,' Mrs Coniston muttered under her breath. Either Mr Newington didn't hear or chose not to. Caroline ignored the remark, refusing to show how it tore at her self-esteem, pushing her lower – back into the gutter. If the snide woman only knew what Caroline had been dealing with, she'd have more compassion. Or perhaps she wouldn't. She clearly revelled in other people's misery and would only look down on her more if she knew her brother was in prison. His guilt or innocence would have nothing to do with it.

As everyone returned to their work, the clattering of typewriter keys and the scraping of filing cabinet drawers growing louder again, Barbara whispered, 'Cor, that was a bit nasty, wasn't it?'

'Mrs Coniston or Mr Lascelles?'

Barbara giggled. 'Both actually. But I meant Mr Lascelles. Don't expect anything else from old grot-bags over there.'

'He was right. I didn't do a good enough job.' She studied the paper seeing where he'd marked up errors. 'The worst thing is, I didn't even notice I was making mistakes. I should have paid more attention and read it all through before I gave it back to Mr Newington. It was my fault.'

'You have seemed distracted today. Is everything all right? You look pale too, and tired,' she added, a note of concern cutting through the unthinking remark. 'If I can help you will say, won't you?'

'Thank you. There is something bothering me, but it doesn't matter. Thanks for asking. I haven't asked if you're all right today. Sorry. Did you have a nice weekend?'

'Me? Oh, I'm fine. I'm always fine. Going to meet a nice young fella when I finish here.' She said the words loudly, wanting Mr O'Keefe to hear, but he didn't respond. Caroline hadn't expected him to, but Barbara looked disappointed. 'Going to treat me to a slap-up meal, he says.'

'I hope you have a wonderful time.'

'Oh, I intend to.'

Within half an hour, everyone was packing up to leave the office. As they walked to the door, Caroline bid Barbara goodnight as well as Mrs Coniston, though the older woman responded with nothing more than a slight nod of her head and a jab at her glasses, pushing them up the bridge of her nose.

Mr Newington paused on his way out. 'You won't be long, will you? You don't want to miss Milly's party.'

'I promise I'll finish this and be right over.' She'd all but forgotten that it was Milly's twenty-second birthday today. She'd wished her many happy returns at breakfast, when they'd eaten together, but there hadn't been much time to celebrate. Luckily, Caroline had bought her a gift long ago and it was already wrapped, waiting to be collected from her room and taken to the party that evening.

'Caroline . . .' She looked up to Mr Newington's kind smile. 'We all have bad days. I once typed entirely the wrong minutes and the Press Secretary received everything the Chief Archivist was expecting and vice versa. Everyone was quite bemused. Don't let today get you down.' He placed a hand gently on her shoulder and she returned his smile, his words providing the comfort she had desperately needed.

'Thank you.' Emotion welled inside her. 'I needed that.'

He withdrew his hand, wishing Mr O'Keefe goodnight and left, closing the door behind him.

Now it was just the two of them and Caroline returned to her work. After her experience with Timothy, she worried she might feel trapped, vulnerable, and she waited for the fear to rise. It had happened before when she'd been alone with a new footman or butler. Nothing had ever transpired, but it didn't stop her worrying. As she waited for the feelings once more, she was surprised when only tiredness and annoyance at her mistakes crept up on her. Whatever Mr O'Keefe was doing, she felt safe being in the same room as him. Perhaps it was because he disliked her so much and was therefore happy to have nothing to do with her. The thought made her a little sad, but it was probably for the best as she didn't much like him either. Yet earlier he'd helped her. He'd spoken out to Mr Lascelles – the Queen's private secretary, one of the most senior men in the palace – to save her blushes. She tried to hold her tongue, to forget about it, to keep her mouth shut, but curiosity drove her on and she couldn't stop herself from spinning in her chair and asking, 'Why did you help me when Mr Lascelles was here? You never had to change the keys for me, and they haven't been sticking.'

He stood and began tidying his desk, readying to leave. 'I might not like that you're getting all the top jobs, but you just seemed . . .' He searched for the words and she felt her breath hitch. 'You seemed down today.' Her eyebrows rose in surprise and Mr O'Keefe bent to the floor behind his desk. She couldn't see what he was doing and assumed he was tying his shoelaces. When he stood, he said, 'Listen, I'm no communist but we're not machines and they shouldn't treat us like ones. He wouldn't like it if you marched into his office and embarrassed him in front of the Queen. It's not fair that he thinks he can do it to us just because we're lower than he is. Or because of where we come from.'

She hadn't ever thought he felt the same way she did: out of place, the wrong class for a job like this; but he must have. Prejudice against Irish people was still rife in London, just as prejudice against those whose skin was a different colour was too.

'I'm not sure it's possible to embarrass Mr Lascelles,' she replied with a smile.

'Oh, everybody gets embarrassed sometimes.'

'If he does, I reckon he twitches his moustache like this . . .' She demonstrated, scrunching up her nose and wiggling it. He laughed and it was genuine and heartwarming.

After a second, he said, 'Well . . . goodnight.'

''Night,' she replied and returned to her desk. From the corner of her eye, she watched as he grabbed his coat from the coat stand, slinging it on to his broad shoulders and adjusting the collar before opening the door and leaving.

As unexpected as that exchange had been, it had left her less raw, and Caroline returned to her work with gusto. The others would be waiting for her, and she didn't want to be too long. Within half an hour, she'd finished the document, read it through and made the relevant copies on the giant machine with the tiring crank-handle at the back of the room. She took it to the office of Mr Lascelles, knocking on the door. When there was no answer, she opened it gingerly only to find the Queen standing beside his desk, rifling through a stack of papers.

'Oh, Your Majesty, I'm so sorry, I—' She dropped into a curtsey as she'd been taught to on the first day she arrived.

'Caroline,' the Queen replied, her warm, wide smile filling her face. Although she was the most important person in the entire country, there was something very personable and welcoming about her. She was impeccably tailored as usual, not a hair out of place, wearing a pale grey skirt and a lemon-coloured, fine-knit jumper. 'I was informed you were working temporarily in the offices. How are you enjoying it?'

'Very much,' Caroline replied, dumbstruck, before remembering her manners. 'Thank you, ma'am.' Although she'd been in the same room as the Queen on a few occasions and had cleaned her private quarters, direct conversations were few and far between. In fact, she couldn't recall ever having one before. Despite her rank, Caroline had the feeling of being truly seen by the woman in front of her.

'And still working now? How diligent of you.'

'I made some mistakes,' she said without thinking, her cheeks colouring as soon as the words were out of her mouth. 'I wanted to get it right and back to Mr Lascelles as soon as possible.'

'Mistakes are inevitable,' the Queen replied kindly, her head tilting to the side. 'One would never learn if one did not occasionally make mistakes.' As she emphasised the word 'occasionally', the wry humour that made her so well liked shone from her eyes. She picked up a piece of paper and read it far quicker than Caroline was able to. 'Ah, here we are, just what I was looking for. Now, I must go. Do wish Milly a happy birthday from me, if you please.'

'Yes, of course. And . . .' The Queen paused. If she was

surprised, she didn't show it. 'We hope Prince Charles had a nice birthday.'

Caroline marvelled at how much the Queen managed to pack into her days. She took her role as monarch seriously, but also her role as a mother, even though that often had to fit around other concerns.

'He did, thank you. How very kind of you to ask.'

Caroline curtseyed again as Queen Elizabeth passed, smiling fondly over her. She left and, with a sigh of relief, Caroline placed the papers on Mr Lascelles's desk and hurried to the party.

Chapter Nine

In the Household Lounge, all the butlers, footmen, cooks, cleaners and maids had gathered to celebrate the birthday of one of their own. The sound of Duke Ellington rang out of the gramophone, occasional notes audible under the chattering voices. Robert had made a wonderful cake and Caroline was relieved to see she hadn't missed out on any as she found her friend and handed over her present.

'Happy birthday, Milly.'

'Oh, Caroline, thank you!' Milly took her friend in a hug, almost squashing the carefully wrapped parcel. 'What is it?'

'Open it and see!'

Milly did and a smile spread across her face as she took out the record Caroline had purchased for her: a copy of *When Irish Eyes Are Smiling* by Bing Crosby. He was Milly's current favourite singer. Since the launch of the *New Musical Express* in March, Milly had found a love for music and read the weekly paper diligently, often sharing snippets of information on the latest goings-on.

'How marvellous! It's absolutely perfect. Thank you so much.' She hugged her again and, after placing a kiss on her cheek, went off to show Robert, who was in the corner speaking to some friends. She watched as Milly showed it to him and he wrapped his arm around her waist.

Caroline found Helen sitting by the window and, grabbing a cup of tea on her way, sat with her. 'Everything all right?' she asked.

Helen clasped her hands in her lap, the roundness of her tummy visible despite her attempts to hide it. A half-empty teacup sat on the low coffee table between them. 'Yes, as well as they can be.'

'You feeling ill again?'

'No. It's not that, it's – what are we going to do about your brother? I can still go and see the solicitor but I'm worried that if we tell him a crime's been committed, he'll have to report it to the police, which Johnny doesn't want us to do. I don't really know what to do.'

'I've been thinking about this all day.' Caroline didn't mention she'd had to redo some of her work as she'd been preoccupied with the matter. The less she spoke about that the better. 'I don't really know what we can do either. I suppose I could go and see Arthur Whitelock, see what he knows. Johnny's denying to the police that he took the van so unless Mr Whitelock actually saw him do it, I might be able to convince him Johnny had nothing to do with the robbery of Mr Oclee. He might speak up for him – with the police, I mean – and then they might let him go.'

'I'm not sure that's how it works,' Helen replied glumly.

'What else can I do? The only other person I can talk to is Don – who Johnny says is only doing what he has to for his family, but I know he's as dodgy as they come – and see if he has any idea who might have done the Oclee robbery. Then I can send the police their way instead. Give 'em an anonymous tip-off or something.'

Helen thought for a moment. 'You're right. I suppose that's all we can do. But you shouldn't go alone. I'll come with you.'

'You will not!' Seeing Helen's eyes widen at her tone, Caroline lowered her voice. 'Mrs Barnes would never forgive me if anything happened to you in your condition. I'll get Pa to go with me.' She'd had no intention of doing that either – her pa was in no fit state to speak to him – but it would stop Helen worrying. At least she had agreed with her plan. With nothing more to be said, she asked, 'Have you been back to the doctor's yet?'

'No. I know I need to. I need to find a midwife. But honestly, all doctors scare me and I'm not sure I can put up with any more rudeness about being a single mother.' She twisted her mother's ring again, staring down at her ring finger. 'Even with pretending my husband died, most people don't believe me. They've heard it a thousand times before.'

'Ma knows a midwife,' Caroline said after sipping her tea. 'She might be able to help. I'll ask her to find out.'

'I don't want to add to your worries.'

Caroline waved her friend's concerns away. 'Ma'd be more annoyed if you carried on without asking. You need someone to look after you. What're you going to do when you go into labour if you don't know what to look out for?'

'R-right everyone,' Robert said loudly, shouting above the din and stepping into the middle of the room. He was holding Milly's hand and she had never looked as happy or content. 'Can we all r-raise our glasses to Milly Hendry and wish her a happy b-birthday?'

Everyone did, followed by three cheers and hip-hip-hoorays. Caroline and Helen stood, raising their teacups in toast.

'And before everyone m-makes a dash for c-cake – which I made by the way, so it should be scrumptious' – there was a round of chuckling laughter – 'there's something I n–need to ask Milly.' He let go of her hand, lowering on to one knee and pulling a small ring box from his pocket.

Milly's hand shot to her mouth and Caroline and Helen looked at each other, as pleased for Milly as she was for herself. They'd wondered when this moment would occur and it was a wonderful gesture that Robert had done it on her birthday. Caroline and Helen stood up and moved to get a better view.

'M-Milly H-Hendry,' Robert said, his stutter becoming more pronounced as nerves took over. 'Will you m-marry m—?'

'Yes,' she shouted before he had finished asking. 'Of course I will!'

Robert stood and the couple embraced, tears falling down Milly's face. Mr Newington, whose smile couldn't be wider, offered Mrs Barnes his handkerchief and she wiped a tear from her eye. He watched her for a moment before placing a kiss on the top of her head. It was such a beautiful, loving gesture that Caroline too had to stifle a sob. The emotions of the last few days rose to the surface, and she struggled to dam them. A tear trickled down her cheek, and Helen rubbed her back.

'Well, that's wonderful, isn't it?' Helen said, smiling at her. 'I had no idea he was proposing today, did you? I thought – hoped – it might be soon, but he never said anything to me. Did he tell you?'

Caroline shook her head, drying her eyes again. 'No, nothing. But I'm so happy for them. She deserves every happiness. They both do.'

'I wonder when the wedding will be?'

'Who knows? It'll be a squeeze to get it in before the coronation but what's the point in waiting, I suppose?'

'So now we've got two things to look forward to: the Christmas dance and planning a wedding.'

Caroline smiled, hoping it reached her eyes.

As soon as she'd left his embrace, Milly raced to her aunt and then straight towards them. They shared in her congratulations, hugging and crying together, but all the while, Caroline's heart remained heavy. If only her mind wasn't burdened with other problems, she'd be able to fully enjoy this moment. She'd made a fool of herself at work, now seemed incompetent to the Queen's private secretary, and had let down Mr Newington, not to mention the fact that her brother was locked away in prison for a crime he didn't commit. Yet he was in no way blameless and now she had to return to the East End to ask awkward, possibly dangerous questions to try and save his neck.

Chapter Ten

The following night, Caroline trudged through the snow towards the docks and Whitelock's Warehouse. She shivered in the bitter wind, her toes almost numb in her sensible, low-heeled shoes, every step precarious. Her body ached from being held rigid, trying not to slip on the black ice. Even her ears were cold under the headscarf she'd tied beneath her chin and no matter how she bent her head against the onslaught of the weather, it penetrated her bones right through to the marrow. She'd never known a winter like it.

Despite a few of the shops beginning to show signs of the Christmas to come, if any part of London still looked like it had after the war had ended, when devastation and destruction reigned, it was the East End. Missing houses, or rows of houses, left gaping wounds in the landscape. Piles of rubble where homes and families had once lived scarred many of the streets. The remains of lodgings, now empty shells of dwellings with roofs missing or one side fallen away, still stood, precarious and dangerous, looming over them.

The East End of London had been one of the worst-hit areas: a constant target for the Luftwaffe aiming for the docks with the intention of disrupting Britain's trade. Despite the constant fear and dread, the people she knew had pulled together, as they always did in that part of London, and somehow they'd all got through it. Yet, all these years later, the land, like its people, still hadn't fully recovered. Poverty, even penury, abounded, and there were times when it felt like every effort made to move forwards, to put the past behind them, was thwarted, pushing them backwards, burying them further in deprivation and strife. She passed slums and overflowing tenements, families huddled inside trying to keep warm. Some children played out in the snow, their clothes thin and threadbare. The air was smoggy, as it always was in London, making visibility poor. Though the snow had eased off for the moment, there was no telling when the heavens would open and it fall from the sky again. Luckily, Caroline knew this area of London like the back of her hand. The smell of the Thames drifted into her nostrils, a potent mixture of sewage and silt, and before long she could hear its sludgy, lapping tide, the dragging of the shingle.

She was nearly there.

Ships and boats were soon in sight. The tall necks of cranes reached high into the night sky though no stars were visible through the clouds and smog. It wasn't late – only six thirty; she'd come straight from work – but the docks were busy, as they always were. Voices echoed in the gloom. The tread of heavy boots mingled with the tapping of horse's hooves and the rumbling of a cart's wheels. The hum of a car, its headlights penetrating the frosty wind, rumbled beneath the unnamed sounds of the darkness.

She passed a small set of stone steps leading down to the banks of the Thames. Come the morning, children would go mudlarking down there, seeing what they could find beneath the seaweed-covered legs of the jetties. Unlit and dark, she could make out two forms in the half-light of the passage-way, a man and a woman. From the sighing and moaning it was clear what they were doing. She hurried on towards the warehouses.

Burly men surrounded her as she manoeuvred past barrels and boxes being unloaded from the ships. Some wolf-whistled; some asked if she was lost, calling her a snobby cow as she marched on without answering.

'Someone thinks they're Lady Muck, don't they!' a particularly vocal man shouted to the jeers and cheers of his friends.

'If she's at the docks in the dark, at night, she ain't no lady, is she?' another replied.

Caroline's stomach constricted with apprehension. She shouldn't have come alone. Though the East End was her home, it didn't mean it was free of danger or that everyone who lived there was kind like her ma and pa. She wasn't even sure she could run in these shoes on icy streets, but she pressed the fear down. She was here now, and she'd soon be safe at her destination.

The sign for Whitelock's Warehouse came into view and she hurried towards it. Next to the huge double doors of the warehouse was the entrance to the office, the name etched into the glass in gold lettering. A light was on and through the window she could see a chap bent over a messy desk piled high with papers. Heavy male voices sounded from inside the warehouse, and she poked her head gingerly around the large double doors, trying not to be seen.

Three men in dirty blue overalls over shirts loaded boxes into Whitelock's vans. As Johnny had said, there were two vehicles, both identical: dark blue with numberplates obscured by grime. She'd seen several similar vans as she'd walked through the docks. Most of the warehouses around here had vans like them, it seemed. That was surely good news. It meant that whoever had seen the van couldn't be sure it was a Whitelock's one and, therefore, couldn't be sure it was the van Johnny had taken to help Don Green move black-market meat. In fact, any dark van, from any of the warehouses, could have been used in the robbery of Mr Oclee's.

Caroline stepped back, relieved not to have been seen, leaving the calls and shouts of the men behind her. She knocked and entered, a wave of heat hitting her from the small four-bar heater that buzzed and hummed from the floor, glowing with a bright, unnatural orange light.

'Can I 'elp ya?' asked the man behind the desk. His flat cap hid most of his untidy greying hair and his long face was weathered from years spent working outside. He had enormous hands scarred from manual work, yet his clothes were neat and tidy.

The heat and the safety of being inside relaxed her. 'I hope so. I'm looking for Arthur Whitelock.'

'That's me.' He placed the piece of paper he'd been reading down on the desk and flattened it with the palms of his hands. 'What can I do for ya?'

'You employ my brother, Johnny Stratton—'

'Employed,' he clarified. 'I won't have no thieves working for me.'

'He's not a thief,' Caroline said without thinking, wishing she'd kept her mouth shut as Mr Whitelock pinned her with a malevolent look. In truth, Johnny *was* a thief, but not of the kind Mr Whitelock referred to: the type that burgled jewellers and beat up defenceless old men.

'Been charged, ain't he? As far as I'm concerned, he's a tea leaf and a cowardly one at that.'

'I went to see him,' Caroline continued as Mr Whitelock stood up from behind his desk and moved to a shelf at the back of the room. He pulled down a file and added the sheet of paper to it, not bothering to look at her as she spoke. 'He told me he had nothing to do with the business at Oclee's jewellers.'

Mr Whitelock finally looked up, amused. 'Well, he ain't gonna come right out and say it, is he? Not to his own kin who most likely won't never speak to 'im again. Course he's gonna say he didn't do it.'

'But he didn't. Please, Mr Whitelock, you have to believe me. Is there no way you can speak on his behalf to the police? He's always been a good employee, hasn't he?'

He shrugged a shoulder, using his other hand to steady the file, the papers almost falling to the floor. 'He's been all right. Far too lippy for my liking. Thinks he's clever, that one.'

'I know Johnny has his faults,' she said. In his youth, he'd had an answer for everything and sometimes he couldn't stop himself standing up for something he thought was wrong. But he was never disrespectful. 'But he's a hard worker. You've had no complaints, have you? Please, Mr Whitelock, he'd never hurt anyone. You do know that, don't you?' she pleaded.

'Who knows what people is capable of?' He snapped the file shut, placing it back on the shelf. 'I'll not speak for him,

Miss Stratton. And he better not show his face round 'ere looking for work neither.'

'What about innocent until proven guilty?'

'What about it?' he replied with a scoff. 'The police think he did it, they've charged 'im, end of. Now if you'll excuse me . . .' He began to move back towards his desk.

'Johnny didn't do it,' Caroline stated again firmly. She didn't plan on coming here again so this was her last chance to convince him to help her brother. Mrs Barnes had once told her that flattery can go a long way and she changed tack. 'If you could speak up for him, Mr Whitelock, the police might reconsider the evidence against him. It's all just coincidence. A respectable man like you – your word means a lot around here.'

'I'll not be swayed by pretty words, Miss Stratton. Your brother's no good and now he's been caught. It ain't nothing to do with me.'

Her temper finally frayed, and she snapped, 'If you won't help me prove it, then I'll find someone else who will.'

At this, Mr Whitelock's demeanour changed. He took three rapid steps towards her, closing the gap between them in a second. The room felt suddenly hot and stuffy, the overly warm air from the heater clawing at her skin, reaching under her headscarf and making her scalp prickle. Memories of another man's unwelcome hands flooded her, strangling her wits.

'Now you listen 'ere, missy.' One long, meaty, disfigured finger was in her face, jabbing at her with every word. 'Ain't no one gonna 'elp prove your brother is innocent, 'cause he ain't. And if you go sticking your nose in, disrupting my business or blackening my name, I'll have ya, d'you hear me?' He grabbed her arm with his giant hand, making her gasp in shock. She'd always been tall and slight, but even with her jumper and coat, his hand wrapped completely around her arm, his vice-like grip forcing her wherever he wanted her to go. 'Out ya go! Go on!' With his other hand he opened the door and pushed her outside, slamming it shut in her face.

The glass panel shook with the force of it, and she stood trembling in the dark. Her legs were like liquid. She couldn't move, couldn't trust them to bear her weight, yet all she wanted to do was run. She'd felt this before. Been trapped by her body's lack of strength. She had to run. To get as far away from this awful man and this awful place as possible.

Hearing the door slam, the men from the warehouse emerged. She turned her head, fearing more taunts and threats. With a stumbling step backwards, her legs almost gave way, unwilling to hold her up.

'You all right, miss?' one of them asked kindly, but as he took a step towards her, her thoughts raced from Mr White-lock back to Timothy. To the first time he'd tried to take things too far and to the second when he'd forced his way into her room and left only because Milly had helped her. Fear gripped her throat, tightening, stealing her breath. She couldn't get any air, yet her heart beat so fast she thought it might give out. The muscles of her stomach spasmed uncontrollably and she forced her iron-heavy legs to run.

The smog followed her through the streets, the cold wind biting at her face. Her teeth chattered and if it hadn't been so cold, she might well have cried, but her nose and eyes stung too much for that. The burly men watched her go, none of them uttering a single word that she could hear, and soon she was away from the docks and entering the streets of friends and neighbours. She thought about stopping at her parents' house, but she could never tell them where she'd been. They'd chastise her for going to the docks at night, for getting involved. They'd want to know what Johnny had been doing and she still wasn't sure whether to tell them or not. Johnny had begged her not to and she'd given her word. They'd go straight to the police. Her ma's need to see her boy free would overrule his wishes.

No, she couldn't go to them. Her only choice was to go straight home to the palace and as she dashed towards the tube stop, her heart sang at the thought.

Chapter Eleven

Mrs Barnes glowered at Caroline as she removed the napkin from her lap and placed it on the table. She tutted. 'I still can't believe you did that, you silly girl.'

'It turned out all right in the end, didn't it?'

It had been two days since she'd been at Whitelock's and she felt, or at least pretended to feel, far more confident about her escapade. It wouldn't do to share her fear or the memories of Timothy it had stirred. Milly had been as affected by him as she had, and she didn't want to ruin Milly's happiness by bringing those difficult recollections back up, especially as she was sitting gazing at the small diamond on her ring finger.

'Turned out all right in the end?' Mrs Barnes said. Her pitch was far higher than normal. 'I'm startin' to worry you've gone mad, my girl. I hope you don't plan on goin' back there.'

Caroline shook her head emphatically and pushed a lock of curly red hair back from her face. She was wearing it down today, pinned back at the sides with combs. She'd never have bothered before when working in the Royal Household, but things were different now and she felt the style made her look older than her twenty-one years. 'Why would I? Gave me the creeps, he did. And he hurt my arm.' She took the tender spot in her other hand and rubbed it gently. 'Reckon it's going to bruise.'

To say her palace family had been appalled by her actions was an understatement. Mrs Barnes and Milly had found out everything the night she'd returned and had accused her of being foolhardy and downright ignorant. She'd tried to defend herself, but she knew she'd been stupid and naive. Helen, who had only just heard the news, gave her a wide-eyed stare across the table.

'I understand why you felt you had to go, Caroline, and it was very brave of you, but you really should have taken someone with you. I'll come next time.'

'Give over!' Mrs Barnes exclaimed, leaning over the table. 'You sound like that man who waltzed up to the gates convinced he'd have a little chat with the Queen. What on earth am I hearin'?'

They were having lunch together in the Household Dining Room. Usually this was time that Caroline cherished, given her new work colleagues, but today wasn't as welcoming as it normally was.

'If anyone goes with her, it'll be me.' Mrs Barnes tutted again. 'Honestly. In your condition.' Her eyes skittered over Helen, who adjusted her posture. 'But I will give you that it does sound like this Arthur Whitelock's reaction was a bit suspicious. Why grab you like that? Why not just call you a silly girl and send you away? That's what most men would've done.'

Robert nodded. 'Or w-why not threaten to tell your pa? You s-said your pa knows him. It'd make more sense to threaten to tell him so he could speak to you.'

'Exactly,' Mrs Barnes agreed. 'It all sounds a bit over the top to me.'

'Me too,' Caroline agreed.

'Johnny did say he wasn't as respectable as your dad thinks he is,' Helen added. 'Is there something in that?'

'I don't know. How would I even find out? I can't ask Pa. He'll want to know why I'm asking questions and if he thinks I'm getting myself involved in something I shouldn't, he'll tell me to stay away. I don't want to lie to him, but the coppers have already decided Johnny did this and I don't trust 'em to do a good job.'

Milly added, 'It would be so much easier if he told the truth.'

'But then he'd still end up in gaol and so would someone else. He won't do it.' Even though she'd asked him to do the same thing at the prison when faced with the horrid surroundings he was living in, Caroline wished her friends could understand that things were different in the East End. You didn't grass on neighbours – you didn't grass on anyone. Getting a reputation as a snitch wasn't something to be risked. There were repercussions. Violent repercussions.

'We could ask Jake,' Helen said coolly, but her eyes remained on her hands, her fingers interwoven. 'I could ask him.'

An uncomfortable, heavy silence descended. Though Jake, the father of Helen's child, was a reporter for the *Daily News*, no one wanted her to have anything more to do with him. Suddenly, their voices erupted, and everyone began to say no, or variations thereof, in unison.

'Absolutely not!' Mrs Barnes declared. 'After what that

blighter's done to you? Not on your nelly. What's best left is soonest mended in my opinion.'

'Does that apply to Johnny too?' Caroline asked, worried Mrs Barnes was telling her she should leave well alone. She seemed surprised at Caroline's reaction, but rather than berate her, she softened.

'I don't know. Part of me thinks you should let justice take its course, but I know what police can be like. I just want you to be safe and not go gallivantin' round the docks in the dark.'

'Jake's been a reporter for a while,' Helen said, feeling the tension but carrying on regardless. 'And he'll have sources. The *Daily News* will also have archives of past stories. Perhaps there's something in there? Or maybe one of his colleagues will remember Arthur Whitelock's name? I think it's worth a shot to find out all we can about this man. His reaction to you was a warning, and a warning is only needed if he's done something wrong. He clearly doesn't want you sniffing around, and we have to ask why. It might be totally unconnected with the theft from Oclee's jewellers, but we haven't got any other way of finding out. Also, Jake might have heard something else about the robbery. Some piece of information we can feed to the police.'

Milly took a sip from her glass of water. 'I really don't think talking to Jake is a good idea, Helen. You don't *want* to see him again, do you?'

'Absolutely not. I'll be happy if I never have to see that man again in my life, but we need to help Caroline and it could be a possible, and safe, route to do so.'

'Is it really safe for you?' Milly's eyes were focused on

111

Helen but not angrily and Helen gave a small smile, grateful for her friend's concern.

'As safe as houses, I promise you. And I don't have to meet him alone.'

'I'd come with you,' Caroline agreed.

'Me too,' Milly added.

Mrs Barnes interlaced her fingers under her capacious bosom. 'Three of you together I approve of.' Her gaze shifted to Caroline. 'Alone, I don't.'

'So I'll telephone him?' Helen asked.

'Yes,' Caroline replied. 'Do. Whenever he wants to meet, I'll be there. Let's see if he knows something. Lord knows it won't be long till Johnny's in court and once that's started, it'll be even harder to get him out.'

Caroline glanced at the clock on the wall and sadness washed over her. 'We haven't even talked about your wedding, Milly.'

'It's only been three days since Robert proposed,' she replied with a chuckle. 'I haven't had time to think about it myself yet. But someone did recommend a book to me. It's called *The Complete Guide to Wedding Etiquette*, so I think I'm going to get that as they said it tells you everything you're supposed to do.'

'Good idea,' Caroline replied. 'Right. Time for me to go.' She stood up and brushed her hands down her skirt. She wished she could stay in the dining room with its thick carpet, white tablecloths and familiarity. 'Wish me luck. Mrs Coniston has been sourer than a lemon this morning and Mr O'Keefe keeps watching me, waiting for me to make a mistake.'

'Are you sure that's why he's watching you?' Milly asked. She and Robert were holding hands – her left in his right – and they both kept glancing at the delicate gold band with a small solitaire diamond that shone in the light.

'What do you mean?'

'He c-could be looking at you for a different reason,' Robert added, blushing.

Caroline scoffed at the thought. 'I don't think so. He hates me and no mistake. Thinks I've come to steal all his work, like there ain't—'

'Isn't,' Mrs Barnes corrected.

'Isn't enough for everyone,' Caroline finished, giving Mrs Barnes a tender glance. 'Don't talk about the wedding without me, all right?'

Milly giggled. 'I promise we won't. The only thing we've decided is that we'll marry late summer next year. There's just too much on with the coronation and I can't face planning a wedding on top of that. So maybe August when the Royals are in Balmoral.'

Caroline smiled. 'That's a nice idea. I love a summer wedding.'

'It gives us time to save up too,' Milly added. 'And I want a nice dress for this Christmas dance first.'

'We all need to save up,' Helen agreed. 'I'd like to get you a nice present to say thank you for all your help.'

'You don't need to do that.'

'I really better be off,' Caroline said, stepping away from them all, and with a gentle wave she began to make her way through the corridors towards the office.

Just as she turned one of the corners, she saw Mrs Coniston

making her way towards her with a face like someone chewing a nettle, as her pa would say. She pushed her small spectacles up the bridge of her nose as if focusing in on Caroline, ready to attack. Deciding she couldn't possibly deal with the obnoxious woman any longer than she had to, Caroline turned to double back, running headlong into a solid chest.

'Oh, I'm so sorry.' She pressed a hand against her forehead, then looked up to see Mr O'Keefe frowning at her as he restraightened his tie.

'You really should look where you're going, you know.'

'Sorry,' she replied, trying to edge around him. She would have protested but it had actually been entirely her fault.

'Umm . . . you're going the wrong way.'

'I forgot something, that's all. I need to fetch it.'

He studied her, his pale blue eyes narrowed, then darted his head around the corner, spying Mrs Coniston. 'Ah, I see. What were you planning to do? You've got to see her some time.'

Caroline thought about continuing with her lie but there was a softness to Mr O'Keefe's features as he looked at her now. A kindness to his eyes and teasing hint in his smile that gave her the courage to admit the truth.

'I just can't stand seeing that woman before I absolutely have to. I was going to use the secret stairs and avoid her.'

'There're secret stairs?' he asked, his eyebrows raising.

'Everywhere. Didn't you know that?'

He shook his head. 'I've never needed to use them. Wouldn't be allowed anyway and all the offices are so close

114

to each other, I don't think I'd even know where to look for them. I don't get to see other parts of the palace.'

'But you must have known they existed?'

'I know the Queen uses some, but I thought they were just for her between certain rooms. I didn't know there were lots, and everyone uses them.'

'Not everyone. And we're not really supposed to unless there's a good reason, but I think Mrs Coniston is one.'

'She certainly has been in a difficult mood this morning.' He gave a warm, friendly grin. The musicality of his Irish accent enveloped her and to her surprise he said, 'Can I join you?'

She met his gaze; his eyes were alight with a twinkle that she was sure could melt hearts but wouldn't touch her own. 'All right.' Mrs Coniston's heels clicked on the floor, growing louder. 'Quick. This way.'

Caroline led them a short way back down the corridor and identified the secret door that looked like any other section of wall with a painting fixed to it. By pressing a concealed button near the skirting, the door popped open, and Caroline led them through.

'Where does this lead?' Mr O'Keefe asked as they began to climb a narrow, curving staircase.

'All the way to the second floor and the Queen's wardrobe, but you can go off here . . .' She stepped on to a landing where a new, narrow corridor led away from the stairs. 'And this takes you to the first floor. We can then go down and approach the offices from the other side, avoiding her altogether.'

She glanced behind her and smiled at his open-mouthed expression. He was running his hands over the walls as if the plainly painted surface were somehow magical. A laugh bubbled up into her throat.

'What?' he asked.

'You just look so amazed, that's all. Like a child at Christmas. That's how I looked when I came downstairs Christmas morning and there was a present for me. Maybe a couple if Ma'd been saving.' She felt suddenly self-conscious at this remark, remembering how judgemental Mr O'Keefe was of her accent and background.

'I remember when I was little and Mammy would stand so proudly in front of the fireplace where the presents were piled, just wanting to see us happy.'

'Us? How many of you were there?'

'Eight.'

'Blimey.'

'But . . . I'd rather you didn't say anything to anyone else. I get enough comments about where I come from as it is.' This was surprising. She hadn't thought he'd ever speak so openly, so unguardedly in front of her. Before she could say she had no intention of doing so, he stopped. 'What's that?'

Raised voices could just be heard through the wall. They must have been level with the Duke of Edinburgh's suite as it was definitely his voice Caroline could hear. She'd know it anywhere. He said something she couldn't quite make out, as though he were over the other side of the room. Then the Queen answered, her voice calm but strong with a steely edge to it.

They paused and listened.

'It's outrageous, Lilibet. You have to do something about it.'

'There is nothing I *can* do, Philip. It is tradition.'

'But if it was the other way around, you'd be walking beside me. As the man, I don't see why I have to walk behind you. It's emasculating.'

Behind the wall, Caroline whispered, 'What does that mean?'

'It means it makes him less of a man. He must be talking about the coronation and having to walk behind the Queen. If he were the King, she'd walk beside him, but it doesn't work the other way around. I heard he was unhappy about it and wanted it changed but Queen Elizabeth won't have any of it. She says it's tradition and a tradition that *has* to be honoured.'

The Queen's voice reached them, and they held their breath. 'There really is no point in discussing this again, darling. Things have to be a certain way. You know it is simply how they are done. I know you disagree with it, but it is not emasculating—'

'Oh, don't give me that guff, Lilibet, I'm not one of your subjects.'

'Philip, it is our wedding anniversary.'

'And you're working. As you always are.' She said nothing. 'Will you at least think about it?'

Her voice grew colder. 'There is nothing to think about. And please, Philip, can we not have this discussion today? The Duke of Windsor's visit didn't go well. It was awfully hard to have to tell him that he is not welcome at the coronation and to say he has taken the news badly is an understatement.'

'What can the man expect? He turns down the throne to marry some American trollop and then expects to be invited to, and take part in, all the pageantry and nonsense. He simply wants to steal the limelight from you and get back into the public's good graces.' Philip snorted a laugh. 'That's not likely to happen.'

'Tommy said he stormed out of here and almost frightened a footman to death. I must go and see him and make sure he is all right.'

'It's right he doesn't come, but, Lilibet, can't you see that I should walk beside you as you become queen? I'm your husband!'

'Philip, please—'

'Oh, fine!'

Caroline shuddered as if the cold atmosphere in the room were leaching into the corridor. After a second of silence, footsteps pounded and a door slammed.

Caroline released her breath slowly. 'Blimey, I ain't never heard them like that before. Not with each other, anyway.'

'It can't be easy, can it? Being queen, I mean.'

She suddenly realised how close their faces were as they leaned against the cold, grey wall, their heads almost touching the freezing stone. Mr O'Keefe looked down at her and Caroline was struck again by how handsome he was: his dark, chocolate-brown hair pomaded and well combed, his jaw clean-shaven. He had nicely shaped lips and unexpectedly she wondered what it would be like to kiss them, shocked by her body's physical reaction to him. She hadn't thought she could ever be in such a small, enclosed space with a man and feel safe.

Then suddenly, as her mind and body replayed the fear and terror Timothy had instilled in her, panic rose into her throat. It clamoured inside her, pulling at her lungs, and she grew hot. She had to get away, to get out of there before things turned nasty. Before risk became reality. Mr O'Keefe raised his hand and she flinched, though it didn't come anywhere near her and instead touched the back of his head to scratch an itch. His eyes narrowed in concern, his forehead knitted with lines as confusion pinched his eyebrows together.

Without a word, she pushed herself away from the wall and hurried past him to the end of the corridor where a second set of stairs led back down to the ground floor.

'We better hurry or we'll be late,' she said, pushing the words up and past the rock that had settled at the base of her gullet.

She didn't risk a look back, uncertain what she'd see, or how it would make her feel. The physical memory of Timothy lingered in her body, making her feel vulnerable, and the flash of attraction she'd felt to Mr O'Keefe confused her senses. Thank God she'd trodden these corridors a hundred times, or she'd be in danger of losing her way. As the shadow of Timothy's touch faded, she worried she'd never be able to love anyone again. He'd damaged her in ways she hadn't even realised, leaving scars that might last forever. Scars that might never fully heal.

Chapter Twelve

On the walk from Buckingham Palace two days later, it felt as though the temperature was plummeting with every step. Milly, Caroline and Helen wrapped their coats around them as they went to meet Jake Walker, *Daily News* journalist and reluctant father to Helen's baby.

The icy wind whipped around them on this particularly bleak and grey day. The bare branches of trees in Green Park appeared stark and dead, and the grass frozen, still covered in a thin white film. The pale, weak sun did its best to break through the clouds. Milly was quiet, Helen unusually chatty and Caroline quietly seething, ready to give the no-good man who had used and abused her friend what for. She felt stronger in their company – more like herself – and wished she could tell them what had happened in the corridor with Mr O'Keefe. Discuss the way memories of Timothy haunted her. But no matter how much she wanted to, she couldn't bring herself to open up about the effect he had on her still when, until recently, she believed she'd put it behind her.

Though it was hard to speak against the buffeting wind, the palace was full of gossip about the Duke of Windsor's visit and Caroline told her friends what she'd overheard in the passageway.

'According to Davey,' Milly said, referring to a young boy who was on the cleaning team with them, 'he arrived marching around the palace like he owned it. That got the Queen's back up immediately. The Queen Mother refused to see him at all, so someone else said.'

'I'm not surprised,' Caroline replied. 'If he hadn't abdicated, her husband might still be alive.'

'That's the general consensus. But the cheek of the man. Thinking he can go off like that and then just come back when the mood takes him and be part of the royal family.'

'Well,' said Caroline. 'The Queen definitely wasn't impressed from what I heard. And did you hear that Princess Margaret's police protection has been increased because some American has threatened her?'

'No!' Helen gasped. 'When was this?'

'Don't know exactly, but she ain't happy being escorted here, there and everywhere.'

'Because', Milly added, 'it means she can't flirt with Peter Townsend. Do you think it's real or just a ploy for them to be kept apart?'

'It's got to be real, hasn't it?' Caroline said.

Helen nodded her agreement. 'Has to be. They wouldn't waste time and money on something like that if it wasn't. There are cheaper ways to keep them apart.'

Conversation died as they negotiated their way through the heavier traffic of the main thoroughfare. Dark cars and red buses filled the wide road of Piccadilly, the traffic moving for a few yards and then coming to a stop again. Even though it was winter, London was busy, the air dark and thick with smoke so dense you could reach out and touch it. On a

Saturday afternoon, the pavements were crowded and the three of them struggled to walk side by side.

Christmas was definitely approaching: in the palace, paper chains were being made for staff quarters: and here, the shop windows were adding festive decorations. In one, a line of paper snowflakes had been hung from a ribbon, and in the next, a cardboard snowman was wearing a bowler hat and a man's scarf.

Helen began to speak as they drew level again, but a bus roared past, drowning out her voice.

'What did you say?' Caroline asked. 'I couldn't hear you over that bleedin' contraption.'

'I felt the baby move today,' she repeated excitedly as the crowd cleared and they managed to stroll together. Milly and Caroline both gasped, their grins wide. 'It's the first time. I mean, I think it might have happened before, but I thought it was just a strange twinge in a muscle. I didn't put two and two together at the time. Today it was the most extraordinary thing. Like a butterfly fluttering its wings in my belly.' She pressed a hand to her stomach. 'It was rather wonderful.'

'I bet it was,' Milly said, smiling.

'Is that why you've been nattering away all giddy like?' Caroline asked. 'I thought it was nerves at seeing Jake again.'

'It's that too, I suppose.'

Milly glanced at her. 'Are you scared?'

'Scared? Of what?' Helen's black hair flicked over her shoulder as she turned her head.

'That you'll fall back in love with him?'

A mirthful laugh escaped her. 'No, not at all. Jake's in the past. Behind me now. I'm moving on with my life and I'm quite looking forward to him seeing that. But I'm glad you two are here with me. It is easier facing him with you beside me.' They huddled closer together, shoulders touching, and the moment of friendship warmed Caroline against the cold winter wind.

They turned off Piccadilly and down one of the smaller side streets. The weight of traffic both vehicular and pedestrian eased immediately, and the tea room came into view with its dark green paint and creamy sign. It wasn't anywhere near as nice as a Lyons' or some of the smaller places they'd been to. The black ashy smoke that stained London buildings had done the same here: the windows grimy, the dark green paint almost black in places.

'This is where he wanted to meet?' Caroline asked, pointing at it and then shoving her hand as deeply into her pockets as possible, the cold nibbling at her fingers through her gloves.

Helen checked the piece of paper she'd written the address on. 'This is the place.'

'Why did he pick here?'

'Perhaps he was already going to be in the area.'

'What did he say when you called?' Milly asked, reluctantly pushing the door open. The hinges squeaked and a little bell jangled as they entered. The warm air hit their cheeks and the place smelled of fresh bread and stewed tea. Half the tables were full. Families squeezed in together, children's faces stained with jam. One old man looked up suspiciously at them but then returned to his newspaper. They took a table in the corner, seating themselves so Helen would be opposite Jake rather than next to him: anything to minimise the physical contact. The chairs creaked and moaned as they sat, and the table wobbled unevenly.

'He was surprised to hear from me, of course,' Helen said, finally answering Milly's question. 'He asked after the baby. After me. Wanted to know if I was looking after myself, if I needed anything.'

'What did you say?'

'I told him I was fine and didn't need or want anything from him at all. Not when it came to the baby.'

'Is that true?' Caroline asked.

Despite being indoors it was still too cold to take their outer layers off. Condensation obscured the view outside the window, and drops of water trickled down the glass, pooling on the sill. Helen gave a wry smile as she loosened the neckline of her coat.

'Not really. Money is tight as usual. To be honest, I could use his help – financially speaking – but I'm determined not to take anything from him. I don't want to be beholden to him or to give him any excuse to turn up on my doorstep. I just feel that . . .'

'What?' Caroline prompted.

'That he'd like me to need him, but once I showed that I did, he'd use it against me.'

'And did you tell him what we wanted?'

'No. I worried he wouldn't come if he thought I was just using him. Once we're face to face, we'll convince him to help us. All I said was that I had something to ask him and that I wanted to do it in person.'

'Thank you,' Caroline said. 'I appreciate you putting

yourself through this for me. For Johnny.' Helen blushed. 'Shall we get a pot of tea? I'm gasping and need warming up.'

'I'll help you,' Milly said. 'It seems we need to go up and get a tray. There aren't any waiting staff.'

They stood and moved to the counter leaving Helen to sit and rest. As they ordered from the burly man who they presumed was the owner, the bell pinged again, and they turned to see Jake arrive. His glasses were steaming up from the change in temperature, obscuring his eyes, and his tawny hair had been blown about in the wind. He really was handsome, and they could see why Helen had fallen for him. Caroline realised he hadn't noticed herself and Milly at the counter and instead dashed towards Helen, throwing himself into the chair opposite her, immediately reaching out for her hand across the table. She recoiled but his hand stayed over hers, holding her firm. Caroline and Milly both glanced at the counter, eager for the man to hurry with their order so they could return to their friend.

'You go,' Milly said. 'I'll wait for the tea.'

Though Caroline's body prickled with nerves, she gathered her courage and went over. She took comfort in the fact that there were enough people here that nothing was likely to happen, and if they needed him to, the owner looked strong enough to throw Jake out. She walked over; with each step his words became clearer.

'Helen, I'm so glad you telephoned. I've been wanting to see you. I can't tell you how much. I've missed you terribly. You're constantly in my thoughts – on my mind. Not a day goes by when I don't think about you, or the baby. How—'

'Let go of me, Jake.'

'But—'

'Let go.' Helen's voice was loud enough that the family at a neighbouring table looked over. He loosened his grip, and she wiggled her hand away from him. He pushed his hair back from his face and removed his glasses, cleaning them on the scarf poking out of the top of his pristine coat.

'I thought—'

The man behind the counter cleared his throat loudly and Milly took the thin wooden tray loaded with three cups and a large white teapot, the spout chipped. She returned to the table and they both sat down. Jake's eyes widened as he watched them, disappointment clouding his face.

Helen's voice was low. 'I'm sorry if that's what you thought this was, Jake. But it isn't.'

His eyes fell to the ring she twisted nervously. 'Are you . . . ?'

Quickly, she whisked her hands to her lap, hiding them under the table. 'It's a precaution. In case people ask questions.'

'So there's no one—'

'I'm not answering those sorts of questions, Jake. I've not asked you here because I miss you and I'm not discussing my private life. I've asked you here because we need your help with something.'

A desolate expression tainted his attractive features. Why was life always so complicated? Caroline hated putting Helen through this, and, though he didn't deserve her pity, Jake too. For everything that had happened, she believed he had loved Helen. Watching him now, Caroline saw that he still did.

He cleared his throat and placed his hands in his lap. 'We?'

'Me,' Caroline replied. 'I do. I need some information.'

'About what?'

The meeting hadn't started how she'd thought it would. The atmosphere was tense and if she didn't do something to defuse it, he'd never agree to help them. She had to get him on their side, or at least willing to listen to what she said. 'Look, before we start, d'you want a cuppa tea?'

'Umm . . . yes. Yes, please.' The question had thrown him and suddenly the atmosphere shifted.

'Then you better go and ask for a cup but there's more than enough here.' She took the lid off the teapot and stirred. The comforting scent drifted into the air. Slightly dazed, he went to the counter.

'What are you doing?' Helen murmured. 'I don't want him to stay any longer than he has to.'

'I know. And I'm sorry but after that start, there's no way he's going to just do as we ask. We need him on our side; otherwise, he'll just say no and walk straight back out. I thought making him a feel bit more comfortable might be the best way. Especially as he's realised you aren't here on bended knee begging him to take you back.'

Milly nodded, impressed. 'She's right. We need him to relax. Good idea, Caroline.'

They quietened as he returned, clutching a cup and saucer. Caroline poured. Milly had been forced to sit next to Jake and looked as if she'd rather be beside a pile of horse manure. Disdain dripped from every feature, and she'd never looked more like her aunt, Mrs Barnes, in one of her moods.

'So, this is what you wanted me here for? Information?'

He looked at Helen and, after meeting her gaze for a second, dropped his eyes to his drink, adding a dash of milk from the jug.

'Listen, Mr Walker,' Caroline said. 'Do you know anything about the Oclee robbery that happened a couple of weeks ago?'

Any hint of loss or grief over Helen was immediately replaced with a quizzical frown. 'I didn't cover it myself, but I know of it. Why?'

'My brother's Johnny Stratton—'

'The chap who's been charged with it all?' He reached into his pocket and took out the reporter's notepad and pencil he carried with him, flipping it open to a blank page. Milly grew even more on edge.

Caroline's earlier sympathy faded: it was clear his career was still the most important thing in his life. She glanced at Helen and saw her cold, unmoving expression; she was clearly determined to keep her emotions in check.

'Yes,' she confirmed, taking the small teacup in both hands and wrapping them tightly around it. 'But he didn't do it. He's innocent.'

Jake looked at Caroline. 'Would he be willing to speak to me, do you think?'

'He might. Maybe he could give you a scoop when he's cleared,' she added.

'But . . .' He was still wearing his hat and, seemingly realising how rude that was, removed it, placing it precariously near the edge of the table. 'I know this sounds callous, but if the police have arrested and charged him, they must have enough evidence against him.'

She shook her head. 'They're wrong. He did go out that night, but he went for a walk, that's all. He didn't go anywhere near the Oclee place.'

'Did anyone see him?'

'Apparently, someone saw him walking but that's all.' They couldn't have seen what he'd really been up to or they'd have told the police that.

'Ah, I see. And are there witnesses who saw him – or whoever it was – at the jewellers?'

'It wasn't him,' she said again. 'But I don't know. I don't think so. The police haven't said anything to Ma and Pa. I don't think there are any witnesses to the robbery itself. Apart from Mr Oclee, who's still unconscious.'

'So the only eyewitness can place him out and about that night, but not near the robbery. If that's the case, they must have more circumstantial evidence they haven't told you about.' He made a note. 'So what is it you want me to do?'

Caroline shuffled to the edge of her seat, keeping her voice as low as possible. The tea room was filled with the sounds of chattering voices, but she didn't want to risk being overheard. 'It's his boss, Arthur Whitelock.' She explained what had happened the night she'd visited him. 'It just seemed a strange reaction to me, and Johnny's always thought there was something off about him. I wondered if the name was familiar to you.'

He scratched his temple. 'All I know is he owns a warehouse down on the docks. I've not come across him personally, but I can ask around, see what some of the more seasoned reporters know.'

Caroline's heart lifted.

Jake glanced at Helen once more before standing and taking his hat from the table. She looked up for a second before turning to a small child at the next table – a baby, its chubby hand clutching a thin strip of buttered toast.

'I'll do what I can,' Jake said. 'But I get the feeling there's something you're not telling me.'

Caroline looked at Helen. She didn't know this man and needed guidance as to whether to tell him the truth of where Johnny was that night. Her friend gave a slight, almost unnoticeable shake of her head. Helen didn't trust him either and that was more than enough for Caroline.

'There's nothing else,' she said, turning back to Jake. 'He went for a walk and came home again, that's all. He didn't go anywhere near Oclee's, and he certainly didn't beat up that defenceless old man. He'd never do such a thing. He'd never hurt anyone.'

'All right then.' He placed his hat on his head, adjusting it slightly. She wasn't sure if she'd convinced him, but he didn't press. 'I'll be in touch.'

With a final glance at Helen he left; the door hinges squeaked and the tinny bell tinkled as he opened the door. He lifted his collar to shelter his neck from the rain and stepped back into the winter cold.

'Are you all right?' Caroline asked Helen. She placed her hand over her friend's where it rested on the table and Milly did the same.

'I'm fine,' Helen replied, though her voice shook. She took a deep breath and let it out in a sigh, lifting her eyes to the ceiling. 'I'm relieved. I've seen him again and he had no effect on me. At least, not the effect he hoped for.'

'He weren't half quick to whip out that notebook,' Caroline said, swigging the last of her cold tea from the cup.

'And he jumped at the chance of a scoop,' Milly added. 'But what do we do now?'

'Wait and see what he can find out, I suppose.'

'And until then?' Helen added.

'Maybe go and see Don Green?'

'I thought Johnny told you not to?'

'He's told me not to do a lot of things over the years, and I've never listened to any of them.'

'Caroline.' Helen's voice was firmer now, her eyes meeting her friend's, clear and certain. 'He said it could be dangerous.'

'What else can I do? I can't just sit around waiting for the police to figure things out. They're not even looking for anyone else now.'

Milly, who was growing ever more like her aunt in character, added, 'Let's talk about it over another cup of tea, shall we? We might as well have another before we head back, and I barely drank the last one.'

'Me neither.' Helen stared at her own, still full cup.

Caroline made her way back up to the counter, her mind racing. She'd never been good at waiting and patience wasn't a virtue she could claim. There had to be something more she should, or could, do to help her brother. Hopefully, this time it wouldn't put her in harm's way, but as visiting Don Green was the next logical step, that didn't look likely.

Chapter Thirteen

When Caroline entered the office on Tuesday morning, she found someone sitting in what she'd come to think of as *her* seat. As she opened the door and took a step towards her usual desk, the back of a head, with long, light brown curls falling down a woman's back, came into view. The woman turned to speak to Mr O'Keefe and the tip of a small, cherubic nose could be seen in profile. For once, Mr O'Keefe was smiling, enjoying the woman's attention, and Caroline felt a sudden hardening in her chest. She blamed it on the annoyance at having to work somewhere else and hoped this wasn't the end of her time in the office. Spying Mr Newington at the in-trays at the side of the room, sorting work, she went to speak with him.

The small, high windows above the trays were closed but draughts crept in through the panes and the room was cold. For once, no one had been smoking, and the air was clear and easy to breathe. As everyone was yet to start work, the clattering of keys didn't reverberate around her skull, though by the end of the day it would be like tinnitus.

'Excuse me, Mr Newington.'

'Oh, Caroline, there you are. Is everything all right?'

'Yes. Course. I was just wondering where I should sit today.'

'Sit?' He turned, suddenly realising the problem, the

crow's feet at the corners of his eyes crinkling. 'Ah, yes, Miss Western has returned to us. If you don't mind, could you move back one desk, next to Mr O'Keefe?'

'Mr O'Keefe?' Mr Newington's head tilted questioningly at her tone and she forced herself to smile. 'Of course.'

'And here. Take these.'

She grappled with the stack of papers he handed to her as some fell, fluttering to the floor. 'Is everything all right, Mr Newington? You seem a little distracted this morning.'

He looked up from where he'd knelt to pick up the lost work. 'Oh, yes. Certainly. We're still very behind but catching up thanks to everyone's efforts and . . . well, actually . . .' Mr Newington stood up and shuffled the papers nervously. 'This is strictly confidential, you understand?' He took a few steps back towards his office and she followed. 'Do you know if Mrs Barnes has a preference for emeralds or sapphires, or perhaps just plain diamonds?'

'For what?' Her mind was blank as to his meaning. Yet when she looked in his eyes, she saw the nerves and love he held for Mrs Barnes dancing there. 'Oh, I see! Do you mean for a ring?' He nodded, flustered. 'Umm . . . I've never really seen her wear any jewellery. But I'm sure whatever you like will be perfect for her. As long as you've chosen it with care, she won't mind a bit.'

'Do you think so?'

'I'm sure of it.' Caroline smiled reassuringly at his worried look.

'Good. Good.' He glanced at the clock and his expression grew instantly more serious. 'Right, we'd better get on. There's a lot to do today.'

'Isn't there always? I didn't realise how much like cleaning this job would be. No matter how much you get done, there's always more.'

He replied with a kindly smile, handing her the odd few sheets he'd collected from the floor, then tugging down his waistcoat. 'Never a dull moment though, hey?'

Caroline moved to the desk next to Mr O'Keefe. Miss Western's eyes followed her, running up and down her body in a way Caroline had come to expect from people in this part of the palace. Her lip curled as she spotted the darned skirt and stockings, the tattiness of her blouse and cardigan. How Caroline would love to go out and buy a whole new outfit: a smart suit so that she fitted in. But her parents needed her money now more than ever. Her feelings of inferiority would have to be ignored until she'd got Johnny out of prison and he was earning a wage again. God only knew when that would be and if anyone would even employ him after this. She ignored the gloomy thoughts and pulled out the chair to sit down.

'That's quite a lot you've got there,' Mr O'Keefe said, glancing over. 'Sure you can manage it all?' She wasn't sure if he was teasing but Miss Western giggled.

'Perfectly sure, thank you. Though I'm not quite sure where to start.' She read the first sheet, and then realised the second was nothing to do with it. 'It's all a bit muddled. I think I'll need to sort it before I start typing.'

'Sounds sensible to me.'

Miss Western suddenly spun in her seat to face them. 'And you are?' she asked as Mr O'Keefe began rifling through his notepad, finding his first piece of work for the day.

'Miss Stratton,' Caroline replied, trying to keep the cockney out of her voice. 'Pleased to meet you.'

'I'm Miss Western. Veronica.' Her accent was decidedly middle-class, like Helen's, but unlike her friend, this woman lacked warmth. Caroline nodded a greeting but followed Mr O'Keefe's lead and focused on her work. She was skimming two more sheets when the whole pile slipped on to the floor again.

'Oh Lord,' Caroline muttered as she bent down and began collecting them. Mr O'Keefe helped her. He'd shaved that morning, and his skin smelled of clean soap. Her cheeks warmed.

'Oops,' Miss Western said. 'Clumsy. Not a great start for you, is it? Have you been here long?'

Mr O'Keefe caught her eye and her heart skipped. They both stood abruptly. 'Only a couple of weeks.'

'Oh dear. You'll have to shape up or—'

'Miss Stratton's joining us from the Royal Household,' Mr O'Keefe added.

'Oh. Really? What did you do there?'

After the other day and the strange moment earlier, she had thought she and Mr O'Keefe were beginning to get used to each other. Yet it seemed he had said it to shame her. To make her admit she was lowly and working class.

'I – I was a cleaner.'

'Really?' Miss Western's tone grew gleeful. 'How interesting.' She meant the opposite. 'Did you get much experience typing while you were cleaning? What about dictation?'

'Miss Western,' came Mr Newington's stern voice from the other side of the room. 'It's one minute past nine.'

'Sorry, Mr Newington,' she purred, giving Caroline one last, smug look before she turned back.

Caroline began to type faster in her anger. Was she never to be accepted here? Would she ever be accepted anywhere? She focused on her work, determined not to make any mistakes, and found herself typing up a report for the Queen on the latest rehearsal of the coronation procession. It had been held on 23 November at seven in the morning and went from the Palace of Westminster to Buckingham Palace. Drummers played throughout the route, followed by troops from the Scots Guards and Grenadier Guards and a landau pulled by eight greys. Household Cavalry (looking magnificent, according to the report) finished the troop and all was described as highly satisfactory.

She and Milly had watched them arrive, marvelling at the sight of them. How splendid they all looked even though it was only a rehearsal. The report she was typing was to be used in a meeting the same week and stated that further, larger rehearsals were to follow. She felt a thrill of excitement as she read and typed. This was exactly the type of work that had excited her ambitions, and satisfaction grew inside her.

More than an hour had gone by when she looked up and realised that Barbara's chair was empty. She hadn't made it in.

'Is Barbara unwell?' she asked Mr O'Keefe, nodding towards the empty desk.

After glancing around the room to ensure he wouldn't be caught chatting, he said, 'Flu, I think.'

'She did seem off yesterday. She was sniffing and pale.'

'And she didn't talk as much as usual.'

The smile he flashed confused her. Perhaps he hadn't meant to shame her earlier. But then, if he hadn't, why mention it? Her mind raced back to the corridor and being in that small space with him – to being in small, trapped spaces with Timothy – and she felt herself withdraw. She turned her attention back to her work, seeing Mr O'Keefe frown in confusion.

They worked on in silence, but Caroline could feel an awkwardness between them. A strange atmosphere that she didn't know how to respond to. Every time she tried to be normal, her feelings overwhelmed her, fear gripping her heart.

When Miss Western left the room to powder her nose, he suddenly said, 'Miss Stratton, are you all right?'

She bristled, only glancing at him, not giving him her full attention. 'What do you mean?'

'I don't know. You just – In the corridor you—'

She recalled flinching as he scratched the back of his head. 'I'm fine,' she replied, sharper than intended, cutting him off. She wanted to say more, to explain, but the words wouldn't come.

'Fine,' he muttered.

And though it pained her to be rude, she settled back to her work, ignoring his presence and the way he occasionally mumbled under his breath. She had just completed another piece of work when Tommy Lascelles knocked and entered the office.

'Mr Lascelles,' Mr Newington said. 'An unexpected pleasure.'

'I was wondering if I could speak with Miss Stratton?'

Caroline's fingers slipped and pressed more than one key, so three type hammers bunched together. She eased the thin metal bands back. She'd have to start again now, but at least she'd only typed a few lines of this new report. The office had grown quiet: even the typewriter keys were being pressed more gently than before, and she could feel the eyes of her colleagues on her.

'In private,' Mr Lascelles added, and Caroline's stomach vaulted. What had she done now? What mistake had she made?

'You're more than welcome to use my office, of course.' Mr Newington motioned towards it.

'I'd like you to join us, Newington, if you have the time? This won't take long.'

'Of course. Yes.' He turned and waved her forward. 'Miss Stratton, if you could come this way, please?'

As she moved between the desks, she saw Miss Western lean in towards Mrs Coniston. The start of their conversation was lost, but then she heard Miss Western's low mumble.

'No, I agree. This is no place for someone like her.'

Her shoulders stiffened and Mr Newington closed the door behind them. Tommy Lascelles leaned against the desk, his small legs crossed at the ankles, the white lines on his pinstripe suit arrow straight.

'Is there a problem?' Mr Newington asked, shifting awkwardly.

Mr Lascelles's moustache twitched, then he gave what Caroline had to assume was a smile, though it didn't seem to come easily to him. 'None at all. I came to thank Miss Stratton for redoing the work I'd had to give back and for delivering it to my office. Queen Elizabeth was very impressed with her diligence and competence.'

'Queen . . . ?' Mr Newington muttered in shock. 'I say. She thanked Caroline for . . .'

Despite the fact the two men were speaking about her as though she wasn't there, she was pleased and relieved to hear something positive. She needed some good news.

'The Queen has asked me to send her warmest regards to you, Caroline, and to encourage you to keep working hard. As you know, the family left for Sandringham today, so she was unable to deliver this message herself. She did, however, ask me to give you this.'

He reached into the inside pocket of his jacket and pulled out a small cream envelope.

Caroline took it in shaking hands. What could the Queen of England possibly have to say to her? Turning over the envelope, she saw her name written neatly in the Queen's own hand. She recognised it from the notepads dotted around the palace – on her bedside, on the dining and breakfast tables – there in case she needed to make a note of something. With shaking fingers, she opened it and pulled out the expensive writing paper that was thicker than the fabric of her skirt.

Dear Caroline,

Your hard work and dedication are greatly appreciated. Remember, mistakes are inevitable. The most important thing is that we learn from them.

Continue to work hard and you will reap the rewards.

Elizabeth R.

She felt lightheaded. Ma and Pa would be so proud of her when she showed them. Not to mention Mrs Barnes, Milly and Helen.

'I say,' said Mr Newington, reading the missive over her shoulder, curiosity proving too much for him. 'We've never had this happen before.'

'No,' said Mr Lascelles, drawing Caroline's attention. Her hand shook and it fluttered the letter in her hand. 'I admit this sort of thing is very unusual. In fact, I'm not sure it's ever happened before. Congratulations, Miss Stratton: it seems the Queen has taken quite a shine to you. And I too am very grateful for your efforts. Keep up the good work.'

With that he left, shaking hands with Mr Newington on his way out of the door. Everyone in the office was craning their necks to see what had happened, though Caroline was willing to bet they'd been watching it all through the small window of Mr Newington's office door.

'Miss Stratton? Caroline?' She heard Mr Newington's voice as though she was underwater. 'Back to work now, I think.'

'Yes. Sorry.' She clutched the letter tightly, leaving him in his office and returning to her seat, placing the envelope on the desk beside her typewriter.

'Is that Smythson's?' Mr O'Keefe asked, eyes wide.

'What?'

'*What?*' Miss Western parroted. 'I think you mean "I beg your pardon?" Or don't they teach you that in Hackney or wherever it is you come from?'

'I'm from Whitechapel, and proud of it,' Caroline answered.

'I live in Whitechapel,' Mr O'Keefe added, forcing Miss Western to blush.

Good. She deserved taking down a peg or two.

Caroline had thought he'd live in Camden or Shepherd's Bush where there were bigger Irish communities, but she supposed Whitechapel was cheap.

Mr O'Keefe nodded again to the letter. 'Is that Smythson's paper? You know, the Queen's stationers from Bond Street?'

'The . . . ? I don't know – I mean, it is from the Queen, but—'

Miss Western scoffed loudly. 'Think you're too good for us, do you? Getting notes from the Queen. All high and mighty. It's a wonder you're working here, in this lowly office, and not up there in her private apartments.'

Caroline, though stung with hurt, found her anger rising. There was no call for her being so rude. They'd only met that morning. They didn't know each other at all, and she had no reason to judge her so harshly.

'Miss Western, I dunno what your problem is with me, but I've been in the private apartments already and they're not nearly as exciting as you seem to think. As to working up there doing this' – she stood and motioned to the room full of desks and typewriters – 'even Mr Lascelles, the Queen's private secretary, has an office on this floor, just down the corridor – where all the offices are. So get your facts straight before you start taking the mickey out of people.'

Mr O'Keefe was smirking, and Caroline felt her anger spark again as he enjoyed her embarrassment. 'And what are you laughing at? You think it's funny that I've cleaned toilets for a living? Well, at least it's an honest living and it's given me better friends than any of you could ever have because you're all too mean-spirited.'

Just then, Mr Newington's door opened, and he peered into the room from his office. 'Everything all right out here?'

'Fine, Mr Newington.' She sat back down, returning to her work, waiting for him to say something, but he didn't and simply closed the door after retreating back inside. Mr O'Keefe's cheeks were red, and he wouldn't look at her. *Good*, Caroline thought again. At least she could have a quiet afternoon focusing on her work. Miss Western was silent though furious, her lips a tight, angry line on her face, the skin around her mouth puckered.

Caroline's gaze drifted back to the envelope on her desk and a feeling of warmth and pride filled her. The Queen knew where she'd come from, knew how hard she'd worked and understood what a struggle she'd had and would continue to face. The thought stirred an inner strength she hadn't known she possessed. One she would use to fight for what she wanted, for herself and for her family. She wouldn't be cowed by those who wanted her to fail.

Chapter Fourteen

Oclee's jewellers on Fieldgate Street was a small, poky shop Caroline had never liked the look of, not even as a girl. The brick beneath the large shop window was stained black with smog and the dark frames, painted that colour to make it appear less dirty, gave the place a less-than-welcoming appearance. Though Christmas was coming to other parts of London and beginning to take hold in the palace with Christmas songs played with more regularity and talk of the presents people were going to buy, there was no hint of it here. The large window, through which she could see cheap jewellery and pawned watches, was divided by three thin wooden grilles, the paint flaking away on to the slushy snow that lined the windowsill. There were large gaps in the display and Caroline assumed this was where the stolen jewellery would have sat. Very little had been left behind.

A man, probably in his early thirties, stood in the door-way, his hands in his pockets, a flat cap pulled down tightly on his head. His features were all wrong: too small and pinched together on his wide face. A cigarette hung from his lips, smoke drifting into the cold evening wind. If only she could have got away from work sooner, she wouldn't have been making another trip in the dark. The man looked down and pulled his trousers up by the waistband. She wondered why the shop wasn't shut like all the others, as it was after closing time.

A stab of fear ran through Caroline, and she hoped it wouldn't be the same as her visit to Mr Whitelock's. Without thinking she rubbed her arm where he'd grabbed her. There were no stars in the sky, no bright moon to guide her way, only the dim glow from the streetlights and the passing headlamps of cars. She approached cautiously and the man took the cigarette from his mouth and threw the stub to the ground before turning and going back into the shop. It landed in a pile of greying, sludgy snow. Caroline hurried on before he could lock the door for the night.

'Scuse me, are you Mr Oclee's son?'

'I am. Who wants to know?' His voice was rough and gravelly, reminding her of the way the Thames water dragged the shingle on the mudbanks.

'My name's Caroline Stratton. I wondered if I could speak to you?'

'Stratton?' His forehead creased with thick mounds of flesh. Then his eyes flashed with anger. ''Ere, you're not related to Johnny, are you?'

'I am, but please—'

He spun to close the door. 'I'll not talk to you. Nor none of your family.'

'Please, Mr Oclee. My brother didn't do this. Please, just give me five minutes of your time.'

'What d'you mean he didn't do it? The police have charged him. They told us there was no doubt.' The door was level with his shoulder, and he spoke through the gap, his hand poised on the knob, ready to close it completely.

144

She walked up the step. 'Johnny swears to me he didn't do it. Please, I just need to know what happened that night. If I don't, he'll spend the rest of his life in prison and who-ever did commit this horrible crime will go free. Please won't you 'elp me?' In her desperation, her accent had changed, returning to her East End roots. Her pleading worked, for he paused and said:

'Five minutes. That's all you've got.'

He opened the door and she walked into the shop. The bright lights provided a sense of safety though it was as cold inside as it was outside and she shivered, hiding it as best she could. She didn't want this man to detect any hint of fear, any vulnerability. She'd learned already that some men would take advantage of that, and she'd been foolhardy enough to come here alone. She hadn't even told Milly and Helen her plans for this evening. She wouldn't risk their safety by dragging them into this mess. Cases with wooden frames but empty of glass panels lined the room. An L-shaped counter ran along two walls ending in a till – a broken one: the cash tray hung out of it and the top was smashed.

'You see this?' Mr Oclee said, lifting back the corner of a dirty, threadbare rug that covered the small shop floor. The pattern was obscured by trodden-in mud. Realising she was standing on the other end of it she stepped to the side. Mr Oclee pointed to a stain on the floor. It was dark brown and oddly shaped, as if a can of paint had been dropped and smattered everywhere. 'That's blood that is. Blood.'

Caroline swallowed down the lump in her throat. She balled her fists in her pockets and glanced towards the door. But as she turned back, it was sympathy, not fear she felt as Mr Oclee Junior's face crumpled. 'This is where they left him – my pa – left him for dead after beating him up.'

'I'm so sorry.'

He regained control of his emotions, eyes narrowing and assessing her for the truth. 'You don't sound like you're from round here no more.'

She ignored the comment, knowing it came from grief. 'Can you tell me what happened that night?'

'Your pa's been in, you know. Asking me to go to the police, tell them I don't think Johnny could've done it.'

'And?' she asked, seizing the opportunity. She was surprised her pa had come. She hadn't known he was going to do anything. His natural respect for authority, for those he saw as better than himself, often stopped him questioning the truth of what he'd been told. The idea that he had come to see the Oclees warmed her. It meant he was fighting for his boy.

'I don't know if he did or he didn't. Your brother, he – he can be daft. Lets people lead him astray. I wouldn't have thought so before this, but people do desperate things sometimes.'

'Johnny wasn't desperate,' Caroline replied. 'He had no reason to do this. He didn't have debts or anything. He had a good job. He was working hard. I know he's made mistakes in the past but he was a boy then. He's not now.' Mr Oclee didn't respond; instead he stared at the bloody mark on the floor. 'Can you tell me what happened that night? Please?'

He scratched his head, his fingers reaching up under his cap. 'I reckon it must've been about midnight Pa came downstairs. He clearly heard something. Something I didn't. I've

146

always been a heavy sleeper. I was out for the count. If only I hadn't been, I—' He swallowed and turned away from the stain to lean against the counter. 'I woke up when some glass broke, probably that counter there.' He pointed to Caroline's left where the case had no glass at all, yet tiny spikes of it still poked from the edges. 'Or this one.' She registered the tall display case she'd seen when she first walked in. 'When I came down, they'd gone – whoever they were – and Pa was on the floor. His head was a mess. I ran into the street and shouted for help. There must've been a policeman nearby 'cause he arrived within minutes.'

'Did you see anyone or anything?'

'A van. I saw a dark blue van.'

'Anything else?'

He shook his head. 'No. I was more worried about Pa and legged it back inside to help him. Ma'd come down and she was screamin' and nearly fainted. I had to sort her out while they were getting him to hospital.'

'How is he now?'

Tears swam in his eyes. 'Touch and go. God knows what we're gonna do. We've been barely scratchin' a livin' as it is.' He pressed his fingers into his eyes and released them a second later. 'I knew your brother. Always thought he was decent. Are you sure he didn't do it?'

'He's sworn to me he didn't, and I believe him. Someone else did this and they're letting him take the blame. You know he'd never hurt anyone. Are you sure there's nothing you can remember about the van or who was driving it?'

He shook his head. 'No.' Caroline waited a moment, but he said nothing else, so she took a step back, readying to leave, when his voice halted her. 'Wait . . .' She lifted her head, her heart squeezing with hope. 'There was one thing.' He closed his eyes as if picturing something in his mind. 'I never saw the man driving the van, but Pa was whispering something when I found him. *Scar*. He said "scar" several times. I had to shush him in the end, told him to save his strength.'

Mr Whitelock had several scars on his hands. Johnny had said he was dodgy, and he'd acted strangely when Caroline had gone to see him, but she'd assumed he was the type of man to get others to do his bidding and not take the risks himself. Could it be that he'd been the one to act?

'Thank you for your help, Mr Oclee, and I'm sorry about what's happened to your pa. I hope he'll be back home soon.'

He nodded briskly and she left the shop. The information she'd gained distracted her from the freezing squalls nipping at her nose and cheeks. Her toes were almost numb, and she took the scarf from around her neck and placed it over her head, tying it under her chin. There was one more place she had to go.

Chapter Fifteen

Thrusting her hands into her pockets, Caroline walked towards the tenements and streets she'd grown up in. She passed a road that had been entirely destroyed by bombs during the war, where children played in the summer, climbing over the remnants of garden walls and the piles of bricks. On she walked as neighbours spoke in doorways. She passed a bonfire, children gathering around it as someone burned rubbish in a metal bin, smoke and fumes curdling the air. She saw the springs of an old mattress through the orange flames, the material ablaze, the fire spreading over it.

Don Green's house was like any other. A shabby, tiny dwelling, squeezed into a terrace. It didn't look big enough considering the number of children he and his wife Mavis had. She knocked and stepped back.

Shouting echoed in the hall on the other side of the door: a mother scolding her children. Then the door swung open. Mrs Green looked older than her years. Her face was lined with wrinkles, her eyes dulled from years of childbearing and worry. She was too thin and too tired, her prominent cheekbones giving her a skeletal appearance.

'Yeah?'

'I was wondering if I could speak to Mr Green?'

'And who are you?'

'I'm Johnny Stratton's sister.'

Mrs Green shook her head. 'Not you. No. Go away. I'm sorry for what's 'appened to Johnny. I am. But I can't 'elp you. I won't say nothin'—'

'Mrs Green, please?'

'No! I had nothin' to do with what Don and your Johnny got up to. I was 'ere with the kiddies. I'm always 'ere with the kiddies. Mornin', noon and night. I don't know nothin'. Now leave me be.'

She was about to close the door as two children walked into view behind her. They were chewing on small pieces of bread, their faces dirty, their clothes torn and too small. It wasn't an unfamiliar sight in that part of London.

'Where can I find your husband?' Caroline asked, realising Johnny was right. She'd taken her life at the palace for granted and had forgotten what it was like to live in the real world. To live in poverty and strife, your belly always empty, parents working themselves to the bone for scraps.

'Where d'you think? Where 'e always is. In the pub.' Mrs Green tilted her head to the end of the street and Caroline stepped away, the door closing in her face.

She followed the road down and as she reached the end, the pub came into view. Men stood outside despite the cold, and they leered at her as she drew closer. She thought about turning around and leaving this visit for another day when Helen and Milly could come with her, but she was here now and as much as she wanted to go home, she had to continue inside.

Ignoring the way the men watched her as she passed,

she opened the door and stepped into the light and warmth of the pub. It smelled of beer and smoke and, in the corner, someone was playing an old, out-of-tune piano. It was nothing like the gold one that had pride of place in the Music Room at the palace, or the smaller one in the Queen's private apartments. Punters joined in singing when they felt like it, their voices fading in and out as they sang songs she'd grown up with. Don Green sat at the bar, and Caroline approached him, untying her scarf from around her face.

'Don? I need to speak to you.'

The pub grew quiet as if they all knew what she was there for. They probably did. News travelled fast in the East End, just as it did in the palace. It was a small community and though everyone normally banded together, there were times when events would tear them apart. Lips curled at her presence, their eyes full of malice and hatred because they believed Johnny had turned on one of their own. They thought Johnny a wrong 'un, and she and her family were tainted by association.

'Caroline?' Don spluttered, surprised to see her. 'We haven't seen you for a while.' He'd aged, just as his wife had. Though he wasn't that much older than her brother, a hard life and years of manual work had taken a toll.

She hated how he was behaving as if everything was fine, and she clenched her teeth. 'I need to talk to you.'

He must have read her anger in her face as he said, 'Let's go over there and chat.'

He guided her to a dark corner, to a tatty seat and a table full of glasses that hadn't yet been cleared. The dregs of ale sat in the bottom, and she pushed the overflowing ashtray away and anxiously fidgeted with her scarf, wrapping it around her hands in her lap.

'Can I get you a drink?' he asked.

'No. You know why I'm here. Johnny's in trouble. You have to tell the police what happened that night. That Johnny was with you.'

He shook his head. 'I can't, Caroline. You know the state we're in.'

'And yet you can afford to come here and drink?'

His tone changed and his posture stiffened. 'What's that supposed to mean?'

'If money's so tight, why aren't you at home spending every penny on your wife and children?'

She knew she sounded judgemental, but Mrs Green had seemed so beaten down by her life. Don should have been there with her, sharing the burden. Yet here he was, messing about with his mates in the pub. Her pa would never have done such a thing. Johnny would never have done such a thing, but it seemed he'd been wrong again in believing in his so-called friend. And Johnny's freedom was on the line.

'Don't speak to me like that, Miss Hoity-Toity.'

It seemed she was to get this treatment from everyone. From those at work and at home too. She didn't fit in anywhere any more. But she wouldn't let him push her around as he did his wife. No matter how much fear was beginning to pool like liquid in her stomach, she had to push on: to convince Don to help her brother.

'Why not? You could tell the police Johnny met you for

a walk. You don't have to tell them what you were really up to.'

'And you think they'd believe that? Especially now? After waiting this long? You're even more naive than you were as a girl.'

'So you're just going to let him take the blame for you? Tell me, did your wife see any of the money you made from selling black-market meat?'

He reached out and grabbed her chin, holding her face firmly as he leant towards her. Her breath ceased and she was paralysed in his grasp, her mind flooding with panic. 'Keep your voice down.'

'Let her go.'

Caroline looked up to see Mr O'Keefe towering over the table. She'd never felt more relieved to see him. His pale blue eyes were fixed on Don Green with a hardness she'd never seen before, and Don did as he was told. He pushed her away and stood up from the table.

'You mind your business, Irish.'

The pub joined in, jeering and calling him unpleasant names. The atmosphere grew tenser, and Caroline's urge to flee was strong.

'I'll not mind my business if it means ignoring you assaulting a young lady.'

Don ignored him and pinned his eyes on Caroline. 'Don't come back here again. Not if you know what's good for you.'

Don pushed past Mr O'Keefe and their shoulders collided. Don stared him down. Mr O'Keefe rocked backwards but didn't move until Don had returned to his seat. The pub was quiet as everyone watched them. Mr O'Keefe slid into the chair Don had vacated next to Caroline and the noise level began to rise as conversations struck up again.

'What was that all about?'

'Nothing. What're you even doing here?'

'I live around here.'

She met his gaze, her body calming from the shock of Don Green's temper, though she could still feel his hand pinching her face.

Mr O'Keefe went on, 'I told you I live in Whitechapel. Now, I think you'd better answer my question, or I won't be able to help.'

'I can't. Not in here.' She wasn't about to tell him the truth and needed some time to think of an excuse. Something that wouldn't make her seem less respectable.

'Then I'll walk you to the tube.'

'You don't have to. I can—'

'The way everyone here's watching you, I can't let you go alone. You might not be safe.'

He stood and Caroline followed, pushing her scarf into her pocket. Her hands were shaking too much to try and tie it now. The chattering voices hushed as they moved through the pub, but more slurs were thrown at Mr O'Keefe. She felt ashamed of her community, of the place she'd been born and raised. When had they become so inhospitable?

Out in the night, they walked along in silence for a few steps until the hum of the pub receded to be overtaken by the quiet of the streets.

'So?' he asked.

Caroline shuddered and he took a long woollen scarf

from around his neck and placed it around hers. She kept her eyes on the ground in front of her, watching her feet as they stepped on the frosty pavement.

'I needed to speak to Don about something.'

There, that wasn't a lie, but it didn't reveal anything either.

'Your brother's Johnny Stratton, isn't he? The man accused of the Oclee robbery? I thought I recognised the name.'

Humiliation flooded her, bringing with it a biliousness that sent water pooling into her mouth. 'He didn't do it.' She was getting bored of saying it and hated that she had to in the first place.

'Does anyone at work know?'

'Are you going to report me? It could mean the end of my job.' It would definitely mean the end of her time in the offices.

'Don't you think you should tell Mr Newington?'

'He already knows.' She knew that from Mrs Barnes but, ever kind and generous, he hadn't spoken to her about it.

'Then if he hasn't done anything about it, there's nothing for me to do.'

His response surprised her. She wanted to trust his word, trust his kindness, but something was holding her back. The memory of Timothy, of being duped and used, told her to be wary. Still, something inside was telling her she could trust him.

'Do you go to that pub often?' she asked to change the subject.

'Not really. I was only in there to buy a bottle of stout. Then I was going to head back to my lodgings. You saw the

155

reception I got. If I go anywhere, it's to the Irish club, but they don't sell stout. When I saw you and that man—'

'Don Green. I'd stay away from him if I was you. He's a snake.'

'He didn't look exactly respectable.'

'Next time you need stout, go to my ma and pa's in Cannon Street Road. She'll give you some. She always keeps a bottle for me pa and it's better than that place. Safer.'

'And she'll welcome an Irish Catholic, will she?'

'Of course she will. She doesn't care about people's religions or where they come from as long as they're nice and treat people right.'

'I'll bear that in mind. What's Don Green got to do with your brother and the Oclee robbery?'

'I – I can't say.'

'But your brother didn't do it?'

'No.'

Silence filled the air and only their footsteps echoed in the dark. 'Does he have a solicitor?'

'Only a useless one given to him.'

'He should hire his own.'

'He doesn't want one.'

'That's not exactly sensible.'

She laughed at this, which, from his reaction, hadn't been the response he'd been expecting. 'No, I know, but it's . . . complicated.'

'I know you don't want me to ask but what exactly are you doing talking to people like Don Green?'

'I'm trying to clear my brother's name, but no one'll help me. And I don't know what to do now.'

She had exhausted all the avenues of inquiry she could think of. She wasn't a policeman. She wasn't clever enough to find out who had done it. All she wanted was a scrap of information that could throw doubt on her brother's guilt. Surely someone, somewhere knew something that could help her? As the panic and fear receded from her body, her spirits were fading and all she wanted was her bed. She walked without looking, her foot hitting a patch of ice and her body jerked forwards, but before she could fall, a strong arm wrapped around her waist and held her firm.

'Steady now.' His soft voice, the beautiful brogue, tickled her ear. She turned to face him, his body and mouth close to hers, and desire welled inside her. This was unlike any feeling she'd experienced before, infinitely stronger and yet somehow completely natural. It frightened her, and as the shadow of past experience circled, she pulled away, stepping backwards. His hands dropped and he cleared his throat.

'The tube's just down there.'

'I know,' she replied, her voice shaking and uncertain. 'I grew up around here, remember?'

With a small smile and a nod, he walked away, and Caroline carried on in the opposite direction. The ghosts in her mind began to recede and her body replayed the feeling that had surged so strongly, providing a warmth that carried her to the tube station and all the way back to Buckingham Palace. If only she could name it, she might be able to trust it, but her instincts were off and her nerves in tatters. She needed sleep, but she had no idea if it would come that night or not.

Chapter Sixteen

'I just don't think the word "scars" is going to be as helpful as you think it is,' Helen said as they walked across Green Park heading for the St James Tavern, a cosy pub on the corner of Great Windmill Street, just off Shaftesbury Avenue.

The darkness felt lighter tonight, less heavy than it had in recent days. A heavy, incessant drizzle had tapped on the windows throughout the day and washed the remaining banks of snow away, turning them to sludge. Tonight, the sky was clearer, the rain clouds drifting away on the strong wind. The streetlamps lit the still busy path through Green Park, people hurrying into the city to go to the theatre, or coming home, eager to trap themselves inside, safe against the beastly weather.

'Why not?' Caroline asked. 'If that's what Mr Oclee said, it must mean something.'

'But that's sort of my point. It could mean *anything*. That the person who did it had scars on their face—'

'Or their hands.'

'Or he could have said "scared" and the son misheard. I just don't think the police are going to take any notice and the courts certainly won't. They'll throw it out within minutes. I do hate to bring you down,' she added, placing a hand on

Caroline's back. 'But I need to be honest with you. I wouldn't be being your friend otherwise.'

'I know,' Caroline replied with a small smile. Inside she was crushed but she appreciated Helen keeping her feet on the ground. Milly too. There was no point in pinning her hopes on something only to be disappointed. 'And I'm grateful. I can't pretend I'm not frustrated though.'

'A stroke of luck Mr O'Keefe turning up though. I still haven't managed to see him yet. Have you, Milly?'

'No. Not yet. It says a lot that he stepped in to help you. Perhaps he's not quite as awful as you thought.'

'He was kinder than I expected,' she admitted.

'What's he look like, Caroline?' Milly asked.

She hesitated, her cheeks burning as she remembered seeing him so closely when he stopped her falling. How for a moment she had thought about kissing him. 'He just looks like a fella in a suit. Same as they all do.'

'But does he have brown hair or blond? Blue eyes or green?'

'Tall or short?' Helen added.

'He's tall with brown hair and blue eyes. Too much hair, actually. He could do with having it cut.'

'Right,' Milly said, smiling a little.

'Handsome?' Helen added.

'If you like that sort of thing.'

'What sort of thing?' Helen giggled as she said it. 'A decent chap who stands up for a woman. That sounds fine to me.'

Caroline decided a change of subject was in order. 'Did

159

you see Mr Newington and Mrs Barnes sloping off for a walk this evening?'

Milly scowled. 'No, when was that? It hasn't stopped raining.'

'As soon as the office closed. He went rushing off saying he needed some air as there was a break in the weather. Next thing I see is him and Mrs Barnes headed out into the gardens for a walk.'

'I was with Robert,' Milly explained. 'My book arrived, and I've been reading all about what you're supposed to do to organise a proper wedding. There's so much. Invitations, decorations, food, bridesmaids, groomsmen. It all seems a bit much to me.'

'What does Robert think?' Helen asked.

'He thinks we should keep it simple. And I agree. We've got plenty of time to get organised though.' Milly turned to Helen. 'I'm still not sure about this though. Jake's playing games with you asking to meet you here.'

Jake had sent Helen a letter, short and sweet, saying he had information and asking to meet her at the St James Tavern. This was where, only five months before, Helen had taken the brave and unusual step of asking him to take her out sometime. It had been the fateful move that had started everything.

She brushed her dark hair back from her face. 'I know he is. And I don't like it any more than you do, but we need to see what he knows. It's worth the risk to help Johnny.'

Milly was right: Jake was playing games, trying to manipulate Helen, asking her to meet there to garner some sort of reaction from her. It was despicable and desperate and Caroline hated putting her friend through this for her brother's sake. But she and Milly would be there to protect her as they had when they'd met for tea. Jake wouldn't get his claws into her again. Not with them around.

The busy thoroughfare of Piccadilly was bustling with people and a steady stream of traffic. The streetlights, shop windows and headlamps twinkled in the darkness, reflecting in the puddles left by the snow and the rain-smattered streets. Though no one Caroline knew had a car, they were everywhere here, along with the familiar London buses that all sounded like they were on their last legs, people hanging off the back as they jumped on at the last minute. They passed a shop window full of beautiful dresses and women's suits. How she wished she could afford one, knowing it would imbue her with confidence the next time she walked into work, but the prices written on the small brown tags were well beyond her. She'd have to make do and mend as usual. Other shop windows were beginning to display Christmas gifts – hat boxes as large as a wheel on one of the palace coaches, toy soldiers for the children, or smiling dolls in need of dressing up, but the event itself still seemed a long way away.

They'd only been in the St James Tavern a few times, and it was as busy as it had been in the height of the summer when she and Milly had first watched Helen approach Jake. The idea of doing such a thing still shocked Caroline. At the time, her mouth had hung open as Helen had told them what she'd said. It just wasn't the done thing for a woman to approach a man. Never mind being so forward as to make the suggestion of a date herself. Caroline wondered if Helen regretted it now given where it had left her, and glanced at her as they entered the busy pub. Helen's smile had vanished as she stepped over the threshold, and there was a tightness to her eyes. She looked around as if replaying the moment in her mind and when she didn't move, they urged her on to an empty table in the corner.

'He'll be late,' Helen said as they settled with a gin and lime each to wait, throwing off their coats and headscarves. Helen had opted for soda water as her body rejected certain things.

'Because he wants to make you wait?' Milly asked.

She nodded. 'I think so.'

'Timothy used to do the same,' Caroline added, staring into her drink, unable to meet Milly's eye. 'I didn't realise at the time, but I've thought about it a lot since. It kept me on the back foot. Kept him in control. That's what it was all about to him. Control.'

Helen reached out and took her hand. 'I don't think Jake's thinking like that exactly, but I do think he's angry that I don't want him back. That I'm building a life without him.'

'Do you think about him much?' Milly asked Helen.

'Not really. I think about his wife more.'

'I keep thinking about Timothy,' Caroline said, grateful to rid herself of the load that had been pressing down on her. She met Milly's eye, sharing the pain. She removed her hand from under Helen's, feeling the need to fidget, and she twisted her glass on the spot, turning it around and around, watching the liquid swirl. 'I never used to, but recently he's started popping into my head more and more.'

Milly sipped her drink before speaking. 'Things are

changing for you. Perhaps it's brought everything to the surface.'

'Maybe.'

Helen said, 'It's important you face these feelings though, Caroline. Don't try and push them away or they'll simply come back up later.'

'I . . .' She faltered, unsure if she even knew how to finish the sentence. 'I don't think I know how.'

'Talk about them,' Milly said softly. 'As soon as I told Robert what had happened, about how Timothy tried it on, I felt better.'

She remembered Milly telling her how she'd confessed everything about Timothy to Robert. It had brought them closer, but she wasn't sure she'd ever be able to speak to someone about it all.

Caroline bit her lip, wanting to release the messy thoughts in her head but also not wanting to face them, fearful of letting go of her control. 'It's strange. It's like there's a shadow of him following me – haunting me like a ghost. We all know the palace is supposed to be haunted – the ghost of a monk from when it was a monastery, that major who shot himself when there was a scandal over his divorce.'

They all knew the tales. King Edward VII's private secretary had taken his own life in one of the offices and now no one ever wanted to go in there. It wasn't even cleaned that often.

'But I know they're not real. Timothy is, though, and he's always in my head somewhere, on the edges of my thoughts, and when I stop pushing him away, he slinks in. I get scared all over again, no matter where I am or who I'm with.'

Milly's voice was calm and reassuring. 'Timothy won't be allowed near the palace ever again. You're safe from him now.'

'Does it happen when Mr O'Keefe is around?' Helen asked. 'Does he make you uneasy?'

'Sometimes. Most of the time I feel all right around him. I don't understand why it isn't all the time.'

'Neither do I,' Milly replied. 'But it was the same for me too and it still happens now sometimes if I'm walking anywhere alone and pass a man. I always worry he's going to do something. But you have to remember that not every man is like Timothy. That's what I've been telling myself. Robert isn't. Your pa isn't. Mr Newington isn't. And, from what you've said, Mr O'Keefe isn't either. Especially given what you said about him walking you home and stepping in with that man.'

'Johnny isn't like that either,' Helen added, immediately dropping her eyes under Caroline's gaze.

'I know what you're saying,' Caroline replied, biting her lip. 'But Timothy wasn't like it to start with either.'

Milly gave a sad smile. 'No, he wasn't.'

'So how do I know things aren't going to go the same way?'

'You shouldn't stop trusting people just because of him, Caroline.'

'Trust has to be earned though,' Helen added, the colour that had flushed her cheeks as she spoke of Johnny fading a little. 'My advice would be to take your time to trust people. Take as long as you need. Eventually, you'll put Timothy behind you and the shadow of what he did won't follow you around any more. I know you can do it. You're one of the strongest people I know. And one of the bravest.'

'Me?' Caroline had never thought of herself as particularly strong or brave. She was a survivor, that was all.

'Yes. You've worked hard to better yourself and your life. You've faced horrible challenges and haven't let them beat you. You're even doing everything you can for your brother. He's lucky to have you as a sister and we're lucky to have you as a friend.'

Warmed by the compliment and the fire burning brightly in the grate, Caroline sipped her drink with her friends until Jake finally appeared. As Helen suspected he was late by twenty minutes.

'Sorry to keep you waiting. I was chasing a story.'

'That's fine,' Helen said, keen to show that his tactics weren't working.

'My editor's giving me better assignments. Articles with my name on them.'

If he thought this was going to impress Helen, it had the opposite effect. She looked away and Caroline spoke instead.

'Did you find anything out?'

'Yes. Quite a lot actually. Let me just get a drink.' He went to the bar and the three of them exchanged glances, knowing it was another ploy to put him in control of the situation. He returned a few moments later with a pint of bitter, the dark liquid sloshing over the side of the glass as he sat down. He removed his hat before pulling out his notebook, then licked his finger and began rifling through the pages.

'So . . . ?' Helen prodded and he glanced at her with both

annoyance and sadness in his eyes. His gaze flicked down to her stomach – to his unborn child – and he cleared his throat.

'It seems Mr Whitelock has a bit of a reputation amongst my fellow reporters.'

'What for?' Caroline asked, edging forwards in her seat. Was this it? The proof she needed that someone other than her brother could have committed this awful crime?

'During the war there was a lot of looting and robberies. Some people – the worst types of people – took advantage of the chaos caused by the bombings and air raids to rob and steal.'

'That's disgusting,' Milly said. 'I remember people talking about it.'

'And they think Arthur Whitelock was one of them?' Caroline asked, her heart leaping at this possible new lead.

'Not exactly,' Jake replied. 'They certainly think he had something to do with a number of cases at that time but not all were in the East End. Some were further afield, and they took different forms so there was never the same MO.'

'MO?'

'Modus operandi. It means the same method of doing it.'

'I don't understand,' Caroline said, frowning. 'Was he involved in them or not?'

'My colleague who reported during the war said that the people he talked to at the time suspected Arthur Whitelock was involved. Not necessarily getting his hands dirty himself but maybe directing operations or running a gang, but the police never even looked into him because he was such a fine upstanding citizen and they were only rumours. No one would openly speak out.'

166

'Why didn't he serve?' Milly asked.

'Flat feet. But he was in the Home Guard. It would have given him ample opportunity to scope out potential houses.'

'Was it always jewellery these people took?' Caroline asked.

'No. It could be anything he could sell on via antiques dealers or pawn shops. Statues, clocks, anything valuable that might make some money.'

Caroline's mind worked through the information Jake had provided. 'But is there anything to connect him to the Oclee robbery?'

'Good question,' Helen added. 'He might have done things during the war but that doesn't mean he still is now. He has a thriving warehouse business, doesn't he? Why would he risk it?'

Jake took a long slug of his drink and wiped the foam from his top lip. 'There are rumours that his business isn't doing as well as it once did. And rebuilding the docks is taking a lot of time and money.'

Caroline added. 'Do the police know anything about all this?'

Jake shook his head. 'Everyone my colleague spoke to back then said no one would grass and the police wouldn't have been interested anyway. There were too few men and too much work to do. I don't think it ever came to their attention. And even if it had, so many crimes of that sort went unpunished. There just wasn't the manpower to chase them all down.'

'But it's not like that now,' Caroline said, her spirits lifting. 'We could tell them.'

'Tell them what? That some people who won't be named

and are most likely dead said something to a journalist almost ten years ago? That they once suspected Arthur Whitelock, but had no evidence to accuse him of anything?' Caroline felt her skin flush with embarrassment, as though the heat of the fire had reached out and touched her cheeks. He softened. 'I'm sorry, Miss Stratton, but nothing was said in the past and there's nothing to connect Mr Whitelock to anything now.'

'He has two vans—' Caroline said and Helen noisily cleared her throat, stopping her just in time. Seizing on her warning, she began again, 'Mr Oclee's son said he saw one being driven away and his pa kept whispering the word "scars", like whoever hit him had scars on his hands as Mr Whitelock does.'

'When did you speak to the Oclees?' Jake asked.

'The other night.'

'And they told you that?' He flicked to a clean page of his notebook and made a note. Helen's face pinched in disdain. 'What else did they say?'

Milly ignored him. 'Everyone who works on the docks has scars on their hands, just as ours are always red raw.'

Caroline looked at her fingers. The nails were growing now she'd moved to the offices and the redness was fading. Her palms were no longer covered with callouses and cuts. However much she hated to admit it, Milly was right. 'So you've not found anything *now* to connect Mr Whitelock with the burglary?'

'There's nothing, I'm afraid. Not that any of my contacts know of. He's squeaky clean. A fine upstanding citizen.'

'So we're back to square one.' She sank down in her chair.

'What you need is hard evidence. Someone to place him

at the scene. A witness to say he wasn't at home at the time of the robbery.'

There was no way she could get information like that.

'And if it wasn't him, then you need to point the finger squarely at someone else, but from what I've read of the case, the fact your brother went out for a walk that night, at the right time, coupled with the police's need to solve crimes quickly, means they're not looking any further.'

'So there are no other suspects?' Helen asked.

'None. Which tells me they either think it was one of the gangs they're already aware of and can't prove it – and they're happy for an innocent man to go to goal – or they do genuinely believe it was Johnny Stratton. I'm sorry.'

Her attempts to clear him seemed doomed. Caroline lifted her head and out of politeness said, 'Thanks for your help.'

Jake nodded before turning to Helen. He opened his mouth to speak but she replied before he could. 'Good-bye, Jake.'

That same regretful look washed over his features. He reached for his hat and walked away. When the door closed behind him, Helen visibly relaxed, her shoulders falling. She cradled her stomach as if it too had survived the ordeal of seeing him again.

Caroline said, 'I'm going to Ma and Pa's on Sunday. Why don't you pop by and Ma can take you over the road and introduce you to the midwife she knows.'

'Would you mind?'

'Course not.'

'So what do we do now? About Johnny?' Milly asked.

'I don't know,' Caroline replied, tapping her fingernails

on the tabletop. They made a pleasing sound where they'd grown, but it did nothing to distract her from the thought of her brother languishing in prison.

'Perhaps', Helen said, concern taming the brightness of her eyes, 'it's time I spoke to that solicitor. If there's no hope of proving he didn't do it, then we need to look at what else we can do. Perhaps they'll be able to get his sentence reduced?'

And though they all looked at each other, none of them had anything to say: no words of encouragement, no new ideas that would help prove Johnny's innocence. In silence, they finished their drinks and left the pub.

Chapter Seventeen

The fire in the parlour of Caroline's parents' house burned low, giving off barely enough heat to warm her cold toes. She watched as the tiny flames flickered and danced lethargically. The snow had eased. On days like this, when the temperature wasn't so bad and the rain trickled lazily down the windowpane, they only used what they had to, saving the rest for the winter to come. With how bad it had been, there was no telling how much worse it was going to get, and her ma and pa had always been sensible.

Caroline hugged a mug of tea close to her chest, realising that the comforting atmosphere she'd always associated with home was all the more notable by its absence. Conversation was laboured, stopping and starting as if they didn't have the energy to speak. Normally her ma would talk nineteen to the dozen about the neighbours, the gossip she'd heard, the comings and goings of the street. Her pa's loud laugh, as big and bold as he was, would fill the house.

Her ma had lost weight. She'd always been thin, but her clothes hung loose around her shoulders and her wrists hadn't looked strong enough to peel the potatoes as she stood in the kitchen preparing dinner. Pa, too, seemed aged by what was happening to Johnny. He was bent and tired, as though the life was draining from him into the floor, disappearing into the depths of the earth. Dark smudges sat under both their eyes. Their cheeks were sallow, their skin lined and deep-set with wrinkles.

This had only ever happened once before, when Caroline's grandma – her ma's ma – had died. Ma had taken it hard – she'd been as close to her ma as Caroline was to hers – but after a week or so, she'd slowly begun to climb out of the sadness, focusing her attentions on her children. Now one of her children was in trouble Ma had no one else to focus on, and it consumed her, blocking the light from her life, leaving her in perpetual darkness.

As the prolonged silence grew uncomfortable, Caroline said, 'Has Nancy been round?'

Ma nodded. 'A few times. You know 'ow busy she is.'

'What's she said about it all? She hasn't even written to me. I wrote to her, but ain't heard nothing back.'

'She's got 'er own life now, Caroline. She said she was sorry about Johnny and to tell her what 'appens.'

'Was that it?' Her ma nodded. 'Nothing about helping or when she'd be over to see you?' She tutted, earning a scowl from both her parents.

Ma defended her. 'She can't be comin' over all the time. And what could she do anyway?'

'She could give you some support. Be here for you. Offer money for a solicitor or something.'

'She probably can't afford to.'

'No, but she can afford to go out with that fella of hers.' Nancy, her sister, had always been a selfish beast. Caroline normally kept her mouth shut about it. They'd been a close family, and it was important that they pulled together now.

'Has Johnny written to you or anything?' she asked, watching her ma carefully to see how she coped with the mention of him.

'Only to say he's fine and that prison food ain't that bad. Nothin' about what 'appens now.' Pa reached out from his armchair and held Ma's arm. She patted his hand in return.

'I've asked your pa to go to the station and ask but he won't.'

'I will,' he said, removing his hand and tapping his pipe, loosening the packed tobacco to refill it. 'It's just I already know what they'll say.'

'That he needs a solicitor,' Caroline added. Her pa nodded. 'Helen said the same thing.'

''E gets one assigned by the court, apparently.'

'But he's rubbish. He needs a good one.'

'I don't know 'ow we'll afford that,' Ma said. 'I'll 'ave to pawn me weddin' ring. It's all we've got.'

The idea stung Caroline deeply. If only she earned more. If only she could get a loan from the bank. 'I heard you spoke to Mr Oclee's son,' she said to her pa.

His head shot up and then he glanced at his wife.

'Where d'you 'ear that?' He was pretending to be offhand, but his eyes flicked to his wife again, and he shook his head. 'I asked about 'im, but I didn't go and see 'im.' He suddenly stood, holding his pipe in both hands. 'Better clean this outside or your ma'll 'ave my guts for garters, won't you, Lils?'

She barely looked up.

Understanding his meaning, Caroline followed. In the tiny garden, nothing more than a patch of a mud with the privy at the end, she shivered. A washing line was strung across the narrow space and when she'd arrived, she and her pa had rescued the line of linen her ma had left hanging in the rain. At least the rain had paused now.

As they hadn't had time to speak about it then, she said, 'It's not like Ma to leave the washing.'

'She almost left it overnight the other day.'

'She always said that was common.'

'I'm worried about 'er. She's finding it 'ard – this thing with Johnny. Some neighbours won't talk to us no more. There's whispers when we walk down the street. Mutterin's. Someone even said they always knew 'e'd go that way.' Using a teaspoon he left in the garden for the exact purpose, he cleaned the old tobacco out of his pipe, took out a pouch from his pocket and began to refill it. A moment later, the sound of a match striking echoed in the quiet garden and a spark of light lit the darkening sky. 'But 'e ain't that bad. I don't understand it, treacle. I really don't. It's killin' your ma.'

'I know.' She glanced back at the house and took the once happy home in again.

The yellowing brick was dark with grime. Tufts of grass grew in the guttering and a few tiles were missing from theirs and a neighbour's roof. Voices could be heard from the nearby properties. Chortles of laughter that had once existed in her own house. From one house, she heard a tired mother encouraging the children to be good or Father Christmas would bring them nothing but a lump of coal.

'You did go to Oclee's, didn't you, Pa?'

He sighed heavily. 'I just wanted to know if they'd actually seen Johnny there.'

She picked up an abandoned wooden peg from the ground and placed it in her pocket. 'They hadn't.'

''Ow d'ya know?' He puffed out a lungful of smoke and she watched it drift away on the air.

'Because I went there too. I just needed to know, same as you. I wanted to see if there was anything that might help Johnny.'

'Ya can't go gettin' involved in this, treacle. I know you wanna 'elp, but you can't risk your job. You've worked too 'ard for it and Johnny wouldn't want you to neither.'

'But he's my brother. How can I leave him in prison?' She felt the tears welling at the back of her eyes and willed them away. The last thing her parents needed was to see her upset. They'd only worry about her too. 'We can't afford a solicitor. What else are we going to do?'

He stepped towards her and wrapped a hand around her shoulder, pulling her in close. 'I'll sort it out. I promise.'

But she knew full well he couldn't keep that oath. The tremor in his voice told her he didn't believe it himself.

'If he were middle-class or lived in Belgravia or Kensington, they'd never treat him like they have. They'd investigate properly. They'd find more evidence one way or the other. I'm no policeman but it seems to me they're assuming a lot.'

'I know, treacle. I know. Come on now, don't upset yourself. Your ma'll see.'

Just then, Ma appeared at the back door.

'Caroline, your friend Helen's 'ere to see you.' She could make out Helen's form in the kitchen doorway and headed inside. 'Well,' Ma said, brightening now they had guests. She brushed her hands down her clothes and, realising she still had her apron on, untied it quickly. 'Make the introductions then, Caroline.'

'Helen, this is my ma, Lillian—'

'Everyone calls me Lils.' She stuck out her hand and Helen shook it.

'And this is my Pa, Terry.' He nodded a greeting and smiled kindly. 'You two, this is my friend Helen Hill.'

'Pleased to meet you,' Helen replied almost shyly. 'I'm terribly sorry about what's happened to Johnny. It's awfully unfair.'

'Would you like some tea, darlin'?' Ma asked as tears pricked her eyes. She spun to grab the kettle and Helen gave Caroline an alarmed look. Caroline shook her head, telling Helen not to worry.

'Tea would be wonderful, thank you. It's still terribly cold, isn't it?'

'Brass monkeys,' Pa replied, signalling to the small table at the end of the kitchen. Helen and Caroline both sat down.

'Caroline said I should pop in because you know a mid-wife who might be able to help me?'

'That I do, darlin'.' Her mind focusing, Ma brightened. ''Ow's the babby gettin' on?'

'Good, I think. I can feel him or her moving now.'

'I always loved that,' Ma said, placing the kettle on the hob and holding a match to the gas. 'Johnny was the worst. Always kickin', 'e was. I knew 'e'd be trouble from the first time 'e moved. Gave me sleepless nights then just as 'e does now.'

'Now, now,' Pa said, moving back to her side and embracing her. 'Don't upset yourself, Lils.'

She wiped her eyes. 'Sorry, Miss Hill. You'll have to excuse me.'

'Please call me Helen.'

Pa took over the making of the tea.

'Now,' Ma continued, gathering herself. 'Let me tell you about Cherry Baxter over the road. She's ever so lovely. Kind as they come but some people don't want 'er lookin' after them, all because of the colour of 'er skin, which is madness to me because she's ever such a good midwife and knows 'ow to look after babies.'

'She's black?' Helen asked.

'That ain't no problem, is it?'

'No! Of course not. Not for me.' Caroline knew she was telling the truth. Helen was, like Caroline's family, unjudgemental and accepted people for who and what they were. If she didn't like someone it was because of their personality, some character flaw, not because of superficial qualities. 'I'd be very grateful to meet her. Have people really refused to have her as their midwife?'

Ma nodded sadly. ''Fraid so. One woman she told me about was awful rude. If I'd used any of the words she'd said, I'd 'ave 'ad me mouth washed out with soap. And it's a terrible shame. She once saved a baby's life.'

'My goodness. What happened?'

'Poor little lamb 'ad the cord wrapped round its neck. It weren't breathin' when it came out and was all blue. Without panickin', she got it breathin' again, wrapped it up and 'anded it to the mother pink and squealin' like any other newborn. These people ought to be ashamed of themselves. Judgin' others when they ain't got no right to.'

'I couldn't agree more,' Helen replied, her hand slipping underneath her rounding tummy.

'Shall we go over after a cuppa tea then? I've told 'er about you and what 'appened, so she already knows your situation.'

Helen nodded enthusiastically. 'Thank you. That saves me explaining everything and feeling embarrassed.'

'You've nothin' to be embarrassed about. That man who was married should be embarrassed.'

Caroline watched the exchange with a small smile. It was about time Helen sorted out some professional care for her and the baby. As the pregnancy progressed, she was going to need support, and there was the birth to think about too.

They drank the tea, making idle chit chat about Buckingham Palace, the telephone exchange and Helen's landlady, who was becoming increasingly curious about Helen's figure, making comments about her weight and the fullness of Helen's face.

'I know I'll have to tell her at some point,' Helen said. By now she was totally at ease in their company, and felt able to speak frankly. 'But I'm hoping by then she'll have some sympathy for me and won't throw a newborn baby out on to the streets.'

'It's a gamble,' Pa said. 'Some people can be nice, but others can be 'orrible. There's no tellin' sometimes.'

'I don't really have any other choice,' Helen replied with a shrug. 'All I can do is hope that she's not as nasty as she seems.'

Ma pushed her empty cup next to the teapot. 'Shall we

get off then? You'll want to be 'eading 'ome before it gets too dark.'

Caroline watched as they departed, Ma fussing as if Helen were one of her own children. She'd be asking after that baby every time Caroline visited, but at least it distracted her. It had been good to see her smiling again, even for this short while. Caroline and her pa returned to the parlour. He threw a couple more coals on to the fire which was nearly out and prodded it with the poker.

Just as they sat down, there was a knock at the door.

'Who can that be?' Pa asked the air as he stood up. 'D'you think your ma's forgotten somethin' and sent Helen across for it?'

'I can't think what they'd need,' Caroline said, standing too. 'But then, I don't know anything about babies.'

'Anythin' I knew I forgot years ago,' Pa said with a grin as he stepped into the hall and opened the door. 'What d'you want now?'

Caroline's stomach dropped. Her pa's tone had changed so rapidly she knew something was wrong. He walked back into the parlour followed by the two policemen who'd arrested Johnny before. A chill ran over her skin, and she drew her arms up and across her chest as if it would protect her.

'We've some news regarding your son, Mr Stratton.'

'What news?'

Caroline's heart jumped into her throat. Was there another suspect? Had someone come forward with information that proved his innocence? Were they now pursuing the man with scars on his hands?

'I'm afraid your son's charge has now been increased to theft, robbery and – murder.'

The word echoed around the quiet room. Caroline became acutely aware of the ticking of the small clock on the parlour wall that had kept time since she was a child. The movement of the hands was overly loud, painful in her ears.

'Mr Oclee Senior died of his injuries in hospital earlier this afternoon.'

Pa crumpled, his legs giving way the moment the words were spoken. Caroline rushed to him and even one of the policemen stepped forward to help. Together they eased him into a chair. His skin was white, all colour faded from his face except for the dark circles under his eyes that were even more pronounced than normal.

Caroline heard the door from the hallway burst open once more and her ma ran in, followed by Helen.

'What is it?' Ma asked, staring between the stony faces of the policemen and the top of Pa's head. 'Cherry saw you through the window. What's 'appened?'

Pa stared down at the threadbare carpet, studying the thin fabric of his slippers and his shaking hands.

'What's 'appened?' Ma asked again, her voice rising, growing shrill and panicked. 'Have you caught who really did it?'

The policemen looked at Caroline as if he expected her to deliver the news. When she didn't speak, he repeated what he'd told them just moments before, using the same words, the same monotonous, formal tone.

'No!' Ma fell to her knees. 'No! Not my boy. 'E didn't do it. 'E wouldn't. Why won't you believe 'im? Why won't you 'elp 'im?' Her body was racked with sobs and Helen knelt down beside her, holding her tightly as she rocked and shuddered.

Caroline stared hard at the policemen.

'I'm sorry,' he said and backed into the hall.

She followed, anger overtaking her. She wanted to shout, to make him feel as powerless as they did. As powerless as Johnny was while all this pain and anguish was inflicted on those around him.

'You're wrong. Totally wrong,' she said to his back. 'My brother never hurt anyone. All he did was—' Again she had to stop herself just in time. She didn't care about Don Green after the way he'd treated her, but his wife would suffer if he were put away. His children would lose out and goodness knows they had so little as it was. 'All he did was go for a walk. Have you looked into Arthur Whitelock? He has scars on his hands and Mr Oclee heard his pa whisper that word before he was taken away.'

At this the policeman paused, assessing her. She lifted her chin, refusing to be intimidated by the man in uniform.

'And where did you hear that?'

'People around here talk.'

'I'm very sorry, miss,' was all he said in reply.

'And what about during the war? It was known White-lock was up to no good back then, but nobody did anything. You should all be ashamed of yourselves.'

They left, closing the door gently behind them.

Caroline returned to the living room and helped Helen pick her ma up off the floor. She was limp and heavy: a dead weight. They moved her to the sofa, and she collapsed down on it, folding over, burying her face in her skirt. Pa still hadn't raised his head.

One thought circled in Caroline's mind stronger than any other, forcing its way to the front and pushing aside all others, driving the pain, anger and fear behind it. Murder was one of the very few crimes that still carried the death sentence.

Murder.

The word resounded in her head like the echo of a drum. It pounded on her skull and sent lights flashing in front of her eyes. She squeezed them shut, yet they remained on the underside of her eyelids, blinding her.

Murder.

Johnny Stratton – her brother – was accused of murder.

Would he hang too?

December 1952

Chapter Eighteen

The night before, Caroline had begged Helen not to tell Milly and Mrs Barnes that her brother's charge had increased. She knew it made no sense and remembered how guilty she'd felt for not telling them when he'd first been arrested. How she could have had their love and support then. But she couldn't stop shame from flowing like blood around her body. Helen had remained calm and unflappable. She'd counselled her against keeping secrets, knowing from her own experience how difficult it made life.

On her return to Buckingham Palace, Caroline had gathered her courage and taken her friends from the Household Lounge to Mrs Barnes's quarters, where she'd admitted the new and shocking turn that had befallen her family.

This morning, on the first day of December, Christmas had suddenly arrived at Buckingham Palace.

Despite her ever-present fears, Caroline, Milly and Mrs Barnes watched from an upstairs window as tree after tree was delivered, ready to be potted and placed in the different areas of the palace. Three trees had already been sited in the Grand Hall, and would soon be decorated by a special team, while others had been positioned in the State Rooms and the royal family's private apartments. Fir garlands would soon be swinging in great, berry-dotted swags from the Grand Staircase and huge floral displays of red poinsettias and deep green foliage were ready to decorate halls, corridors and smaller ante rooms.

Caroline gave Milly a sympathetic look. As beautiful as it was, and though it gave the palace an enchanted air, the pine needles were a pain for those whose role was to keep Buckingham Palace clean. They constantly needed sweeping up and had a habit of hiding under rugs and furniture only to magically appear as soon as you'd finished. She wasn't going to miss that this Christmas, though she still didn't know how much longer she'd be needed in the office. Another person had arrived back that morning, returned from sick leave, and though she hadn't had to change desks, she was becoming increasingly worried her new role was about to come to an end.

With Buckingham Palace becoming even more magical as the smell of pine trees filled the rooms, talk of the Christmas dance was increasing and the palace held a new kind of excitement, though Caroline couldn't muster much enthusiasm for it at present. Her thoughts wouldn't stray from her brother and how he must have crumpled when he'd been told the news.

Milly brushed down the formal dress uniform as Mrs Barnes inspected her.

'Lovely,' Mrs Barnes said. 'Now, the family arrive back from Sandringham any minute, so we better get ready to line up. Caroline, you should get back to your office.'

'I can't believe you don't have to line up outside in this freezing weather,' Milly grumbled.

186

Caroline managed a small smile. 'No, but we do have to line up in the corridor.' She too was wearing her old formal uniform. The navy dress was the smartest thing she owned. 'Will I pass muster, Mrs Barnes?'

'Course you will, Caroline. You look pretty as a picture.' The older woman cupped her cheek and Caroline felt a surge of emotion so strong her eyes teared.

She'd been greeted with words of comfort the night before, as she knew she would be, but they'd done little to assuage her fears and her night had been restless.

'Now, now.' Mrs Barnes pulled her in for a hug, squeezing tightly and then releasing her. 'Let's have none of that. We women are stronger than that, aren't we?' Caroline nodded and took a deep breath before a tear could escape. 'Come and have tea with us later and we'll figure out what to do next, but right now, off you go.'

Caroline trudged towards the office, her eyes down on the crimson carpet beneath her feet, finding Mr O'Keefe along the way.

'No chance of hiding in the secret corridors this morning is there?'

'Afraid not,' she replied, trying to brighten.

'Is everything all right? You look like you've been crying.'

'I'm fine,' she said, turning away from him. She might have told her friends, but she wasn't ready to tell anyone else. Shame closed her throat and she felt as if she were shrinking before him. She changed the subject. 'I quite like seeing the Queen and the royal family up close. It doesn't happen as much in this job.'

'Do you miss it?'

'A bit. But I won't miss standing outside in the Quadrangle in this weather.'

'No.' He chuckled. 'I bet you won't. What's she like? The Queen.'

'I've only met her a couple of times, but she's . . . kind. She remembers you. They all do. Princess Margaret, the Duke of Edinburgh. But Queen Elizabeth The Queen Mother's always been my favourite. She's cheeky. And she likes to laugh.'

'Stuck in that little office, we don't get to hear as much of that as other people.'

'If you don't like it, why don't you go and work somewhere else?' She kept her tone neutral knowing that he could easily take it as a criticism and start a row, and she simply didn't have the energy for that morning.

'An Irishman in London? You think I can just go out and get another job, like that—' He clicked his fingers, though his tone too was calm. There was even a hint of humour in his eyes. 'I was lucky to get this job – more than lucky, thanks to Mr Newington – I don't think my luck'll last anywhere else.'

They walked along in silence, nearing the door to the office.

'What's Ireland like?' Caroline asked. 'I'd love to go there one day. I've heard Irish music and some of the songs you sing. We used to have a neighbour who came from Galway. I loved hearing her when she hung out her washing. She was always singing these beautiful songs.'

'It's a grand place,' he replied, his accent thickening as he relaxed and fond memories lifted his spirits.

'Are your family still there?'

'Most of them. My brother came over to Liverpool, but I don't see him – or any of them – as much as I'd like to.'

'You have a big family, don't you?'

'Five brothers and two sisters.'

'That sounds like hard work,' she said with a laugh that brightened her mood. 'I've one sister and one brother . . .' She couldn't finish the sentence as her mind swam with the possibility that she wouldn't have a brother for much longer if he was executed for murder. She felt sick just thinking about it and looked up to see Mr O'Keefe watching her from the corner of his eye. 'Will you go home for Christmas?'

'No, I don't think so.' His voice rang with sadness. 'I'd like to, but it costs. I'll send some money back though. I always do.'

'So what will you do Christmas Day?'

'I don't know.' He laughed but it was humourless. 'Eat plum pudding on my own, I imagine. Go to church. Maybe go to the Irish club.'

'You should speak to Mrs Chadwick, the cook. If you give her your ration card, she might be able to let you eat here. She's not really supposed to, but she's done it for a friend of mine before.'

Helen often ate meals with them though really only staff who lived on site were supposed to have their meals provided.

'I might do that,' he replied, pushing his hands into his pockets.

'Ah, there you are,' Mr Newington said as they entered the office. 'The cars have just entered the main gates. Quickly.'

He shooed them into the corridor, and they stood side by side waiting.

As Caroline's hand hung by her side next to Mr O'Keefe's she could feel the heat of his skin and had a sudden impulse to stretch out a finger and touch him. She wanted contact. Something physical. A closeness. An intimacy. She pushed the thought away and brought her hands up, the fingers of one hand toying with the other. He glanced over and then turned his attention to Barbara, who was chattering away on his other side. Caroline tried to make sense of her feelings, to understand them in light of the uncontrollable fear that sometimes gripped her, but she couldn't. It was too messy. Too difficult. All she knew was that sometimes she quite liked Mr O'Keefe and found him attractive, and yet at other times he was difficult and unfriendly. She didn't need another relationship where she was always on the back foot, always confused. She needed someone sturdy and honest, like Robert.

Like the ripple of a wave, the row of people fell silent, and before long the Queen came into view. Behind her, the Duke of Edinburgh walked with Princess Margaret. She caught a glimpse of Peter Townsend, one of the Queen's equerries and Princess Margaret's supposed lover. He quickly rushed off in a different direction.

Men's heads bowed and women curtseyed as the Queen made her way along the line. She was dressed in her travelling clothes of a tweed skirt and jacket with sensible shoes. Princess Margaret looked more fashionable in a day dress with matching coat and a string of pearls at the base of her throat. She was laughing and smiling, though looking to see where Peter Townsend had gone.

When it came to Caroline, the Queen paused. 'I am very glad to see you still here, Caroline.'

'Thank you, Your Majesty.'

'And how are you finding things?'

'Very good, ma'am. I'm enjoying it a lot.'

'Good.' The Queen studied her, her eyes lingering on Caroline for a moment too long, though her expression didn't change. Caroline wondered what she was thinking. Was it her clothes, or her sallow pallor and tired eyes that had drawn the Queen's attention? Whatever it was, the Queen moved on, and Caroline was left wondering if she had imagined the whole thing. Perhaps she was just paranoid, or imagining an intimacy that wasn't really there.

Mr O'Keefe seemed surprised when the Queen greeted him by name too. He stammered a reply and Caroline had to smother a laugh. He seemed bemused, like a child staring at snow for the first time.

Within seconds it was over, and they went back to their desks.

'Told you she was kind,' Caroline said as they both returned their attention to the piles of papers on their desks.

'I'd no idea she knew my name.' His features softened, and his pale, almost water-blue eyes lit up, making something inside her flutter.

'You seem a bit star-struck.'

'She's never spoken to me before.'

'Maybe you're doing better than you think here?' She

risked a smile to show she was teasing and again something stirred inside her. 'I meant to ask, does the office get decorated for Christmas? All the State Rooms do. It would cheer this place up a bit to have a paper chain or two.'

'Not normally, but you could ask Mr Newington. He seems excited for Christmas this year. You should ask him.'

Caroline resolved to – if she was still there when the time came – and then work began in earnest. Caroline was absorbed in her task of typing up various reports and press statements when a footman in full uniform who looked decidedly put out entered the office.

'The Queen would like to see Miss Stratton.'

Caroline swallowed. Her face grew hot, and she glanced at Mr Newington.

'Oh, right. I see. Well, off you go, Miss Stratton.'

'Someone is the Queen's pet, aren't they?' Miss Western added, earning a throat-clearing from Mr Newington.

Caroline stood, her legs shaking, and followed the footman out of the room. She knew the Queen wouldn't have given any indication as to why she wanted to see Caroline, so there was no point in asking. Head down, as if she were being sent to the headmaster's office, she followed through the corridors, studying the plush red carpet, taking note of the priceless pictures on the walls.

Eventually, she came to the Queen's study and the footman knocked, waited for a response and, once the word 'Enter' was heard, opened the door with a soft click.

'Ah, Caroline. Do sit down.'

The Queen sat behind her large mahogany desk complete with two telephones and the notorious red despatch box. She placed some papers back inside it and closed the lid. Behind her was a large undecorated Christmas tree, the heavy green branches beginning to drop from where it had been tightly wrapped for transportation.

Caroline slid into the wooden chair opposite and her limbs began to tremble. She'd watched the Queen from a distance and had even once seen her speak to Milly very personally, but this sort of contact was out of Caroline's depth. She was a girl from the East End, and up till recently had been a cleaner. What had separated her out for such special attention? She hoped she wasn't about to get sacked.

Clasping her hands together, the young Queen smiled warmly. Her eyes were kind and the smile she gave genuine.

'I wished to speak with you and make sure everything was all right.'

'With me, Your Majesty? Yes, yes, everything's fine. Absolutely fine.' She tried to smile but knew it hadn't reached her eyes and was entirely unconvincing.

The Queen said nothing and took a deep breath. 'Caroline, it has come to my attention that . . .'

She waited, her heart pounding in her chest, imagining the next words to come out of her mouth. The Queen had heard about Johnny, and she couldn't work here any longer. Panic crept into her heart like ice.

'. . . you might be finding it rather more difficult than you imagined moving to a different team and occupation within the palace. Is that correct?'

The fear left her in one heavy exhale. Seated before the Queen of England she couldn't lie. 'It is, ma'am, but I'm working hard and doing well.'

The Queen assessed her with her shrewd eyes. 'You will often find in life that there are those who like to remind you of what you once were, not of what you can become.'

She glanced at the window and Caroline wondered if she was referring to the Duke of Windsor's visit. She'd heard rumours from Mrs Barnes that he'd said some horrible things, reminding her that she was once nothing more than his niece and wouldn't even be Queen if things had worked out differently, if he'd been allowed to marry the woman he loved *and* keep his throne.

Caroline couldn't help but see similarities between him and Princess Margaret, who now wanted to marry a divorced man twice her age. Would they allow her to marry a divorcee because she wasn't Queen or in direct line to the throne? The decision had just been announced that she was to accompany Elizabeth to Rhodesia after the coronation. Were they making plans for when the rejection finally came to try and cheer her up? Speculation was rife in the palace about secret plans, but nothing had been confirmed.

'Are you sure there is nothing else bothering you? I have always noticed you around the palace. Your beauty is very striking.' She'd never thought of herself as beautiful. Her brother used to tease her that she was so pale she looked like a ghost. 'But you have seemed rather sad lately and I hope you don't mind me saying but you do look tired. If you would prefer to move back to Mrs Barnes, I will ask Mr Lascelles to speak to Mr Newington.'

'No, no! Please don't. I do really like the work and won't let anyone else bother me.' She opened her mouth, about to admit that Johnny was being charged with murder but bit her lip and let her courage fade. Footmen stood around the room, and she didn't need anyone else knowing her family's private business. 'Some women in the office don't think I'm up to the job, but I'm determined to prove them wrong. There's nothing else. Honestly. But thank you for being so kind to me.'

The Queen gave a smile that made her seem older than her years. 'Very well then. You may go.'

Caroline left in a daze, giving an unsteady curtsey before she left the room, aware that her whole life might implode if Johnny were found guilty. A shorter stay in prison for dealing in black-market goods was surely better than swinging from a rope. She had to go and see Johnny again and convince him to tell the police the whole truth. There was no other way for it. Don Green's family would have to survive somehow. She wasn't sure her ma would cope with losing her son. She had to be selfish and damn the consequences for others.

Chapter Nineteen

By Saturday afternoon, a smog unlike anything anyone had ever known descended on London. While Buckingham Palace was lit within by golden light and the decorations for Christmas had now extended into the staff quarters, with bright glass baubles and ribbons of gold; in contrast the world outside appeared cold and bleak, if any of it was visible. Excited chatter about Christmas and the dance had died down as the staff spoke of the weather instead.

Caroline had looked from the windows of Buckingham Palace, unable to make out the gold-topped gates that surrounded the palace or anything further than a few yards from the window. Jane, the new coffee maid, had commented that it was frightening. At the time, Caroline had thought it was just typical British weather and supposed she'd need to wrap up warm when going to visit Johnny in prison the next afternoon. November had been particularly cold with heavy snow, and it wasn't a great surprise that, with more people burning coal at home to keep them warm, there'd be more smoke than usual. But as Sunday rolled around and Caroline waited at the gates of Buckingham Palace to meet Helen, who had insisted on accompanying her, the world felt different. There was no wind, which meant the wisps of smog didn't move, they simply floated in front of her. The air had a strange colour – a greenish hue – and was growing darker and denser as she stood in the cold. A strange smell, like bad eggs, stung her nose and forced her to place a hand over her mouth. Visibility was so poor cars were moving slowly, if they moved at all.

That morning, the Queen and Duke of Edinburgh had advised all staff to stay at the palace unless travel was absolutely necessary. When the announcement had been made, Mrs Barnes had put down Milly's marriage book and said, 'Do you really need to go, Caroline? Can't you put it off till next week? I've never seen anythin' like this before.'

She wished she could, but plans had been made and, with Helen meeting her, she couldn't change her mind now.

'It'll be fine, Mrs Barnes. I'll be careful.'

Now she wished she'd taken the older woman's advice. As they all so often did.

Shivering in the cold, Caroline looked around for Helen. If she didn't get there soon, she'd have to head off on her own.

The guardsmen at the gate were marching as usual and she was glad of their protection. The Changing of the Guard had continued as normal, and though the faces of the guards remained passive, their steps had been a little shorter, more unsteady. The London she'd soon be stepping into was going to be dangerous. The weather was perfect for pickpockets, and she refused to let her mind wander to any worse possibilities. After a few more minutes, Helen arrived.

'Sorry I'm late. There aren't any buses at all.'

'What, none?'

Helen shook her head. 'They can't see to drive. I waited

for ages and realised it wasn't ever going to come, so then I had to rush to the tube.'

'Are you sure you should be coming with me?' Caroline asked. 'Travelling in this sort of weather's going to be difficult. And in your condition—'

'I wish you'd all stop going on about my condition,' Helen replied tersely. Then her tone softened. 'Honestly, I'll be fine. I have a torch.' She produced it from her handbag. 'We'll use this if we need to.'

'We better get to the underground then if there aren't any buses.'

They began to walk in the direction of the nearest station, seeing the eerie sight of abandoned cars on the way.

'I don't mind the not being able to see,' Caroline said, placing a gloved hand over her mouth and nose. 'But it's the smell that's getting me.'

'Awful, isn't it? Like rancid eggs. It's making me feel queasy.'

'Another reason you shouldn't be here.'

'Don't let's fight,' Helen said, threading her arm through Caroline's. 'I want to come. I want to help.'

'Why? Johnny's a pain in the backside.'

Helen chuckled. 'He's also one of the only men I've met who knows my situation and hasn't judged me for it. That says a lot about someone, if you ask me. He's a good man, Caroline. And what's happening isn't fair. I want to help you and your family. If I can.'

Rather than walking across Green Park, they chose to take the route down Constitution Hill that was better lit and from there get the tube at Hyde Park Corner. In the summer, this road had been lined with bushy green trees offering welcome shade from an unprecedented heatwave. After a cold autumn, the trees were virtually invisible beyond the wall of smog that surrounded them. Both Caroline and Helen coughed every few paces as the horrid, thick air clasped at their throats, stripping them so they felt rasping and raw.

As they walked, barely speaking as they tried not to breathe too deeply, they heard a scream over the other side of the road.

'What was that?' Caroline asked, hoping Helen would say an animal of some kind even though it was clear it wasn't.

'Where was it might be a better question.'

'Help! Help me, please!'

They both looked around unable to see anything.

'I think it's coming from over there.' Helen switched on the torch and shone it in the direction she suspected.

Moving gingerly, they crossed over the road, hearts pumping. The woman was still pleading, her voice muffled by the fog, but they managed to locate her. She was on the floor, her stockings wet, her hair falling out from under her scarf. She didn't seem hurt but was most definitely shocked and trembling.

'Are you all right?' Caroline asked, diving forwards. Both she and Helen helped her up to stand.

'Yes, yes, I think so. Oh, thank goodness you're here.' Closer, the woman was older than them, but only a little. Through the rips in her stockings, they could see her knees were grazed.

'You're all right now. Here, lean on me.'

Helen shone the torch around the ground at their feet. 'I can't seem to find your handbag.'

'It's gone,' she said, wiping her eyes as tears began to fall. 'Some lads stole it from me.'

Caroline instantly peered around, looking for signs or sounds that they were still there.

'The little beggars have run off,' the woman said. 'That way.' She pointed in the direction Helen and Caroline were soon to follow. No doubt they'd be a good distance away by now, probably robbing their next victim. 'It's this blasted weather. My husband warned me not to go out.'

'Will you be all right to get home?' Caroline asked. 'We can walk you if you'd like some company.'

'That's all right. Thank you, though. That's very kind.' Her voice was growing stronger as she regained control of herself now she was safe. She brushed the remnants of the murky puddle from her coat. 'They've got my ration book and my purse. They were both in my handbag.'

'That's very annoying.'

'Nothing that can't be fixed,' Helen said comfortingly. 'The important thing is you're all right.'

'You girls should be inside.'

'We will as soon as we can.' Helen glanced at Caroline, a warning that they weren't to linger once the woman had gone on her way. 'Are you sure you're all right to continue alone?'

'Absolutely. We should all move along. This is only going to get worse.'

With the woman dispatched, they hurried on to the tube. As they descended the first few steps, grateful to be out of the weather, they stopped, unable to get any further. People were queuing on the stairs, waiting to buy tickets. Helen brushed a tinge of black soot from her coat and Caroline suddenly noticed hers too was covered in a film of dirt. Gripping their handbags tightly they edged forwards and eventually, after much waiting, were on a train and arriving at Caledonian Road, ready to walk the short journey to the prison.

The horrid building looked even more menacing as they approached through the gate. Danger seemed to lurk around every corner, veiled, yet ready to pounce. Unlike the last time they'd come, there were barely any other visitors. The woman with the children wasn't here and few men and women walked past them. They walked around the corner to the entrance, relieved to see a guard at the open door.

'Surprised you or anyone else made it today,' he said with an attempt at warmth, but his hard features and suspicious eyes gave the statement an accusatory feel. 'Open your bags please.'

They did as asked, and after he'd rifled through, were led in.

'Who are you here to see?'

'Jonathan Stratton.' A sudden need to cough overtook Caroline, her chest tight and her throat tingling. She doubled over, covering her mouth.

'Names?'

Helen answered as Caroline composed herself and they were passed through to another man who asked similar questions and pointed to a table.

'Are you all right?' Helen asked as the cough became persistent again.

'I think it's just the change from outside. I'll be all right in a minute.'

The room felt darker as little light penetrated the windows. Having been through this all once before, Caroline had hoped she'd feel more at ease but being one of the only people there made the experience even more surreal. A man arrived to visit someone shortly after they sat down, but otherwise, they were alone. In the cold room, the hard faces of the guards made it even more frightening. She glanced at Helen who, from the nervous look in her eye, seemed to feel the same way.

Johnny was led out looking downcast, thinner and tired. Caroline kept her emotions under control. Johnny sat down and her heart swelled as he and Helen smiled at each other. It was clear Helen and Johnny couldn't fight the attraction they felt towards each other.

'How are you?' Caroline asked and Johnny reluctantly drew his attention away from her friend.

'I'm getting by. The food's not as good as Ma's but it's better than some people get. I've even been allowed some books to read.'

'You've always hated reading,' Caroline replied, surprised by this comment and the unexpected brightness of his tone.

'I'm learning a few things being in here.'

Unable to stop herself, Caroline got straight to the point. 'You have to tell them the truth now, Johnny. You have to. There's no other way out of this mess.'

'Caz, I—'

'Don't tell me you can't. I don't want to hear it. You *can* and you *must*. Ma's fading. Pa too. I don't know what'll happen to them if you don't. Murder's no joke, Johnny. You could hang.'

'Don't you think I know that?' he snapped, his expression immediately changing to one of regret and shame.

The words echoed in the empty space, the weight of them settling between them.

'It really is the only way, Johnny,' Helen added calmly. She placed her hands flat on the table, leaning forwards towards him. 'I know you'll go to prison, but it won't be for as long as if you get convicted of murder.'

He suddenly reached out and took her hands. The guard looked over and stirred, but Johnny let go before he could come over. 'If I ever get out of here, I'll never step a foot wrong in me life. I promise.'

Startled at this outburst, Helen stilled, then the hint of a grin lifted the corner of her mouth.

'Then tell the police the truth,' Caroline insisted.

'Do – d'you really think I should?'

The question was directed first at Caroline and then at Helen. They both agreed.

'I know you'll go to prison for stealing the works van—' Helen said.

'And Don Green won't be happy with you either—' Caroline added. 'But it's better than the alternative.'

'I was only trying to help him,' Johnny said, his voice small as he considered their advice. 'But you're right. I won't be accused of murder, and it doesn't look like the police are trying to find out who really did it.' He glanced at them both then lifted his chin. 'Guard?'

The prison warder pushed himself off from the wall and came over. 'What d'you want?'

'I need to tell the police something.'

His eyebrows lifted. 'You done with these two then?' He motioned to Caroline and Helen.

'Yes,' Johnny replied though it was clear he wanted to remain with them for longer. Maybe he knew his strength would fail if he didn't speak up now.

'Come with me.'

'I love you, sis,' he said. 'And, Helen, I . . .' But his words died as he was led away.

The meeting over, they shuffled out, back into the smog and the darkness. It had grown thicker since they'd arrived and most of the journey home was spent in silence, with one or the other occasionally coughing. They'd just managed to get a ticket for the tube and were standing on the platform when Caroline's attention was drawn to the crowd.

As her eyes assessed the tall man's head of dark hair, his bearing and, finally, his profile when the crowd parted and she could see him fully, her heart pounded. A cold sweat began to break out on her forehead and that familiar need to escape took hold.

'Caroline, are you all right?'

She couldn't take her eyes off him, needing to keep him in focus: to know exactly where he was so he couldn't get near her, so she could run if need be.

'Caroline, what is it?'

Helen followed her gaze just as the train pulled into the station. She inhaled sharply. 'Timothy.'

There was such a crush for the train, Helen pulled Caroline

aside and they let others shove their way on. He boarded and the train sped him away into the darkness of the tunnel. He hadn't seen her. Hadn't even noticed her. He probably never thought about her, yet seeing him had paralysed her and she was back where she'd been all those months ago.

Helen pressed her hands to either side of Caroline's face as she began to come back to the moment, realising where she was and that she was safe with her friend.

'It's all right, Caroline. He's gone. You're shaking,' Helen said, rubbing her hands up and down Caroline's arms. 'Lean against the wall.'

Mechanically, she moved backwards, directed by Helen.

She should have known she'd see him again at some point. He was never going to leave London, but she'd always felt safe in the knowledge that the city was large and sprawling. The chance had seemed so small, but luck hadn't been on her side lately. Her erratic breathing grew calmer as she looked into Helen's bright blue eyes.

'I – I'm all right,' she replied, her voice tremulous. It was a lie and Helen saw through it immediately.

'No, you're not, but he's gone now.'

But for how long?

All she could do was hope that she'd never, ever see him again. But was that likely? Regardless, she closed her eyes and prayed that it was.

Chapter Twenty

Caroline looked out of the window of the Household Breakfast Room on Monday morning but could see nothing. The
smog was thicker than ever, the greenish, yellowing tinge
the world had assumed the day before growing stronger as
more smog thickened. With no wind, it settled on the ground,
the air thick and unmoving like a blanket.

'Any sign of her yet?' Mrs Barnes asked.

They'd all worried about Helen making her way in in
this weather. Traffic was at a standstill. No buses were running, yet more cars had been abandoned in the street, and
Mr Newington had told them he expected many of the staff
would be unable to make it in.

Caroline hugged her teacup closer to her, warming her
fingers. The Household Breakfast Room was cosy from
the heated breakfast trays that lined one side of the room.
The thickly upholstered furnishings, deep red curtains
and carpet all helped keep the room warm. It lacked a
Christmas tree, but one had been installed in the Household Lounge for the staff to enjoy. Caroline wished her
friend were with them and didn't have to travel in from
Whitechapel.

'Nothing yet, Mrs Barnes, but I can't see anything out
there. Shall I check at the exchange?'

'If you don't mind, my girl. It'll put my mind at rest.'

Mine too, Caroline thought.

'I'll come with you,' Milly said, popping the last piece of toast into her mouth. She closed the wedding magazine she'd been looking at and Caroline noticed several dog-eared pages that had been marked for future reference.

Together they set off through the corridors towards the exchange, leaving behind the comforting smell of eggs, toast and marmalade. Occasional tables in the corridors were decorated with small flower displays of red flowers and deep green foliage, and it was hard to believe Christmas was so near.

'I know clothes rationing ended in '49,' Milly said. 'But it's still hard to get a wedding dress. London has more shops than most but it's difficult to find what I want on my budget.'

'Oh?'

'Everything's so expensive. Did you know lots of dresses are still made out of parachute material like they were during the war?'

'If you wanted something made, I could speak to Ma. She is a seamstress after all. And she can get material for you too.'

Milly suddenly brightened. 'Do you think you could? I keep seeing all these pictures in magazines but they're all so glamorous and expensive.'

'You'll look lovely in whatever you wear, and Robert won't mind a bit.'

'I know. I still want to look like me or I'll feel silly, but I'd love my dress to be extra nice.'

'I understand,' Caroline said as they stopped outside the exchange door. They both stood for a moment, Caroline playing with her nails, Milly smoothing down her white dress. Mr Marshall, Helen's boss, was an intimidating man with frog-like features and a military bearing. What would he say to them?

'You knock,' Milly said.

'Me? Why me?'

'Because this was your idea.'

'You offered to come.'

They began to chuckle, knowing how ridiculous they sounded. Caroline checked her watch. It was already a quarter to nine and Helen would normally have been there by now. In fact, she'd normally have been there early and joined them in the breakfast room for a cup of tea. Caroline took a deep breath, knocked and opened the door.

It always surprised her how small the telephone exchange at Buckingham Palace was given how crucial a service it provided. The room was stuffy and loaded with machinery: two large banks of equipment lined each side, wires sticking out from them, and Mr Marshall was currently marching through the middle like an army commander on parade. After a quick glance he came towards them.

All Caroline and Milly could hear were the repetitious words the operators were saying: 'Hold the line, please, caller'; 'Go ahead, caller'.

'Can I help you?' he asked, coming to a halt in front of them.

'Apologies, Mr Marshall,' Milly said. 'But we were just looking to see if Helen had arrived yet.'

'Helen Hill?'

'Yes.' She glanced over his shoulder but couldn't see her dark hair or familiar form.

Some of the men who worked the night shift were still there and several chairs were empty where others hadn't made it in. It was going to be a tough day for those who had managed it.

'No.' His moustache twitched as he pursed his lips. A habit they knew he had from Helen's impressions. 'No, I'm afraid not. Don't fancy her chances either. Never seen anything like it in my life.'

'Nor have we,' Milly replied. 'Well, thank you, Mr Marshall. Have a nice day.'

'You too, young lady.'

He about turned and began marching back between the banks.

'What shall we do now?'

Caroline checked her watch again. 'I'm going to wait outside for her.'

'Are you sure?'

'Yes. I'll give it ten minutes then I'll have to get to work myself. I'd like to know she's here and safe before I go though.'

'OK. I'll join you.'

After appraising Mrs Barnes of the plan and fetching their coats and scarves, they went outside and found their way to the guarded gate at the staff entrance. Outside, they had to walk with one hand against the building and then head in the direction of the guards' marching feet and racking coughs.

'I hope you're not on long,' Milly said to one of the guardsmen on duty.

'They've shortened our shifts. Everyone who's out here for more than an hour comes in unable to breathe.'

'It's awful, isn't it?'

At that point, Caroline started coughing just as she had the day before. 'It's the smell that's the worst,' she spluttered, but she couldn't catch her breath and a strange fear rose inside her that it would never come back. Eventually, the cough abated, and she was able to breathe normally again.

Just then, they heard footsteps and some women appeared, showing their staff passes. Helen wasn't one of them and Caroline's stomach began to knot, fearful that something terrible had happened to her and the baby on the journey. Just as she was about to return inside and get to the office before she was late, Helen appeared, a handkerchief pressed to her mouth, her other hand holding a torch.

'What are you two doing here?'

'Waiting for you!' they answered in unison.

'Well, that was silly. You should be inside where it's safe.'

The guard was just closing the gate behind her when Caroline recognised Mr O'Keefe's voice. 'Hold on! Wait for me.'

They turned and Helen's torch illuminated the fuzzy shape of a man. Mr O'Keefe was nearing the pavement when a screech of tyres was followed by a horrific thud. In the wisping cloud, Caroline could just make out his body being thrown from the bonnet of a car that was driving too fast. She gasped, pressing her hands to her mouth. He ricocheted off the windscreen, his limp figure falling back down the car and landing in front of it as the tyres halted centimetres from his face.

An eerie quietness surrounded them, and the world seemed to slow. Something stabbed at Caroline's heart as suddenly everything sped up, the world restarting and coming back into focus. A guard leapt forwards. The man who'd been driving the car climbed out and Caroline, Helen and Milly ran over to Mr O'Keefe.

'I'm so sorry. I'm so sorry,' the man repeated. He pressed his hands to his head. Then, without warning, he climbed back in his car, reversed and drove away into the gloom. As the other guardsman couldn't leave his post, all they could do was shout and demand he stop but he paid no attention.

'Is he breathing?' Caroline asked. Mr O'Keefe's handsome face was battered and bruised, blood pouring from a cut on his forehead. A surge of emotion leapt through her, fear mixed with panic, and her heart throbbed.

Helen felt at his wrist. 'Yes, he is. We should telephone for an ambulance.'

'Right.' Caroline stood. 'I'll run inside and—'

'An ambulance won't get through this fog,' the guard said. 'We need to take him to the surgery in the palace.'

'Inside the palace?' Milly repeated incredulously. 'But that's just for the Royals—'

'He needs a doctor, miss. Now.'

Milly ran inside and before long a troop of people were rushing over to help them.

Four men carried him through the corridors towards the surgery. Footmen, butlers, maids and clerks dived out of the way as they rushed him inside. Word had clearly spread as they drew closer, and the doctor appeared. He had a white coat on and a stethoscope around his neck.

'What have we got here then?'

'He's just been hit by a car,' Caroline said, her voice sounding tinny and stretched.

'He's breathing,' Helen added in her calm way. 'But he has a head injury and he's out cold.'

'In here then, please.' He held the double doors of the surgery open for them.

If the doctor was surprised, he hid it well and his calm demeanour helped to still Caroline's racing heart. She didn't know exactly what she felt for Mr O'Keefe, but she knew it was different to anything she'd felt for Timothy. She'd thought of his arms around her, as he had that night when she'd slipped on the ice. She'd thought of what it would be like to kiss him. She prayed he'd be all right and have nothing more than a headache and sore ribs. His head lolled as he came in and out of consciousness, and fear sent icy fingers down her spine.

Whether it was rushing to keep up with the men carrying Mr O'Keefe or because she was finally away from the noxious gas outside, Caroline began coughing again, doubling over as she struggled to catch her breath.

'I want to look at you too,' the doctor said, pointing at her as they placed Mr O'Keefe on a medical bed in the fully equipped surgery. 'It's Miss Stratton, isn't it?'

Just over a year ago, this place had been made into an operating room for King George VI when his lung had been removed. He hadn't wanted to go to a hospital, possibly for fear of the press finding out. As the thought occurred to Caroline, and she remembered watching his health fail, a shudder rippled through her body, causing her to start coughing again.

'I don't like the sound of that cough at all,' the doctor said. 'You can wait outside for now and I'll check you over once I'm done with him. Nurse?'

A middle-aged woman appeared from a side room, and she entered with brisk steps, ushering everyone out of the room and then closing the doors behind them. The doctor's voice faded as he barked instructions at her.

Caroline, Milly and Helen all sat on the wooden chairs that lined one side of the corridor. It had the horrible feel of a hospital waiting room.

'I'm sure he'll be all right,' Milly said, taking Caroline's hand.

'Yes,' Helen added. 'He might have a concussion, but it didn't seem like anything too dreadful.' She shook her head. 'What was that man thinking driving like that in this weather?'

'And then driving off!'

Caroline could hear their words, but they were muffled by her own, confusing thoughts. She kept glancing at the door, wishing it would open and the doctor come out to say he was awake and ask if she could sit with him a while. The feelings were powerful and overwhelming. She didn't even know Mr O'Keefe.

'I need to go to work,' Helen said. 'Mr Marshall won't like me just sitting here, but I will if you need me to, Caroline.'

'No, no.' She gave her a small smile. 'It's fine. Go.'

'I'll go and tell Mr Newington,' Milly said. 'I'll tell him you're waiting for an update from the doctor.'

'Thank you. If he needs me to work, someone can come and fetch me.' She began coughing again.

'And let the doctor examine you,' Milly added. 'Like he said, I don't like the sound of that cough.'

Milly and Helen departed, leaving Caroline alone in the corridor. She stood and paced backwards and forwards. She tried to glance in through the door of the surgery but couldn't see anything. A blind obscured the other side of the window, blocking the view. She sat down again, trying to make sense of her feelings.

The only conclusion she could come to was that she liked him. She liked Mr O'Keefe in a way she hadn't thought she'd ever feel about anyone again. There was no denying her physical attraction to him. The trouble was, she liked him how she'd first liked Timothy, when she had been too young and naive to see the warning signs. She was younger then, she told herself. She was older now and had learned from her experiences. And if Milly and Helen had shown her anything, it was that it wasn't how old you were, but your experiences that gave you wisdom.

She turned at the sound of footsteps in the hall and leapt up when she saw the Duke of Edinburgh striding towards her. He looked dashing in his dark grey double-breasted suit, his arms swinging by his sides.

'Now, what's all this I hear about someone getting hit by a car and being treated in the surgery, hmmm?'

'Your Royal Highness.' Caroline ducked down into a curtsey, but her legs were unsteady. Lightheaded from the all the coughing, she wobbled, woozy and off balance. The Duke's hands gripped her arms, gently guiding her back to a chair.

'Now, now. Have a seat, you look like you're about to faint and we don't need another patient to deal with, do we?'

'I'm—' She began coughing again, covering her mouth with both hands. Her breathing became shallow, her lungs unable to take in any air. It was terrifying in a way she'd not known before. Her body refusing to do what it should naturally.

'Take some deep breaths. That's it. Head between your knees.'

She did as instructed until her breathing calmed. 'I'm fine, sir. Really.' She swallowed, trying to moisten her throat. 'The man in there is Mr O'Keefe—'

'Irish chap, works in the clerks' office.'

'Yes, Your Royal Highness. He was hit by a car near the staff entrance. The guardsman said an ambulance wouldn't get here in time so we should bring him here.'

'Quite right too. Anyone inform the police?'

'I don't think so, sir.'

'Not much point, I wouldn't have thought. The man who did it is probably long gone by now. I heard he ran off pretty quickly after seeing what he'd done.'

'That's right.'

'Bad form, I say. Well, I'll report back to Her Majesty. You stay and get yourself seen too as well. Do you live on site?'

'Yes, sir.'

'Good. Then you can go and rest without having to travel in this. Who knows how much longer it's going to go on for.'

He turned and walked away and, before she'd had a chance to compose herself, the surgery doors opened, and the doctor called her.

'You can come in now, Miss Stratton.'

Mr O'Keefe was sitting up on the bed, a bandage around his head, a plaster over his eyebrow. He was fastening the top buttons of his shirt, and she caught a glimpse of the dark hairs on his chest, poking from the top of his vest.

'Nothing too much to worry about,' the doctor continued. 'A slight concussion and some bruising. Mr O'Keefe should be back to work soon.' Caroline glanced at him, and he smiled sleepily. His eyes were heavy from the shock and possibly the concussion. The doctor moved to speak to the nurse and Caroline edged closer to the bed.

'How are you feeling?' she asked, knowing it was a stupid question.

'Like I've been hit by a bus.'

'It was a car, actually, but you're not wrong about what happened.'

He laughed and pressed a hand to his head. 'Hadn't you better call me Connor, given that you're sitting at my bedside like Florence Nightingale?'

'I'm not a bit like Florence Nightingale. I won't be treating you for one thing.' He chuckled again and this time ran his fingers over the plaster on his forehead. It was clear the wound was still bleeding – a tiny pinprick of red was beginning to show through – and causing him some pain. 'Do you remember anything?'

He shook his head. 'Not really. All I remember is fog and then waking up here.'

'Maybe that's for the best.' She often wished she couldn't remember some things.

He gave her a strange look and yawned before resting his hand on his ribs. 'I'm sorry for causing you any distress.'

'You didn't get hit by a car on purpose, did you?'

'I don't think so. It wouldn't be the stupidest thing I've ever done in my life, especially if I was trying to impress a pretty girl.' Did he mean her? She felt her cheeks warm, and he seemed to realise what he'd said, blushing too. He cleared his throat. 'Thank you for checking I'm all right, Miss Stratton.'

'You should probably call me Caroline if I'm calling you Connor.'

His sleepy eyes met hers, a lopsided smile playing on his lips. They were caught in a moment, and she didn't feel worried or scared. She felt calm, excited by the attraction between them.

The doctor was suddenly by her side. 'That's enough time. Mr O'Keefe needs some rest. It's you I'd like to check over now.'

'Oh, I'm fine, really. It's just this weather. If I'm out in it, it makes me cough.'

'Let me just listen to your chest then. Come with me.'

He led her to another small examination room. 'Just undo the top button of your blouse please.' She did as she was told, and the cold stethoscope was pressed to her skin. He listened without speaking and the tickling started again. Her lungs seemed suddenly heavy, her throat tight, her chest ratcheted closed. He frowned. 'I don't like this at all. I'm going to give you an adrenalin shot and put you on bed rest.'

'What? No, I—' She began coughing again and the doctor

merely stopped and stared, one eyebrow raised as if she were making his point for her. It took her some minutes before she was able to take a breath and, in that time, he'd loaded a syringe and injected it into her thigh.

Her breathing calmed and she looked at the doctor. 'Was that really necessary? Honestly, I think it's just the weather.'

'Your heart was racing an unusual amount. Bed rest, please. I'll have the nurse inform your superiors and I don't want you going out in this weather. Not at all.'

'I won't,' she replied.

'Go to bed, sleep and stay warm.'

Defeated, she nodded, fastened her blouse, and moved back into the main room.

'Are you off then?' Connor asked, his eyelids heavy with fatigue.

'I'll let Mr Newington know you're all right.'

'Will you come back and see me later?'

Caroline's heart pulsed. 'I've been put on bed rest for my cough.'

'Oh, I see. Soon then, maybe?'

She looked to the doctor.

'We'll see. Depends if you've been coughing.'

She turned to Connor. 'All right then. If you want me to.'

'I can probably put up with you for a bit longer.'

The surgery door swung closed behind her and Caroline smiled, feeling the time they'd spent together fill her entire body with joy like a shaft of sunlight penetrating the gloom. She decided to hold on to it as tightly as she could. Bed rest wasn't ideal, but at least Connor was OK. Connor . . . she liked the sound of his name.

Chapter Twenty-One

'Here,' Robert said, handing Caroline a small, battered short-bread tin. 'Y-you can give Mr O'Keefe these biscuits. They're f-from all of us in the kitchens.'

Mrs Barnes patted his arm tenderly. 'That's very kind of you, Robert, and Mrs Chadwick too. Mr Newington's very fond of Mr O'Keefe. He'll be pleased to know he's being looked after.'

After returning to her room, as ordered by the doctor, she'd slept for a good couple of hours. Whether that was due to the awful side effects of the adrenalin shot, or tiredness from the horrifying events of the morning, she wasn't sure. But after lying in bed for a while she'd grown bored and was eager to get back to work. She didn't want anyone else taking her spot and, though Mr Newington wouldn't hold it against her that she hadn't been able to work, she didn't want to risk losing this opportunity. An opportunity she was beginning to enjoy.

Despite the queasiness brought on by the adrenalin, she'd made her way to the dining room earlier in search of food. The doctor need never know. Her chest and throat were a little sore from the coughing, but that was to be expected. Otherwise, she felt back to normal, and she couldn't waste time being sick when she needed to get home and find out how Johnny had got on with the police. She wanted to be there to meet him when he was let out and she wouldn't know more until she went home to see Ma and Pa. However, once she'd reached the dining room, Robert had sent her straight back to bed with a tray and told her to follow the doctor's advice. It seemed he'd spent the afternoon making something for Mr O'Keefe and something for her.

After a few more hours' sleep, Caroline had returned to the Household Lounge that evening. Off-duty staff were gathered at the windows, watching the hidden world outside, exclaiming that it was all far worse than they thought it would be. There was always fog in London, thick pea-soupers that darkened the day, but this was unlike anything anyone had ever experienced. As their curiosity and morbid excitement grew, their conversations became even more animated.

Caroline took the shortbread tin from Robert, feeling both nervous and excited. Whenever she'd been alone with Timothy conversation had been difficult, and she'd always felt stupid. She'd say something and he'd look at her and pity her lack of education. At first, she'd thought his corrections were kindly meant. That he didn't want her to embarrass herself in front of others. How wrong she'd been. Timothy's responses had fallen quickly into disdain. He'd make comments that deliberately made her feel stupid, though he wasn't really any more educated than she was. In fact, now she'd been to secretarial college, she was probably more qualified than him.

Helen and Caroline had decided not to tell Milly about

seeing Timothy at the tube station. He'd hurt her as much as he'd hurt Caroline and they didn't want to spoil her happiness as she made wedding plans with Robert, discussing food, dresses, flowers and everything else they could think of.

'Go on,' Milly said, a mischievous look on her face. 'Don't keep him waiting.'

'He's in a hospital bed, he's not going anywhere,' Caroline retorted.

It was a good job she'd grown up with teasing and taunting or she might have found their words embarrassing. As it was, it reinforced to her how much she was loved, how important her palace family were. She hadn't heard anything from her ma and pa or Johnny, though it had only been a day and she supposed it would take a while for the police to decide what to do with the new information he had told them.

'Remember,' Helen said as Caroline began to walk away. 'Take your time to trust. No one can make you do anything you're not comfortable with and even if that means you don't stay long with Mr O'Keefe, follow your instincts.'

Grateful for her friend's advice, she said: 'I will. I promise. Are you staying here tonight?'

'No, I'm going to try and make it home. The last thing my landlady needs is another reason to moan at me. She's already asking questions and getting suspicious. I need her to like me.'

Mrs Barnes turned to join their conversation. 'I do wish you'd stay here, Helen. I don't like you travellin' about in all that. We can find you a room, it's not a problem, and the

Queen said that if anyone needed to stay, they'd be looked after.'

The announcement had come shortly after Mr O'Keefe's accident. Clearly the Duke of Edinburgh had reported back to Queen Elizabeth and, as always, she'd thought of the welfare of her staff.

'I know,' Helen continued. 'But I know my landlady already thinks I'm a slattern and I won't be able to hide this bump under my coat forever. I want to try and get her onside so that when I do come to tell her about the baby, she'll like me too much to send me away. I know that sounds calculating.' She brushed her hair back from her face, a tinge of pink colouring the apples of her cheeks.

'It's survival,' Mrs Barnes said. 'You've got to think of yourself and this baby.'

Caroline placed a hand on her arm. 'Take care, won't you?'

'I will, I promise. Now go!'

Caroline left the Household Lounge, with its comfortable chairs and relaxed atmosphere, and made her way to the surgery. As she arrived, the doctor was removing the bandage from Connor's head, revealing his ruffled dark hair. He looked pale but his soft blue eyes were more focused than they had been earlier.

'Hello,' she said, nerves biting at her stomach. She cursed herself but tried to keep her feelings in check. 'I've brought you some biscuits. They're from Mr Newington really. He said how fond of you he was. Mrs Chadwick, the cook, and my friend Robert baked them for you.'

'Robert . . . ?'

'Prior. He works in the kitchen. He's recently become

engaged to Milly Hendry, my friend. She's Mrs Barnes's niece.'

'Right.' He seemed to relax at this, and Caroline hid the smile racing over her face. Had he been worried she was stepping out with Robert? She ignored the thought and sat in the chair next to the bed. He took the tin from her and opened it, picking up a biscuit and taking a bite. 'They're very good. Here.'

He offered her the tin. She reached for one. 'Robert's turning into a very good cook. Mrs Chadwick's very pleased with him.'

'What did he do before?'

'Kitchen porter.' She took another bite.

'He's worked his way up? I admire that.' She glanced at him, raising her eyebrows. 'What?'

'I've worked my way up and you didn't seem that impressed when you met me. You hated me when I started working at the offices.'

'No, I didn't.'

'Yes, you did. You thought I was nothing but a stupid cockney who should stay in the Royal Household cleaning toilets.'

He popped the last of the biscuit into his mouth and crossed his arms over his chest. For the first time she noticed he was wearing hospital pyjamas. 'That's not what I thought at all.'

'Isn't it?' Her tone was dismissive.

'No. I thought . . .' He met her eye, and something sparked in the air between them. As his eyes scanned her face, she wondered what he was going to say. 'Well, it doesn't matter.

223

But I admit maybe I was a little jealous of Mr Newington being so fond of you. I thought you were going to steal my promotion.'

'What promotion?'

'There's talk of a senior clerk role coming up soon. I was hoping Mr Newington might put in a good word for me and then you came along and were suddenly getting all the highly confidential jobs.'

'I don't want to be a senior clerk,' she said honestly. 'I want to get used to being a normal one first. And I don't know if that'll even happen for me.'

'Why not?'

'I'm only there temporarily. As soon as people come back from the flu and now this fog, I'll be gone. I mean, I wouldn't mind managing an office or something one day but not yet.'

'So you won't be stealing my promotion then?' His eyes were brighter now, and the corner of his mouth twitched into a smile.

'Definitely not. And I've only been given some of the confidential work because we hear so much as cleaners. Mrs Barnes always said discretion is the most important part of the job. I know some of the women in the office hate me because of it.'

'They don't hate you. They might be jealous but that's because they've been caught gossiping before, so Mr Newington's careful what he gives them. Barbara isn't too bad. For all her chatting she knows when she shouldn't talk about things.'

'I like Barbara. She was kind to me when I first started.'

'I'm sorry if I wasn't.' He suddenly chuckled. 'And if I

hadn't been very nice, I certainly learned my lesson when you gave me what for, even though I was on your side.'

'When was that?'

'When you told Veronica Western off for being rude to you.'

'You were smirking at me,' she replied in her defence.

'I was smiling at seeing Miss Western taken down a peg or two. She's always had a mean streak.'

'Oh.' She'd taken his response to mean something totally different. Could she have mistaken other conversations?

'Can I ask you something?' he said, taking another biscuit. Though he was trying to seem unconcerned, from the way he glanced at her she could tell something difficult was coming and her stomach knotted. 'When we were in the secret corridor, I raised my hand to scratch my head and you winced. Has someone . . . Is someone . . . Are you all right?'

Without warning, the moment she hadn't been ready for arrived. She'd always known that at some point, when she became attracted to someone, she'd have to tell them about Timothy and all that had happened between them. About the invisible scars he'd left on her. But she didn't know if she was ready for that yet. A lump formed in her throat and silence wrapped around her.

'It's all right if you don't want to tell me,' he said gently. 'I just thought—'

'There was someone,' she replied, the words forming and leaving her mouth before she could stop them. 'I – I thought he liked me, but he just wanted to – to see what he could get. He was forced to leave the palace when he didn't get what he wanted.'

'I'm sorry.' She was aware of his eyes on her but couldn't raise her own. 'What a rat. Back home, he'd have lost more than his job.'

She couldn't believe that she'd told him as much as she had or that she'd felt comfortable enough to do so. Did she really trust him that much? Apparently, she did, and that trust had grown naturally between them. He knew about Johnny too. Not the latest developments, but certainly he knew more about her than she'd ever thought she could give away to a man.

'So what's the day's gossip?' he asked, changing the subject.

'I don't know much. I've been on bed rest all day. But Robert said everyone's talking about the dance and Christmas coming up. Most can't wait for the family to leave for Sandringham. Televising the coronation still seems to be an issue. There're grumblings about what they should and shouldn't do. Some of the Scots Guard arrived this morning to help protect the palace in the smog. I guess they're worried someone might try and get in.'

'Like that lunatic last month?'

Caroline nodded. 'Apart from that, it's business as usual. The Queen's still been seeing people.'

A knock at the door drew her attention and she turned to see Helen, Mrs Barnes and Milly arrive. As soon as they walked in, she stood, noting their concerned faces, their glances at one another.

Mrs Barnes pressed a hand to her chest. 'I remember when this was all changed for the King. God rest his soul.'

'What is it?' Caroline asked.

Helen held out a small envelope. 'This was left at the gate for you. The guard knows we're friends and asked me to deliver it to you. I was just leaving but came straight back.'

Caroline took the note, recognising her ma's writing. The letters were spidery and small, written in an unconfident hand. Caroline opened it and read the words, and then fell back into her seat as her legs shook, unable to bear the strain she was under. Mrs Barnes was by her side in an instant.

'What is it, my girl? You've gone white.'

'It's from Ma. She said she's heard from the police again. Johnny told them everything – he told them the truth about where he was – but Don Green's denied it, so they don't believe him. They think he's just making up lies to save his neck.'

Her lip trembled. Tears swamped her vision. She'd finally convinced him to tell the truth, and this was the result. He'd left it too late. Bitterness swept over her like sickness. If he'd just told them everything from the beginning this could all have been so different.

Milly darted to Helen's side. She too had gone pale and seemed unsteady on her feet. Connor tried to get up but winced. Seeing everyone else try to help Helen, he lay back.

The doctor appeared from his office and went straight to Helen. 'Everything all right?'

'Yes, fine. I just felt a little woozy.'

'Let's get you a chair.' He pointed at one on the other side of the room and Milly carried it over. 'Take some deep breaths,' he instructed. 'Perhaps one of those biscuits?'

Caroline handed one over to Helen who nibbled it, glancing at the doctor. 'I'm all right now. Really.'

He eyed her and then, seeing her colour return, said, 'I'm just over there if you need me.'

When he'd gone, Caroline lowered her voice. 'Ma also says there was another robbery Sunday night—'

'They can't think Johnny had anything to do with that,' Helen exclaimed. 'He was in prison at the time.'

'That's what Ma said.' She turned the letter towards them with a flick of her wrist. 'But according to the police Johnny's now in a gang. So, while he was banged up the others carried on without him. They want him to tell them who the other gang members are.'

'This is ridiculous.' Milly threw her hands into the air.

'It's all because he's poor,' Caroline replied, growing angry. 'If we were richer, they wouldn't just assume Johnny had something to do with it. I know he hasn't helped himself, but this isn't fair.'

'Where was your brother?' Connor asked, calmly.

She'd almost forgotten he was there – where they all were. She sighed. There wasn't much point in lying now. 'He went out that night. He took one of his boss's – Arthur Whitelock's – vans to help a friend move black-market meat.'

'And now he's come clean that friend's denying he had anything to do with it?'

'Yes. He's the man you found me with the other night. The one who grabbed my face.' Mrs Barnes gasped. 'It's all right, Mrs Barnes. Nothing happened.'

'We're gonna have serious words when this is all over, missy. Believe me.'

'Arthur Whitelock,' Connor said, his tone one of confusion. He suddenly started. 'Arthur Whitelock! That's why I was calling out to you this morning, coming to speak with you. Your brother worked for him, didn't he?'

'That's right.' She hadn't mentioned this in their previous conversations, but everyone knew and they were surely the subject of all the gossip in their neighbourhood.

'I overheard someone in the pub saying something about him.'

'When?'

'Last night. I'd gone for another bottle of stout. I was at the bar, waiting to be served and I could hear people talking. Someone – I don't know who – said something about Arthur Whitelock and his midnight drives. I didn't know what they meant at first, but what if he was driving one of his vans at the same time your brother was using the other one?'

'He does have two vans. I saw them myself at the ware-house. If he'd seen Johnny take the other van,' Caroline reasoned, 'then it'd be in his interest to stay quiet. The police would think only one van went out that night and that Johnny was the one to use it. But if the other van was driven by him then he could be behind all of this.'

Helen, revived by the biscuit, straightened up. 'Jake said he had a reputation, but nothing could be proved. What if he's always been up to something but just hasn't got caught yet?'

Mrs Barnes nodded along. 'That would explain why he was so intimidatin' to you, Caroline, when you went to see him. He was probably scared you'd go pokin' around and he'd then have the police on his back.'

'But wouldn't they have noted he has two vans and thought that was a possibility?' asked Milly.

Caroline shook her head. 'Lots of warehouses and shops

have those vans, and they think Arthur Whitelock is a fine, God-fearing man. That's what Jake said, wasn't it?' Helen nodded her agreement.

Connor shifted and reached for the small glass of water on his bedside. Caroline helped him as he winced and clutched his ribs. 'It doesn't sound like the police have done much investigating. They found your brother and didn't look any further. Sounds like someone on the force might be being paid to turn a blind eye.'

Could that really be the case? She'd only met the two policemen who'd come to the house to arrest Johnny and then to tell them that the charge had been increased to murder. Could there be someone at the local nick who was keeping the attention elsewhere? Or was it just a case of Johnny being the easy target and lazy police work?

Whatever it was, she needed to find out exactly how involved Arthur Whitelock was. If there'd been a robbery the night before, there was every chance he still had hold of the goods. Surely it would take some time to move them. She turned to the window. The smog was proving dangerous and deadly, but it could also provide the perfect cover for her if she could get to the docks and Arthur Whitelock's office.

'What are you thinking, Caroline?' Helen said gently.

If she said anything, Helen would go with her. Milly too. Even Mrs Barnes would come along if she asked her for help. But she wasn't going to ask them to risk anything by coming with her tonight. She had to do this alone.

She began coughing again, the doctor appearing from a side room as everyone crowded around her in worry. She tried to breathe deeply but her lungs were spasming. No air could move in or out and she thought she was going to be sick. A cold stethoscope was pressed to her back and a mask was slipped over her face.

'It's some oxygen. Deep breaths, please.'

A moment later, she felt more like herself, and her lungs were suddenly expanding and taking in air.

'Back to bed with you,' the doctor commanded. 'Now. You can't keep exerting yourself like this. I'm afraid I'll have to ask all of you to leave.'

'We'll help her back to bed,' Milly said, and Mrs Barnes nodded.

'Nurse, go with them please.'

Caroline was vaguely aware of Connor's concerned glance, but her eyes were tearing so much she couldn't make out his face. Mrs Barnes's hands were under her arms on one side, Milly on the other, and she was being led away, out of the room. She didn't have time for this. She had to use the smog to her advantage and who knew how much longer it would last? Tonight might be her only chance and no matter what the doctor said, she wasn't going to waste it.

Chapter Twenty-Two

Sneaking out of Buckingham Palace was almost as difficult as sneaking in. The staff were free to come and go as they pleased, but creeping out late in the evening, when the Queen had declared everyone was to stay inside and not venture out in this weather, was going to be difficult.

After being put to bed by Milly and Mrs Barnes, tucked up with a rubber hot-water bottle and a large glass of water, Caroline had thought long and hard about her plan for the evening. She knew it was dangerous and it was doing herself more harm than good, given the state of her health and how the thick smog was affecting her. But as far as she could see, she didn't have any choice. The fog could clear just as quickly as it descended and she didn't fancy doing what she had planned without the protection of its cover.

Caroline watched the clock tick by. She'd have to get past the guards on the staff entrance. They were there all day and night and she'd need a good excuse to manage it. It would be best to try and head out at ten o'clock. That was when the palace really began to slow down for the night. As the Queen liked to settle at eleven, a natural hush descended, and the staff would often retire to their rooms for some peace and quiet too. What she was planning was risky in the extreme – foolish some would say – but she couldn't see any other option. Her chest hurt, her lungs were sore from coughing, and the pressure on her ribcage and the tickling in her throat remained. The doctor had given her some cough medicine but it tasted foul, like bitter liquorice, and she'd always hated liquorice. It didn't seem to work either, though she could feel it coat her throat as it went down, soothing it a little.

In her room, Caroline dressed, leaving her coat lying on the bed beside her. As she'd suspected, there was a gentle knock on the door at nine thirty. She knew without look- ing that it was Mrs Barnes checking on her. When Caroline didn't reply, and instead sat still on the bed, unmoving and pretending to sleep, she heard her speak to Milly.

'She must be out for the count. Good. It's the best thing for her right now. Poor lamb.'

Caroline muffled the cough that was tickling her throat and squeezing her chest. The noxious fumes would start her coughing again as soon as she stepped out of the comfort of the palace, but she'd just have to bear it. She waited another half an hour and, after wrapping a woollen scarf around her neck, covering her mouth, and tying another over her head, she opened the door a crack and peered out.

The corridor, half-strewn with paper chains made by the staff in effort to bring some of the Christmas glamour from the State Rooms downstairs, was empty, and she crept along and out of the staff quarters, stepping lightly on the gravel, trying her best to remain silent. The night was eerie. Cold and dark, and she couldn't see the velvet sky overhead. Even her hand in front of her face was invisible and when she looked down at her feet, they were shrouded in mist. The horrid smell of eggs was as strong as it had been earlier, and she could feel the smog leaving black, sooty stains over her clothes. The temperature was dropping and it seemed as if the dense fog would turn solid, just as water turns to ice. She took a moment to find her bearings, to remember where she'd come out from and which direction she should be heading in. Hoping it was the right one, she started off.

'Who's there?' demanded the guardsman on the gate.

She couldn't see him but was pleased she'd headed in the right direction. Only when she drew to a stop directly in front of him did he come into view.

'It's Caroline Stratton, cleaner in the Royal Household.' She said it by accident but didn't bother clarifying that she now worked in the offices. Perhaps her heart was still there with Milly and Mrs Barnes. 'I need to go home.'

'You shouldn't be out in this, Miss Stratton,' the guard said, clearly recognising her. 'Specially this late at night.'

'Believe me, I don't want to be,' she replied. The smog was making her lightheaded and she planted her feet firmly, hip width apart, to steady herself. 'But there's an emergency at home. I need to get there as soon as I can.'

'It ain't safe to travel, miss. Not at all. Queen's orders were that everyone should stay inside unless absolutely necessary.'

She gave a mirthless laugh. 'If there was any other way, I wouldn't be going anywhere but my ma's ill.' She hated making up lies like this, always fearful that God might hear and make it true as a punishment, but she didn't have a choice. Johnny was relying on her. 'She needs me now and I can't not go. I'll be all right.'

'Are you sure, Miss Stratton?'

'Absolutely.'

The guard hesitated and she worried he was going to send her back inside or ask for her to prove it somehow. Her stomach roiled and she pulled the scarf further up over her nose and mouth.

'Go on then but get back here as soon as you can.'

'I will. No doubt about that.' She passed him and hurried down Constitution Hill, not bothering to cross Green Park and get the tube from there. She much preferred to get on at Hyde Park Corner, as she had with Helen, even though it would mean changing lines. She didn't fancy walking across the green in this weather and shivered as her courage nearly failed. Memories of the woman getting mugged that she and Helen had come across the day before were still vivid, and she found herself looking around, listening intently to the noise. The echo of her heels was the only sound in the gloom, but it rang eerily around her as though someone was walking close behind. Caroline clenched her fists in her pockets until . . . Surely no one would be stupid enough to attack her near Buckingham Palace where police and soldiers were on duty all the time? A tap on her shoulder sent a scream pouring from her mouth.

'Caroline, it's me!'

'Milly!' She pressed a hand to her heart and crumpled over. 'What the 'eck are you doing here?' Frustration took hold, her cockney accent rising to the surface. 'You shouldn't be 'ere. Go back.'

'No!' Milly's kind and pretty face hardened with indignation. 'Whatever you're up to, you're not doing it alone.'

'I'm not—' There didn't seem much point in lying. She'd

sneaked out of the palace late at night when the doctor had told her to stay in bed. There was no way her friend would believe one of her horrid lies. 'It won't be safe and . . . How did you know I was up to anything anyway?'

'I'm not sure. I just knew after you read that letter. There was something in your eyes. I knew you were plotting something.'

'What about Mrs Barnes? Does she—'

Milly shook her head. 'I convinced her you couldn't possibly move from your bed in the state you were in. She's gone to bed none the wiser.'

'I really don't feel well,' Caroline said, pressing a hand to her chest. 'But you should go back. I don't want you getting into trouble.'

'Why should I get into trouble? What are you planning to do?'

'I'm going to have a look around Arthur Whitelock's office.'

'What?' Milly's eyes widened. 'How?'

'I haven't figured that out yet, but I will by the time I get there. You don't need to be involved in this. Not with Robert and the wedding to think about. Turn around and go home.'

'Absolutely not. You'll need someone to act as lookout. You can't do this on your own and what if you start coughing again and need some help?'

'I'll be fine. I can manage—'

'But you don't have to.' Caroline met Milly's gaze. Milly's face was softer now, but steely determination shone in her eyes. 'I'm not going anywhere so we might as well get moving or we'll be out in this all night.'

They began walking quickly, side by side, their shoulders touching so they didn't lose track of each other. The tube was unnervingly empty. Where all the theatres had closed their doors, the usual crowds were gone. Only locals were venturing to the few pubs that had remained open, but restaurants were closed, bookings cancelled. The city was deserted as the night gripped the normally bustling metropolis.

'It reminds me of when the King died,' Milly said as they waited on the platform.

Caroline peered around, checking for Timothy, or anyone else who might pose a threat.

'The world seemed to stop, didn't it?' Milly continued.

'It was very strange. It's been a strange year really. So much as happened. I feel like a different person now than when I started working at the palace.'

'I do too. But perhaps that's just life. We grow and change, like children do.' Milly eyed the ring on her left hand.

'Do you think Helen will have a boy or a girl? Ma says it's too early to tell but she thinks she'll know once her bump's properly developed. I kind of hope it's a girl.'

'Do you? I hope it's a boy. Boys have to be easier than girls, don't they? Look at the trouble we've both got ourselves into.'

'Yeah, but Johnny's showing us all what boys can be like. Girls have to be nicer, and their clothes are prettier.'

Milly agreed as the train arrived on the platform, and they made their way to the poorest part of London.

The familiar world of the East End now seemed alien to Caroline, shrouded in the dense, yellowing fog that appeared as solid as a loaf of stale bread. Immediately she began to cough.

'I don't like you being out in this,' Milly said, spluttering herself. 'What would the doctor say?'

This time, she was able to catch her breath before the cough grew too strong. 'I'll be fine. Hopefully we won't be very long. Come on, it's this way.'

They headed through the streets, the poverty of the tenements hidden by the unusual weather. Everyone was inside and only occasional voices penetrated the night: male voices mostly shouting, cursing and ultimately fading away. Caroline's nerves spiked like daggers. Milly stayed close, wrapping her arm through her friend's. The smell of the Thames was only just noticeable under the wretchedness of the fog, the sewage scent an unpleasant undertone to the eggy, sulphurous air. Caroline's hand found a gap in the buildings, and she knew this was the steps down to the banks of the Thames. Though they couldn't see down the narrow alley, the panting sounds of a woman and the grunts of a man made Milly blush and Caroline hurried them on. It seemed not even the fog or the sub-zero temperatures could put the woman off the world's oldest profession.

Soon they were at Arthur Whitelock's warehouse. The building lay in darkness, the office lights out. The docks were silent as no ships could moor in the foul weather. It was as if the world had ended and they were the only two left in it. She could have turned back. Could have retreated to her parents' house. But where would that leave Johnny? Where would that leave her? She'd come all this way and, screwing up her courage, she ploughed on.

Caroline tried the front door but wasn't surprised to find it locked.

'What now?' asked Milly.

'We'll try round the back.'

With one hand against the wall so she didn't get lost, Caroline led them to the back of the building. The only way in was through a small top-light window. She found a pallet piled up against a nearby building and moved it closer, hoping it would bear her weight.

'What are you doing?' Milly whispered.

'If I can get to this, I should be able to jimmy it open. My brother showed me how.'

It wasn't any wonder the police hadn't thought twice about arresting him, Caroline thought as she pulled a dinner knife from her pocket.

'Where did you get that?'

'I borrowed it from the Household Dining Room.'

'Did you? When? How did we not notice?'

'I took it earlier when we called in for Robert to find us a hot-water bottle. I hid it up my sleeve when you were talking about Princess Margaret being carted off to Rhodesia after the coronation and the Duke of Edinburgh having another row with the Queen.'

Caroline manoeuvred the knife between the window and the sill. As she'd hoped, the wood was old, flaking and warped, giving her enough room to slip the blade in and push up the catch. Using the tips of her fingers she eased it open as wide as it would go. It didn't give her much room, but there was just enough for her to squeeze through, though she didn't much fancy the drop. With the place in darkness, she couldn't see what was on the other side and she hoped she wouldn't have to fall all the way to the floor.

'I've got it open,' she whispered to Milly.

'What now?'

'Give me a leg up. Cup your hands.'

Milly did as she was told, and Caroline placed her foot down. Milly then hoisted her high enough to pull her body through the window. Reaching out her hands, she found a surface and, shifting her weight forward, used that to lever in her legs. She landed with a soft thud, then lowered herself to the ground from what seemed to be a workbench.

'Are you all right?' Milly whispered. Caroline moved to the door and slid open the bolts to let her in. 'So? What's the plan?' she asked, stepping inside with a quick glance about.

'We need to find some evidence he was involved in the robberies.'

'Like what?'

'I don't know. Let's get looking.' She pulled out her torch and shone it around.

They were in a small back room attached to his office. To her right, a staircase led to the upper floors. To her left was the door to the warehouse proper. She undid the bolts on that too and pushed it open, shining the torch into the large, cavernous space. Boxes and pallets were stored on one side and in the centre, one of the vans was parked. She went to it, Milly following behind. She couldn't see into the back and there were no windows on the rear doors. There was nothing on the driver's or passenger seats either. Disappointment stung. She hadn't known what she might find, yet it was still discouraging that there were no jewels sitting there waiting for her.

'Anything?' Milly asked, coming to her side.

'Nothing.'

'What now? I've checked the drawers over there but there's nothing useful. Just invoices and delivery notes and useless bits of paper.'

'We better check the office.'

They moved back inside, through to the office. In the cold, inky blackness, the ghost of Mr Whitelock and the way he'd treated Caroline lingered. She could see his outline in the dark, hear his voice in her head. The little heater that had cast a golden glow around the room lay silent and cold. She shuddered. What on earth was she doing? This was madness. If she were to get caught, she'd lose her job. She'd never live it down. And what would happen to Milly? Her friend was risking so much for her. She wasn't sure that she deserved it. The tight feeling in her ribcage grew stronger.

Milly began to search the piles of correspondence on the desk while Caroline, urged into action, checked the drawers.

'Remember when we found the King's handkerchief?' Milly asked.

Almost a year before, they'd found a bloody handkerchief of King George VI's wedged behind his bed when they were cleaning his private apartments. The find had been disturbing on many levels, not least because it showed that he wasn't recovering as well as they'd been told he was. Yet Caroline couldn't understand why Milly was bringing it up now.

'Course I do. What about it?'

'Well, if you were going to stash jewellery you'd stolen, you wouldn't do it somewhere the police might look, would you?'

'So where should we search?'

'I don't know, but maybe we should check for loose panelling or around the skirting boards. Somewhere less obvious.'

'Good idea.' They started checking the edges of the office, searching for any possible hiding places, but found nothing. 'Let's check in the garage again.'

They moved back to where the van was, searching on hands and knees behind workbenches, boxes and crates. She was just about to give up hope when Caroline saw a loose brick in a dark corner. The box in front of it was too heavy to move, but she managed to wiggle herself behind it. She pressed the knife she'd brought with her into the loose mortar and eased the brick forwards. The torchlight caught on something, reflecting and brightening the beam.

'Milly! I've got something.'

Milly scrambled to her side and Caroline reached in, stretching her arm and her fingertips to pull out a beautiful gold necklace. The chain was nothing special, but the pendant was fan-shaped and set with diamonds. The ornate art deco style must have been worth a bob or two, and in the centre was a large teardrop-shaped emerald.

'Crikey!' Milly exclaimed.

'He must have kept it for his wife or to sell later,' Caroline reckoned. She couldn't imagine any other reason for keeping stolen goods. Surely he'd want to sell them on as quickly as possible and get rid of them: make the profit he so desperately wanted.

'What do we do now?'

'I don't know.' Caroline's fingers slid over the bright, shining stone. 'Should I take it to the police?'

'And tell them you got it by breaking into Whitelock's warehouse? That won't go down well. They'll just think you're as bad as Johnny. Or that you've planted it to frame Whitelock and get your brother off.'

'But I haven't!' Caroline protested, her voice growing louder.

'But they won't know that. And I'm not sure they'll care.'

'So what do we do?'

A voice, male, loud and angry, sounded from outside. They'd been so absorbed in their task, they hadn't heard the men approaching. Behind it came the sound of an engine: the other van returning.

Caroline started.

'Quick, put it back,' Milly ordered.

Ramming the piece of jewellery back into the hole and pushing the brick in as quickly as possible, Caroline struggled to think. Her hands lacked coordination while fear and panic swirled in her brain. A key was placed in the padlock on the opposite side of the door, the chain rattling, the metal scraping as the latch clicked round. She swung the torch towards the open door of the back room, illuminating the way they'd come in. But the voices were growing louder. It was too far away. The front doors were beginning to move as they heaved them open. There wasn't time to get there. First one door began to open, then the other, and the headlights of the car started to flood the dark garage with light.

Caroline's heart raced. 'Quick,' she said, pulling Milly

down. 'Over there. We'll have to hide behind the crates and sneak out when they've gone.'

'What? No! We have to get out of here.'

'If we move now, they'll see us. Just come with me, quickly.'

Crouching, they hurried along to a stack of crates in a dark corner and edged in behind them. Pulling her skirts closer, Caroline tried to calm her breathing. Blood pounded in her ears and her heart raced. Her breaths were ragged and noisy but, using all her strength, she took slow, steadying breaths, her lungs protesting. The cough that had been plaguing her began to tickle her throat and she grabbed it with her free hand, pressing down gently as though the pressure would stop the cough emerging. She couldn't lose control now, but her breathing was growing quicker.

Two men walked into the garage, chatting between themselves. They were talking about the weather like a couple of washerwomen. Then the car headlights lit the garage with bright white light. Caroline and Milly ducked lower and Arthur Whitelock's voice echoed around them as the engine was switched off and he exited the car. He turned on a light. The unshaded bulb in the middle of the ceiling cast their corner in deep shadow.

'Not a bad night's work, fellas. Now, back 'ome with ya before yer missed.'

'All right, guv,' one replied.

''Ere,' Arthur said. 'Which one of ya left that door open.'

Caroline glanced at Milly, her chest tightening.

'Not me, guv.'

'Nor me.'

'Well, one o' ya must have 'cause I didn't.'

Squeezing her eyes shut, Caroline felt Milly's hand touch hers, their fingers entwining, hoping everything would be all right. She was going to cough. Her lungs protested at every breath; her thighs burned as she crouched but she didn't dare move.

'I swear it weren't me, guv.'

'Nor me.'

Silence.

'Just have a check round,' Whitelock ordered, and Caroline's body began to tremble.

She turned to Milly and mouthed: 'We have to run.' Milly nodded her understanding, her skin as pale with fear as Caroline's own. Caroline risked a look around the edge of the crate. Arthur Whitelock had headed into the office. One man had followed him to the back room and the other was working his way around the garage. He was on the other side of the car, placing it between them, checking the corners and behind the crates. It wouldn't be long till he found them.

The garage doors were still open. This was their only chance. They couldn't go back the way they'd come. They had to head out of the front and hope the smog and gloom would aid their escape, help them hide.

She looked at Milly, nodding towards the doors and widening her eyes to ask if she was ready. Milly nodded and, taking her hand, she mouthed, 'One. Two. Three.'

They both stood up, Caroline a fraction faster than Milly. They made it to the other side of the car as the man exclaimed, 'Oi! You!' and began to chase after them. He caught hold of Milly's arm and their momentum suddenly halted. Tugged backwards, Caroline was vaguely aware of Arthur White-lock's large form filling the doorway to the back room.

Milly gasped, whining and wriggling. Some strange impulse for survival took over and without thinking, Caroline spun back and kicked at the man holding Milly. She hadn't aimed for anything in particular, swinging her leg wildly, but the top of her foot collided with the man's body, squarely between his legs. With a groan, he crumpled, releasing Milly's arm and falling to the floor. Caroline grabbed Milly and they made it out on to the street as Arthur White-lock rounded the car and came for them.

The light from the warehouse was swallowed in the gloom but as she ran, she could make out Arthur White-lock's bulky form sprinting after them. At first it seemed he was gaining on them, his long legs making easy work of the distance, but Caroline pumped her legs, running faster and Milly had no choice but to keep up.

Unable to see her hand in front of her face, they continued to run holding on to each other. Mr Whitelock's curses followed them as he hurtled behind. Their low heels wobbled on the uneven paving. At one point, Caroline lunged to the side as her ankle turned, but Milly pulled her upright and they carried on, turning this way and that until they could barely breathe. Caroline's lungs burned, the need to cough fierce, but they had no idea where Arthur Whitelock was, how near or how far. For all they knew he could have been around the next corner or just a few steps away. They hid in a doorway, pressing themselves into the gap and stood in silence. Caroline pressed her hand to her throat again, breathing deeply, the air hot in her lungs. She covered her mouth with her scarf and her arm, hoping to cover any noise, yet her gasping breaths were loud, echoing in the night.

After a few moments, they braved a glance from their hiding place. The docks had returned to the eerie quiet that had existed before. The distant Thames lapped on the riverbank, the shingle hushing gently as it moved. Carefully, they edged out and into the street.

'Where are we?' Milly asked, glancing up and down.

'I don't know,' Caroline replied, completely disoriented by the fog and the way they'd run in whatever direction had seemed the safest. She'd always thought she knew this area like the back of her hand, but nothing was familiar in this strange, unknown light. Every street seemed new and unwalked; every destroyed house and pile of rubble was novel. 'Let's walk along here until we see a road sign.'

Most road signs were high up on the sides of buildings, so it wasn't until they reached one near enough to a streetlight that they had any idea where they were.

'We're nearer Helen's place than Ma and Pa's. We better head there.'

'Shouldn't we head back to the palace?'

'Let's get to Helen's first and catch our breath. I need a drink of water.' Caroline began coughing, her throat and lungs stinging with the effort. This time, she couldn't catch her breath. She doubled over, barely able to breathe in or out. A cold sweat covered her temples and all Milly could do was rub small circles on her back. Panic gripped her as it seemed this would never end. What would happen to Milly if she keeled over here? Her breaths grew ever more shallow but after a few moments, her lungs eased and air filled them.

'We need to get you back to the palace and to the doctor again,' Milly said.

'Let's just get to Helen's. I need some water.'

They began walking and Milly slipped her arm into Caroline's. 'Thank you for saving me back there.'

'Wasn't about to leave you, was I?'

'I know, but you . . . well, you could have run to get help or something, but you didn't. You stayed with me.' She giggled. 'You got that poor man right in his bits and bobs.'

'I did, didn't I?' Caroline laughed too, though, from the high-pitched sound of her voice, she sounded hysterical due to the shock. 'My foot don't half hurt.'

'Helen won't believe it when we tell her.'

'Neither will Mrs Barnes.'

Milly sighed, her head dropping. 'She's going to kill me when I get back to the palace.'

'Me too. At least we're in it together. And it was worth it. We found proof that Mr Whitelock's involved in these robberies.'

'Yes, but what can we do with that information?'

'I don't know yet,' Caroline replied. 'Let's just try and get to Helen's flat in one piece first.'

With one hand pressed against the walls and gates of houses to guide their way, the smog as dense as ever in front of them, Caroline led them away from the docks, towards their friend's home and safety at last.

Chapter Twenty-Three

They climbed the stairs to Helen's flat, aware of their heels clacking on the linoleum floor in the silence of the night. Most people were sleeping, or at least tucked safely inside their homes. Caroline felt her chest tighten with each step. Her heavy breathing turned into a wheeze, and she doubled over halfway up, covering her mouth as retching and hacking sounds filled the hallway.

'Crikey, Caroline, this cough of yours is getting worse.'

'It's OK. I'll be all right in a minute.' The words were forced out between breaths and didn't sound convincing. It didn't help that the smoggy air was seeping through the loose windowpanes and holes in the damp walls, filling the building.

A woman opened her door and scowled at them in the dim light of the empty corridor. Her eyes roved up and down them both and then she closed the door, watching through the crack until the very last moment. They knocked at Helen's flat as quietly as possible. When there was no answer, Milly tried again, louder. As Caroline leant against the wall, taking long deep breaths and trying to quieten her cough, Milly bent down and called through the letter box.

'Helen? Helen, can you hear me?'

Soft, light footsteps sounded from the other side and

Milly stood back as it opened and light poured on to their faces. Helen's hair hung around her shoulders, mussed up and knotty from sleep. Her eyes were half closed but widened as she focused on them.

'Wh-what are you two doing here? It's the middle of the night.'

Caroline began coughing again. Taking a breath in, she made a strange sound like a goose honking. She had no control over her body.

'We'll tell you everything inside,' Milly said, holding her friend under the elbow and leading her into Helen's flat.

'I'll get you some water.' Helen closed the door behind them, then edged past and into the kitchen.

Her voice rang with concern and, for the first time, Caroline began to worry less about her brother and the trouble they'd only just escaped and more about her health. How would she explain the worsening of her symptoms to the doctor? She'd never had anything like this before. She knew others who'd suffered with their chests were coughing because of the weather, but this had come from nowhere. What if it never went away? She could only hope that it would pass as soon as the fog lifted.

Caroline took the water gratefully and sipped, trying not to splutter. Eventually she said, 'That's better,' and her voice sounded more like her own.

'Where've you been?' Helen walked the short distance to her living room and sat on the small sofa that had come with her from her father's house. Milly took a seat beside her and Caroline sat opposite on the small armchair. She placed the water down on the low coffee table between them, eager to have it near in case she should start puffing again. Helen's place was yet to be decorated for Christmas too and Caroline couldn't help but think that was a good thing. Right now, knowing her brother would most likely be spending it in gaol, it might have made her cry.

After a few deep breaths and more water, Caroline outlined everything that had happened that evening while Helen stared agog, her mouth hanging open.

'You're going to get yourself in trouble, Caroline. Or worse. If these people are up to no good – if they'll rob and steal, and beat up defenceless old men – what do you think they'll do to a woman?'

A shiver passed down Caroline's spine at Helen's words, which rang inside her head. 'I had to do something.'

'The question is what do we do now?' Milly asked.

'First things first, you'll have to stay here tonight.' Helen looked between them both. 'One of you can share with me and the other can sleep on the sofa – I've got enough blankets – and I can always light the fire if need be.'

'Shouldn't we try and get back to Buckingham Palace?' Milly was stricken, her face pale.

'I'm not sure I can,' Caroline admitted. 'My chest and throat hurt so much and as soon as I step outside, I'll start coughing again.'

'Not to mention', Helen added, 'that it's not safe for two young women to be roaming the streets at this time of night in this fog. A neighbour of mine was attacked the other day on his way back from work. And a lady three doors down said she had to run all the way from the tube station because she was sure someone was following her. Even then she took a wrong turn and nearly missed the flats all together. It's not safe. Stay here tonight and head back early in the morning.'

'And Arthur Whitelock might still be looking for us,' Caroline added.

'I'm due to start work at six,' Milly said. 'I'll have to leave by five to get back before Aunt Edie discovers I'm missing.'

Helen adjusted her dressing gown, tightening the collar against the frigid air in the flat. 'You can at least get a couple of hours.'

'And what do we do about Mr Whitelock and the jewellery?'

'What are our options?' Milly asked.

Caroline took another drink of water and began to count on her fingers. 'Tell the police—'

Helen shook her head. 'You illegally broke in. And as they don't believe Johnny now he's told the truth, they won't believe you. They'll arrest you too. And there's every chance that as Mr Whitelock saw you, he'll have moved everything just in case you report it. He won't take any chances.'

'So the information's useless?' Caroline felt tears sting her eyes. After everything she'd gone through, everything her friends had gone through, it was for nothing.

'I don't know. Maybe. I hope not. Oh, I can't think right now.' Helen rubbed her tired eyes. 'Let's try and get some sleep and talk again in the morning. I'll set my alarm for just before five, Milly. Let me get you those blankets.'

Soon Milly was asleep on the sofa, her gentle snores sounding through the paper-thin walls. Helen too was snuffling quietly, uttering occasional moans as she rolled over, but Caroline couldn't rest. Not because her chest was unyielding and heavy, but because she knew there must be a way to use the information to free Johnny. She just had to think clearly. A solution was dancing somewhere in the back of her mind, but before she could grasp it her eyes closed and, for a few hours at least, she slept.

The next morning, the alarm woke Caroline with a start. She sat up and looked over at Helen, who was slowly stirring. Caroline reached across to her friend's bedside, trying not to disturb her more and turned it off.

'Go back to sleep, Helen. We can talk later.'

'No, no, it's fine.' She sat up, pushing her long black hair back from her face. 'I'm awake. I'll make tea.'

They left the bedroom to find Milly already filling the kettle and spooning tea into the pot. She'd washed her face, and her skin was pink from the cold water, her eyes tinged underneath with a blueish hue. Caroline knew she didn't look much better. She'd never been a great wearer of make-up, only since she started her office job, but what little had been on her eyes was now plastered on her cheeks, her eyelashes clumped together. She went to the bathroom and washed her face, using the small remnant of Palmolive soap. The tiny green slice slid in her hands, almost falling down the sink, but she managed to catch it and work up enough of a lather to remove the traces of mascara.

When she returned to the kitchen it was to find her friends sitting in the living room. The dark outside was visible through a gap in the curtains but some of the smog seemed to have lifted and visibility was a little better.

'So,' Helen said as Caroline sat down. A tea tray had been laid out on the coffee table and she poured Caroline a cup, passing it to her. 'I've been thinking about what we should do and I've struggled to come up with any answers.'

'Me too,' Milly replied.

Caroline nodded her agreement. 'There was something in my mind last night but I'm blowed if I can remember what it was.' Milly looked up from her tea, her head tilting to the side. 'It wasn't an idea as such. Just . . . Oh, I don't know. A thought that might have led to an idea. I'm too tired to think right now.'

'There's nothing we can do this morning,' Helen said. 'We all just need to get to work and get on with the day. We can meet again tonight. I'll stay behind and meet you in the Household Lounge after dinner.'

'Meet us *for* dinner,' Milly said. 'It's the least we can do after disturbing you late at night. Robert will sort it out with Mrs Chadwick.'

'If you're sure.'

Milly nodded.

'He's a good man,' Caroline said. 'And he's lucky to have you. I'll speak to Ma about your wedding dress when I see her next. It'll give her something else to think about.'

Caroline's mind drifted to Connor and the conversation they'd had yesterday evening. How could it have only been the evening before? It seemed far longer. She stifled a yawn, pressing a hand to her mouth. How was she to get through today? She'd have to pay twice as much attention as usual. There wasn't room for mistakes.

'We'd better get going,' Milly said, placing her cup on

the tray and standing up. Caroline did the same and Helen showed them out.

They had just stepped into the hall, bidding Helen goodbye as quietly as possible, when a door further down opened and the woman who had watched them arrive last night stepped out. She wore her hair in rollers and an old pink flannelette dressing gown tied tightly around her waist, the fabric pilled and worn, as were the flat, broken slippers on her feet.

She marched over to them. 'What's going on here?'

'Nothing, Mrs Puddifer,' Helen replied. 'My friends got caught in the smog last night and had to stay with me, that's all. They couldn't make it back to the palace.'

'The palace,' she scoffed. 'You know, I'm not sure I believe you work at Buckingham Palace. Any of you.' She looked Caroline and Milly up and down, sneering as she did so. 'What kind of palace work requires you to be out so late at night?'

'I had to visit my ma,' Caroline replied. 'She's sick. Then we got stuck in the smog.'

'Really.' The woman clearly didn't believe a word of it and the lines on her face pulled together as she pursed her mouth. 'I'm no fool. I know what type of girls you are.'

Helen protested. 'We're not any type of girls—'

'I won't have your sort living in one of my flats.'

'We're not—'

'You think I don't know you're pregnant? You think I haven't seen that bump of yours?'

Where Helen's robe was tied, it emphasised the roundness.

'I was going to tell you,' Helen said quietly.

'And that ring? You weren't wearing it the first time you came here and then all of a sudden it's shining bright as day? You think I missed that detail? I might not have had much schooling but I ain't no fool.'

'Mrs Puddifer, my husband died—'

'I'll not listen to lies.'

'I'm not lying. I assure you I was married and he passed away!'

'Nonsense. I know your sort. Found yourself a fancy man and then you got knocked up. Couldn't wait till your wedding day – or was he married?' Helen recoiled. 'Ah, that's it, is it?'

'I assure you it's not.' Though Helen lifted her chin, her confidence had vanished, and tears glistened in her eyes.

'Low morals, that's what it is. Disgusting. You should've kept your legs crossed. You've got till this smog clears, then I want you out.'

Helen was stricken and guilt surged so fiercely through Caroline she thought she might be sick. She hadn't meant to bring even more problems to Helen's door. 'Please, Mrs Puddifer, this isn't Helen's fault,' she pleaded. 'We got lost in the smog on the way back to the palace and I couldn't stop coughing. Please, don't blame Helen for us turning up late at night and—'

'It's really not what you think,' Milly added calmly, but the old woman was not to be moved.

'Until the smog's cleared,' she said again, jabbing a finger towards Helen. 'I'll not have tarts and unmarried mothers in my flats. Shame on you. Shame on you all!' She turned on her heel and marched back into her apartment.

Helen fell against the doorframe, sniffing, wiping tears from her cheeks.

'What have we done?' Milly said, looking at Caroline.

'Helen, I'm so sorry.'

She dropped her eyes to the floor. 'She would have thrown me out sooner or later – once I told her about the baby, or the bump became more pronounced. It's just happened earlier than I thought.'

Caroline shook her head. 'No, this is my fault. She might have changed her mind if you'd had a chance to speak to her, if we hadn't turned up in the middle of the night giving the impression we're . . . working girls.'

'What will you do?' Milly asked. 'Maybe Aunt Edie can find you somewhere at the palace?'

Helen shook her head. 'They're already allowing me to keep my job; I can't ask them for more.'

'Then what can we do?'

Helen's voice wavered as her eyes went to Mrs Puddifer's closed door. 'Nothing. There's nothing you can do.'

Chapter Twenty-Four

By the time it was nearing eight o'clock, Caroline was starving, her stomach growling and empty. She and Milly had parted to their own quarters at the palace and were now meeting Mrs Barnes at the Household Breakfast Room.

After the previous night, and perhaps from lack of sleep, the room looked different. The finely upholstered chairs, the shining silver cutlery and fine white china all spoke of a world that didn't exist anywhere else. Where else would a poor East End girl eat in such finery? How had she come to take it so for granted? She joined the queue and loaded her plate with eggs and her fair share of bacon, adding plenty of toast to fill the gaping hole in her stomach.

'Blimey, Caroline,' Mrs Barnes said. 'Woken up hungry, have you?' She glanced at Milly, whose plate was equally loaded. 'You too? Crikey. Well, it's nice to see you growin' girls eatin' and not starvin' yourselves like some of these young 'uns do.' When neither of them responded, Mrs Barnes continued: 'Well, we've got a lot to get on with today, Milly. You look ever so tired though. And you, Caroline.' She took a bite of toast covered in marmalade and chewed thoughtfully, her eyes glancing between them both and the cloth-covered tabletop. 'Right,' she said, tossing the crust on to her plate, crumbs scattering on to her lap. 'What's going on?'

'Nothing, Aunty,' Milly declared.

'It was just a difficult night that's all – with my cough.' Caroline touched her throat for additional effect. It wasn't a total lie. She did feel out of breath and her lungs were sore. 'I found it hard to sleep last night.'

'I see.' Caroline began to relax; then her relief faded as Mrs Barnes went on: 'You think I was born yesterday, do you? Think no one told me you two slipped out of the gates last night and didn't get back till the early hours of the mornin'?'

Milly's mouth hung open and Caroline sat speechless.

'You knew?' Milly asked, resting her hands on the table, her knife and fork paused.

'Of course I knew. Nothin' gets past me and everyone knows you here. Did you think the guards wouldn't tell me?'

'But they don't tend to come in here. They—'

'They told a footman who told me. You can't get away with anythin', my girl. I'd have thought you'd have learned that by now. So . . .' She turned to Caroline, whose stomach knotted under Mrs Barnes's accusatory gaze. 'Do you want to tell me what you've been up to?'

Caroline lowered her eyes, ashamed of her deceit. 'I'm sorry I lied, Mrs Barnes, but I had to. I didn't want anyone to follow me, but then Milly did and . . . I told her to go back, but she refused.'

'Quite right too,' Mrs Barnes replied, folding her hands in her lap. Milly gave her aunt a relieved look.

Voices swelled as more and more people joined them in the breakfast room. They brushed past the enormous flower displays that had been added by the specialist team who decorated the palace. With the noise level rising, Caroline felt it

259

safe enough to speak. No one was paying attention to them, deep in their own conversations and plans for the day.

'I went to Arthur Whitelock's warehouse and had a look around.'

'You mean you broke in and rifled through his stuff?'

She nodded.

Mrs Barnes's tone carried disappointment, but not exactly surprise. 'And what did you find? The man wasn't stupid enough to leave somethin' lyin' around, was he?'

'I found some jewellery hidden in the wall behind a crate. He's guilty, Mrs Barnes. I just need to prove it to the rozzers. The trouble is, he saw us . . .'

'He did more than that,' Milly added. 'He chased us.' She blushed under her aunt's disapproving gaze. 'We were lucky to get away. But then we got lost in the fog and ended up near Helen's so stayed there. And now she's getting thrown out because of us.'

'Slow down.' Mrs Barnes held her hands out, palms up, to both of them. 'I can't keep up with you gallopin' at that sort of speed. First things first. You found somethin' at Mr Whitelock's? What did you do after that?'

'Nothing but get to Helen's.'

'So you haven't told anyone.'

'No. The police won't believe me, and I don't want to get arrested for breaking in. Helen said he'll have probably moved it by now.'

'Most likely. And what's all this about Helen gettin' thrown out?'

Milly continued. 'Her landlady saw us enter and leave. She thinks we're working girls and knows that Helen's pregnant. She said Helen can stay till the smog's cleared and then she has to find somewhere else to live. I feel terrible.'

Caroline wiped her mouth with the napkin and crumpled it in her hands. They should have come straight back here and not involved her. Helen had had a rough enough time of it over the last few months and didn't need any other worries in her condition.

'Now that is a problem,' Mrs Barnes said, glancing at the clock.

'She's joining us for dinner,' Milly replied. 'I'm going to square it with Robert.'

'Good. We can talk then. For now, we need to get on with the day. One thing at a time.' She stood and placed a hand on Caroline's shoulder, giving it a good squeeze. 'I'm not happy at you takin' such risks, but I understand why you did it. We'll figure out what to do next. For now, drink your tea, and eat up, we've work to do.'

She bustled away, running into Mr Newington. He drew her into a corner, whispering to her. From the smile on Mrs Barnes's face, he was saying something sweet. Milly smiled, and then stared at Caroline.

'I thought she'd explode.'

'Me too. Your aunt is full of surprises, Milly.'

'Isn't she just.'

As Caroline entered the offices, she was amazed she'd made it back here and to work on time. Her eyes were tired and gritty, the lids heavy. It was going to be a long day.

She scanned the room and was surprised to find not only

a floral display fit for the Queen's apartment, but a few sprigs of holly had been placed in the corner of the room. Connor was back at his desk. The cut on his head was still covered by a plaster and angry purple bruising lined his cheek, just above the contour of his well-defined jaw.

'You're back?' Caroline said, eyes skimming the pile of papers already laid out on her desk.

'Yes. The doctor said I could return to work and go home.'

'That's good.'

Mr Newington flitted about the room, handing out work. He smiled when he saw her, and she responded with a grin of her own. The last thing she needed was him asking questions and checking she was all right. As tired as she was, her defences were lower and the smirks and angry glances from Mrs Coniston and Miss Western were already affecting her. She ignored them as Barbara turned around.

'Crikey, are you all right, Caroline? You look like death warmed up. You're not coming down with this flu, are you?'

'No, I'm fine. Just tired.' She settled down into her seat. 'Are you feeling better?'

'Much. Thanks.'

'So,' Connor said without looking at her, instead holding up two documents and seemingly reading them both at the same time. 'Where did you get to last night? Gossip is that you left the palace late.'

'Who else knows?' She hadn't thought that whoever had told Mrs Barnes would have mentioned it to other people, but she should have realised that would have happened.

Connor shrugged. 'That I don't know, but I'm guessing it's to do with your brother?'

Since she'd spoken to him in the surgery, something had shifted in their relationship and for some reason she couldn't explain, she wanted to tell him the truth and seek his advice. Out of all the people she knew, she wanted him to help her to figure out what to do now.

'I can't tell you here,' she said. 'Do you—' She faltered, wishing her courage hadn't all been spent the night before. It wasn't for women to ask men such things but, somehow, she found a bit of the bravery she'd shown the night before. She leaned in so the others couldn't hear. 'Do you want to join me and my friends for dinner? They're going to help me figure out what to do now.'

His eyes widened in surprise. 'I'd like that very much.'

The warmth of his smile filled her, chasing away some of the fatigue and worry. She began to work, aware of his occasional glances and those of Miss Western, who clearly wasn't happy Caroline was still there.

After a few hours, just as Caroline's energy was fading and her stomach rumbling loudly for lunch, a footman entered.

Mr Newington looked up in surprise, the papers he was sorting almost falling from his grasp. 'Mr Walsh, what can I do for you?'

'I've been asked to fetch Miss Stratton for Mr Lascelles.'

'Oh. Right. I see.' He looked at Caroline, who was already standing and pushing her chair in.

She didn't know what she'd done and was sure she hadn't made any mistakes in the work she'd produced that morning, but the chance of her making errors grew stronger every time her mind wandered.

'Off you go then, Caroline,' Mr Newington said cheerfully, though there was a note of concern in his voice.

Caroline followed the footman through the corridors, expecting to stop as they hit Mr Lascelles's office, but Mr Walsh continued up to the first floor, towards the Queen's study. Caroline's nerves tied into a knot that sank to the pit of her stomach. What could the Queen want with her? Surely if she'd made a mistake in her work, Mr Lascelles would be the one dealing with it?

The footman knocked and a second on the opposite side of the door opened it. Mr Walsh walked in first, formally announcing Caroline.

Behind her large dark wooden desk, the Queen sat, head down, writing furiously. Mr Lascelles had taken the chair opposite her and a second, empty one had been placed beside it.

Mr Lascelles stood and motioned Caroline towards it. 'Take a seat, Miss Stratton, if you please.'

She sat, folding her hands into her lap and toying with her fingernails. The Queen stopped writing and looked up, placing the pen down carefully in line with the sheet of paper. With her iron-rigid posture, she sat upright. She was wearing a different shade of lipstick then normal, Caroline noticed. A coral pink that looked more like something Princess Margaret would wear. She couldn't decide if it suited her or not. Perhaps it was because the Queen was unsmiling, and her eyes were stern.

Caroline's chest, which had improved since being back inside, felt tight and the cough that had been plaguing her tried once again to emerge. She forced it down, swallowing heavily, aware that her throat had moved with the effort. She pushed her hands together in her lap.

'Now, Miss Stratton.'

That the Queen hadn't called her Caroline, as she had done before, sent a shiver of fear down her spine. This meeting felt far more formal than any of the others they'd had.

'I'm aware that despite my request for all members of staff to remain in the palace until the smog has cleared, you ignored this and went out last night. Is that correct?'

Caroline froze. How did she know? Why did she care?

As if sensing her unease, she said, 'I asked the guards to inform me of anyone who left the palace after my express wish that they do not.'

'I . . .' She couldn't think what to say and shrank under Mr Lascelles's hard eyes. The Queen waited for her to respond, her expression neutral and unchanging.

'I—' Caroline swallowed again. 'I had to go and see my ma. She's sick. It – it was an emergency.'

Lying had never come easily to her and she'd never once thought she'd be lying to the Queen of England. But her ma *was* sick – in a way. Her heart was breaking, and the longer her son was in prison the more she was fading.

The Queen studied her, bringing her hands up from her lap and placing them on the desk, still clasped together. 'I am sorry to hear that. What is wrong with her?'

'She's tired. Not eating.' Caroline tried to think of other symptoms that would warrant her to disobey the queen's commands. 'She can't keep anything down.'

'And how did you know?'

'A note was left at the gate for me.'

'And you didn't return until very early this morning?'

'The fog – it's been giving me an awful cough. I stayed at home and came in first thing.'

'I see.'

'I ain't done nothing wrong, Your Majesty. I swear. I'm sorry I left but I had to. I—'

The Queen held up a hand, which instantly silenced her. 'I understand. Thank you. You may go.'

She began to stand, surprised at how quickly the meeting had ended. Did the Queen believe her? She couldn't tell.

'Thank you, ma'am.'

'Please follow my instructions in the future, Caroline.' The use of her name reassured her, though the Queen's tone was less than friendly. 'I have been taking an interest in you. You have worked hard and done well for yourself. I do not want that interest to be in vain.'

'It won't be, ma'am. I promise.'

She curtseyed and left, the footman opening the door for her. Mr Walsh had gone, but she passed him and made her way back to the office, unsure what to make of it. The Queen had been taking an interest in her? What did that mean? And what would happen if she let her down?

Chapter Twenty-Five

Settled in the Household Lounge after dinner, Caroline watched as Helen's hands rested atop her stomach, her eye roving to the Christmas tree now fully decorated in the corner of the room. Dark green and bright red glass baubles glittered, and swathes of ribbon circled the tree. Her pregnancy was evident now and Caroline wished again she hadn't gone to Helen's flat.

For the best part of an hour, they'd been discussing her predicament and what could be done to solve it when Caroline bolted upright, an idea occurring to her that, had she been less tired, would surely have struck much earlier.

'Go to Ma and Pa's,' Caroline instructed her friend. 'Johnny's room's spare at the moment and even when he comes home' – she couldn't imagine any other possibility – 'he can sleep on the sofa till you find somewhere else, or he does. They'll help you. I know they will.'

'I – I couldn't—' Helen shook her head, her dark hair tumbling on to her face. 'They already have enough to worry about and they're too kind to say no. I don't want to be a burden to them.'

'You wouldn't be. You're a friend in need and you've met my ma. She'd be offended if you didn't ask her for help.

Having you there might even be good for her. Give her some-one to fuss over.'

'What a marvellous idea, Caroline,' Mrs Barnes said.

Mr Newington had joined them, As had Robert and Milly. The wedding book sat on the small table between them, pages dog-eared where Milly and Robert had been study-ing them. Caroline's gaze drifted to the door for Connor. She wondered where he'd got to. At the end of their day, as they'd been leaving the office, he'd said he had an errand to run before meeting them but had promised he'd be there.

'You really think I should?' Helen asked. 'You don't think I'd get in the way?'

'Of what? Ma and Pa don't exactly have a whirlwind social life at the best of times. They'd be happy to have you there. And it'd be handy for the midwife.'

'She's been wonderful,' Helen replied, beaming. 'She said everything seems fine. The baby's growing well, and I'm as fit as a fiddle. Just a little tired.'

'Then Ma and Pa's might be the best place for you. You'll be able to go home and relax. Ma loves to cook. They really will be happy to have you there.'

'I'll pay rent of course. I can give them what I was giving Mrs Puddifer.'

'They won't take that much,' Caroline replied, shaking her head. 'Not when you've gone from your own flat to a small room. And it will be small. Not sure what we'll do with all your furniture.'

'That's a point.'

They fell into a contemplative silence, everyone mulling over the latest problem. Caroline's idea suddenly seemed to lose momentum. When they'd moved Helen from her father's house into the small flat, they'd left a lot of furniture behind but what she had now still wouldn't fit into a small single room.

Mr Newington looked at Helen. 'I say, I can look after some of it for you.'

'Can you?' Milly asked, glancing at him and then her aunt.

'There's room in my house and I also have a small garage where some things can be stored. I'll happily look after it until you're back in your own place.'

'I'd almost forgotten you lived off site,' Caroline added.

'Oh, Mr Newington!' Helen's eyes were shining with gratitude. 'I don't know what to say. Caroline, your family are welcome to anything of mine they can use.'

'That's kind of you, Helen. Ma and Pa'll help you move. We should probably go and see them tomorrow as that evil woman said you have to be out so soon.'

'At least the fog's lifting now.' Helen glanced out of the window and, though it was dark, they could see the smog had cleared.

'It'll have to be after work,' Caroline said. 'And no telling them what I've been up to. They'll have kittens if they know.'

Helen nodded as Caroline and then Milly stifled a yawn.

Mrs Barnes pointed at them both. 'You two need some sleep.'

Caroline had never wanted her bed more than she did in that moment. Then Connor appeared in the doorway, and she became suddenly more alert, unable to keep the smile from her face. Where her attraction to Timothy had been driven by his good looks and smooth words, with Connor she saw a kindness in his eyes that spoke to his good character. Something Timothy had been lacking. Though it didn't stop some of the people in the room staring at him and whispering to each other.

'Hello,' he said. 'May I join you?'

'Of course.'

He pulled a chair over and Caroline began the introductions. Mrs Barnes and Mr Newington smiled warmly. Robert and Milly, holding hands, nodded a greeting and even Helen mustered a grin.

A slightly awkward silence ensued and Caroline, eager for Connor to feel welcome amongst her friends, said, 'We were just talking about last night.'

'You said you'd tell me what happened.'

There hadn't been a chance at work, especially after her chat with the Queen. When she'd returned, Miss Western and Mrs Coniston had eyed her suspiciously, but she'd refused to give them any idea what the meeting had been about.

Let them wonder, she'd thought as she'd sorted her papers, prioritising her work.

She outlined everything, including Helen's predicament, though Caroline was careful to stick to the official story – that her husband had died in a car crash. Perhaps one day she'd tell him the truth about Helen, but it wasn't her secret to share. To Connor's credit, if he suspected anything contrary, he didn't say so and simply nodded his understanding, smiling sympathetically at Helen.

'So what are you going to do?' he asked Caroline gently.

She'd been thinking about it all day. The elusive idea that had shadowed her mind as she'd fallen asleep had danced with her thoughts, but whenever she tried to remember what exactly it was, it fluttered away. As Mrs Barnes poured Connor a cup of tea and began to talk with him about where in Ireland he came from and if he had any family, her eyes wandered to Helen. She was sure it had something to do with her, but she couldn't put her finger on it.

'My family all live in Malahide, near Dublin. It's beautiful. I came here for the work, but I'd go back there in a heartbeat if I could.'

'I've always wanted to visit Dublin,' Mr Newington said. 'I'm sure my father once told me we had family out that way.'

Something to do with the word 'father' flashed into Caroline's mind and her eyes once more wandered to Helen. Was it to do with her? The thought remained abstract, but one thing she did know, she'd have to go and see Johnny again. She had to tell him what she'd found. At least then he'd know she was doing everything she could for him.

'Caroline?' Connor said, tilting his head to catch her eye. Clearly, she'd been lost in thought. 'Is everything all right?'

'Fine,' she replied with a weak smile. 'I just realised I'm going to have to go and see Johnny again. Let him know what's happened.'

'Perhaps he'll have some thoughts on it himself. You never know. Do you want me to come with you?'

'I'll go with her,' Helen said, colouring a little and then turning to stare out of the window.

'Thank you, Connor, but I think it'd be best if Helen came.'

She could only imagine what Johnny would say to Connor and she didn't want him meeting a member of her family for the first time in prison. She turned to Helen, 'We can tell him you're staying at Ma and Pa's. He'll want to know what's happened and you can reassure him you're fine.' She turned back to Connor: 'You don't mind, do you?'

'No. Of course not.'

The decision made, conversation moved on to palace gossip. The Christmas dance was less than a week away and it was all anyone was talking about: what they'd wear, who might dance with whom, if the Queen would be there. The Coronation Commission had met again, and the Duke of Edinburgh had been in a foul mood afterwards, though no one knew why. A short while later, Helen headed home. Robert and Milly settled together a little further away to talk about their wedding plans, and Mrs Barnes and Mr Newington huddled in a corner discussing something secret, heads bowed together as if they too were hatching a plan.

'So,' Connor said. 'That's Mrs Barnes, is it? The woman who's stolen Mr Newington's heart?'

She chuckled. 'It is. Is that what people are saying in the office?' She suddenly began to cough, and Connor looked worried. 'It's all right. It's getting better,' she reassured him. 'Are they saying Mrs Barnes stole his heart? I bet Mrs Coniston and Miss Western think she's tried to trap him to further her own ends.'

'It's meant kindly. Well, by me and Barbara it is.' The use of Barbara's first name sent a sting of jealousy through her, but she kept her expression neutral. 'You're not that wrong about Coniston and Western, but you shouldn't listen to them. Most of us are glad to see him happy. He's a nice man. He deserves it.'

'Mrs Barnes is a good judge of character and if she likes him, then he must be good.'

'You respect her a lot, don't you?'

'I do. She's always looked out for me. Milly and Helen too.' She pushed her wild red hair back from her face. She hadn't had a chance to wash it since going out the night before and it smelled musty from the fog.

'Mr Newington's done that for me. He used to ask me out for a drink after work if he thought I was homesick.' She'd always known Mr Newington was a kind man and he clearly had good taste as he liked Mrs Barnes, but to know he'd tried to help Connor cemented her good opinion of him. Connor continued: 'Your friends are nice. I like them.'

'I think they like you too.'

'You're all very close. Not like in the offices.'

'Maybe it's the work. It's hard and tiring so we support each other. I know I'm lucky to have them.'

'They're lucky to have you.' Their eyes met and Caroline had the feeling of being exposed – yet safe. He seemed to see her in a way no other man had and her stomach flipped. 'So, Caroline Stratton, is life in the palace always this boring for you?'

She threw her head back and laughed. 'There's never a dull moment, as Mrs Barnes would say. I bet you're wishing you'd never met me.'

'Oh, I wouldn't say that.'

Her breath hitched and her skin prickled, suddenly aware

273

of the air around her, of the cigarette smoke lifting the delicate hairs on her arms.

'What are they talking about, do you think?' Connor asked, nodding to Mrs Barnes and Mr Newington.

'I don't know. But whatever it is, it seems to be important—'

'And secret.'

She'd have to ask Milly – see if she knew.

'I'd better get going,' Connor said, standing up. Caroline did the same, though a part of her wanted him to stay. She searched for something to say – a reason for him to remain so they could talk longer. 'I'll see you tomorrow. At work, I mean,' he added.

'Yes,' she replied, forcing this unknown happiness from her tone. 'Nine o'clock on the dot. And thank you for not judging me – about Johnny.'

'If you knew some of the things my brothers have got up to in their time, you'd be the one judging me.'

'And you had nothing to do with it, I suppose?' She crossed her arms over her chest, pretending she wouldn't believe his answer.

He laughed, took his coat from the back of the chair and shrugged it on. 'Nothing at all. I was always a good boy.'

Caroline felt four pairs of eyes on her. Mr Newington and Mrs Barnes were smiling fondly while Robert and Milly stared as if they were at the pictures watching a film. She ignored them.

'Goodnight, Caroline.'

''Night, Connor.'

She watched him leave, enjoying the swagger in his walk, his upright bearing, the strength in his shoulders. He still received disdainful looks from some of the people and she was sure a comment was made as Connor's head spun towards a young man in the corner, but he didn't stop.

A physical longing began to burn within her. She wanted to feel his arms around her, holding her close. To feel his lips on hers. She shook her head, trying to displace the thoughts that she'd worried would never touch her again. Yet in her heart she held tightly to them, protecting them from the shadows and scars of previous experiences that, for the first time, weren't able to reach her.

Chapter Twenty-Six

'Caroline,' her ma said, opening the front door of the house. 'And Helen too. Come in, come in.' She took her daughter in a hug, the fake cheer failing almost instantly; then she gathered herself and embraced Helen too. 'What a lovely surprise. Are you stayin' for dinner?'

'If that's all right,' Helen replied.

'I said it would be,' Caroline added.

'Course it is. Come on inside out of the cold. Pa,' Ma called back towards the kitchen. 'Helen's 'avin' tea too. Ain't that lovely?'

'Wonderful,' he replied, leaning back so his head was visible around the doorframe. ''Ow's that baby of yours?'

'Fine, thank you. I've been seeing the midwife and she's happy with how things are progressing. Apparently, I'm as fit as a fiddle – now the morning sickness has gone, anyway.'

Ma took over the conversation. She was just as thin as she had been before, her cheeks sunken, and there was an almost manic edge to her cheerfulness. 'Oh, that can be 'orrible. Glad you're feelin' better though. We've got mince for dinner and boiled potatoes and carrots. That all right?'

'It sounds lovely,' Helen replied.

'So, what's the gossip in the palace, Caroline?'

They moved towards the kitchen, where steam billowed

from the pans on the hob, misting the windows with a sheen of condensation. Caroline noted the lack of Christmas decorations in the house. They'd never gone overboard. Even as children, her and Johnny's attention hadn't lasted long when it came to making paper chains, but the house seemed desolate without any at all. Caroline could understand her parents' wish not to celebrate, but perhaps it might cheer them to put up a small tree in the parlour? The neighbours, she'd noticed, were beginning to decorate windows and hang wreaths on their front doors. Her ma was acting strangely, as if she'd never been happier, and Caroline caught her pa's worried glances towards her.

Ma took the kettle, filled it and placed it on top of the last, empty gas ring. The water over the potatoes was boiling fiercely and she took a knife, piercing one to check how long they had left.

'Not much to talk about really,' Caroline replied, taking a seat at the table. 'Did you see the announcement yesterday that the whole coronation will be televised?'

'I did. Very excitin'. Not that we'll be watchin', but your pa's tryin' to persuade old Geordie down the pub to buy one.'

Geordie was the landlord of her pa's local, so nicknamed because he had a strong Newcastle accent.

'That'd be good. Then you can all watch it down there.'

'That's what we were thinkin'. We don't want to miss out. There's been talk of a street party too. No one's spoken to us directly of course . . .' The note of sadness was clear in her voice. 'Only our true friends have mentioned it. Apparently, the rest of the street don't want us there because of – well, you

277

know. I told 'em 'e's innocent and it's all a mistake but what can you do? People'll believe what they want to believe.'

Caroline brushed a few crumbs of bread from the table-top into her hand and placed them in the bin. It wasn't like her ma to miss something like that. 'It's still months away. A lot could change by then.'

'People have long memories round 'ere,' she replied bitterly.

Ma busied herself in the kitchen and, despite their attempts to help with dinner, they were told firmly to remain in their seats. Caroline risked her ma's displeasure to grab cutlery from the drawer under the sink and lay the table. When they'd all enjoyed the meal – her ma managing to turn gristly mince soft and tender – and they'd discussed the goings-on in the street, Caroline caught Helen's eye, silently informing her she was going to bring up the matter they'd come here for.

'Ma, Pa, there's something I need to ask you.'

'Cor blimey, that sounds serious,' Ma replied. 'It's not about Johnny, is it?' Her voice wavered as she said his name and she kept her eyes averted, standing up and beginning to clear the table.

'No, but try not to worry, Ma. We'll hire a good solicitor for him. There must be something they can do. It's about Helen here actually.'

'Oh?' Ma placed the plates on the counter and retook her seat.

Pa removed his pipe where he'd just lit it.

'She's been kicked out of her flat now the landlady knows she's pregnant. She's got to move out as soon as possible.'

'Oh, Helen!' Ma leapt up from the table and engulfed Helen in a hug. Helen, unused to such exuberant contact, started and Caroline smiled, knowing she hadn't had a mother around to give her such affection. 'You poor thing. When did this 'appen?'

'Yesterday morning,' she replied, tears shining in her eyes. 'Mrs Puddifer's never been a nice woman, but I have to admit, it's sooner than I expected. I thought I might at least get another month or two. I've been trying to hide the pregnancy as much as possible.'

Ma returned to her seat. 'You can't hide it forever. Your body's changin'. You don't just look like you've had a big dinner or put on a bit of weight. It's the roundin' that does it. Gives it away every time.'

'We were wondering', Caroline began, 'if she could come and stay here for a bit? Johnny's room's going spare, and Mr Newington's said he'll store her furniture for her. What do you think?'

'Of course she can!' her pa said. 'And Johnny can sleep on the sofa when 'e gets 'ome if she hasn't found anywhere better by then.'

'I can't imagine anywhere will be better than here,' Helen replied. 'And I'll pay rent of course. I'll give you exactly what I was paying Mrs Puddifer.'

Pa shook his head. 'No, no, no.' As Caroline had expected he added, 'We can't take money for a whole flat when you've only got a room. A bit to cover your food will be more than enough.'

'Please,' Helen protested. 'Let me give you what I was paying before. You're taking me in at short notice. I can't tell you how grateful I am.'

279

He shuffled and stroked his beard. 'Well, we can talk about that later, I s'pose.'

Lillian beamed at Helen. 'I'll change the sheets first thing tomorrow. And flick a duster round while Pa comes and 'elps move some of your stuff.'

'Oh, that's so kind of you, but I've got till Saturday. Mrs Puddifer can't expect me to move all my furniture before then – she knows I work – and with Mr Newington working too, he won't be able to do anything before then either. But if you want to use any of my furniture, you're more than welcome to. You're being so kind to me, and I'd prefer it to go to good use than sit in a garage or Mr Newington's spare room.'

'Well, that's somethin'. Caroline, why don't you show Helen Johnny's room, so she knows what she wants to bring with 'er? And I'll make some puddin'. I think this calls for a bit of a celebration, don't you? Tinned pears and custard?'

'Smashin',' Pa replied.

They stood and Helen thanked them once again.

'We'll be 'appy to 'elp you as long as you need it,' Caroline's ma said.

Already her cheeks contained more colour than they had when Caroline and Helen had arrived, and her eyes were brighter. Her fears and worries over Johnny were still there, and they were ever present for Caroline too, but this gave Ma something else to focus on.

Upstairs, Caroline opened the door to Johnny's room with mounting nerves. Their house was small, in need of decoration, draughty in winter and nothing like the posh, two-bedroomed detached house Helen had lived in with her father, or the flat she'd occupied alone. It would be a disappointment to her: a step down in the world.

'It's not much,' Caroline said as she opened the door, hoping to pre-empt Helen's dissatisfaction. 'I know it's not—'

'It's perfect,' Helen said, reaching out and touching her arm.

'There's not much of a view.' Caroline stepped forwards and flung the curtains apart allowing the light from the streetlamp to spill in. Johnny's room was at the front of the house with a view over the street. Though night had descended now, the day had been brighter than it had been for a long while. The smog had all but gone. A few children played in the street in front of their house, jumping a hopscotch that had been chalked on to the ground. A small girl skipped with a skipping rope, the handle of one end missing, the rope tied in a knot. Caroline wondered if she'd get a new one for Christmas.

'It's perfect,' Helen said again. 'And all the better for your ma and pa being such lovely people.'

'They're not bad, are they?'

'You're lucky to have them. Will you tell them what you found at Arthur Whitelock's?'

She shook her head. 'Not until I know for sure I can do something with it. There was something floating in my head the other day, but I can't remember what it was.' Caroline perched on Johnny's bed and Helen sat beside her. Helen toyed with her hands, running her index finger along the rim of each nail. 'Are you sure you want to come to the prison with me on Sunday?' Caroline asked.

'I don't mind. I – I want to see Johnny.'

Caroline had wondered for a while if there was something between her brother and her friend. Now she knew for sure. 'You like him, don't you?'

Helen looked at her almost apologetically. 'I do. When he helped me move that day, he never judged me. He knew my situation but didn't care and since then, he's done all he can to help me, bringing me food . . . even flowers. He's a good man.' A tinge of pink crept over Helen's cheeks, making her look even prettier with her dark hair and blue eyes.

'Oh, Helen, you do have terrible taste in men.' Caroline burst out laughing. 'I know Johnny can be cheeky and charming but he's not good enough for you, and I say that as his sister. I love him to bits but look at the mess he's got himself into here.' Their laughter subsided and silence filled the room.

'You don't approve?' Helen asked quietly.

'Of him!' Caroline clarified, grabbing her arm in both hands. 'I worry he'd let you down.'

'Why, because of what's happened to him now?' Caroline nodded. 'He's in prison because he was helping someone and their family. That that person has let him down isn't Johnny's fault. He's kind and considerate and has a generous spirit.'

'I know he's a good man and he really has tried to leave his past behind him, but you need someone with a job. A good job, earning decent money. Someone reliable.'

'Johnny can get a job again. He had one before and was a good employee. He just made a mistake, Caroline. And I don't need someone who earns lots of money. I need someone who makes me happy – and Johnny does.'

'I suppose he'd be less inclined to make mistakes if he had someone like you and a baby to look after. And he likes you. I know he does. I knew it the moment he saw you.'

'You have to prove Arthur Whitelock's guilty,' Helen said, her expression growing serious. 'And get Johnny out of prison. He makes me feel . . . happy. Content. Just as Connor O'Keefe makes you feel.'

Caroline looked up sharply, feeling her own cheeks redden. 'It's true,' she confided, grateful to have the chance to talk about it with someone she trusted implicitly. 'I don't know when it happened exactly – Lord knows I didn't like him at all when I first met him – but as I've got to know him, I've realised there's something kind about him. Something gentle. After Timothy I didn't think I'd ever like anyone again or want to be alone with them, but Connor makes me feel alive inside, you know? But safe as well.'

'I do know.' Helen moved her hand over Caroline's where it sat in her lap, and they held hands together. Caroline rested her head on Helen's shoulder, just as she'd done with her own sister, while her friend continued: 'I like him very much, you know – Connor. I think your instincts are right about him. And he clearly likes you.'

'Really?'

'Of course! Why else would he join us last night and offer to go with you to see Johnny?'

The idea made Caroline smile, though Helen couldn't see it. It was a smile that filled her entire body, shielding her from the cold and protecting her from the draughts inching in through the gaps in the windowpane. Her brother was a good man too but if she succeeded in getting him out of prison, he'd have to prove he was worthy of her friend. She couldn't allow him to let Helen down as Jake Walker had, and she was sure that Helen's love would be the making of him. Not to mention how pleased it would make her ma and pa.

If she could find a way to get him out of prison.

Lillian knocked on the door, and they both stood up.

'The room's perfect,' Helen said.

'Good. I've got somethin' for you, Caroline.' She held out a dress that had been folded over her arm. 'I've altered it for you. It should fit like a glove now.'

It was the dress she'd seen before: the one she'd hoped to wear for the ball. Taking it from her ma, she held it up, letting the fabric fall so she could see the full length of the dress. The old-fashioned puffball sleeves had gone and in their place were two thin straps. The V-neck remained and the navy satin dress looked elegant and sophisticated.

'Oh, Ma!' she said breathlessly. 'It's beautiful.'

'You'll look smashin' in it. And, Helen, I've got somethin' for you too.' She dashed out of the room and returned a moment later with another dress. 'It's second-hand but I've washed and pressed it and let it out. It's gathered under the bust now, rather than at the waist, so it should be more comfortable for you.' The pale pink dress would suit her colouring and Helen stood in a daze, moving towards it as if it had put a spell on her and was drawing her closer. She touched the fabric gently with her fingertips.

'Oh, Mrs Stratton—'

'Lils, dear, please. Or Lillian if you prefer.'

'Lillian, it's – I don't know what to say. Thank you.'

'Now you'll both look the belles of the ball.'

'What about Milly?' Caroline asked Helen. 'Do you think Robert's brought her a dress?'

'I have a dress she can wear. Especially now I have this.' She beamed at Caroline.

'Tea!' Pa called from downstairs, and they moved back to the kitchen, Caroline hoping that the moment of happiness would last for them all.

Chapter Twenty-Seven

It was Sunday afternoon; shallow patches of fog marred their vision as they reached the prison.

Caroline coughed but was able to calm it before it grew into something more. She didn't know how she felt about the information she held. Would it make it worse for Johnny to know there was evidence that he was innocent but that no one might ever see it? If she were in his position, she'd want to know no matter what and was using that to guide her. If only she could remember the idea that had occurred to her before she fell asleep that night at Helen's. No matter how she concentrated on it, it remained at a distance, flitting away from her fingertips every time she tried to grab it. It did the same now as Helen's voice came into focus.

'I can't tell you how much I hate this place. I know prisons aren't supposed to be friendly looking but there's something about here in particular that gives me chills.'

'I know what you mean. What worries me most is that I might have to get used to it.'

'You won't. Johnny's innocent, we know that for sure, and we'll find a way to prove it.'

She couldn't help but admire her friend's determination. It was exactly that which had got Helen through the hardest times over the summer and was helping her now.

'Do you think they allow Christmas decorations or a tree in prison?'

'I don't know,' Helen replied. 'But we'll have him before you need to think about that. There's still time. Ready?'

Caroline nodded and they joined the queue and went through the same procedure they'd grown accustomed to. Before long, they were sitting with Johnny.

He didn't look any better than he had the last time they'd seen him. She'd have to lie to her ma, Caroline thought. She'd have to pretend he was doing well, and his spirits were up.

'Hello,' Caroline said as Johnny sat down.

'I do wish you wouldn't come. Both of you. You shouldn't be here. It's no place for girls like you.'

'People who care about you?' Caroline asked.

'Good girls. Honest girls. The people here, they're . . . dangerous. You shouldn't be exposed to this sort of place.'

Before she could reply, a ruckus burst out near them as a man leaned across the table and tried to attack the man who'd come to see him. Guards were there in an instant, separating the two, the visitor's hand pressing against his cheek where the inmate had landed a blow. Though her attention had been drawn to the fight, from the corner of her eye Caroline had seen Johnny flinch, his features contorting in fear, and pain had stabbed her heart.

'You should both leave. Now.'

'We're not going anywhere,' Helen replied calmly. They gazed at each other for a moment and Caroline could see Helen was battling to control her emotions. 'Caroline has something to tell you.'

He turned his attention to her, and Caroline outlined everything that had happened over the last few days.

'You could have been hurt. I told you – Arthur Whitelock's a dangerous man.'

'But now we know for sure. We just need proof.'

'And how will you get that? No one'll believe you, or me, or Ma or Pa or anyone associated with us.'

'So we need someone not associated with us.'

She suddenly straightened, her eyes darting to Helen. That was it. The idea that had been elusive in her tired and busy mind suddenly crystallised.

Jake.

She'd been thinking about Jake and how he could help them.

'Jake Walker!' she declared loudly. The people at the next table turned around and she lowered her voice.

'What about him?' Helen asked nervously.

'He could help us. He has a camera, doesn't he? Or he can get one? If we can get photographs of Mr Whitelock robbing somewhere, or handling stolen jewellery, then I'll have actual evidence I can take to the police. Or Jake can take it to the police. They're more likely to believe him anyway. He'll get a story, and we get Johnny out of prison. It's a win-win.'

'Who's to say Arthur Whitelock will do anything else?' Johnny asked. 'It could be a wild goose chase.'

'Especially now the fog has cleared,' Helen added.

The smog would have proved the perfect cover for him, but surely someone like Arthur Whitelock wasn't going to stop being a criminal simply because the weather had cleared.

'What other option do we have? Time's running out.' Caroline turned to Helen, taking her hand. 'I hate to ask, Helen, I really do. But you don't have to see him. I can talk to him alone.'

'Perhaps Connor can come with you.'

'Who's this Connor?' Johnny asked, livening. 'You got yourself a fella, Caz?'

'No! Shut up.' Her cheeks blazed and a small smile lit her brother's face, especially when he looked at Helen. Caroline continued: 'Jake might have information on this last robbery. I'm sure Arthur Whitelock must have got back from doing something dodgy the other night. Where else could they have been so late? I can't remember much about what they said. I was too scared that we weren't going to make it out of there, but he must have been up to something and, given what we found, I doubt it was anything legal. Perhaps Jake can find out something about that.'

'I'm not afraid of seeing him,' Helen said, glancing at Johnny. 'Not any more. But . . . is there really no other way?'

'None that I can think of. Can you?' She asked the question gently. If her friend had other ideas, she was more than happy to listen but now the notion had solidified, she was sure it was the only way forward.

'All right,' Helen agreed with a small nod. 'I'll telephone him.'

'You're sure you don't mind?' Johnny asked.

'I agree it's the only way. We need evidence and Jake's in the best position to help us get it.'

'But what evidence can you get?' Johnny asked. 'Whitelock's not stupid. He'll have moved the jewels by now.'

'Is there anywhere else he could be storing stuff?' Caroline asked. 'Anyone else he could be working with?'

Johnny thought for a moment. 'There is a chap. He's got a warehouse further down, near Wapping. He and Whitelock have been mates for years. He told me they go way back to the war. I assumed they served together or worked on the home front but maybe it was something else. His name's Mulberry. Sean Mulberry.'

'Good.' Caroline felt a spark of hope. 'I'll see what Jake can find about him.' Helen glanced at her, flashing her eyes. 'There's something else we need to talk to you about.' She took her brother through Helen's change of circumstances. The move had gone well the day before and everyone had pitched in to move Helen's belongings.

Helen smiled. 'You're sure you don't mind?'

'Nah.' He shook his head. 'Better you use the room while I'm in here and when I'm out, well . . . I've been saving up for a place of me own anyway. 'Bout time I moved out of Ma and Pa's, so you'll be able to stay as long as you need to.'

Caroline suddenly had the feeling her brother might have more to him than she'd realised. She'd had no idea he'd been saving up for a place and, knowing how he'd been checking on Helen, even bringing her flowers, it was clear he'd been trying to get his life in order for her.

For the short time they had left they spoke of other things, but when they stood to leave, Johnny said: 'Don't do anything stupid, Caz, d'you hear me? And you stay out of it, Helen, please? Promise me you will.'

'I . . .' She faltered. Had she been planning on going with Caroline to get the pictures they needed?

'She promises,' Caroline said for her. 'Don't you, Helen?'

She nodded. 'I do.'

Johnny sat back in his chair, his skin pale under the harsh prison light. 'Good.'

'Ma and Pa wouldn't let her out of their sight anyway.'

'I've never felt so looked after,' she added. 'Not since Dad was well.'

The guard announced visiting time was over and the room grew busy.

'It'll be all right, Johnny,' Caroline said as she prepared to leave. 'I swear it.'

'Just don't land yourself in here as well. It's worse for women. I couldn't stand that.'

And on that melancholy note, they were shepherded out by a warden.

Chapter Twenty-Eight

Milly had caught Caroline the minute she returned from the prison visit, eager to be filled in on everything that had been discussed. When Caroline mentioned her feelings for Connor, Milly had smiled widely.

'I knew you liked him. I knew it. It was clear as day as soon as you looked at him.'

'Like you and Robert?' Caroline had teased in return.

'Exactly like me and Robert. And Helen and Johnny . . . ? How do you feel about that?'

'I'm happy for them as long as my brother doesn't mess it up. That's if he gets out of prison. Gosh, I do hate saying that.'

Milly had rubbed her arm. 'Hopefully you won't be saying it for much longer.'

They'd looked over to see Mrs Barnes having more secret discussions with Mr Newington and she and Milly decided to leave them to it.

Now, as she entered the offices on Monday morning, having admitted her feelings for Connor O'Keefe to both her friends, Caroline felt suddenly self-conscious. As she walked back to her desk, Connor caught her eye and she didn't know how to act. It had been easier when she'd kept her barriers up and he was teasing her. She'd expected him to smile and ask how her brother was, but instead, he lowered his head, his eyes on his work.

'Hello,' she said tentatively.

'Good morning.' He didn't look at her and his tone lacked its normal warmth.

She busied herself with her normal routine: sorting and beginning her work. When he didn't say anything more, she spoke again. 'I might have thought of a way of helping my brother.'

His eyes widened in surprise but he quickly returned to his work.

'Helen's telephoning someone she knows. A reporter. He works for the *Daily News*. He gave us some information before and I'm hoping that he can bring his camera and get something solid the police will believe.'

'Right.'

'We've got a new name for him too,' she continued, fear beginning to mount in her stomach at Connor's reactions. 'Sean Mulberry. I'm just hoping there'll be something there. Helen's telephoning at lunchtime if you want to join us?'

'No, no, thank you. I . . . I'd better keep working.'

'Of course,' she replied, hiding her disappointment. 'Are you feeling unwell? Is everything all right?'

'Fine. I'm just . . . busy.'

They worked, speaking occasionally, conversation begun by Caroline and shut off quickly. When the sounds of the Changing of the Guard faded, the noise of the trumpets and drums lessening as the Guard marched away, Miss Western turned around, narrowing her eyes at Caroline, who'd been trying to speak to Connor again, discussing another word he couldn't make out on his notes.

'What a lovely dress, Caroline,' Miss Western said, catching her off guard.

'Thank you,' she said, though she knew from the tone it wasn't a compliment.

'I do love an old-fashioned style, don't you, Mrs Coniston?'

'I do. I do.' The old lady looked up from her work, assessing Caroline for a moment. 'Though there is a difference between old-fashioned and just old, isn't there?'

'True. True.' Miss Western cast her eyes up and down Caroline's body.

Connor stood and walked past her. Before, he might have told her to ignore them but instead he continued with his work.

'I'm surprised at you, Mr O'Keefe,' Miss Western said, her voice soft but her eyes cold as they focused first on him and then Caroline.

'Oh, why's that?' He'd stopped by the duplicating machine at the back of the room but didn't look round.

'Well, you need to be careful how you choose your friends, given you're hoping for the senior clerk role that's coming up soon. Maybe you should think about who you're spending time with. You wouldn't want fraternising with the wrong sort to damage your prospects.'

Caroline's breathing quickened and heat crawled over the back of her neck. Miss Western shot her a sneering smile, but she refused to meet her eye. Was that why he'd been so cold and distant this morning, when only days before she'd thought they were finally getting to know each other?

'And what is the wrong sort?' he asked, his voice firmer than Caroline had ever heard it before. A flash of something passed over Miss Western's face and she clearly wished the response she'd received had been different. 'I'll spend time with whomever I like, thank you very much, and I don't see what business it is of yours.'

Caroline had never heard him speak so assertively and pressed down the relief filling her whole body. Barbara turned around, smiling, speaking loudly.

'Well, that told you, didn't it?'

'Be quiet, Barbara,' Miss Western snarled.

'Excuse me, Miss La-di-dah. Like Mr O'Keefe said, I'll talk to whoever I like, thank you.'

Miss Western spun back to her work, but muttered, 'It must be nice to have other people to fight your battles for you.'

The comment was meant for Mrs Coniston, but Caroline leapt on it, fuelled by her own irritation. 'I don't need anyone to fight my battles for me. But this isn't a battle. This is just a miserable woman trying to make everyone else as miserable as she is. Oh, and Miss Western? You've got lipstick on your teeth. Did you know? Just here.' She pointed to her own front tooth and sat down, the anger bubbling inside her belly calming with satisfaction and pride.

His copies made, Connor returned to his seat but still he didn't smile.

*

At lunchtime, Caroline went to the staff telephone where she had arranged to meet Milly and Helen.

'Ready?' Milly asked as their friend seemed nervier than usual.

Helen nodded, but Caroline wasn't convinced. 'Do you want me to do it?'

'No, I'd better speak to him.'

Luckily no one else was waiting to use the staff telephone and they could speak without being overheard.

'What is it, Helen?' Milly asked as she prevaricated.

'I don't know. Perhaps it's because I can feel the baby move now, but speaking to him – my baby's father – I don't know if I've done the right thing in cutting him out of our lives. Should I let him be a father?'

'I don't know,' Milly replied.

Caroline felt the same. 'All you can do is see what happens. There's plenty of time to decide if you want Jake involved before the baby arrives. You don't have to do anything now. Just don't make any hasty decisions. You're a good person, Helen, so I know you want to do the right thing.'

'You're right. I need to think more about it.' Helen picked up the receiver and asked for the *Daily News*. When the call connected, Helen angled the receiver so they could all hear the conversation.

'Helen!' Jake said, his voice high with surprise. 'Is everything all right?'

'Yes, we just . . . We need to ask for your help again.'

'Helen, I really can't keep—'

Caroline cut to the chase to make this as quick as possible

for Helen. 'I found some stolen jewels hidden at Arthur Whitelock's warehouse.'

'What?'

His curiosity piqued, she continued, telling the story again.

'Goodness me, that would have made a decent article.'

Helen, Milly and Caroline shared a knowing glance. The story was all Jake Walker was ever interested in.

'And we have another name for you too,' Caroline continued. 'Sean Mulberry. He owns a warehouse in Wapping.'

'Hmm . . . I'm not sure if that rings a bell or not. I'll see what I can find out. Wait to hear from me.'

She hung up and they stared at each other in silence. Waiting had never been Caroline's strong point. After a few seconds of unpicking the phone call and checking Helen was all right, they began to walk in different directions: Helen to the exchange, Milly back towards the State Rooms (though they weren't allowed in the ballroom as it was being prepared for the dance that night), and Caroline back to the offices. She'd hoped Connor would be there with her. That he might offer to go with her. But now, she wasn't sure where she stood with him.

She wondered if he'd ask her to dance later that evening but from his mood earlier it didn't seem likely. Sadness washed over her as she wondered what it would feel like to have his hand on her waist, to feel his body near to her own. A tiny flicker of unease tried to creep into her thoughts but was soon extinguished by excitement and hope. Whatever hold Timothy Ranger had had on her before, it was faltering. She just wished she knew what had ruined this . . . whatever it was that had grown between her and Connor. There was every possibility that at the dance tonight she'd be standing on the sidelines while everyone else danced around her, and the man she was growing attached to moved further and further away from her.

Chapter Twenty-Nine

That evening, Caroline stood in front of the mirror in her small room, adorned with the Christmas decorations she'd brought with her when she first arrived at the palace, admiring the dress her ma had given her. The gown, made of navy satin, had been altered so it caressed her body. She felt like Princess Margaret. She'd added the pair of black satin high heels Helen had given her and a black clutch bag. Her red hair had been pinned loosely so some tumbled down. She felt pleased with what she saw in the mirror and knowing that she would be amongst friends gave her greater confidence. Mrs Coniston and Miss Western would get a lot more than they bargained for if they tried anything while Mrs Barnes was around.

Caroline left her room and knocked on Milly's door. There was a general air of excitement thrumming in the staff quarters and the smell of perfumes, hairsprays and tonics permeated the air. Milly answered and Caroline couldn't help her eyes widening in wonder.

'You look beautiful, Milly!'

In the dark blue dress that Helen had given her, she ran her hands over her hips. 'It isn't too much, is it? I don't want to be in something fitted when everyone else is in something poofy.'

'It's beautiful – you look beautiful and Robert's gonna be proud as punch to have you on his arm.'

'Connor won't be able to take his eyes off you in that either.'

Caroline blushed and dropped her eyes. 'I doubt he'll be looking at me at all.'

Milly frowned and Caroline told her of his reactions earlier.

'Maybe he was just having a bad day. Shall we go and get Aunt Edie?'

They walked along the corridor to Mrs Barnes's room. She opened the door a crack and peered through the gap.

'Is everything all right, Aunt Edie?' Milly asked.

'I'm – I'm not going. Tell Leonard I'm sorry but I don't feel well.' She shut the door leaving Caroline and Milly staring at each other in shock. When she'd gathered herself, Milly knocked on the door again.

'Aunt Edie, what's going on? Let us in. I'm not moving until you tell me what's wrong.'

'I told you I don't feel well,' she shouted through the closed door.

'Aunt Edie, please.'

A second later, just as they both thought it was hopeless, the door opened wide enough to let Milly and Caroline edge through. Mrs Barnes stood in her dressing gown, her face made up so she looked like a movie star, though her hair was still in rollers secured in a headscarf. Dresses covered the floor and, as the girls surveyed the desolate scene in front of them, Mrs Barnes trudged to her armchair and flopped down. 'I can't go in any of these,' she said, gesturing to the mess on the floor. 'I look like a frump. Leonard won't want me on his arm lookin' like a sack of potatoes, will he? I'll embarrass him and I'll not do that.'

'Of course you won't, Aunty,' Milly said, moving to her and crouching by her chair. Caroline followed.

'What's the problem, Mrs Barnes? My ma's taught me loads of tricks for clothes that are too big or too small. There must be something here you like.'

'I like my uniform, that's what I like.'

Caroline realised that dressing for the dance was pushing Mrs Barnes so far outside her comfort zone, she was panicking. She'd never seen the solid, stoic older woman anything but confident in herself, and it made her heart ache to see her so rocked.

'What about this one?' she said, standing and picking up a long-sleeved green velveteen evening dress.

'It's too big. I hadn't realised I'd lost weight.'

'I thought you were looking trimmer,' Milly said. 'It must have been with all the preparing for the party. You've worked your fingers to the bone.'

'And you and Leonard go for lots of walks, don't you?' Caroline added. 'Pop it on and I'll see what I can do.'

Caroline knew that, fitted properly, it would show off Mrs Barnes's hourglass shape. She had an ample bosom, and the cross-over dress would show off her neckline and skim over her tummy.

'It's no good,' she argued. 'I'll look a fright. Better to stay here and have an early night or somethin'.'

'No,' Milly said in such a sharp tone it was if their roles were reversed. 'Mr Newington will be so disappointed if you don't come, and you'll regret missing out. It can't hurt to try it on and see what Caroline can do?'

Mrs Barnes chewed her lip and begrudgingly pushed herself up to standing. 'All right.'

As the room was open plan with a bathroom at the end of their corridor, Caroline and Milly moved into a corner and turned around to face the wall, giving Mrs Barnes some privacy.

'See?' she said when she was ready, and Milly and Caroline turned around. The sleeves were a little loose on her arms and there was definitely some extra room around her waist.

'Do you have any safety pins?' Caroline asked.

'There's a box over there.' Mrs Barnes pointed to her knitting basket near her armchair and Milly fetched them.

'Sorry to ask, Mrs Barnes, but can you take it off again?'

They spun back and a moment later, Mrs Barnes, now in her robe again, handed Caroline the dress. She set to work, turning it inside out and placing two of the pins at the back of the waist. 'Can I use a bit of that wool?' she asked, and Mrs Barnes agreed. Cutting a length, she went back to the dress and threaded it through, tying it tightly. The waist was now gathered and a couple of inches tighter. Then she took the sleeves, folding the fabric and gently inching in the pins, careful not to tear it. 'There,' she said. Her ma didn't know much, having left school to work at a young age, but what she did know was coming in handy now.

Mrs Barnes changed into the dress and when she said, 'Oh my Lord,' Caroline and Milly spun around.

'Caroline!' Milly exclaimed. 'You're so clever. It fits perfectly.'

The dress now fitted as intended and Mrs Barnes looked elegant and beautiful.

'Aunty, you look wonderful. But we should just . . .' Milly unwrapped the headscarf and took out the rollers, securing the sides with tortoiseshell combs.

Caroline gasped. Mrs Barnes appeared as they'd never seen her before. Her hair, falling in soft curls to her shoulders, pinned gently back from her face, made her look elegant and stylish. With her soft make-up she looked utterly beautiful.

'Caroline, I—' Mrs Barnes pressed a hand to her mouth. 'I don't know how to thank you.'

'You've done so much for me, Mrs Barnes, it's the least I can do.'

After they'd put the final touches to Mrs Barnes's outfit, they walked through to the Grand Hall where everyone was meeting. It felt strange to enter as a guest so dressed up. A huge Christmas tree twinkled with golden candles in small glass baubles and giant swathes of red ribbon had been wrapped around it. Every alcove overflowed with festive flowers: beautiful red blooms vibrant against lush green foliage. The scent of pine, so strong she could almost taste it, filled the air, the unmistakable smell of Christmas. Butlers and footmen had changed into suits; other cleaners, maids and clerks were in their finest attire; the room filled with chittering voices as the excitement level rose.

Jane the coffee maid made her way over to them, her cheeks already pink with the extravagance of it all.

'I can't believe we're here to dance – like guests!'

'It's going to be a wonderful evening,' Milly replied, and Jane bounced off back to the rest of the maids, who were all laughing and joking, comparing frocks and bags.

Near the Grand Staircase, bedecked with swathes of holly and fir, red berries shining brightly, the ladies spied Helen speaking to Robert, Leonard Newington and Connor. Caroline's breath hitched and she admired the lines of his jaw, the smile on his lips. He was wearing a dapper three-piece suit, the waistcoat emphasising his tall frame. He hadn't seen her yet – what reception was she going to get?

They cut through the crowd and as he saw her, he paused, drinking her in. Timothy's eyes had roved over her with wanton lust, and it had frightened her, but a shy smile grew on Connor's mouth, one of affection and admiration. There was, she was sure, a hint of desire, and felt the same towards him, but it wasn't lurid or aggressive as Timothy's had been.

'Hello,' she said as the group stopped in front of them.

'Hello,' he replied. 'You look – Sorry, I—' His cheeks reddened with embarrassment. 'Sorry. You look very beautiful.'

'Thank you.' She turned to see Mr Newington puffing with pride as Mrs Barnes took his arm and stood beside him.

Helen was wearing the gown her ma had given her. It settled under the bust before hanging loosely over her bump. She was already receiving disapproving glances from some of the people in the room. The gold band was still on the ring finger of her left hand, but the rumour mill of Buckingham Palace never really stopped working. It simply moved from one person to another, finding new fodder each week. No doubt someone would do something embarrassing that evening that would be the talk of the palace for weeks to come. Caroline just hoped it wouldn't be her.

An announcer declared the Royal Household Social Club Christmas Dance open, and the heavy crowd of hundreds began to edge forwards up the Grand Staircase and through to the ballroom. She bumped shoulders with Connor and the atmosphere that had developed between them – the mutual attraction and need to be near each other – grew stronger.

Though Caroline had seen the room a hundred times, had cleaned it just as many, with the Christmas tree that reached as high as the ceiling in the corner, and the band playing lively music, it felt completely different. Atop the columns lining the room, giant flower displays spilled over; the great candelabras had been filled with white candles and all were lit, casting everything in a warm, magical, golden light. That light shone on the gold and crimson chairs lining the sides, away from the dancing. She could only imagine this was what it was like for visiting dignitaries and guests of the Queen, only better because the atmosphere was not one of duty or etiquette, but one of frivolity and joy.

People began to dance – couples moved around the floor, even Mr Newington and Mrs Barnes taking a turn – and yet Caroline and Connor remained standing motionless next to each other at the side of the room, in silence. Only when a young man was making his way towards Caroline did Connor turn to her and said: 'Would you like to dance?'

She tried not to show how much his question pleased her and instead nodded solemnly. They moved to the dance floor and she allowed herself to be swept along in the festivities.

'Are you feeling better?' she asked. He looked at her, puzzled. 'After this morning. You didn't seem yourself.'

'No, I – I mean—' He dropped his eyes, seeming almost ashamed of himself. 'I'm fine, thank you.'

Conversation died, and she was about to press again when he commented on the room. They talked about the atmosphere, about how different everyone looked in their evening attire, but there was still something in his manner that concerned her. Perhaps he did care so much about his promotion he didn't want to fraternise with her any more than he had to.

When the dance was over, though she longed for another one, she also needed a drink as the tickling cough, which still hadn't abated since the smog, reared its head.

'I'll come with you,' Connor said. They moved to the Ball Supper Room where tables had been set at the side with bowls of punch and Connor ladled one for himself and one for her.

'You're a pretty good dancer,' Caroline said, regaining her breath.

His shoulders dropped and he relaxed. 'Pretty good? I'll have you know my sisters say I'm the best out of all my brothers.'

'Is that so? Maybe they're lying.'

'Oh no. If I was rubbish, my sisters would've told me. They'd have warned me against asking you to dance in case I put you off.'

'Well, you haven't, and I'd be quite happy to dance with you again, actually.'

A new voice entered their conversation, shocking her into

silence. 'But Mr O'Keefe promised he'd dance with me,' Miss Western said, moving closer and latching her arm on to his. Connor shifted uncomfortably but Caroline noticed he didn't step away. 'Isn't that right, Mr O'Keefe?'

'I – I can't remember.'

'Yes, you can. It was before Miss Stratton started working at the offices. You said that when we went to the Christmas dance, you'd be only too delighted to dance with me. In fact, you said you weren't sure one dance would be enough.'

Caroline met Connor's gaze and she could tell immediately that he had said those words. It didn't matter that it was before she'd started at the offices – before they'd met – he'd clearly been flirting with Miss Western and, given that she was such a nasty, snide woman, she wasn't sure how he could do such a thing. She wondered if it also explained his behaviour that day. His pulling away from her.

'Don't let me stop you,' Caroline said, turning away from them and sipping her drink. Her heart felt torn in two, bruised and beaten.

Miss Western took a step towards the dance floor, Connor moving robotically with her.

'Caroline, I—'

'What a lovely dress, Caroline,' Miss Western said, interrupting him. 'Isn't it awful though how one can never quite remove the smell of mothballs?'

Caroline's cheeks flamed and tears stung the back of her nose. 'Excuse me.'

She stepped away and forced her way through the throng into the East Gallery. She thought she heard Connor shouting her name but there was so much noise she couldn't be sure. She headed in the opposite direction to the ballroom. At the top of the stairs, she stopped and took a deep breath, staring at the ceiling to try and dry the tears before they escaped and ruined her make-up. The last thing she needed was mascara staining her cheeks. She brushed her hands down her dress and couldn't help but try and covertly sniff the fabric. She hadn't noticed any smell of mothballs and surely her friends would have told her if there had been? She hated herself for taking Miss Western's words so to heart.

'There you are,' Helen said as she and Milly dodged people to reach her. 'Where've you been?' Her light and jovial tone suddenly changed. 'What's wrong?'

'Nothing. I just needed some air.'

'You can't lie to me,' Milly retorted. 'What's happened? Has Connor upset you?'

'No – yes. He's dancing with Miss Western.'

'That horrible woman from your office? Why?'

'Apparently he promised he would, months ago.'

'Did he want to?'

'I don't know. But he is, so he must do. And he's been strange recently. Like he doesn't want to know me.' All her fears and self-doubt crashed in. 'I'm the wrong sort, aren't I? Too common. Of course he's going to want someone better than me.'

'Better than you?' Milly asked, astounded. 'There is no one better than you. You've every right to be here and don't you forget it.'

'Perhaps', said Helen, 'he's just being a gentleman. If he said he'd dance with her, he couldn't very well not.'

'The way he looked at you tonight?' Milly added. 'There's no way he wants to dance with anyone else. He was besotted.'

'I wish I could believe you, but he doesn't even want to talk to me.'

Knowing he was in the other room dancing with Miss Western, his hand on her waist, laughing or staring into her eyes, sent a chill down her spine.

'What's happening here?' Mrs Barnes asked, coming to join them. She looked utterly radiant, and it wasn't just from the fine dress. She was the happiest any of them had ever seen her. Not just from the love of Leonard Newington, but from the love and respect of her friends around her. Milly told her why they were hiding away from the fun.

Mrs Barnes rounded on Caroline. 'Well, I've just seen him and he ain't looked so miserable in all his life, I'd wager. She's simperin' and gazin' at him adoringly, but he looks so awkward Leonard almost offered to go and save him and pretend there was an emergency.'

'Really?' Caroline asked, hope rising again.

'Really. Now come on. You can't linger by the staircase all night. Let's go and have some fun. Who knows when this will happen again?'

Together they moved back to the heat and drama of the ballroom. Robert and Milly went to dance, as did Helen and a young man they recognised as one of the butlers. A moment later, Connor found her.

'There you are. I've been looking for you everywhere. Where did you go?'

'To get some air,' she replied, unable to fully look at him.

'Caroline, I—'

'It's fine, Connor. I know we're not friends. You don't have to stand with me.'

He couldn't meet her eye. 'No, Caroline, I'm sorry. I do want to be friends, it's just . . . I don't want you to have an even harder time by being friends with me.'

'What are you talking about?'

'Me being Irish. I get a lot of abuse at times, and you don't need to be dealing with all of that on top of everything else you have going on. Listen, I did say that to Miss Western. It was when the ball was announced, and we were all joking and being silly about it. I know it sounds bad, and I suppose I was a little flattered by her attention, but it was before I met you and as soon as I did – well – I . . . I do want to be friends.'

'Friends,' she repeated, her heart tearing as she understood that he was rejecting her. She was just about to speak when a drunken man fell into her from behind, his arms circled around her, sending her body into a panic. Fear flooded her system so strongly she couldn't breathe, and the memory of Timothy and his attempts to bed her appeared in her mind with startling clarity. The emotions of those moments were as real and visceral as if they were happening for the first time. They swamped her, and though Connor had already pushed the man away, telling him to drink some water and watch what he was doing, the terror remained.

'Come on,' he said gently, leading her back out into the East Gallery, full of priceless pictures and statues, and down towards the staircase. 'Quick, in here.' He pushed open a door and they entered the Silk Tapestry Room.

As the noise abated, so did her heart rate. She was safe.

For a while she couldn't speak. Then she looked at Connor and managed to say, 'We shouldn't be in here.'

'No one'll mind. We'll go back to the party soon enough. Do you need some water?'

She shook her head and sat down, burying her face in her hands as she took slow, even breaths. Her lungs fought against it, pulsing with fright, but she focused on filling her body with air and letting it out slowly, enjoying the empty feeling each exhale left.

'What happened there?' he asked gently. 'Was it . . . ?'

She knew it was a difficult thing to ask about – it was a difficult thing to talk about. But she wanted him to understand that sometimes things just made her remember.

'You know I said there was a man?' He nodded. 'His name was Timothy. He was a footman. He told me he loved me, that I was special – like no one he'd ever met before. I thought he was wonderful at first. But he got controlling, secretive, and he became a bully. He manipulated me and though I never slept with him he tried to make me and . . .'

Connor balled his hands into fists, the knuckles white.

'I know he's gone now, and I'll likely never see him again, but sometimes I can't help the memories coming back. I felt so helpless and alone. It's hard sometimes to remember that's not real any more.'

Connor knelt before her and took hold of her hands. 'You're the bravest person I know, Caroline, and not just because of what you're doing for your brother. You've clearly been to hell and back and I want you to know that I'll—' He stopped himself. Caroline looked into his eyes and saw his expression was sincere, almost . . . loving. 'I'll wait for as long as you need me to. I'll never ask you to do anything you don't want to do. Ever. If you think you can bear being out with someone like me. Most people are nice, but some aren't and I don't want you being spoken to how they speak to me.' He sighed and turned away. 'I'm not good enough for you, Caroline. I wish I were, but I'd only bring you trouble.'

She couldn't fathom that this was why he'd withdrawn from her. If he only knew what she, Milly and Helen had been through over this last year, he'd know he was good enough for her. If anything, it was the other way around – she wasn't good enough for him. From somewhere inside, she gathered courage.

'I'm tougher than I look,' she replied, her voice brittle.

He pressed a finger to her chin, lifting her head so their eyes met, and despite everything she found she wanted him to kiss her. She felt herself leaning towards him, closing the small gap between them. Tentatively, their breath hitching and mixing as they drew closer, his lips swept hers and she closed her eyes as a feeling of warmth, comfort and then desire swept through her, pushing away all the fear and doubt of moments before. He was just about to kiss her again when from the opposite side of the room, she heard: 'I say, must you really do that in here?'

She turned to find the Queen and Duke of Edinburgh watching them.

Caroline and Connor leapt up.

'Your Majesty.' She ducked into a curtsey as her eyes fell on the Queen. As usual, her implacable face showed no sign of emotion. She curtseyed again for the Duke of Edinburgh. 'Your Royal Highness.'

'You shouldn't be in here, you know,' the Duke said.

'I apologise, Your Royal Highness. I—'

'She had a fright,' Connor interjected. 'She just needed a moment to gather herself. It was my fault. I—'

The Queen halted him with an upheld hand. 'Are you all right now, Caroline?'

'Yes, ma'am. Perfectly. I'm so sorry.'

'We shall give you a two-minute head start before entering and greeting everyone. Does that sound fair, Philip?'

'More than,' he agreed, rocking on to the balls of his feet and back again.

'Off you go.'

As Caroline left, she saw the Queen and the Duke share a mischievous glance.

'We were like that once, Lilibet,' she heard him say as the noise of the crowd overtook her once more. She hoped they would be again. They'd always been a remarkable couple, clearly in love, but the coronation planning had strained them both.

In the corridor, Connor and Caroline burst out laughing.

'Wait till I tell Mrs Barnes about this. Come on, let's go and find them.'

A moment later, the Queen entered and began chatting with everyone, Philip walking a few steps behind and at ease with the staff, as he always was. They found Mrs Barnes and her friends and waited with them. There was no way the Queen was going to be able to speak to them all, but it was wonderful she'd made an appearance, especially as she'd only returned from Windsor earlier that day.

Caroline slid her arm through Connor's, noticing Miss

Western's consternation from the corner of her eye. The troubles of her everyday life were far away in that moment, dressed as she was in the ballroom of Buckingham Palace with the Queen and Duke of Edinburgh nearby. Reality would come crashing in soon and she'd be back to waiting to hear from Jake Walker and worrying about her brother, but she hung on tightly to the magic of the evening. She committed every moment to memory: the sensation of her dress on her body, the feel of Connor's hand at the base of her back, the love and support of her friends.

She might need them more than ever in the months to come.

Chapter Thirty

Five days later, Caroline entered the Prospect of Whitby pub, wondering why Jake had insisted they meet there, in Wapping. Connor was with her and the gentle pressure of his hand on the base of her back as she moved through the crowd was reassuring.

The pub was one of the oldest in London and it too had been decorated for Christmas. A small garland lay on the mantelshelf above the fire and sprigs of holly hung from the corners of the ceiling. A public house of some description had stood on the site since the 1500s and, being on the banks of the Thames, it was often frequented by dock workers. Like most of the pubs she'd been in – which wasn't that many – the inside was a mix of dark wood, pewter or glass tankards, and dark oak beams that lined the ceiling. Immediately next to it were a set of stone and wooden steps leading down to the riverbank. Pa had told her tales of its bloody history: of how this area was the site for many a pirate-hanging. That she was here to prevent her brother from being hanged hadn't escaped her notice and a slight chill ran down her spine as she wondered what the evening had in store for them.

Jake's telegram hadn't said much, which wasn't surprising given the cost of sending them, but what little had been written carried a tone of excitement. On Wednesday morning, just as Milly and Caroline were leaving the House-hold Breakfast Room, they'd met Helen racing down the corridor towards them, the chit in her hand. Caroline could see immediately she had something important to share from the tense expression darkening her face.

'What is it?' Caroline had asked as Helen handed her the telegram.

'This arrived for me at home this morning, just as I was leaving. It's for you.'

Caroline had read it quickly. 'Jake wants us to meet him Saturday night. He says he's found something.'

His reporter's instinct must have kicked in quickly for him to respond so soon, or perhaps the name Sean Mulberry meant more than she'd first thought. Whatever it was, hope had risen for the first time in weeks, and she'd immediately run to the offices and asked Connor to go with her. He'd agreed willingly and, after their kiss, she was more certain than ever that she would be safe with him. The days had passed slowly, yet the palace hadn't been exactly quiet.

Since the dance, every member of staff had talked of nothing else, picking over the night's events. Upstairs, there'd been further discussion regarding coronation dresses, crowns and when the next rehearsal would be. The Duke of Edinburgh was still petitioning to walk beside the Queen, causing untold tensions. Then today, news broke that Peter Townsend had been granted a decree nisi: his divorce from his wife Rosemary was now finalised. He was a single man. As his wife was the one accused of adultery, their children were awarded to him, but it was clear she would still be the one looking after them. Caroline wondered how much she was taking the blame to allow the handsome group captain to follow his desire for Princess Margaret.

Speculation was rife as to what this would mean for all the royal family. Would the Princess now be allowed to marry him? There had been a definite shift in tensions, according to Mrs Barnes and Milly, who had the most contact with the royal family. Princess Margaret seemed to expect it all to be plain sailing from here, but everyone knew that the problem wasn't so much the man, but the fact he was a divorcee. However, one question remained: was Princess Margaret ready to give up everything she had for love? If indeed that's what it came down to.

'Shall we sit there?' Connor asked, pointing to a table near the back of the pub. Caroline nodded. It was already late – nearly ten o'clock – and she presumed Jake would want to be as inconspicuous as possible. 'What would you like to drink?'

'Just a soda water, please.' She wanted to keep her wits about her, not knowing what the evening had in store. Connor came back with the same for him. 'You could've had a beer. I wouldn't've minded.'

'I know, but I'd prefer to be on top form with this Jake. He sounds like a snake.'

'I think he is, especially after how he's treated Helen.'

'He's the father of her baby, isn't he?'

The question took her by surprise, yet it shouldn't have. He was an intelligent man, and they must all have been giving things away.

'He is. It's not my secret to tell, but I suppose with the

bump showing more and more, it isn't much of a secret any more. Jake duped her. Told her he loved her, but he's actually married to a woman called Emily.'

'What an absolute dog.'

'Don't judge her, please?' Caroline pleaded, and his face softened. 'He really didn't let her know till it was too late, and she was going through a lot at the time.'

Connor smiled and placed his hand over her own, his fingers slotting between hers. 'I won't. I like her. You're very loyal to your friends. I like that.'

'They've been loyal to me. And they're good people.'

He took a sip of his drink. 'I won't judge anyone. It's easy to make good choices when life's simple. We've all made mistakes when life's hard.'

'What mistakes have you made?'

'Nothing too drastic. Don't look so worried. But I did once steal an apple from a teacher.'

She was feigning outrage when the door opened again, and Caroline watched for Jake but as her eyes focused on the man who'd entered, her blood ran cold. Connor must have noticed the change in her. Her body stiffened and she was sure the colour had drained from her face.

'Is that him?' Connor asked.

'No,' she replied, quietly.

'Who is it then?'

'It's Timothy.' Her voice shook and was muffled as though his mere presence had gagged her.

'The man who took advantage of you?' His expression had grown hard with anger and he rose out of his seat. Caroline grabbed his arm, pulling him down.

'No, don't. Just ignore him. He hasn't seen me. I – I don't want to talk to him.'

Timothy sat down with some friends, oblivious to her presence. He wasn't even looking around the room; instead, he was deep in conversation with the man opposite him, a beer already on the table waiting for his arrival.

Jake arrived a few moments later, weaving through the crowd and adjusting his glasses. When he saw them, he paused, peering around for Helen; then, frowning at finding her absent, he stopped at the bar before making his way towards them. With pint in hand, he sat down and took off his hat, dropping it on the table. He removed a camera from around his neck and placed it on the empty chair.

'Helen's not here,' Caroline said before he could ask anything about it. 'I don't want her involved in this, and certainly not in her condition.'

'She didn't tell me.' He gave a sardonic chuckle. 'She worried I wouldn't come if she said she wouldn't be here, didn't she?'

'Would you have?'

'I would. This could be a big story.'

The implication that he might not if the story hadn't been big enough wasn't lost on her or Connor, who tilted his head to catch her eye. She couldn't stop her gaze drifting towards Timothy, checking he hadn't noticed her. She ducked down in her chair, ensuring she was shielded by Jake.

'So what did you find out?' Caroline asked, her anger at Jake's callousness giving her strength. 'Did the name Sean Mulberry mean something?'

'He's a friend of Arthur Whitelock's all right, but it's not him that's the most interesting thing.' He checked his watch. 'We'd better be quick. I want to get in position with plenty of time to spare.'

'What do you mean get in position?' Connor asked.

'Who's this?'

'He's a friend,' Caroline answered coldly. 'He works at the palace. You didn't think I was going to meet you alone, did you?'

Jake couldn't stop himself glancing at Caroline as though she were so far beneath him, he'd never dream of talking to her. Timothy had looked at her in a similar way whenever she hadn't acquiesced to his wishes. The fear and pain that had plagued her turned to rage, burning in her gullet. She glanced at Timothy and for the first time, she wanted him to see her. To see she wasn't the same person she'd been before, easily manipulated and used. She was still alive, still there, stronger than she had ever been before. She turned her attention back to Jake.

'Sean Mulberry owns a warehouse down here in Wapping. He stores coal from Newcastle, delivered on a boat called the *Blue Moon*. The boat's what caught my attention. I started looking for any connections between Arthur Whitelock, Sean Mulberry, the robberies and the docks, and it turns out that the *Blue Moon* has moored at Sean Mulberry's dock the day after – or at least very soon after – each robbery.'

'What about during the smog?' Caroline asked.

'No, not then, but I think I know why. There was a robbery in that time, and it was an auction house, not a jeweller. I think if Arthur Whitelock was involved in that it must have been a spur-of-the-moment thing. Him doing what he thought he could get away with while the police were busy trying to stop people getting killed in the smog. There was another robbery a few days ago though – a jeweller in Limehouse – and tonight the *Blue Moon* docks again.'

'So you think Arthur Whitelock and Sean Mulberry are in it together?' Caroline asked.

Connor added: 'And they're sending the stolen goods to Newcastle on the *Blue Moon*?'

'That's exactly what I think.' Jake sat back, pleased with himself, and took a drag of his beer before lighting a cigarette.

'So, what's your plan? Have you told the police?'

He blew a long stream of smoke into the air. 'Not yet.'

'Why not?' Caroline asked. 'If you're sure, they'll be able to raid the warehouse before he has chance to move the goods or can catch them in the act?'

'That's what we're going to do.'

'What?' Caroline didn't fancy sneaking into any more warehouses or being grabbed by burly men who wanted to hurt her. Her eyes shot to Timothy.

'I need evidence – a good photo for a front-page feature. I've briefed my editor already and he's promised me a whole page if I can get a photo of it happening. We'll telephone the police station as soon as we know they've got the goods and the boat has arrived.'

'That sounds far too risky to me,' Connor said.

'Maybe it is. But it's what's happening.'

Caroline felt decidedly uncomfortable. 'Why can't you just tell the police? Surely it's better to have them there to support you?'

'They'd go in like a bull in a china shop. Too much room for error with lots of flat feet running about. This is the only way to prove their involvement. This will free your brother, Caroline. Trust me.'

She turned to Connor and, after a second, he nodded his agreement. 'All right then.'

'Good.' Jake checked his watch again and downed the last of his beer. Picking up his hat, he left the cigarette on the ashtray and lifted his camera. 'We'd better get going.'

The three of them stood and the scraping of chairs drew Timothy's attention. A wave of panic washed over Caroline, and she began to cough, her chest protesting at the sudden emotion. Connor's hand was on her back, guiding her, protecting her. He watched Timothy and, as recognition dawned, Timothy stood and came towards them.

'Caroline?' he asked, as if they were old friends. 'Well, look at you. Pretty as a picture as always.'

'Go away, Timothy. I have nothing to say to you.'

'I'd listen to her if I were you,' Connor added as they made their way through the pub.

'And who's this? I remember you,' he said with a grin. 'Irish boy from the clerks' office. Still typing away like the ladies?'

Connor moved past him, placing himself between Caroline and Timothy and shepherding her towards the door.

'How's Milly?' Timothy asked with a maliciousness that made her blood run cold.

The fear that had crowded her mind fled as his remarks chilled her. The flame of fury she'd felt earlier began to rise again. He was nothing more than a bully. Nothing more than

322

someone like Miss Western or Mrs Coniston and Caroline had stood up to them on more than one occasion.

'You want to know how Milly is?' she asked, taking a step towards him. She allowed her shoulders to roll and she stood up to her full height. She'd always hated how tall she was but now she was glad of it, and she met his eye. 'She's getting married to Robert. Remember him? You used to tease him about his stutter. She's over you, Timothy. We both are. We were over you long ago. You don't exist to us any more. You're nothing more than a nasty memory that's faded away to nothing. You're pathetic and you'll always be pathetic.'

As all the pain she'd experienced filled her voice with vitriol and menace, Timothy's smugness drained away. She was more than her past, more than where she came from or how she spoke. Whoever Caroline had been, that wasn't the woman stood in front of him now. In her place was a warrior, and Caroline felt powerful and, for the first time, in control. He took a step back, clearly realising he'd misjudged her.

'Let's go,' Connor said, and they left the pub.

She didn't even look behind her to see what he was doing now. Timothy Ranger had no power over her any more.

Chapter Thirty-One

By eleven o'clock they were standing in a small, cramped alleyway with a view over the dock and Sean Mulberry's warehouse. The ship was due to dock at around midnight, but they needed to get evidence the stolen goods were in the warehouse. The large building was empty, but no doubt Sean Mulberry and Arthur Whitelock would be arriving at any moment. Snatches of noise circled around them. Some men were still working, their voices carrying on the night air.

'What do we do now?' Caroline asked.

'I need to get in and make sure the goods are there. I won't touch anything. We need Whitelock and Mulberry to move them. I just need to get inside and find them first because if they're not there, this is all for nothing. How did you get into Arthur Whitelock's place before?' Jake pushed his glasses up the bridge of his nose, surveying her. The lens of the camera, hanging from a strap around his neck, caught the light.

'I jimmied a window,' she admitted, keeping her eyes away from Connor.

'You are full of surprises, Caroline,' Connor said with a smile.

Not least of which was standing up to Timothy, she thought. Her body still buzzed from the thrill of it.

'Can you do that again?' Jake asked.

'Maybe,' she admitted begrudgingly.

'Let's go.'

Keeping to the shadows cast by streetlamps, they moved to the back of the warehouse. The layout of the building was similar to Arthur Whitelock's and, using a barrow that had been left outside, Caroline was able to climb in through a small top window and unlock the door for Connor and Jake. Without switching on any lights, they searched the small office, and both floors of the warehouse. Fear inched further into Caroline's body. She felt sick with nerves now and her stomach felt heavy. If they were caught now, Jake would get out of it all right. He was a reporter; he was middle class. He'd be able to worm his way out of any trouble. But she and Connor . . . ? They'd be prosecuted. They'd lose their jobs. She moved quickly, eager for this to be over with.

After a thorough search, Jake returned to them. 'There's nothing here. Damn it.'

'What now?' Connor asked as Caroline's heart sank.

'Let's get back outside. The boat's coming, which means Mulberry will be too. We don't want to be in here when he arrives.'

They left and Caroline locked the door behind them, before climbing back out of the window. Just as she did, the headlights of a car pierced the darkness, the light growing stronger as it drove towards them. They ran back to the alleyway and hid in the shadowy recesses.

She was wrong. It wasn't a car that had drawn up. It was a van. Arthur Whitelock and a man Caroline presumed to be Sean Mulberry exited. Mulberry – skinny, with receding hair and tatty clothes – opened the office door at the front of the building as Whitelock unlocked the back of the van and took a small cloth bag from inside. She couldn't hear what they were saying but, from their tone, it was clear they were chatting easily with one another as they stepped inside Mulberry's office.

'That's it,' Jake whispered excitedly to them. 'That has to be the goods. I'm going to check.'

Before Caroline could stop him, he ducked away, and she watched his figure as he crept along the wall and around the front of the building.

'What did Helen ever see in this man?' Connor asked.

'He was charming once.' But his ambition had turned him into someone whom Helen never would have been interested in.

Jake was out of sight for no more than a minute before he returned.

'It's definitely jewellery in that bag. I heard it clink when Mulberry moved it off his desk and could see gold shining through the fabric.'

'So what do we do now?' Connor asked.

Jake adjusted his glasses. 'We wait for the boat. As soon as it arrives, Caroline, you go and call the police from the police box down there.' He pointed at the end of the road and Caroline could just make out the blue telephone box in the darkness, its light dimmed by gathering mist from the river.

'What if they don't get here in time?' Connor asked.

Caroline interjected: 'They have to.' There wasn't any other option.

As they waited for the *Blue Moon*, the cold, damp air seeped into her clothes. She'd worn an extra layer, not knowing what the night would bring, but it wasn't enough to fight the December chill. She shivered but refused Connor's coat. He needed it himself. Eventually, the slow chugging of a ship engine brought the boat to the dock.

Mulberry and Whitelock came out to meet it and before long it was moored. The dock was flooded with men.

'It's time,' Jake whispered, his eyes pinned on the action ahead of him.

She worried she'd be seen if she didn't get to the telephone box quickly enough.

'Ready?' Connor asked, placing both hands on her shoulders and looking her in the eye. 'You can do this, Caroline. Just stay in the shadows and move as quickly as you can.'

She nodded before sprinting into the darkness. She'd worn flat shoes and ran on tiptoes to minimise the noise, all the while checking behind her that no one had followed. She arrived out of breath, and lifted the receiver, reciting all the information they needed.

The police were on their way.

A modicum of relief helped her regain her breath, but Jake's plan was risky and if the timing didn't work out, she'd be back to square one. After taking a few deep breaths, she made it back to the alleyway with more care, not bothering to run, but moving between the shadows of the buildings until she eventually darted across the road and back into the alleyway.

'What's happening?' she asked as Jake watched on from the darkness.

'I need to get closer. I need to be able to tell the police where the bag is. Wait here.'

He crept out again and, despite his instructions, Caroline followed. She had to see this through. Had to find the evidence they needed to free her brother. There was no way she could wait in the darkness of a lane wondering what was happening, her fear growing rapidly.

'Wait!' Connor whispered, reaching for her, though she was out of his grasp. She followed Jake and they ducked down behind the remnants of a wall that was partially demolished.

Connor was suddenly next to her and there didn't seem to be enough room for everyone. She was sure they'd be discovered: that the two tall men would give their position away, but clearly the noise of the men unloading the ship, along with the dock workers' whistles and jeers, had masked their steps. Whitelock and Mulberry had no reason to suspect anyone would be watching and didn't so much as glance in their direction.

Piercing the darkness, sirens sounded in the distance, growing ever nearer, and Caroline's heart began to thud. The men shouted obscenities to one another, working faster, harder, and Whitelock and Mulberry left the office. Caroline couldn't hear them, but their actions indicated panic. Mulberry grabbed a sack of coal, cut it open and placed the bag of jewels inside. He adjusted the dark, sooty rocks so that nothing could be seen before lifting the sack on to the ship.

Two police cars raced towards them, then screeched to a halt just in front of the wall. Policemen in blue uniform, blowing their whistles or shouting at everyone to stop, climbed from the car like ants from a nest. They swarmed everywhere, forcing the dock workers to cease unloading.

Some looked genuinely confused, their hands in the air, while others, Caroline was sure, must have known what was happening as their expressions were pinched with worry.

'What's going on, officer?' Arthur Whitelock asked calmly.

'We have reason to believe that stolen goods are being moved via this boat.'

He scoffed. 'What stolen goods exactly? I've no idea what you're talking about.'

'Goods taken from Oclee's jewellers amongst others.'

'And who told you that?'

The officer shifted. 'We received an anonymous tip-off.'

Whitelock and Mulberry shot each other a look, a hint of concern creasing their brows.

The policeman began searching the ship and the warehouse, yet they were missing the one place they needed to look. Caroline's nerves mounted, biting at her to stand up and tell them. If she didn't do something soon, they were going to get away with it. She glanced at Jake, who stood and strode forwards.

'I tipped them off,' he said calmly, his broad frame illuminated by a streetlight.

As the police, Mulberry and Whitelock, turned to him, Caroline and Connor ducked back down.

'Jake Walker. *Daily News*. I think you'll find, officer, that what you're looking for is here.' Whitelock and Mulberry both went to move, but the officer blocked them. Jake grabbed the sack of coal and removed the lumps, pulling out the cloth bag and revealing gold and silver necklaces, bracelets and watches.

'Why you—' Arthur Whitelock lunged towards him, but

the two policemen had him firmly in their grasp, yanking his arms behind his back.

Sean Mulberry began to run for it, charging towards her and Connor. He hadn't seen them, she was sure. He was simply attempting to escape in the opposite direction. As he came alongside the wall, Caroline stuck her leg out and tripped him. He fell heavily, his body thudding against the ground.

'Well done,' Connor muttered as Mulberry rolled and scrambled to get back up, but the police were on him, hauling him to his feet.

'Who are you?' they demanded, catching sight of her and Connor.

They stood and gave their names, confirming they were with Jake.

'You!' Arthur Whitelock screamed, his face pinching in anger. 'You little bitch—'

'Hey!' Connor stuck a finger out towards him. 'You watch your mouth.'

'Arthur Whitelock,' the officer in charge said, 'I'm arresting you on suspicion of burglary and handling stolen goods.' The same charges were read to Sean Mulberry.

Jake removed the camera from around his neck and took a photograph of Arthur Whitelock being manhandled into the back of a police car. Then he grabbed his notebook from his pocket and began asking the officer in charge questions. Within seconds, the action was over, the world calmer, though police were still canvassing the area. Caroline was told she'd need to make a statement at the police station. They all would. She'd do so gladly.

330

'You'll have to let my brother go now, won't you?' she asked.

'Yes, miss. I think we will,' the officer confirmed, and the breath left her body in one fast swoop. She began coughing again but it didn't last long. Connor wrapped an arm around her waist to support her as tears flooded her vision.

She'd done it.

She'd saved her brother from hanging. It wouldn't be long, and he'd be home. Perhaps in time for Christmas.

Chapter Thirty-Two

On Monday morning, Caroline made it to the office to find herself one of the last to arrive.

'Ah, Caroline,' Mr Newington said, 'there you are.' She glanced at the clock on the wall. 'Don't worry, you're not late. I've just been waiting for you.'

'Oh, is everything all right?'

Connor had raised his head too and she caught his eye, sharing a look of concern.

'Shall we speak in my office?'

He strode off and Caroline quickly placed her handbag on the floor under her desk. Mr Newington's office was tidier today and more in keeping with the meticulous man she'd come to know. They were clearly catching up with the workload.

'Do sit down.' He gestured to the chair opposite his desk and sat in his own chair, which creaked and rasped.

Folding her skirt beneath her, she crossed her legs at the ankles and placed her hands in her lap. He already knew about Saturday night as Mrs Barnes had relayed everything to him, but what else could he need to speak to her about?

After the excitement with Arthur Whitelock, Connor had escorted her back to Buckingham Palace before returning to the East End himself. He'd been a perfect gentleman and had kissed her gently on the cheek before he'd left. She pushed the memory aside and focused on Mr Newington, trying to guess from his expression and body language what this might be about.

'The royal family are off to Sandringham for Christmas shortly, so this'll need to be quick, but I'm happy to say that we'd like to make your new role at the palace permanent, if you're willing to keep working with us.'

'Really?' She couldn't keep the grin from her face. 'Are you sure?'

'Of course I'm sure. You've done a marvellous job and, most of all, when you've made any mistakes, you've not stopped until you've put them right. That shows me a dedication most people are lacking. The Queen is most pleased with your work. As is Mr Lascelles.'

'I was sure he didn't like me.'

Mr Newington laughed. 'That's just his way. He's an old-fashioned chap but a good judge of character.'

Caroline wondered what he made of Peter Townsend's divorce and the future of his and Princess Margaret's love. He'd have definite views on that.

'You'll be allowed to continue living here too. I know most people in the offices live off site, but the Queen was most insistent you be allowed to stay in your room.' That was more than she could have hoped for. More than she had dreamed possible. 'We'll shortly be recruiting someone new,' Mr Newington continued, 'as Mr O'Keefe will be taking over the role of senior clerk in another department.'

'Will he?' Caroline was over the moon that Connor had secured his promotion too. 'That's wonderful news.'

'I was hoping you'd help to train up the new person when they arrive. I could ask Mrs Coniston or Miss Western, but between you and me, I'm a bit worried they might scare them off and I'm not sure Barbara's up to the task.'

'I'd be delighted, Mr Newington, if you think I'll be any good at it.'

'I know you will, Caroline. You should have more faith in yourself. We all believe in you.' She dipped her head, embarrassed. 'Well, if you're happy to accept a permanent position, I'll get things sorted.'

'Oh, yes, definitely, Mr Newington. Thank you so much.'

'Good, good. Now, off you go. Lots to do today and we'll shortly have to line up to say goodbye to the Queen. Better get moving.'

She walked back into the main office in a sort of dream, noticing for the first time how additional paper chains had been strung across the ceiling from corner to corner and a homemade wreath hung on the wall. Miss Western sneered at her, but the annoyance radiating from her bounced off Caroline as if she were wearing a shield. Mr Newington followed and made the same announcement to the team.

'Can I have your attention, please, everyone. Just to let you all know that Mr O'Keefe will shortly be leaving us to take up a position as Senior Clerk in the Press Office and Miss Stratton has kindly agreed to take a permanent role here.'

Barbara turned around, smiling widely, while Miss Western and Mrs Coniston shared disapproving glances.

'Congratulations,' Connor said, grinning.

'Congratulations to you too.'

'I was wondering . . .' He seemed suddenly nervous. 'Would you like to have dinner with me after Christmas?'

'I'd like that very much,' she replied, her heart beating furiously.

The world had spun on its axis – turning on a dime, as the movies said. It was hard to believe so much had changed in such a short space of time when she'd been through weeks of worry and strife.

'Right,' Mr Newington announced. 'Time to line up.'

They all began to move into the corridor and Caroline took the opportunity to speak to Miss Western, leaving Connor to walk ahead so she could catch her.

'Miss Western, can I have a word?'

'What do you want?'

Mrs Coniston walked past with a sneer.

'I wanted to say that, as we're going to be working together from now on, I . . .' She struggled to find the words and decided to speak how she normally would. 'Oh, look, you don't like me and, to be honest, I don't particularly like you, but we need to be professional and treat each other with respect. We don't have to like each other but we don't need to make life difficult for everyone else by sniping and snarling at one another from across the office.'

Her eyebrows had shot up to her hairline at Caroline's brisk words, but then, surprisingly, her expression softened. 'You're right. I can't say we'll ever be best friends, but I don't like working in a hostile atmosphere and you've shown you're more than capable of doing the job.'

Caroline hadn't known what to expect in reply and suspected that was the best she was going to get. An apology would have been out of the question. Miss Western wasn't the sort to admit she was wrong or to be friendly towards someone she thought below her, but this was a step in the right direction. Caroline knew she herself was a kind person and a worthy friend, and if Miss Western didn't recognise that, that was her loss.

'Thank you,' Caroline said and went to stand next to Connor in the corridor outside the office, ready to say goodbye to the royal family.

'Everything all right?' Connor asked.

'As fine as they'll ever be.' Which was all right with her.

She spotted Tommy Lascelles first, leading the Queen and Duke of Edinburgh down the corridor from the direction of his office. One by one they bobbed into curtseys or bowed their heads. The Queen spoke to them all, even eliciting a smile from Mrs Coniston and Miss Western. She stopped in front of Caroline.

'Mr Lascelles has just informed me that you will be working permanently in the offices.'

'That's right, Your Majesty.'

'How marvellous. Though Mrs Barnes will miss you, I am sure.'

Caroline was hit with a twinge of sadness. She'd been so consumed with excitement, she hadn't thought what she'd be leaving behind. Was she really ready to move on?

'I'll miss them, ma'am, but I'm excited about this new opportunity.'

'I am very pleased for you.'

With a fond smile, she moved away, and Caroline's body hummed at the life opening up before her. Of course she would miss working with her friends, but she'd still be living here, and she'd see them every day.

The Queen and Duke of Edinburgh, already in their travelling clothes, left and, as they filed back into the office, Mr Newington called to Caroline and Connor.

'Is everything all right, sir?' Connor asked.

'Yes, fine. I just ... umm ...' He reached into his pocket and took out two small filing cards. 'Mrs Barnes asked me to give you these.'

They both took them, reading the address printed in Mr Newington's neat handwriting.

'What is it?' Caroline asked.

'Or should we say where is it?' Connor added.

'Can you both meet me there on Wednesday at three o'clock?'

'But it's Christmas Eve on Wednesday,' Caroline said, confused. 'Shouldn't we be working?'

'No, no. If you could please meet us there at three o'clock, that would be marvellous. Oh, and Sunday best, if you can.'

He disappeared back into the office before they could ask any more about it.

'What's that all about, do you think?' Connor asked, his brow creasing attractively in confusion.

'I've no idea,' Caroline said, reading the address on the card as if it would suddenly give her a clue. She'd just have to wait and see.

Chapter Thirty-Three

The following evening, Caroline and Helen waited inside the grounds of the prison before the small side door they'd used to visit Johnny. When they'd stepped inside the gates this time, it was with hope rather than fear. The building loomed before them, still intimidating, but Caroline looked at it knowing she'd never have to see it again. They shifted their feet in the dark and gloom, but it didn't diminish the joy inside them. The London fog had cleared and the stars shone overhead. The cold wind still gripped their bones, however, and Caroline glanced at Helen.

'I wish you'd stayed at home.'

'I'm fine, honestly. It's just a bit of wind. I won't die, and neither will this baby. Besides, I wanted to be here.'

The door before them opened and Johnny, in the clothes he'd been arrested in, walked out. He wrapped his arms over his chest, tucking his hands in against the cold. Ma would need to feed him up, but he'd soon be home and back to his usual self.

'I should've brought you a coat,' Caroline remarked. 'I didn't think about it.' It hadn't even registered that the clothes he'd been arrested in might not stand up to the weather of his release.

'It's all right, Caz,' he said as he stopped in front of them.

He pulled his sister into a tight embrace. 'How am I ever gonna thank you?'

She closed her eyes and committed the feel of her brother's hug to memory. He annoyed her at times but he was her family – her flesh and blood – and she loved him.

'Oh, don't worry,' she joked as he let go. 'I've got a lifetime of favours to call in now.'

'I knew I'd be in for it.' He laughed and switched his attention to Helen. 'Hello, Helen. You're looking well.' His voice was softer now, tentative.

They couldn't stop looking at each other and Caroline took a few steps away, giving them some space.

'Thanks for coming,' Johnny said.

'I couldn't not,' she replied.

'I'd offer you my jacket if I had one.'

'We'd still both be freezing, I think. Oh.' She pressed a hand to her stomach.

Johnny leapt forwards, his hands out as if the baby was suddenly going to appear and he'd have to catch it. 'What is it? Is it the baby? Is it because of the cold? Is everything all right?'

'Everything's fine,' she replied with a chuckle. 'He or she is moving, that's all.'

He relaxed and his sallow cheeks lifted into a grin, filling with colour. 'Really? What does it feel like?'

'Like a fluttering. It's hard to explain.'

'Helen, I—' He glanced at Caroline, who turned away from them and pretended to tie her shoelace. 'I got to thinking when I was in there that life's short, ain't it? Too short. I know I'm not clever and I'm not . . .' He suddenly tugged the hat from his head and held it in both hands. 'If I get a good job and a flat and show you I'm worth it, do you think you'd like to – Maybe we could – step out together – or summat?' he added.

Caroline couldn't help herself and turned around to watch the scene unfold.

'You'd like to take me out?' Helen asked tentatively. 'Even with this baby on the way?'

'I'd like it more than anything,' he replied, blushing to the roots of his hair. 'I know what happened with Jake Walker and I don't give a tuppenny bit about it. I like you and I always wanted kids myself.'

Helen stared, shell-shocked. 'I – I don't know what to say.'

'Just say you don't mind being taken to the pictures, or for a walk out and about sometime.'

'I'd like that very much.'

'Good.' Johnny's shoulders dropped. He placed a gentle kiss on Helen's cheek and they gazed at one another.

Smiling, Caroline said, 'We better get you home, Johnny, or Ma'll have my guts for garters. Come on, the bus stop's just down here.'

Helen linked her arm with Johnny's, and they walked through the cold December night towards the bus stop and home.

'There's my boy!' Ma shouted as she opened the door and the three of them stepped inside.

Johnny was immediately engulfed by both his parents, and Helen and Caroline watched on with tears in their eyes as the joy of the moment consumed them all. The fire had been lit and the heat from it permeated the house. The deep, savoury smell of beef filled the air and Caroline felt a comfort that was only ever associated with home. She spied a few decorations in the hall. Tatty paper chains brought out year on year, patched up in places but no less beautiful. A small tree had been placed in the parlour, decorated with salt-dough decorations made over the years. A few presents were already wrapped and placed underneath it, hasty gifts bought in the nick of time for Johnny, since no one had been able to bring themselves to be so presumptuous before now. With relief, Caroline allowed the feelings that only ever came from her home at this time of year to envelop her.

'Now,' Ma continued. 'I've made steak and kidney puddin', though it's more kidney and puddin' than steak. Still, beggars can't be choosers and I'm sure it's better than that prison slop you've been eatin' – or not eatin', by the looks of you.' She assessed him once more, seeing, as they all did, the dark circles under his eyes, the weight he'd lost from his face. His belt had been tightened as much as it would go, and his trousers hung loosely around his legs.

'Good to 'ave you 'ome, boy,' Pa said, giving him a pat on the back as they moved towards the kitchen.

As they came closer, Caroline's mouth watered; as they squeezed in together at the table, she couldn't help but feel she had the best family in the world. A family that was about to get bigger with Helen living with them. One day, she was sure, Helen would be a sister to her, as long as her brother could keep himself out of trouble. Caroline had no doubt now that he would, and she realised that she hadn't given him enough credit before for leaving behind his tear-away teenage years or how difficult it must have been for him. Seeing him so smitten, she smiled. She was sure Helen would be the making of him.

'Now . . .' Her ma began dishing up pie and mashed potatoes. 'There's even blancmange for puddin' as it's a day for celebration.'

Pa winked at her from across the table and she knew the celebration was as much for her new job as it was for Johnny's freedom. As they toasted the meal with cups of tea, she allowed herself to be immersed in the family around her.

Over the last two months, people had made her question her worth. They'd made her feel less than others because she was working class, because she had a cockney accent, because she came from the poorest part of London. But the people around the table were the kindest, most loyal people she knew. Her ma would do anything for anyone. Her pa was gentle and hard-working. Johnny had made mistakes, but he'd done so to help a friend. Not that Don Green was his friend any more. Johnny had already said he was staying away from him and his ilk, and tomorrow he was out to find a new job. Caroline vowed not to let anyone make her feel 'less than' again. She was worthy of a good life, worthy of a good job, worthy of love. She promised herself that the next time someone like Mrs Coniston or Miss Western tried to make her feel small she'd ignore their jibes. As far as she was concerned, the only time you looked down on anyone was to help pick them up.

Chapter Thirty-Four

Caroline and Connor approached the address Mr Newington had given them. She wore her best dress, shoes and gloves. Connor looked handsome in the same three-piece suit he'd worn to the dance, and she enjoyed walking along with her arm tucked into his. He'd complimented her as soon as he'd seen her. His words had been kind, but it had been the way his eyes had widened as he'd taken her in that had pleased her most of all. Still, she couldn't help but wonder what they were all doing there. Was it to do with Milly and Robert? Or something to do with Helen and the baby?

As they approached, they saw Mr Newington, Helen, Milly and Robert all waiting outside a red-brick building.

'What's going on?' Caroline asked the crowd gathered outside. 'Is Mrs Barnes joining us?'

Mr Newington, whose face bore a strange, nervy expression that pinched his features, tried to answer just as a taxi pulled up. He suddenly leapt forwards to open the door and Mrs Barnes emerged. She exited gracefully, clad in a beautiful, fitted cream dress that swept out over her hips. The ruffles of her petticoat shifted as she brushed her hand down her skirt. A cream clutch bag hung from her wrist and she held a small posy of fresh flowers. Her hair had been caught up into a low bun similar to that which she normally wore, but with tendrils hanging down, curling in the misty winter day. She looked beautiful. She'd even worn a smattering of make-up, subtle but enough to highlight her almond-shaped eyes and smiling mouth.

'Aunty!' Milly declared. 'Are you ... ?' She glanced between Mrs Barnes and Mr Newington, watching as they beamed at each other.

'Gettin' married?' Mrs Barnes answered. 'Yes, we are.'

'On Christmas Eve,' Caroline said, pressing her hands to her mouth. 'How romantic.'

'I rather thought so,' Leonard replied. The bride and groom couldn't stop smiling at each other. 'You look beautiful, Edie.'

'You don't look bad yourself,' she replied bashfully.

'When did you decide all this?' Milly asked. 'And why didn't you tell me? I could've—'

'We can talk about all that later. I didn't want a big show. Just my friends and family around me.' She cupped Milly's cheek. 'Now, shall we get a squiggle on, or we'll miss our slot.'

They headed into what was clearly a register office. The room was small and office-like, with only one desk and two smiling men behind it, one seated, one standing. A small vase of flowers had been placed on the windowsill to brighten it up.

'I'm the Registrar of Marriages,' the man sitting said. 'And this is the Superintendent Registrar.' The standing man nodded a greeting.

The ceremony began and, after reciting her vows, Mrs Barnes slipped a ring on to Mr Newington's finger, her eyes

344

shining as he, in return, made a solemn vow to love, honour and protect her. Milly had to wipe the tears from her eyes as she watched her aunt make the same promise, though Mrs Barnes herself couldn't stop smiling. When they were pronounced man and wife, they shared a gentle kiss.

'Now,' the registrar said. 'The two witnesses?'

Mr Newington turned to Connor. 'Would you mind, Connor? I was rather hoping you would . . .' He signalled to the paper.

Clearly moved by the request, Connor cleared his throat. 'I'd be delighted, sir.'

Mrs Barnes turned to Milly. 'Would you, my girl?' Milly nodded, wiping an escaping tear from her eye.

Finally, the newly married couple turned to their friends who showered them in congratulations.

'I'm so happy for you, Aunty,' Milly said, embracing her. 'But why didn't you say? I'd have brought some rice.'

'We'll give you a few moments alone.' The two registrars excused themselves, closing the door softly behind them.

'We could have helped you organise everything,' Milly added.

'We didn't want any fuss and what was there to organise? Leonard and I decided that at our age we wanted somethin' simple. We don't need a church or bells and whistles. All we wanted was to marry each other – that was what was important.'

'When did you propose?' Helen asked Leonard.

'Wait a minute,' Caroline said, remembering seeing Mrs Barnes beaming back in November although she tried to hide it with everything that was going on after Johnny's

345

arrest. 'Quite soon after Robert did? When you were smiling all the time – both of you.'

'It was,' Leonard agreed. 'I've always been a private person and I knew Edie wouldn't want a big announcement. And to be honest' – he turned to Robert – 'after you'd done such a good job proposing to Milly, I wasn't going to be able to do anything as romantic as that.'

'Nonsense,' Mrs Barnes said, threading her arm through his and leaning into him. 'We went for a walk, and he stopped under Victoria and Albert' – referring to the two tall trees that had been planted by that couple and now stood entwined in the gardens of Buckingham Palace. Caroline, Helen and Milly all said, 'Aww,' as Mrs Barnes continued – 'and he said, "Now, Edie, I know this may seem fast, but I really think we should get married!" He told me loved me and that was that!'

'I'm so happy for you both,' Milly said, embracing them in turn. 'But what will you do about work?'

'I don't know,' Mrs Barnes replied matter-of-factly without a hint of sadness.

It was standard practice that once two people employed at the palace married, one had to leave, as both parties couldn't work there at the same time. Normally it was the woman, who went to set up home and have children. Mrs Barnes and Mr Newington's situation was slightly different with them both being older and Caroline doubted Mrs Barnes would want to give up the life she'd created for herself. A ray of hope was that things were changing at the palace: Helen had been kept on after falling pregnant and Caroline was making her way in a different department with the Queen's blessing.

'I'll speak to the Chief Housekeeper and see what's what, but I will definitely be movin' in with Leonard now we're married. It's time for me to have more of my own life. I've lived and breathed the Royals for far too long. It's a new chapter for me and one I'm very much lookin' forward to. Until then, let's away back to the palace. Mrs Chadwick's prepared a special afternoon tea for us.'

'She was in on it too?' Milly declared, a little outraged that she'd been left out.

'She was, my girl, but only because she winkled it out of me.'

'I thought something was going on, but I never thought it was this. Oh, Aunty, what a wonderful day.' She embraced her aunt again as a gentle knock on the door told them their time was up.

'I'm sorry to intrude,' the registrar said. 'But my next appointment is here.'

Mr Newington shook his hand again. 'We're just leaving. Thank you so much.'

Back outside, the sky was a pale grey. There was no sign of the snow of earlier months, leaving the winter rainy and damp. Any hopes of a white Christmas had soon faded, and drizzle began to fall. They hunched their shoulders against the wind, but the bride and groom didn't care.

'Shall we get a taxi?' Leonard said, hailing one. They all stared in disbelief. It would cost a fortune. Far more than any of them had, but it was a special occasion. 'I insist,' he said and raised his hand to hail one. A black cab pulled up and he began to usher everyone inside. 'We can't have Edie's beautiful dress ruined. Not when she looks so wonderful.'

They clambered into two cabs and the driver of Caroline's almost didn't believe them when they asked for the staff entrance of Buckingham Palace. He was full of questions, but they avoided them with vague answers, knowing that, as usual, they couldn't give anything away.

The Household Lounge had been decorated with bunting and fresh flowers gathered from the garden. The Christmas tree given to them by the Queen and decorated with shining glass baubles in green and red shone from the corner of the room and the scents of vanilla and cinnamon from Mrs Chadwick's baking joined that of Christmas pine and lush red poinsettias. Christmas had arrived in all areas of the palace, both above and below stairs, making everyone giddy with excitement.

When Mrs Barnes challenged her friend on where the flowers had come from, Mrs Chadwick informed them that with the royal family now in Sandringham for the duration of the Christmas period, they'd be none the wiser.

'They ain't gonna miss 'em, are they? And they'd all be dead by the time they got back. The flowers that is, not the Royals. Least I hope not. I quite like the ones we've got. Better than some of the others who come here on state visits giving it "I can't eat this and I can't eat that".' Her cheeks were a deep red and plump as she smiled.

'You really shouldn't have,' Mrs Barnes said. 'Not for little old me.'

'Well, it ain't just me who wanted to do this for you. The gardeners were more than happy to oblige. Oh, and I know you wanted it to just be this lot' – she motioned to Helen, Milly, Robert, Connor and Caroline – 'but when I was telling everyone why I needed the room, they insisted they offer their congratulations too, so you've got an hour on your own and then everyone else is joining us for a party. Don't worry!' She silenced Mrs Barnes's protestations. 'It won't cost you a penny. In fact, most people have dashed out to get you both a wedding present.'

'They didn't need to do that,' Mr Newington said.

'They wanted to! And you can't stop people showing their appreciation. It'd be rude.'

'She's right,' Milly added. 'A party to celebrate your wedding will be wonderful.'

'We better get on with this afternoon tea, then,' Mrs Barnes replied, smiling at them all.

Mrs Chadwick bustled off, Robert being told to sit down after he'd offered to help. 'You're part of the wedding party. Don't be daft.'

'You are too,' Mrs Barnes said to Mrs Chadwick and the woman placed a hand to her chest. 'Sit down and join us.'

'Maybe for a few minutes,' she replied, wiping a tear from her eye.

Before long, sandwiches, cakes and pastries were piled in front of them on delicate cake stands worthy of the Queen, the table decorated with holly and red ribbon that swam between the platters. With small plates and napkins, they ate a delicious wedding breakfast and soon others were arriving bearing gifts for the happy couple. Someone placed a record on the gramophone and the jazzy notes of a swinging Christmas song filled the room. Tables and chairs were pushed to the side, and dancing and festive cheer reigned.

Caroline watched as Robert and Milly spun around the

floor and Edie Barnes – now Newington – danced with her new husband. She went to sit with Helen.

'I wish Johnny were here,' Helen said shyly, sipping an orange juice.

'I'm not sure Ma'll be ready to let him go anywhere before New Year. The only place she's let him go is the flat he was eyeing up before – well, before all this rubbish happened. He wants to get settled in a place. Get a good job so he can look after you.'

'I don't know how I'll ever be able to thank your family for all they've done for me,' Helen replied, her eyes glassy with tears.

'They wouldn't have it any other way. I hope they're not too over the top tomorrow at Christmas dinner. Ma's cooking up a right feast. You need to eat for two, she said, and Johnny needs feeding up. She won't be happy till he's put on a stone.'

'It's wonderful to be included. I never thought my first Christmas without Dad would be so full of . . .' She searched for the word. 'Love.' Caroline touched her hand. It was hard to believe it was only three months since Helen's father had died. 'And what about you?' Helen asked, glancing at Connor who was now talking with Robert and Milly, but kept looking their way.

'He said he's going to take me dancing after Christmas. We're going to take things slowly though. I'm over Timothy and what he did to me. I haven't felt scared or trapped with Connor, but I still worry it'll come back when I'm not expecting it. When I let my guard down. Yet I do feel like I'm leaving it behind me, and that's a good thing.'

'I understand. But you are different now, Caroline. You'll always be our wonderful friend, but you've grown in so many ways these past few months. You've found something new inside you. We all have.' She looked at Milly who, given that Connor and Robert were now talking about football, had come to join them.

'Shall we have a toast?' Milly said, raising her teacup. 'To friends and family.'

'Friends and family,' they chorused.

They'd all been through so much over the last year and while last Christmas had been fraught with tension over the King's health, this year they were all ready to celebrate and enjoy the festivities. The year to come, with a new job for Caroline, Helen's baby, the coronation, and Robert and Milly's wedding, would undoubtedly be a good one. Caroline glanced at Connor and, seeing his eyes crinkle as he smiled, her body warmed inside. She took Helen's hand and Milly's. The New Year was going to be busy, but wonderful, she was absolutely sure of it.

Acknowledgements

First of all, thank you to everyone who's picked up a copy of one of the Palace Girls stories. I really hope you enjoyed a behind the scenes peek at Buckingham Palace and a bit of Sunday night drama in book form! I think all authors know they wouldn't be anywhere if it weren't for the people who pick up their books and choose to spend some time with their characters, so thank you from the bottom of my heart.

Thank you to my agent, Kate Nash, and my editor at Century, Susannah Hamilton. I'd also like to say how grateful I am to the team who've worked on this series. Richenda Todd for her amazing copy-editing and Laurie Ip Fung Chun for managing the whole process with such seamless efficiency.

Finally, I really must thank my family, especially my husband who's been there for me through thick and thin, always supportive and always loving, even when I've been tearing my hair out. And to my children, for understanding when deadlines are looming, and dinner might be chicken nuggets and chips yet again!

Discover more from

THE PALACE GIRLS

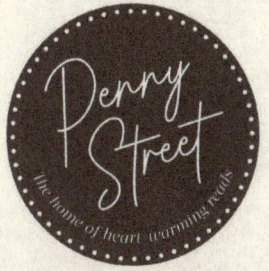

On a station platform, with nothing to read,
and a four-hour train journey stretching ahead of him...

That's where the story began for Penguin founder Allen Lane.
With only 'shabby reprints of shoddy novels' on offer,
he resolved to make better books for readers everywhere.

By the time his train pulled into London, the idea was formed.
He would bring the best writing, in stylish and affordable
formats, to everyone. His books would be sold in bookstores,
stationers and tobacconists, for no more than the price
of a ten-pack of cigarettes.

And on every book would be a Penguin, a bird with a certain
'dignified flippancy', and a friendly invitation to anyone who
wished to spend their time reading.

In 1935, the first ten Penguin paperbacks were published.
Just a year later, three million Penguins had made their
way onto our shelves.

Reading was changed forever.

—

A lot has changed since 1935, including Penguin, but in the
most important ways we're still the same. We still believe that
books and reading are for everyone. And we still believe that
whether you're seeking an afternoon's escape, a vigorous debate
or a soothing bedtime story, all possibilities open with a book.

Whoever you are, whatever you're looking for,
you can find it with Penguin.